Firefly Diaries
© 2021 C.C. Warrens

This novel is a work of fiction. Situations, scenarios, and characters in this book are a reflection of creative imagination and not representative of any specific person, group, situation, or event.

Editing by Deb Hall at TheWriteInsight.com.

Scriptures taken from King James Bible.

A COMPLETE LIST OF WORKS BY C.C. WARRENS

Holly Novels

Criss Cross

Winter Memorial (A Short Story)

Cross Fire

Crossed Off

Seeking Justice Novels

Injustice for All

Holly Jolly Christmas

Imperfect Justice

ACKNOWLEDGMENTS

A special thank-you to my local sheriff's department for answering my many questions.

· · ·

A special thank-you to my pastor, his wife, our pastoral counselor, and our church elder/scholar for continually sharing their spiritual wisdom.

· · ·

And I'm so very thankful for my Jesus, who is with me during every step of the writing process, even when I feel discouraged and confused.

This book contains subjects and situations that might
be difficult for some readers.

Firefly
Diaries

PROLOGUE

The dashboard rattled as the car idled at the intersection, and Maddie smacked it a few times.

Like beating up the old piece of junk would make it work better. This car had more sound effects than her cell phone.

She blew out a breath and brought a finger to her mouth, biting down on a nail. The taste of fresh nail polish made her wince in disgust.

Mom liked to joke that she'd been chewing on her nails since she grew her first tooth.

Maddie informed her that nail biting was better than other nervous habits like smoking, overexercising, or stuffing her face with five pounds of chocolate, and she should quit nagging.

Really, who didn't have bad habits and flaws?

If I was perfect, I wouldn't need Jesus, she thought with a smile. She'd thrown that gem in her mother's face a few times too. She should have a T-shirt made with that slogan.

She checked her nails, relieved to see that the sliver of polish her teeth had taken off was barely noticeable.

Her nails were a rainbow, each one a different color. She questioned some of God's creations—like mosquitoes, gnats, and annoying little brothers—but He was on point with rainbows.

She squinted at the red light, then glanced at the no-turn-on-red sign. "Come on already. Before I'm a grandmother."

The light bounced to green, and she turned onto the side street. She wasn't familiar with this area, but the Maps app on her phone had gotten her this far.

When she arrived at her destination, she idled. There were no nearby lights outside, leaving everything beyond the glow of her headlights doused in darkness.

An uneasy feeling squirmed in her stomach, urging her to put the car in reverse and leave, but guilt overshadowed her unease.

Not everyone grew up in a home like hers, with two parents and two incomes. For some, having a roof over their head at all was a luxury. This was where he asked her to meet him, and she wouldn't judge him for it.

Maddie turned off the car and tugged the keys from the ignition, trying to ignore the trepidation whispering in the back of her mind.

Stretching to see her reflection in the rearview mirror, she fixed a few wild strands of her blonde hair and then tapped the unicorn dangling from the mirror.

"Wish me luck. I could use a friend."

Nerves fluttering, she grabbed her purse and climbed out of the car.

CHAPTER One

Dry leaves stirred around Noelle's feet as she climbed the bowed and weathered steps onto the wraparound porch.

A chill clung to the night air, and a puff of steam swelled from her parted lips as she sighed and dropped her suitcase and duffel bag at her feet.

She straightened the red-rimmed glasses on her nose and swept her gaze over the old house.

From the moment she had stumbled across the photographs on the auction website, she felt a connection with this place, one that tugged her across the country.

At this hour, most of the house's features were cloaked in darkness, but she remembered every detail from the photos. Abandonment and neglect dulled its white paint, and a lifetime of storms left it worn to the bone and leaning with exhaustion—a condition that resonated through her to her soul.

This past year had stripped away everything that mattered to her, and she felt as damaged and exhausted as the structure before her.

She ran a gloved hand along the paint-chipped porch railing. "We're going to heal together. One day at a time."

As she whispered to the house, the words of the pregnant waitress from the local diner drifted through her mind.

Are you sure you want to live there? It's got a bit of a history, and some people say it's haunted . . . if you believe in that sort of thing. And sometimes it sounds like the walls are crying.

The house had an ethereal beauty that would lend itself to ghost stories. With chipped siding, floor-to-ceiling windows—most of which were boarded over—and a door knocker fit for a castle, it was no doubt the centerpiece of many spooky tales whispered around campfires.

Every old house has a story, written by the people and events that unfold within its walls. This house, Noelle suspected, ended on a dark chapter.

The lawyer who facilitated the sale wished her luck, but there was a glimmer of foreboding in his eyes as he said it, as if he expected something unfortunate to happen tonight.

Noelle should've investigated the house's history before purchasing it, but the auction was nearly at its end when she stumbled across the listing. She had to make a split-second decision. Hopefully it wasn't one she would regret.

She turned to survey the darkness that stretched as far as the eye could see. Something the auction site had neglected to mention was that her only neighbors were the spiders weaving their silk in every corner of the porch.

A web sparkled in the moonlight above her, a spider working to add new strands. "Hello, Charlotte." She cocked her head. "Or are you a Charles?"

Charlie. She could almost hear her little boy's voice whispering the name, and grief ricocheted through her like a bullet, ripping open wounds that had only just begun to scab over.

Tay loved every creature, though he had a special place in his heart for spiders. He named them as if they were part of the family. That was her sweet boy—exuding love everywhere he went.

Tears skated across her vision at the memory of him, blurring the beautiful web, but she blinked them away. "Charlie it is."

She turned her back to her busy neighbor and fished the flashlight from the cluttered depths of her purse, clicking it on so she could see the keyhole on the front door.

A chill whispered down her neck, drawing her back around, and she swept the flashlight beam over the rustling trees and moonlit reeds of grass.

This country village in Ohio was supposed to be safer than Seattle, where she'd spent her entire life, so why did she feel exposed and vulnerable standing alone on this porch?

The only things she should have to worry about here were car accidents and the occasional deer who took a wrong turn and ended up lost in Walmart.

Still, that uneasy feeling lingered.

You're imagining things, as usual.

Tyrese's accusatory voice surged up from her memories, leaving a bitter taste in the back of her throat. Somehow, even thousands of miles apart, he managed to make her doubt herself.

5

Pushing him from her mind, she drew the key from the side pocket of her purse and slipped it into the old lock.

The dead bolt released with a clunk, and the door drifted inward on its own, sagging unevenly and scraping across the floor until it bumped into the wall.

Noelle's eyebrows pinched.

The door was barely hanging onto the frame.

At least there is a door, she silently countered, trying to focus on the positive.

But as she swept the flashlight beam over the foyer, she was *positive* she was in over her head. She wasn't as experienced at renovating houses as her parents, and this place was in a desperate state.

"Home sweet home."

She set down her luggage inside, but before she could follow, a screech pierced the quiet, sending goose bumps down her arms.

It's probably the porch swing drifting in the breeze, she reasoned.

A storm was blowing in, a light wind rattled the treetops as a sheet of dark clouds stretched overhead.

Another screech, louder this time. Noelle walked to the corner of the house to check on the swing, and the beam of her flashlight glinted off the rusted chains the lawyer had captured in his photos. But then it landed on something the lawyer *hadn't* captured, and Noelle's throat tightened against a scream.

A dead man slumped in one corner of the swing.

6

CHAPTER Two

The man's eyes were sunken, and his cheekbones jutted out above dark hollows. Mud caked his boots and the bottoms of his pants, as though he'd been dragged from a grave.

Noelle shoved away the wild theories that left the beam of her flashlight shaking and focused on the most likely explanation: he was an old man crossing through the property, and he stopped to rest on the swing.

He couldn't be dead.

She was certain she saw the subtle rise and fall of his chest, though that could have been wishful thinking.

Should she check for a pulse or leave that to the local authorities? Before she could decide, a deep voice crackled from his throat.

"So you're her."

Fear sucked the feeling from Noelle's extremities, and the flashlight tumbled from her grip. She tried to catch it but only managed to slap it farther away with fumbling fingers. The beam of light spun wildly as the flashlight rolled across the floorboards, jolting to a stop beneath the man's boot.

Noelle's pulse pounded in her temples. "Who . . ." She tried to clear the nerves from her throat. "Who are you? What do you want?"

With a quick snap of his wrist, a flame ignited between the man's fingers. Moving leisurely, as if he hadn't heard her question, he pressed a cigarette between his lips and lit it with the dying match.

He lifted his head to look at her then. His face, cast in shadows from the beam of the flashlight, appeared even more gaunt, like a macabre mask, beneath the straw hat he wore. "You're the woman who stole my family's house."

Noelle stiffened at the accusation, some of her fear giving way to indignation. "I didn't steal anything. The house was up for auction."

Then the rest of his words registered: my family's house. The lawyer who handled the property for the deceased woman hadn't informed her of any local relatives who might take issue with the sale. She should've thought to ask.

The old man took a drag from the cigarette, and smoke swirled from his mouth as he replied, "No one had any business selling this place. It should've stayed in the family."

"I'm sorry. If I'd known there was family in the area, I would've tried to reach out." If only to avoid this awkward situation.

He flicked ash from the end of the cigarette. "Did you even bother to learn about the woman who used to own this property?"

Again, that accusatory tone, as if she'd committed an unforgivable sin. "I know her name was Elizabeth Bechtel."

She intended to research every person who had ever lived here, to uncover their personal stories, but she hadn't had the opportunity yet.

His gaze drifted into the distance. "Lizzy." He took another puff of his cigarette, blowing smoke into the silence that stretched.

Noelle had no idea how the man was related to Elizabeth Bechtel, but the grief in his voice was unmistakable.

"Losing someone you love is . . . excruciating," she said, because she couldn't bring herself to utter the hollow condolence that had poured in from every direction for months after the funeral of her son: "I'm sorry for your loss."

"I lost Lizzy fifty-three years ago. In that room back there." The old man reached back and rapped a knuckle on the wall behind him, which must've enclosed one of the five bedrooms.

"But I thought . . . she died recently."

"There's more than one way to die."

His words sent a chill crawling down her neck to linger at the base of her spine. "I see." What else was there to say to that disturbing remark?

"I don't think you do." He leaned forward, resting his elbows on his knees, and fixed her with a look that made her want to take a step back. "If you could see the truth, you would run back to wherever you came from."

The only place she wanted to run back to was the past—eight months and three days ago, to be exact. Unfortunately, no one had invented time travel yet.

"I'm staying."

"No one wants you here." The disdain in his tone made her wonder what it was about her that he found so distasteful, though she had an inkling.

She'd been apprehensive when she first arrived in this village because she seemed to be the only drop of color in a sea of white. She wasn't sure how the small community would respond to a black person moving in.

"You city people think that because you have money, you can buy what should belong to us and destroy it. I can hear it in your voice—the *city*." He spat the last word.

So it was her origins rather than her complexion that he took issue with. This man knew nothing about her, and yet he had the nerve to judge her because of her city roots?

"I'm sorry if my buying this house adds to your grief. That wasn't my intention. But I'm not some developer who wants to level the house and build a department store. I only want to restore it and make it livable again."

The old man pushed up from the swing, the easy movement revealing more strength than Noelle expected of his matchstick frame. He closed the distance between them, his voice dropping to a menacing level. "You will not change so much as a lightbulb in this house."

Noelle stepped back, the sleeve of her sweatshirt snagging on the rough wood siding. She yanked the material free and straightened her shoulders, determined not to be bullied. "I understand you have an emotional connection to this place, but I will make whatever changes I need to make."

A vein pulsed in his forehead. "You might have some signed piece of legal paper, and you might be able to change the locks . . ."

A warm cloud of breath and smoke from his mouth fogged the lenses of her glasses, and her heart hammered against her ribs as he all but blinded her.

"But this house will always belong to my family. My ancestors built it with their bare hands. Every pet we loved and lost is buried in that backyard. My family's blood is on these walls and in these floors."

His family's blood? Surely that was a figure of speech and not a reference to a family massacre.

"You can try to remove the bloodstains by scrubbing the floors and peeling off the wallpaper, but you can't remove the dead. And they don't like to be disturbed, Ms. McKenzie. They don't like that at all."

Noelle wasn't sure what unsettled her more—that he knew her name or that he spoke about the dead as if they were still in the house, buried beneath the floorboards like some Edgar Allen Poe story.

Please tell me I didn't move into a serial killer's house.

She slipped a hand into her purse and wrapped her fingers around the handle of her revolver, the solid, cold metal bringing her a measure of comfort.

The old man flicked the nub of his cigarette over the railing into the wet grass and reached for something in the shadows.

Noelle's heart stuttered when he grabbed a rifle that she hadn't even noticed was leaning against the side of the house.

He slung the gun over his shoulder, the barrel pointing up at the night sky. "I expect you gone by morning."

Noelle held her breath as he stomped down the side staircase and melted into the darkness. With a relief that nearly took her to the floor, she exhaled and sagged against the side of the house.

CHAPTER
Three

Noelle's nerves calmed as she locked the front door from inside. She hooked a finger around the dusty curtain to her left, lifting it to see through the window.

She half expected the old man's gaunt face to materialize on the other side, but the only movement on the porch were leaves skittering in the wind of the growing storm.

She released the curtain and dropped her head back against the door, closing her eyes. She'd never been easily startled, but the past eight months had shaped her into someone different—a woman she didn't recognize.

A series of thumps nearly sent her through the ceiling, and then she realized it was the drumbeat she'd set as her phone's email alert. She rolled her eyes and pulled the phone from the pouch of her sweatshirt.

She stared at the email icon on the notification bar. To open it or flick it off the screen and pretend she never saw it . . .

Begrudgingly, she tapped the icon to call up the message. The email was from Amy, her agent and friend, and the subject line read:

Elle, I know you're not feeling inspired to write, but I thought this story might spark your creativity.

Noelle bit back a sigh and scrolled down to the information Amy had pasted in the body of the email. Her insides twisted at the details. A man had been convicted and sentenced to life in prison for assaulting ten women in the state of Pennsylvania. Following the gruesome article, she found Amy's personal thoughts.

I think this would make an outstanding piece of fiction. The victim who finally stood up to this monster and got the legal ball rolling is a bit of a ghost. And apparently she refuses to speak to anyone, but I might be able to swing something if you're interested.

Ordinarily, this kind of real-life horror would have Noelle pulling out her storyboard and pinning up pictures of potential characters and note cards with plot twists. But her passion for writing had died along with her son, buried in a coffin so small it shouldn't exist.

The haunting memory of that casket sinking into the ground clawed its way to the surface, tendrils of grief wrapping around her heart like chains. She pushed the memory back down before it could reduce her to a puddle on the floor.

Amy meant well with her monthly emails, but all they did was remind Noelle that she was a shell of the person she used to be. Silencing her phone, she tucked it away and then turned her attention to the house, something that—unlike her life—she might actually be able to fix.

She switched on one of the battery-operated lanterns, and the warm glow brought shadows to life on the walls.

Noelle tipped her head back to look at the ceiling. Cobwebs hung down like cartoon ghosts caught between two floors, their tails swaying back and forth in the draft that seeped through the house. It would take her ages to find and seal all the cracks letting in cold air.

If she managed to make friends in town, she could assemble a hunting party and arm everyone with caulk guns. It wouldn't be the prettiest fix, but with winter huffing and puffing on Ohio's door, functionality was more important than appearances.

She drew in the scent of her new home, a combination of mustiness, damp wood, and dust.

It reminded her of childhood, of every long-vacant house her parents purchased in order to renovate. A mixture of nostalgia and regret blossomed inside her.

Those had been difficult, bittersweet years.

Despite the renovation business, money had been tight, and they usually had to live in the house they were fixing up because they couldn't afford the up-front costs of the project as well as rent for an apartment.

They moved to a different place every six to eight months, and those months between purchasing the house and selling it were full of uncertainty—would there be enough money for food, electricity, water?

Noelle had promised herself that she would never live with that kind of uncertainty again, and yet here she was, moving into an abandoned house with no electricity, water, or heat, and hoping she could make it livable.

She stuffed her hands into her sweatshirt pocket and considered how to tackle the mess she'd gotten herself into.

She would have to scrub every inch of the house, and then set up dehumidifiers to dry it out . . . once she had electricity.

If only I could convince the critters living in here to clean it for me, she thought, watching another spider rappel down from the ceiling on a silky rope. But she wasn't a Disney princess, and her singing voice would be instant death to any critter within earshot.

Lightning flashed outside, and a few heartbeats later, thunder rumbled overhead.

Noelle cast a cautious glance at the high foyer ceiling, listening to winter and fall battle it out in the sky. "Let's hope the roof doesn't leak."

She didn't have any pans or buckets to catch the water, and she doubted the previous residents left anything useful behind. People had a tendency to leave miscellaneous nonsense that was too inconvenient to pack.

Of course, that was part of the fun when she was little. Mom and Dad would purchase a house to flip, and Noelle would set off in search of hidden treasures, like the necklace she wore.

The silver pendant rested below the hollow of her throat, a reminder that sometimes the most beautiful, worthwhile things required hard work and determination. She'd dug through a lot of dirt before finding this necklace.

Another flash of lightning ignited the sky, closer this time. The old bones of the house crackled under the growing pressure of the storm, and the wind whined as it cut through the trees and into the cracks of the siding and windows.

Sometimes it sounds like the walls are crying, the waitress had said.

The sound—like a child whimpering in the night—raised the hairs on Noelle's arms. If she believed in ghosts, she would be flinging open the door and bolting back to her car, even if it meant sleeping in the backseat.

"It's an old house. Old houses are . . . chatty."

But she still found herself reaching for the lantern like a child desperate for a night-light that would drive away the monsters.

Armed with light, she set out to take stock of her new home. All the photos on the auction website had featured the house's exterior, leaving the inside a mystery.

Broken glass and bits of plaster crunched beneath her feet as she walked down the hall, and something bounced off the tip of her shoe, skidding across the floor. A plastic horse lay in the middle of the hallway. Picking it up, she brushed the plaster dust from the waves of colorful hair. It looked like a party favor, one of those gift bag decorations for little girls.

She doubted there were too many birthday parties happening in this house. Unless they were Casper themed.

She tucked the toy into her sweatshirt and continued to the end of the hall, her footsteps slowing as she approached the formal dining room.

Five chairs and a long wooden table sat in the middle of the room, a half-burnt candle at the center.

Confusion tugged at her brows as she stepped into the room that probably once hosted holiday meals and family gatherings.

Why would the family who lived here before her leave behind such an exquisite dining set? Her confusion twisted into anxiety when she noticed the open window on the far wall.

Thrusting the lantern at the surrounding shadows and finding no one lurking in the corners, she crossed the room to close the window.

As she gripped the dusty frame, a flicker of light drew her eyes past the rain-splattered glass to the woods. The warm glow seemed to hang in the branches of the far-off trees.

"What is that?"

She pushed up the window, but it slid back down like a guillotine blade, catching in the same position an inch from the bottom. The track must be damaged. She pushed it back up and leaned out of the screenless opening to get a better visual.

She squinted against the cold mist spraying her face as raindrops pelted the porch, but whatever the light was, it was too far away to identify. She would have to check it out tomorrow morning.

After wrestling the window shut, she locked it. She needed to make sure all the doors and windows were locked and then find a spot to settle in for the night.

CHAPTER *Four*

Harsh winds slapped rain against the Justice Center building, and lightning pinballed through the overhead clouds, the rolling rumble swallowing the quiet shuffle and hum of the sheriff's department.

The storm stretched over the entire county, sweeping upward from a category 5 hurricane down south. Ohio might not need to worry about hurricanes or tropical storms, but they wouldn't escape the fallout.

Derek ignored the stack of reports and requisitions on his desk awaiting his signature as he watched the power lines whip back and forth in the storm.

The sheriff's department was going to be busy tomorrow, responding to calls about fallen trees and power lines, someone's roof or trampoline in the middle of the road. Most of the three cities and twelve villages that made up the county had their own police departments, but by the time this storm blew her last breath on Wade County, there would be a lot of cleanup to do.

Derek rubbed at his eyes and leaned back in his chair.

He already felt guilty about taking tomorrow off, especially with it being Monday, but he needed a break. With the rash of burglaries and homicides lately, the paperwork was starting to feel like a bad game of Jenga. One bump and the wobbling stack would topple off his desk.

When he set his sights on law enforcement as a teenager, he expected to be tackling mountain-sized criminals, not mountain-sized stacks of paperwork. And he certainly never expected to become a division captain before his hair was gray.

Though this job might be what was *turning* it gray.

Dragging his focus away from the storm, he opened a file to review the report of a homicide outside the small town of Smithvail. He was reading the deputy's notes on the suspect interrogation when his desk phone rang.

He plucked it from its cradle. "Captain Dempsey."

"Hey, Captain." Wind crackled down the line, but he recognized the voice of his oldest and most experienced deputy. Rusty had a distinct voice—deep with a touch of John Wayne. He would've fit in nicely as a laid-back sheriff in the old West.

"I'm guessing you found something interesting during your visit to the Cherry Creek Developmental Center."

Rusty was helping out the village police department by responding to a trespassing complaint. Occasionally, out-of-towners came to the closed asylum searching for the ghosts rumored to haunt the empty hallways.

'I found something interesting, but it wasn't at the asylum."

"What did you find?"

"An abandoned car on the dirt trail behind the cemetery." The wind nearly carried away Rusty's words, and

Derek strained to catch them. "I stopped at the ice cream stand for something sweet, and I overheard this lady complaining about a car blocking the dirt trail behind the cemetery. Apparently she likes to jog back there after work."

Joggers and walkers ignored the No Trespassing sign, but the chain across either end of the trail discouraged vehicles.

"I decided to check it out, and sure enough, there's a car in the middle of the trail. Engine is stone cold. The lady said it's been there since at least Friday night."

"Any visible damage?"

Silence stretched as Rusty examined the car. "The front is a bit torn up. No surprise, since they drove straight through the chain. Snapped it in two."

"Maybe they left the car there because it ran out of gas or the engine failed and they didn't want to foot the bill for a tow truck." Or *couldn't* foot the bill for a tow truck, Derek thought. "Did you run the plates?"

"Sure did. They're registered to a Eugenia Banks from Cleveland, Ohio. But seeing as she's ninety-seven years old, I don't think she was driving it."

Derek let out a low whistle. "Ninety-seven. Let's *hope* she wasn't driving it." Though that might explain why she drove through the chain barricade.

"It could be borrowed or stolen."

"Anything in the car to help identify who might have been driving it?"

"A few girly stickers on the glove compartment and a silver cross keychain dangling from the ignition, but nothing with a name."

Derek sat forward in his chair. "Are there any other keys on the ring?"

"Looks like one other. Could be a house or apartment key."

Abandoned cars weren't unusual, but an abandoned car with the keys still in the ignition was practically unheard of. The fact that there was a second key, possibly a house key, was cause for concern.

The squeak of a car door opening filtered down the line. "Based on how close the driver's seat is to the steering wheel, I would guess our driver was on the smaller side, between five foot three and five foot six. I'm guessing female. Hang on, I think . . . yep, there's a long blonde hair tangled around the headrest of the driver's seat."

"Any signs of a struggle?"

"Not that I can see on the inside, and anything on the outside would already be washed away."

"Does the car start?"

Rusty grunted, noise crackling over the line as he shifted the phone, and then the car's engine sputtered, coughed, and died in the background. "Nope. It's not catching."

Dispatch hadn't received any calls from or about someone wandering through town, stranded or injured, so it was possible the driver had called someone to pick her up.

"Have the car towed to the impound lot for now." He checked the time. It was late. "Call Eugenia Banks in the morning and find out whether her car was stolen or if she lent it to someone."

"Sure thing, boss."

Derek ended the call and dialed the police department. The trail behind the cemetery fell under their jurisdiction, but between storm calls and the flu sweeping through the ranks, their small department was overwhelmed tonight.

"This is Captain Derek Dempsey from the sheriff's department," he said when the line was answered. He relayed Rusty's observations and probed for information, but the car and its driver were as much a mystery to the police as they were to him.

A butterfly-light tap on the door frame of Derek's office came as he returned the receiver to its cradle, identifying his visitor before he saw her.

Carol's husband used to work in Derek's division, and even though he passed away four years ago, she still dropped by every week with something sweet.

Derek closed the file he'd been reviewing and smiled. "Carol, are you fattening up my deputies?"

The fine skin around her eyes crinkled with delight. "I might be. I have to make sure they're all too chubby to catch me if I commit a crime."

Derek laughed. If that was her goal, she had a lot of work ahead of her. His deputies were the epitome of fitness.

"I brought in some homemade coffee cake for the evening crew, and one of them mentioned you were still here."

"It's been a busy week."

She nodded, her short auburn curls bobbing. "I saw. I watch your weekly videos on Facebook updating everyone on what's happening in our county."

He disliked that part of his job almost as much as the paperwork, but it helped with community relations.

"I hope I'm not being a nuisance by interrupting, but I wanted to make sure you got a slice of cake before there was nothing left but crumbs."

"You're never a nuisance, and I appreciate you thinking of me."

She carried in a paper plate with a slice of cake and handed it to him. "My friend from church called to tell me the Bechtel estate changed hands today."

He'd heard a rumor it would be auctioned after Elizabeth Bechtel passed away from cancer. She'd set things in motion after her health started to decline a few months back. "Do you know who bought it?"

"I don't know her name, just that she's not from around here. I do hope she knows what she's gotten herself into with that house, though." Carol's thin lips pinched in concern.

Derek doubted the woman had bought the house with a full understanding of its history or the complications that came with it. He would give it an hour before she called in, panicked and raving about ghosts and possessed scarecrows.

CHAPTER
Five

Noelle had seen some strange houses during her childhood—some with doors that went nowhere and others with so many different styles and colors that their decorator could've been the Mad Hatter.

But this place was a museum, each room a haunting exhibit of a family's life decades before.

Their belongings were protectively cocooned in cobwebs, waiting for them to return—a basket of yarn and knitting needles beside the rocking chair in the living room, reading glasses and a magazine on the coffee table, a kitchen sink overflowing with dirty dishes.

It was as though the entire family left and never came back. But this room suggested a much darker version of events.

Noelle rubbed at her upper arms as she stared at a brown stain marring the creamy floral wallpaper of the main bedroom, the old man's ominous words echoing through her mind: *My family's blood is on these walls and in these floors.*

The words had unsettled her then, but they chilled her now as she stood face-to-face with old blood spatter.

And the dark stains on the mattress . . .

Something awful happened in this house, and the old man spoke as if he knew the details intimately. He considered himself part of the family. If she could find a family portrait, he might be in it, but all she'd seen were faded patches on the walls where frames once hung.

She checked the blanket chest at the foot of the bed for photo albums, but it was empty except for a few tufts of lint. Not even a blanket. The nightstand drawers were cluttered with magazines, books, and other miscellaneous items.

Her nightstand drawers had always managed to become a catchall too. She lost track of all the times she found a stray sock or an unfinished granola bar smashed between books.

Finding nothing, she closed the drawers and walked to the window, studying the darkness that had wrapped around the old man like a cloak when he stepped off the porch.

He could be a ghost, her rusty imagination coughed up.

"He's not a ghost."

He couldn't be, because God would never allow a human soul to slip through His fingers and wander the earth for all eternity. Noelle's relationship with Him might be strained, but she knew that much.

The shiver lingering at the base of her spine slithered to life again, awakened by the sense that someone was watching her.

That's ridiculous. No one in their right mind would be out in this storm, she told herself, watching the trees twist wildly. But the feeling clung to her as tightly now as it had when she stood on the porch.

She tugged the thick drapes shut, as much to block out the feeling as to stop the cold air from seeping through the rotted window seals.

She changed out of her jeans into sweatpants and wiggled her toes into three pairs of wool socks. Shivering to sleep in a sleeping bag on the floor of an unfinished house when she was a child destroyed her tolerance for the cold. She would rather be sweating than shivering.

The relaxing patter of rain on the roof increased, deepening into a sledgehammering torrent, and Noelle eyed the bedroom ceiling.

Please don't leak, please don't—a drop of icy water landed on her chin and her shoulders drooped—*leak.*

————

He leaned against a tree, the hood of his coat covering his head to deflect the rain, and watched the house.

The white light that had bounced from room to room finally settled on the second floor—the main bedroom.

The woman was nervous. She'd checked every unboarded window in the house, making sure they were locked, before settling in upstairs.

People always thought locks could keep them safe, as if glass couldn't be shattered and flimsy doors couldn't be knocked down. And when the locks failed, they held on to the hope that the police would save them.

The woman stood in front of the bedroom window, but she would never be able to see him. Not in this storm. He could barely see her from this distance with rain coating his binoculars. As though she sensed him, she whipped the drapes shut, cutting him off.

He ran his tongue over his teeth. The woman was an unexpected irritation, like the sausage stuck between his top molars.

He pulled a flossing stick from his pocket and worked the bit of pork loose. He couldn't stand the feeling of something caught between his teeth. He shoved the flossing stick back into his pocket and tried to clear the lenses of his binoculars.

He wanted the woman gone, but he wasn't quite sure what to do about that. If he made the wrong move, it would draw the attention of the authorities and the media, and the last thing he wanted was more people getting in his way.

————————

Noelle nudged a pot with her foot, centering it beneath the slow drip coming from the ceiling, then readjusted the plastic cup on the nightstand.

This house was the opposite of weatherproof. It invited cold air and rainwater inside like they were old friends.

The rhythmic sound of water tapping against the empty bottom of plastic cups and clinking into metal bowls tickled a memory she hadn't thought about since she was a child—a group of men making music in the street by tapping on milk crates and trash can lids.

Most adults walked by, unable to appreciate the performance, but Noelle and had been drawn to it like a magnet.

Her roof might be hemorrhaging rainwater from a dozen different places, but the memory of that performance brought a certain beauty to the noise.

It was going to make for an interesting night, though. She moved her makeshift bed of blankets for the third time when rainwater splashed on the pillow.

She could find an inexpensive motel to sleep in for the night—one that at least had a working bathroom and solid roof—but it could take weeks to finish the roof and update the plumbing, and she needed all her money for the repairs.

Besides, immersing herself in the house and its history was a part of the experience. Even if that meant pumping water from the artesian well to fill buckets so she could dump them into the toilet to flush it for a week or two. Hopefully, doing that wouldn't further damage the plumbing.

Noelle settled onto the nest of blankets a few feet from the propane heater and stretched out her legs, warming her toes. She eyed her laptop and notepad. After driving all day, the only thing she wanted to do was sprawl out and relax, but there was too much to do.

Begrudgingly, she dragged her notepad into her lap so she could start compiling a list of repairs and necessities.

She barely uncapped her pen before her phone rang. A picture of her father lit up the screen, and guilt riddled her. She'd forgotten to call and let her parents know she arrived safely.

She swiped the screen to answer and pressed the phone to her ear. "Hi, Dad."

"Hi, pumpkin. How's the house?"

She opened her mouth to answer, but her mother's voice broke in from somewhere in the background.

"Tell her that geometric wallpaper is all the rage right now, and it will look great in her new living room."

"I did not call our daughter to give her wallpaper advice."

"It's good advice," her mother said, the volume of her voice indicating she had moved to hover over Dad's shoulder.

"Then you call her and give it to her."

"How am I supposed to call her when you're on the phone with her?"

"If you hadn't been flipping through wallpaper samples, you would've called her first."

An outraged huff from Mom.

Would they notice if she hung up, or would they carry on arguing without pause? She decided to jump in before her mother could start in on paint colors.

"The house is in rougher shape than I anticipated." *A bit of an understatement*, she thought, casting an uncomfortable glance at the murder mattress across the room. "So I have a lot of work to do."

"Of course you do," Dad said. "But safety first."

Her mother chimed in about goggles and masks to protect from asbestos, but that wasn't the kind of safety her father was talking about.

"Make sure you lock all the doors and windows, leave a light on to discourage a break-in, and if anything happens or someone bothers you—"

"Call the local authorities. I know." She was thirty-three years old, but he still treated her like she was thirteen. "And I have my gun."

A pause, and then he cleared his throat. "Good. That's good." He'd encouraged her to buy one and take some classes after the rash of violent break-ins in her last neighborhood, but he hadn't picked up a gun since he quit the police force and started renovating houses when she was four. "A gun can be useful, but I would rather you call the police if anything strange happens. Promise me."

"Dad—"

"Promise me, Noelle."

Relenting, she promised. She told her parents she loved them and then disconnected. They were wonderful people, but they could be exhausting.

Noelle tapped her pen on her blank notepad, mentally compiling a list, and then started jotting things down.

She added "blueprint," because it hadn't been included in the documents the lawyer gave her, and it would be necessary for renovations. When she spoke with him next, she intended to bring up his deception about the condition of the house as well, though she doubted it would matter. She purchased it in as-is condition, and the sale was final.

"Pathetically useless front door should be at the top." She circled the sixth item on the list and drew an arrow to the top of the page.

Another lap around the house would help her fine-tune the list. Being able to see what she was looking at would help even more.

She made a note to check into local utilities tomorrow. The electric shouldn't be too hard. It was the underground water and sewage pipes that concerned her. Tree roots let nothing stand in their—

A crash came from downstairs, the resultant vibration rippling through the entire house, followed by a sharp crack that was swallowed up by rumbles of thunder. Noelle stared at the closed bedroom door.

What was that?

CHAPTER Six

The gun was cold in Noelle's grip as she crept down the old staircase, every creak shooting more adrenaline into her veins.

She wished she could flip a switch and light up the house, but all she had was the lantern dangling from her left hand. She lifted it, scrutinizing the shadows beyond its glow.

A chilly draft swirled around her ankles, carrying with it the crisp scent of fall and damp earth. She'd checked all the windows and doors before settling in upstairs, so where was the smell coming from?

A dry leaf skipped across the floor, stirred by the invisible breeze coming from the back of the house. The foyer was littered with leaves that had managed to make it inside over the years, blowing through open doorways and hitching rides on shoes.

Her focus shifted past the leaf to the patch of floor it danced on, noticing something she hadn't earlier—a clean trail through the dust on the floor that traveled from the foot of the staircase and down the hall.

What could've caused something like that? A piece of furniture being dragged or . . .

A *creak-tap, creak-tap* from the back of the house nearly made her miss the last step. She managed to plant both feet on the bottom floor without spraining an ankle, and held her breath as she listened.

Was that a loose shutter rattling against the siding or a tree branch tapping on a window? Neither of those possibilities explained the reverberating thump she heard from upstairs.

The *creak-tap* came again, and Noelle followed the disconcerting sound down the hall toward the kitchen, her fingers tightening around her gun.

Something skittered across her foot, and she shrieked, nearly flinging the lantern out of reflex at the tiny attacker. A small brown mouse, as terrified of her as she was of it, scampered through the obstacle course of debris on the floor and disappeared into a hole in the plaster.

A mouse. She'd screamed and nearly climbed up the wall because of a fuzzy critter with adorably large ears.

Pull yourself together, Noelle.

She turned the corner into the kitchen, and her sneakers froze on the linoleum floor, her heart slamming against her ribs as she absorbed the sight.

The door that led into the backyard stood wide open, creaking back and forth in the breeze.

Possibilities raced through her head—a burglar, a vandal, a murderer—and she rushed forward to slam the back door. But even as she did so, it occurred to her that the intruder might still be inside.

CHAPTER
Seven

Derek's headlights brightened the two-story house as he bumped along the gravel and dirt driveway, reeds of grass slapping the hood of his cruiser.

He'd been locking up his office when a call came in for this address—a break-in, no assailant on the premises. To his surprise, the woman sounded rational and calm as she explained the situation.

Since the house was half a mile down the road from his, and he was headed home for the night, Derek decided to respond to the call rather than send a deputy out this far.

He'd been to this place many times as a kid—riding over on his bike with his friends to peer through the windows, hoping to catch a glimpse of something ghostly—and the passage of time had only made the structure more eerie.

Why would anyone want to live here? he thought, slowing to a stop behind the car parked near the porch.

A dim glow appeared in the foyer window as a hand brushed aside the curtain. The woman said this wasn't an emergency, but if she was watching for him, she was more nervous than she let on over the phone.

Derek double-checked the name in his notebook, and then eyed the Bubblicious-pink car in front of him with bumper stickers plastered around the Washington license plate. He strained to make out the words through the rain.

I'M NOT TALKING TO MYSELF.
I'M TALKING TO MY CHARACTERS.

And . . .

I'M NOT SPACED OUT. I'M PLOTTING.

The last one surprised a smile out of him.

WATCH OUT FOR PLOT HOLES.

It sounded like Ms. McKenzie was a writer, which was bound to make things interesting. The last writer who came to town was a journalist looking to exploit the tragic history of this place with no regard for the surviving family members. He'd gone to great lengths to gather material for his article, but he hadn't been desperate enough to move into the two-story relic.

If Noelle McKenzie was here for a similar reason, there were easier ways to gather backstory material than purchasing the property. Unless she had a morbid fascination with death.

Derek tucked his notebook into his pocket as he pondered the woman's motives. This was his hometown, and these people were his neighbors. He didn't want them harassed by another writer with an agenda.

Reserve judgment, he reminded himself.

All he really knew about Noelle McKenzie was that she was a possible victim of a break-in, and he needed to make sure she was safe.

Before he could open the driver's door, his phone rang, dragging his attention to the cup holder between the seats.

His baby sister was calling, but as much as he adored her, he didn't have time to talk right now. He ignored the call and zipped his phone into his jacket pocket.

He would get an earful from her later for not answering, but he doubted it was anything more important than another lecture on his stagnant love life, and he was still recovering from her last lecture:

"You've been single for half a decade, and you're pushing forty. Midlife crisis is right around the corner, and you do not want to be looking for a girlfriend when you're in midlife crisis. You'll end up with a twenty-year-old who thinks a pound sign is a hashtag, and she'll be hashtag-pounding your personal lives all over social media."

Trudy was determined to find him another wife, but he had no interest in dating or remarrying.

He plucked his hat from the passenger seat and climbed out of the car, ducking his head against the wind and rain.

The front door opened as he climbed the steps, and a woman dressed in pink sweatpants and an oversize sweatshirt appeared in the opening. He pegged her at about five foot eight, early thirties, with a warm complexion, and black hair secured by a pink hairband on top of her head.

Normal enough, he thought. *Probably not here out of some morbid fascination with death then.*

"Ms. McKenzie?" He brushed water from his jacket sleeves. "I'm Captain Dempsey from the Wade County sheriff's department."

"Noelle." She gripped the door with her left hand, revealing an indentation on her bare ring finger, and visually dissected the darkness behind him before saying, "Come on in."

She shifted to give him room, and he caught sight of the revolver that had been concealed between her body and the wall a moment earlier.

Tension rippled through him, and his hand dropped to his sidearm. "You mind putting that away?"

She sucked in an audible breath. "Oh, of course." She tucked the gun into the pouch of her sweatshirt, the weight dragging the shirt down to her hips. "Sorry about that."

It didn't bother him if the locals carried around him—he'd grown up with many of them—but he didn't know anything about this woman.

He stepped inside, and she wrestled the door shut. She checked the front window again before resettling the curtain.

"You called about a break-in?"

Noelle blew out a breath and ran a hand over her hair, leaving a few shorter pieces sticking up at odd angles. "I did, but I think I might have overreacted."

Considering her chosen residence, Derek wouldn't be surprised if someone let themselves in. "You called, so you must have had cause for concern."

"Yeah, um . . . my father made me promise to call the local authorities if anything weird happened. And it's certainly been a weird night."

He removed his hat, glanced at the coat rack to his left covered in spiderwebs, then plopped the hat back on his head. Water dropping from the brim was better than spiders. "Why don't you fill me in."

"There was an old man on the porch when I got here. I thought he was dead, which was probably his intention now that I think about it. No one sits that still by accident." Two thought lines, like delicate quotation marks, formed between her eyebrows.

Appropriate, considering she was probably a writer.

"But then he struck up a disconcerting conversation, grabbed his rifle, and walked off into the night. I don't suppose you know who he is."

"Sounds like the Scarecrow."

That statement earned him an incredulous stare. "Should I be on the lookout for a cowardly lion and a tin man too?"

A smile tugged at the corners of his mouth, but she clearly wasn't amused, so he restrained it. "That's what the kids call him because he's as thin as a scarecrow, wears a straw hat, and makes it his mission to scare away anyone who comes to vandalize or loot the place."

"That description's practically a portrait. I assume Scarecrow is not the name his mother put on his birth certificate."

"That would be Walter Bechtel. He's Elizabeth's younger brother."

"He was telling the truth when he said this was his family's house." She folded her arms and sighed. "At least that's one mystery solved. Maybe you can solve another?"

"I'll do my best."

"Where are all the family pictures?" She gestured to the faded rectangle of wallpaper beside him, where a framed photo once hung.

"You might find some pictures still tucked away in albums and boxes, but the obvious ones have been stolen over the years."

"Why would someone steal pictures of a family they're not a part of?"

"Kids have been sneaking into this place for the past fifty years, but they need proof to show their peers that they were actually inside the 'haunted house,' so they take something. A picture of the family is irrefutable proof."

A few pictures were taken by the last writer who came to town hunting for information on the Bechtel tragedy. He published them in a journal article alongside quotes and details he pestered out of the locals.

"I suppose that makes sense," she said, her expression still pensive. "Anyway, I don't want to keep you longer than necessary. I'm sure you have someone to get home to." She scooped up the lantern from the floor. "The door I found open is in the kitchen."

41

Derek followed her down the hall. "Can you tell me about the events leading up to finding the door open?"

"I was upstairs, compiling a list of repairs."

That'll be a long list, Derek thought, noting the holes along the lower hallway wall. Probably from kids kicking in the plaster for fun.

"I heard a loud bang followed by a crack, which I thought might've been a gunshot." She glanced back at him with concern.

"Gunshots aren't uncommon in the country. Usually it's someone trying to scare wild animals from their property."

She made a thoughtful sound. "You hear a gunshot in Seattle, it usually means someone died."

That he could believe. He followed her into the kitchen and scanned the room for anything out of the ordinary, his attention landing on the laptop open on the counter.

He recognized the face glowing on the screen. It was a picture of Elizabeth Bechtel, the one displayed at her funeral three weeks ago. Noelle must have been doing research while she waited for someone from the sheriff's department to arrive.

"I came downstairs to investigate, and I followed the creaking sounds into the kitchen. That's when I noticed the door standing wide open," Noelle explained, drawing his attention away from the laptop.

She indicated the door, which now had a chair wedged beneath the knob, a trash can tucked into the corner, and a broom lying across both of them.

42

Derek tried to hide his amusement as he approached the unusual barricade. Did she really expect a wooden broom to keep out an intruder?

"You told dispatch you think someone kicked in the door, but now you think differently?"

She set the lantern on the counter. "There was a string of break-ins in my last neighborhood, so when I came downstairs and found this door open . . ."

"You made an assumption based on past experience."

She crossed her arms and shrugged self-consciously. "I guess so. The front door is hanging by a thread, so it makes sense that the back door would be damaged too. It was probably broken before I even moved in. I wouldn't be surprised if a gust of wind blew it open tonight."

Her tone suggested she wanted to believe that because it was easier to cope with, but she hadn't been able to convince herself. Hence the awkward barricade and the gun in her hand when he arrived.

"You mind if I take a look?"

"Go ahead."

He removed the broom from the top of the pile and handed it to her, fighting a smile. People made strange and illogical decisions when they were anxious.

Pushing aside the trash can and chair, he clicked on his flashlight and studied the area around the door. Slivers of wood littered the floor.

He flicked the beam toward the wall, noting the recent contact point where the knob had punched through the plaster, and then opened the door. The area around the door jamb was broken and splintered. Something had impacted the door hard—a foot, a shoulder . . .

Derek shone his flashlight over the back porch, illuminating smudges of muddy shoe prints. "Have you been outside since the rain started?"

"No, why?"

He crouched for a closer look. Either someone had fallen in their haste to flee, or they intentionally disfigured their shoe prints, making it impossible to determine size or tread. The former possibility suggested a neighborhood kid, which wasn't much of a concern. The latter, however, could mean an intruder was trying to cover their tracks.

Derek swung the flashlight beam left to right over the yard, but the grass was high enough to conceal a person who didn't want to be seen. "I don't think it was the wind that sent the door flying open tonight."

"I only heard one crash. If someone was kicking down the door, I would've heard that too."

"If the door was already compromised, which I would say is a strong possibility considering kids have been breaking into this house for decades, then a solid shove could pop it open, and I doubt you would've heard that over this storm. The thump you heard was likely the door connecting with the wall."

"But . . . who would do something like that?"

"More than likely, a curious teen who didn't realize the house is no longer vacant until after they shoved open the door." Derek stood, his knees creaking in protest. "But to be on the safe side, I'd like to take a look around. And

I'll have a chat with your neighbor first thing in the morning."

"I don't have a neighbor."

He indicated the back of the house with a tilt of his chin. "Walt lives in a camper on the other side of the trees."

She sagged against the counter, fingers still curled around the handle of the broom. "Of course he would be my neighbor."

CHAPTER
Eight

Noelle set aside the broom she was absently twisting in her grip and ran her hands over her hair, her fingers coming to rest on the messy bundle she'd scraped her hair into.

Her first night in her newly purchased house and someone had kicked in the back door.

If she believed in curses, she would be researching ways to break the one that was wrecking her life.

She dropped her hands with a sigh and gripped the edge of the counter.

"What am I even doing here?" She lifted her eyes to the ceiling, the furthest her prayers reached these days.

She couldn't explain why she'd felt drawn to this old house or what truly drove her to pack up what few belongings she had and move across the country. It was illogical and senseless, but something told her things would be better here.

That *something* was a liar.

Depression and grief packed their heavy bags and followed her across state lines like relentless stalkers. Depression nipped at her bumper during the drive, blinding her with tears and nearly forcing her off the road. Grief sat with her at dinner and stole her appetite. And now, anxiety danced along her nerves.

46

When you feel overwhelmed, focus your mind on one thing— one thing you can control in that moment—and put everything else aside.

Her therapist's words of wisdom drifted through her mind, and she clutched at them, looking for something to focus on.

She couldn't fix all the brokenness in her life tonight or change the fact that someone had kicked in her back door. But she could make a warm drink for the officer still dripping from the downpour.

A fresh wave of nearly horizontal rain whipped against the kitchen window, drawing Noelle's attention skyward. The mysterious light bobbing in the distance had gone out, leaving a black wall of trees.

Had the light been from Walt's home on the other side of the woods? With these high winds and rains, living in a camper would probably feel like being stuck on the rinse cycle in a washing machine.

Maybe I should check to make sure he's okay. He's old and—

She mentally clubbed the thought over the head. Old man or not, he'd intentionally frightened her, which meant he was either cruel or unstable. What would he do when he realized she ignored his warning to leave by morning?

"Focus," she whispered.

She switched on the portable gas burner, filled the tea kettle with bottled water, and set it on the coil to warm.

47

———

Derek descended the old staircase after clearing the second floor, his mind buzzing with questions about Cherry Creek's newest resident.

He could understand buying this place to renovate it, but sleeping here . . .

It could be research experience for a piece she was writing, or it could be something more.

The only thing he knew for certain was that he would have to be desperate to stretch out on the floor of this drafty, spider-infested house, regardless of how many blankets there were.

Maybe she is desperate.

The indentation from a recently removed wedding ring and her abrupt arrival in town with minimal possessions left him as curious as he was concerned.

He brushed aside a low-hanging cobweb as he walked down the hallway and into the kitchen.

Noelle glanced toward him when he entered the room, then returned her attention to the hot water she was pouring into two waiting mugs. "Find anything?"

He clicked off his flashlight and returned it to his belt. "Just a mouse in the basement."

"That makes at least two mice in the house. I'll have to think of names for them."

One of his eyebrows lifted at the peculiar suggestion. "Names?"

She cleared her throat and returned the tea kettle to the burner. "I kind of meant to keep that thought to myself, but now that it's out there, I doubt anyone gave Walt Disney that look when *he* named a mouse."

"A cartoon mouse. Not a live one that chews through your socks and the food in your pantry."

"True, but I can't kill them." She offered him one of the mugs. "It's a bit late for coffee, so I made tea. It should warm you up a little."

He hadn't intended to stay for a drink, but since she was polite enough to make him one, he could put off going home for a few more minutes.

"Thank you." He took the mug and read the black script on the side: "I kill people for a living." He turned the saying toward her. "Should I be concerned?"

Her lips twitched, as though a smile wanted to escape but couldn't. "It was a gift from a friend a couple of years ago. It's a joke about how authors tend to kill off characters."

An author, not a journalist. He filed that information away for later. "I'm guessing that means you've researched all kinds of interesting ways to kill people."

"Mmm, maybe." She pointedly closed the laptop screen beside her, her expression one of perfect innocence. "But don't worry, I didn't poison your tea."

"Considering your unwillingness to kill a mouse, I'm not worried."

The tea did smell unusual, but then the only tea he ever drank was bottled and loaded with sugar.

Noelle leaned against the far counter and wrapped both hands around her mug, staring into the darkening liquid.

49

Derek wrestled with whether or not to ask the questions still buzzing through his mind like a swarm of gnats.

If you never throw a line into the water, how can you expect to reel anything in? his mentor had asked as they sat on the bank fishing and discussing girls. At fifteen Derek hadn't realized those simple yet wise words would apply to more than just asking out the girl he had a crush on at the time.

He wanted to know more about the mysterious woman across from him, but if he didn't throw out a few questions, he wasn't likely to get any information.

"I couldn't help but notice you didn't bring much with you."

She gave a barely perceptible shrug. "I brought what I need to get by."

She'd brought dirt-scented tea but not an air mattress to sleep on. That made as much sense as a square merry-go-round.

"I guess the house does come fully furnished. Can't ask for much more than that, right?"

She tilted her head. "I could go for some electricity and running water. And a roof that doesn't double as a showerhead."

"Have you thought about staying at an inn or motel until you can get the place fixed up? There's a bed-and-breakfast in Smithvail, which isn't too far from here."

"As wonderful as that sounds, I would rather put that hundred dollars toward repairing windows before winter hits."

There were fewer intact windows than broken ones, one of which he and his friends broke when they were thirteen. He couldn't imagine what it was going to cost to repair this place.

"Besides," she said, taking in the worn-down and filthy kitchen, "this is familiar territory."

Derek took a swig of his tea as he pondered her choice of words, and instantly regretted it. It even tasted like dirt.

Do not spit it back in the cup. Just swallow. Without choking, he thought, silently negotiating with his gag reflex.

He forced the foul liquid down the back of his throat and tried not to cough. "I thought you said you didn't poison it."

A hesitant smile appeared on Noelle's lips—the first one he'd seen since he arrived. "I take it you've never had dandelion tea."

"Dandelions. It's weed broth?"

"Technically, it's root broth, and I happen to enjoy the earthy flavor."

He cleared the lingering *flavor* from his throat and set the mug on the counter. "You were one of those kids who made mud soup and served it to her friends, weren't you?"

Derek's older sister had done that to him when he was four. To this day, he didn't trust her when she came to visit and said, "Try this, it's delicious."

Noelle took a sip from her mug. "I guess dandelion root tea requires a certain kind of palate."

If by palate she means dead taste buds . . . But he kept that thought to himself. She seemed to be enjoying her weed broth.

"I know I'm asking you a lot of questions tonight, and you have better things to do than sate my curiosity, but do you know what happened here?"

"The lawyer didn't fill you in?"

"I got the feeling that having anything to do with this house makes him nervous, especially talking about it. He gave me the keys, minimal details, and practically shoved me out the door."

By her description, he guessed she was referring to Perry Habrams. He was the only lawyer in the village, and he had some strange, superstitious beliefs.

"I'm sorry, I know it's late. I'm sure I can find the information online."

Derek ran a hand over his trimmed beard, considering where to start. "Some people believe this place is cursed."

She gave him the same look she'd given him when he mentioned the Scarecrow.

He suppressed another smile. "It's not unusual for people to associate a string of unfortunate events with the supernatural."

"What kind of unfortunate events?"

"It started in 1848, with the man who designed and built this house—George Bechtel. He was an odd man, antisocial and paranoid, and the few people who lived in the growing settlement avoided him. George wanted to build his family's house on his own, start to finish, with no one looking over his shoulder."

She grunted in thought. "That explains the obscure architecture." At the interested arch of his eyebrows, she clarified, "The structure of the house is beautiful but a bit of a hodgepodge, like the builder pieced together random attributes he liked from different styles."

"You're familiar with architecture?"

"Vaguely. My parents renovate houses, and I learned a bit secondhand."

Other than the offhand mention of her father and her friend who gave mugs as gifts, that was the first truly personal detail she'd shared with him. He wanted to probe for more, but she cut in before he could formulate his thoughts into a question.

"Anyway, I'm more interested in talking about the house's history than my own, so . . ."

Derek swallowed the question he was about to ask, as she slammed a door on personal discussions. "Well, as the story goes, George Bechtel was nailing down the last wood shingle when he slipped and fell off the roof, breaking his neck."

"That's unfortunate, but it doesn't sound like the kind of event that would inspire rumors of a curse."

"If it was just that solitary incident, it would've been long forgotten. But his family lived here for generations, up until 1967, when tragedy struck again. An intruder broke into the house and murdered over half the family—mom, dad, grandfather."

Noelle was about to take a drink of her tea when she froze, the mug suspended below her lips. "That's . . . awful."

"The only survivors were the children. Elizabeth was seventeen at the time, and she was transported to the hospital in critical condition. Walt was twelve, and his situation was a puzzle that no one has ever been able to put together. He wasn't here when the deputies arrived. In fact, he was nowhere anyone could find him until he walked into town two days later, dehydrated but unharmed."

Her brow creased. "How does a child disappear in a town this small?"

Derek shrugged. "That's the mystery. Even more puzzling, the killer who was arrested a month later said there was no twelve-year-old boy in the house that night. Just an empty bedroom."

"What did Walt say happened?"

"Nothing. To this day, he goes out of his way to avoid talking about it."

Bitterness likely contributed to his secretiveness. Before the killer was apprehended, Walt had been a suspect in the murders. He was held and questioned until Elizabeth recovered enough from her injuries to describe the actual assailant. From then on Walt held a grudge against anyone with a badge.

Noelle dropped her eyes to her tea. "Trauma and grief can make things hard to talk about sometimes."

There was a vulnerability in her posture, and despite the clinical nature of her words, sadness slipped into her voice. She might not be garbed in black or mopping tears from her face, but Derek suspected she was in mourning.

Something inside of Derek shifted, reaching out with a desire to comfort her, because he'd been where she was. "Is your family going to come help you fix this place up?"

"No, um, my parents live in Seattle. But I'm sure I can pull this house together in a year." She surveyed the room and amended, "Or three."

Considering its state of disrepair, he would bet on the latter. His plan for tomorrow was to sit by a pond with a fishing pole in his hand and a dog by his side, but if the tug in his spirit had anything to say about it, those plans were about to change.

"I'm off tomorrow, and I'm pretty handy with a toolbox."

She grimaced at the sink full of moldy dishes. "I think this place is going to need a bleach bath and a hundred trash bags before anything else."

"I'm handy with those too."

She offered a ghost of a smile. "I'm sure you are. But I need every penny to fix this place up. I can't afford to pay anyone to help me right now."

"Something about small towns you'll need to get used to—people help each other just because. There's no money involved." He pulled a business card from his wallet and handed it to her. "If you change your mind about wanting help, my personal number is on the back. If you need to borrow trash bags or a hazmat suit, I live a half mile down the road."

He was pleased to hear the note of teasing in her voice when she replied, "I might take you up on the hazmat suit."

It kind of made him wish he actually had one to offer her.

He checked his watch. "I better go. I have a dog eagerly waiting for me to get home. Thank you for the . . . tea."

"Anytime."

Was that a lilt of amusement in her voice?

He rapped a knuckle on the back door. "You'll want to get this secured as soon as possible."

"I will. Let me walk you out." She set aside her mug and escorted him down the hall to the foyer, opening the front door. "Thanks for coming by to check things out."

"Not a problem." He stepped out onto the porch. "I'll see you around, Ms. McKenzie."

He started down the steps toward his cruiser, but paused when she called out, "You'll see me around nine tomorrow morning, if you bring coffee."

He turned back, surprised to hear her accept his offer. "And if I don't bring coffee?"

She tapped his business card against her palm, considering. "Then I'm not sure I'll have the energy to answer the door."

He smiled and tipped his hat to her. "I'll see you at nine with a healthy dose of caffeine then."

CHAPTER
Nine

Derek dropped into the driver's seat of his cruiser and called up the voice mail from his sister.

Her voice, still tinged with a Tennessee accent from the nine years she lived down south, filled his ear, and he frowned at the breathiness of her words.

"Hey, Derek. Sorry to bother you so late, but . . . Joanna had to leave early, and Jared has his night shift at the factory, so . . . I could really use a ride home from the diner tonight if it's not too much trouble."

Joanna was the afternoon and evening waitress, and she'd been giving Trudy a lift home whenever her husband couldn't. If she and Jared were both gone for the night, that left Trudy alone. Derek didn't like her being alone at the diner this late.

He shoved his key into the ignition and was about to back out of the drive when he remembered what Noelle had said about the gunshot.

Gunshots were common in the country, but they were rare at night. Even Walt knew better than to fire his weapon with such low visibility. It could be nothing, but it could also be something.

Sighing, Derek removed the key from the ignition. He could squeeze in a quick conversation with Walt before picking up Trudy. And knowing Walt, the conversation would be as brief as four words: "Get off my property!"

He texted Trudy to let her know he would be there, and climbed back out of his cruiser. Clicking on his flashlight, he started around the house toward the woods, squinting against the icy rain that slapped his face.

He wouldn't be surprised if Walt was hunkered down among the trees or hiding out in some makeshift tent that allowed him to stay close to the house. His attachment to his childhood home surpassed unhealthy, another reason Derek wanted to speak with him. With Noelle living in it, there was going to be friction.

"Walt?"

He scanned the area, but there was no sign of movement. The storm must've driven the old man back to his home.

Derek cut through the woods toward Walt's patch of land. The trees tapered off, and his flashlight glinted off a rusted green-and-yellow camper in the center of a hundred-foot clearing.

The camper had seen better days—the tires completely deflated, patches of metal siding rusted through, the roof covered with tarps to keep out the rain.

Seeing this twelve-foot, broken-down can reminded Derek of how blessed he was to have a functioning house, and compassion squeezed his heart at the thought of the old man who called this place home.

According to the weather predictions, it was going to be a harsh winter, which would turn Walt's metal home into an extra-large freezer.

"Walt?"

He surveyed the area, his gaze landing on one of the metal jaws in the grass.

Animal traps.

Walt used them to deter trespassers, scattering and concealing them throughout his property like land mines.

After what happened to Walt's family, Derek couldn't blame him for being paranoid. He never went anywhere without his rifle either, as if he expected killers to leap out of the shadows. Thankfully, the locals knew to steer clear of Walt and his property.

Lightning brightened the sky, and Derek caught a flicker of movement in the corner of his vision before darkness fell again. He moved his flashlight toward the spot in time to see a figure limp into the trees on the other side of the property.

"Hey! Hang on a minute!"

He took a step, drawn forward by the instinct to pursue the person who was too broad and tall to be the owner of this patch of land, but then stopped. It would take him too long to pick his way through an acre of hidden traps. Judging by his limping run, the trespasser had stumbled into one of them.

He holstered his weapon and grabbed his radio. The man could've been searching for a lost pet, but Derek's gut told him something else was going on. First Noelle's back door was broken in, and then someone was crossing Walt's land, the incidents less than an hour apart.

"Dispatch, this is Dempsey." He waited for dispatch to respond, then explained about Noelle's broken door and the trespasser on Walt's property. "Could be a prowler. And I think he's got a limp. Let units know to keep an eye out tonight, in case he finds himself somewhere else he's not supposed to be."

He released his radio and fixed his attention on the camper. "Walt! You all right in there?"

He half expected the small metal door to fly open and an old man to stumble out into the rain, shouting for everyone to get off his land, but the door remained closed.

Derek surveyed the invisible obstacle course before him. He needed to make sure Walt was all right.

"Some days I hate my job."

As he inched forward, he avoided the tangles of weeds and matted leaves that might conceal a trap, but he was barely out of the woods when a gunshot cracked through the air, sending him to the ground.

CHAPTER
Ten

Puffs of steam escaped Derek's parted lips as he lay facedown in the overgrown grass, heart thundering in his chest.

He'd switched off his flashlight and dropped to the ground, letting the darkness conceal him from the shooter.

The shot came from the east, the direction of the closest road, the bullet missing him by a good six feet as it hissed through the air.

Did the shooter miss on purpose or by accident?

Derek drew his weapon, not that it would do him much good when he couldn't see farther than the blades of grass tickling his nose.

In all his years on the job, he'd never shot another human being, and he prayed that wouldn't change tonight.

As he reached for his radio to call for backup, a bolt of lightning brightened the area like a stage in a school auditorium.

A figure stood at the edge of the clearing about twenty feet in front of him, the tip of his rifle panning left and right.

Derek ducked lower, his chin pressed to the muddy ground.

"That was a warning shot!" the figure called out.

Derek's fingers stilled on the radio clipped to his shoulder, and his heartbeat relaxed even as irritation tightened his muscles. "Walt, is that you?"

The world paused for a beat before Walt's suspicion-laced voice called back, "Deedee?"

"Yes." Derek clicked on the flashlight and aimed it at Walt. "You mind putting the gun down?"

Walt shifted his grip on the rifle and squinted into the light. "That depends. What do you want?"

"I would like to have a conversation without getting shot."

Walt chewed on that for a long second, as if asking not to be shot were an unreasonable request. "Fine." He lowered his rifle to his side, but he didn't drop it.

Accepting that as the best he was going to get, Derek pushed to his feet and picked up the hat that had fallen off his head when he hit the ground. "You need to be more careful with that rifle."

"I have a right to defend my property."

"Guns should be a last resort. What if it had been a kid or one of my officers?"

Or Noelle. But he suspected bringing up her name would be like tossing a match into a puddle of gasoline.

"I fired into the air so no one would get hurt. I'm not an idiot." Walt picked his way through the grass, dodging objects Derek couldn't see. "Besides, your sister gives me a free meal every night. I'm not going to ruin that by putting a bullet in her brother."

Derek slid his gun back into its holster. "Is that where you were headed tonight? The diner?"

"It's meatloaf night."

Derek assumed that meant yes.

"But I barely made it down the road before I heard shouting coming from my property." Walt scrutinized him with narrowed eyes. "You step in one of my traps?"

"No, but I think *someone* stepped in one. I came over to talk to you and saw a man taking off into the woods."

Alarm registered on Walt's face, and he swung the rifle to a ready rest in front of him, both hands positioned to snap it up and fire at a moment's notice. "Are you sure? Which way did he go?" His eyes darted around. "Was he alone?"

Walt was always high strung, but Derek had never seen him this agitated.

He gestured behind the camper. "As far as I could tell, he was alone, but someone else could've gone into the woods ahead of him."

"Did you come straight from the house?"

The house wasn't visible from here, and when he pulled into the driveway, he'd done so without sirens or flashing lights, which meant his initial suspicion was correct—Walt had been keeping an eye on the house from the woods. That was an issue they were going to have to discuss.

"Did you come straight from the house?" Walt asked again, his tone sharp with impatience and worry.

"I did."

The tip of the rifle sagged toward the ground, and Walt dragged a hand over his face, sponging away the rain that plastered his thinning hair to his head.

"What's going on, Walt?"

Walt's jaw muscles twitched beneath his leathery skin. "I don't know what you're talking about."

"You don't usually open fire on random trespassers, especially ones you can't see clearly. Who did you think I was, that you were willing to shoot first and ask questions later?"

"I don't owe you an explanation."

Walt brushed past him and started for the camper, but Derek caught his arm. "You took a shot at me. I could arrest you for that. But I'd rather you answer a few questions."

Walt's face hardened to stone. "You want to arrest me? Go ahead. It wouldn't be the first time you all arrested me for no good reason."

Derek decided not to point out that the first "arrest" had only been investigative questioning, and it had taken place fifty-three years ago before he was even born. "This doesn't need to turn into a fight."

"I'm not the one making it a fight."

"Someone fired off a shot earlier tonight. You know anything about that?"

"Nope."

"You know anything about the back door of your family's house getting kicked in?"

"Nope. Now get your hand off me and get off my property before I decide shooting you is worth losing out on dinner for the rest of my life." A glimmer of madness danced in his eyes.

Derek released his arm. "I know something's going on. If you talk to me, I can help."

"I don't need your help. I can handle my own business. Besides, we both know why you're really here." He jutted his chin in the direction of the house. "That woman."

"That woman has a name, which I'm certain you know."

"I don't care what she calls herself. She's an intruder, plain and simple, and she needs to leave." He stalked away.

"Walt." Derek turned, visually following Walt's furious retreat. "You need to stay away from her . . . and away from the house."

Walt opened the camper door, ducked inside, and slammed it shut.

CHAPTER
Eleven

It was nearly eleven, but a warm glow still shone through the slatted window blinds of Trudy's diner.

Through the glass front door, Derek could see Trudy leaning on the broom in the middle of the dining room, pausing to catch her breath.

She looked exhausted.

He tapped his knuckles on the door, and her head lifted. She pushed blonde bangs back from her forehead, relief flooding her face at the sight of him.

She was barely taller than the broom she carried as she made her way to the door. She was the youngest in the family—and also the runt. What she lacked in size, though, she made up for in heart.

By the time she unlocked the door and pushed it open, she was panting, and sweat beaded her forehead. "I'm almost done."

Derek took the broom from her. "You are done."

Her blonde eyebrows knitted. "There's a giant pile of dirt in the middle of the dining room floor. I can't—"

"Leave it there until morning? You can, actually, and you are. Keys." He held out his hand.

Trudy blew out a breath but didn't put up a fight, a testament to how tired she was. She fished the key ring from her apron pocket and dangled it over his palm. "I suggest a straight trade. Your keys for mine."

"You can't fit behind the steering wheel of my car and still reach the pedals," he reminded her, snatching her key ring.

She scowled and rested both hands on her swollen stomach. "Because I'm carrying a hippopotamus."

"No argument from me. I think you were due five months ago."

"Are you saying I'm fat?"

Indignation heated her voice, and he paused before answering. "I would never say that."

She narrowed her eyes at him. "But you think it. Just because I can't see my feet, and I no longer have ankles, doesn't mean I'm fat."

"I completely agree." He lifted her coat from the hook on the wall. "Where's Brian tonight?"

Brian, her husband, was one of Derek's deputies, and he'd requested last-minute personal leave.

Trudy slipped her arms into the sleeves of the coat he held open. "Cincinnati. His mom is back in the hospital, so he decided to leave as soon as his shift ended this afternoon."

Derek tried to tamp down his rising suspicion, but the best he could do was keep it to himself. His brother-in-law was a recovering gambler, and there were plenty of places in Cincinnati for him to relapse.

"Did something happen with Brian at work?" Trudy turned, concern sparkling in her hazel eyes.

"Not that I know of. Why?"

"For the past several days, he's been unusually stressed."

"And he hasn't given you any idea why?"

She lowered her head and shook it. "He doesn't talk to me about how he's feeling or what he's thinking, but I can tell. And I know he's . . . unhappy."

"He's got a great job, he's married to one of the most wonderful women I know, and he has a baby on the way. What does he have to be unhappy about?"

"I wish I knew, because then I could fix it." She looked down and adjusted the sleeves of her coat in an effort to conceal the hurt in her voice. "He's chronically discontent and always looking for happiness everywhere except . . ."

Right in front of him, hung unspoken.

Tears gathered on Trudy's lashes, and she tried to blink them away as she fastened the top two buttons of her coat, the remainder hanging like parted curtains over her rounded abdomen.

Anger burned through Derek. "He's not going to find happiness in more money, a bigger house, or a nicer car, no matter how much he thinks he will. In the end, all of those things are hollow."

And Trudy deserved better than a husband who was never satisfied.

She smeared away her tears with her fingertips. "He needs Jesus, but I can't exactly hog-tie him and drag him to church."

"Why not? You forget how to hog-tie someone?"

A laugh bubbled out of her. "Last I checked, it would be illegal, and my big brother is the law."

"I can take a day off."

"Sure you can." She grabbed her scarf from the wall hook below where her coat had been. "Oh, I thought you might like to know you have a new neighbor. The woman who bought the Bechtel house came in for dinner. Noelle . . . something. Have you met her yet?"

Derek had hoped to avoid discussions of women with his matchmaking sister, but he couldn't lie. "I have actually. That's why I ignored your call earlier. I was checking on suspicious activity around her house."

"Suspicious activity?" She paused as she was about to thread one end of her scarf through the looped end of the other. "Is everything okay? Is *she* okay?"

"Seems to be."

"Good, because it's her first night in town, and I would hate for something to scare her off."

He picked up on the scheming note in her tone. "Don't start plotting, Tru. I'm not looking for a relationship."

"But she's so cute," she whispered, unable to contain herself. "And I would never plot against you. Only for you."

"Uh-huh. Now let's go before it gets any later. I would like to be home before midnight."

She swung her purse onto her shoulder and snagged her polka-dot umbrella. "Noelle and I did have a chance to chat tonight. She's really nice. Though I got the impression she's a little sad. I would've asked if she wanted to talk about it, but she's kind of quiet."

"So, when you said the two of you chatted . . ."

"I might've done most of the talking."

He offered her a knowing look. "This is my surprise face."

"Ha-ha. She didn't ask for it, but I think she's going to need some help with that house. It's a disaster."

"I know. I told her I would come over and give her a hand tomorrow." As soon as he turned off the restaurant lights, pounding erupted on the metal door on the back side of the building.

"Oh, one second." Trudy shoved the umbrella and her purse at him, pivoted, and headed toward the dark kitchen.

"Tru . . ." He groaned, itching to get home so he could change out of his wet uniform.

When he heard the slide bolt on the metal door open, he frowned and made his way back to the kitchen. Was she letting someone in at this hour?

"Trudy, what are you doing?"

"What does it look like?" As she nudged open the door, synthetic light and rainwater splashed across the red kitchen tile, and she grabbed a foil container from the warming rack beside her.

Derek gritted his teeth. He'd asked her to stop offering free food from the back of the restaurant after closing. While it was helpful for some of the lower income families in town, it also had the potential to draw thieves and drug addicts.

A man in a raincoat shifted into view, the lamplight casting a shadow over his features.

Derek's gaze swept from the man's hood all the way down to his boots half-submerged in a puddle. With a prowler in the area, he didn't trust anyone he couldn't identify.

Trudy held out the food. "Here you go. It's still warm, and the foil should keep it dry until you get where you're going."

The man took the offering and muttered his thanks before turning and heading back to his vehicle.

Trudy yanked the door shut, plunging the kitchen back into darkness, and grabbed a kitchen towel from the shelf to dry herself. She patted her neck. "I can feel your disapproving stare."

"Why do you insist on doing this every night?"

"Because we're supposed to help people in this life. What you do for the least of these, you do for Jesus. Or did you forget that Sunday school scripture?"

"No, I haven't forgotten, but some of those *least* could be dangerous. Why can't you leave the meals in a box outside with the door locked?"

"Because the health department would go ballistic. Besides, in this storm, anything I put out there would end up in the crick."

"Creek."

"Whatever." She tossed the towel at him, and he caught it before it could smack him in the face. "And don't pretend you wouldn't complain about the meals being in a box outside the diner too."

"I worry, especially when you're here alone."

"And I love that you worry." She stretched up on her toes to kiss his cheek. "It's adorably big brothery, but with the factory cutting jobs and the gas station shut down, people are out of work. I'm not going to sell the leftovers tomorrow, and I'm not going to throw them away when there are hungry families."

"I know." But he wished she would be more careful.

Trudy scooped up the last container of food from the rack and a box of what smelled like frosted cinnamon rolls. "Do you think we could stop by Walt's place before you take me home? He didn't make it by tonight."

Because he was too busy shooting at me, Derek bit back.

"And he didn't make it last night either, which isn't like him. It has me worried. I know the only hot meal he gets is from here."

Derek didn't want to have another confrontation with the man, but Trudy was right—it wasn't like him to miss a meal, and he needed the food more than most. "I'll drop it off after I take you home. He's irritable tonight, and I don't want you near him."

She hugged his arm. "You are the best brother."

"Yeah, yeah. It helps that you don't have another brother to compare me to."

"True."

She frowned at the pile of dirt as she passed by it, then glanced at the broom leaning against the wall. Derek pressed a hand between her shoulder blades and nudged her forward.

"Nope, keep walking."

"But it'll only take two seconds."

"Until you see another speck of dirt or realize one of the pepper shakers is empty or notice the fork under the booth."

"There's a fork under—"

He nudged her right out the door, locking up before she had a chance to sneak back in. He would help her straighten up before the diner reopened, but he did not want to be here all night.

———

Derek stepped into his house and flipped on the lights, exhaustion weighing as heavily on his shoulders as on his wet uniform. He hung his hat and kicked off his muddy shoes.

He tried to never bring work home with him, but his mind cycled through the events of the day—the prowler with the limp, the abandoned car with the keys still in the ignition, Brian being in Cincinnati, Walt's heightened agitation.

He wasn't home when Derek stopped by the second time, so he left the food inside the camper. Where had he wandered off to? The diner and the church food pantry were both closed, so it wouldn't make sense for him to walk into town. Was he out in the woods in one of his makeshift hiding places?

Derek rolled his car keys between his fingers, torn between calling it a night and going back out to hunt for Walt. The winds were supposed to reach sixty miles per hour tonight, and the storm was already snapping off limbs along the roads.

It wasn't safe for anyone to be out on foot. But even if he drove all over town until he found the old man, he would never be able to coax him into the car or back to his camper. He was stubborn and distrustful beyond reason.

With a sigh, Derek dropped his keys in the bowl on the entryway table.

The rhythmic thump of a dog tail against the wall welcomed him home, and he bent to greet her.

"Hey, Elsa."

His Labrador was part of a promise he'd made to the woman he loved and lost five years ago. When he and Lacey talked about the future, she dreamed of adopting a white Labrador named Elsa who would grow up alongside their children.

But there never were any children, because Lacey's body wasn't strong enough to fight the cancer spreading through her lymphatic system. They were married for less than a year when they received the prognosis, and six months later she was gone.

Before she died, she made him promise that he wouldn't spend the rest of his life alone and in mourning. To honor her wishes, he tracked down a Labrador puppy so pale that she was almost white, named her Elsa, and brought her home.

God would introduce him to another amazing woman someday, but until then, he was content coming home to Elsa every night.

"Hey, beautiful girl." He bent down and rubbed behind her ears. "I know we were supposed to go fishing tomorrow, but something's come up."

He wished he could bring her to Noelle's house, but with the broken glass and debris all over the property, it wasn't a safe environment for her. He also wasn't sure how Noelle felt about dogs or if she had allergies, and he hadn't thought to ask.

"I met a lady today who needs some help, so I need to go give her a hand tomorrow. We'll go fishing another day, when the weather's nicer."

Elsa chuffed and thumped her tail, her hind legs fidgeting on the tile with excitement. All she cared about was the fact that he was home. After his shower, they would unwind on the couch with some sports recaps and corn chips. Elsa loved her corn chips.

Derek stood and patted her head before heading for the bathroom, Elsa's nails clacking along behind him.

———

Noelle sat against the bedroom wall, her son's black-and-red stuffed spider propped on her knees.

It was his favorite stuffed animal, and one of only a handful of nonessential items she'd packed. She rubbed one of its bead-filled legs between her fingers.

This time of day was always the hardest, when her heart ached for the routine of tucking Tay into bed, reading him a story, and peppering his sweet face with kisses.

Instead, she was alone in this shack with nothing but a stuffed spider and memories for company.

The notification light blinked on her phone, and she tapped the screen to wake it. A Bible verse waited to be read. She'd scheduled the daily reminder when she purchased the phone a year and a half ago, but she couldn't figure out how to *un*schedule it.

She could delete the Bible app altogether, but a part of her feared that would only deepen the rift between her and God.

She tried to flick away the notification, but it expanded, filling her screen. Last night the scripture had been about light shining in the darkness, and tonight it was about joy.

"Weeping may endure for a night, but joy cometh in the morning." She stared at the scripture, then sighed and flipped the phone over on the blankets. "Sure it does."

Joy didn't spontaneously wash over her with the morning light. It was just more of the same—grief, loneliness, and the nagging question: what's the point?

She rested her head back against the wall and let her eyes drift upward, fixing on a knot of wood in the ceiling. "God, if You're listening, I need . . ." She grappled for the right words to express the longing in her spirit.

Something worth living for? A purpose beyond simple existence? A meaning to anchor her so she didn't feel as dried-up and aimless as the leaves tumbling in the breeze?

She sighed. "Something. I need . . . something, Lord."

She slid down onto the blankets and drew her knees to her chest, closing her eyes. And even though she dismissed the Bible verse, a sliver of her heart dared to hope that joy would come in the morning.

CHAPTER
Twelve

He hated unpredictable people. His assault on the back door was supposed to send the woman running, but instead, she pulled out a gun and paced until help came.

Everyone and their blind grandmother had a gun nowadays.

He lifted his binoculars, slapping aside the wet cornstalk leaves that sliced at him like razor blades in the storm. The house was pitch black. The woman was probably asleep.

Scaring her out of the house hadn't worked, which meant he might need to drag *her out. If he buried her body deep enough and disposed of her car, people might assume she left because she was too scared to stay.*

He started to stand, but headlights cut through the cornfield. He shrank back down and waited as the vehicle crawled down the road between the cornfield and house. It was the same car that had driven by four times tonight. It slowed, but this time it turned into the driveway.

The driver's door opened, and a man climbed out, his attention on the house. He took a few steps toward the porch, paused, and then returned to his car, sinking back into the driver's seat and closing the door. He backed out of the driveway and drove off, but there was no way to know if he might circle back a fifth time.

Another unpredictable person ruining his plans.

CHAPTER
Thirteen

The world whipped around Noelle in a dizzying funnel of lights and shouts, people in uniforms pressing in from all directions.

Noelle sat motionless in the street, barely able to breathe. Her little boy's body was too still. Too broken.

"Give us some room," a man demanded, and then strong hands gripped her arms and dragged her away. His tiny fingers slipped from hers, and the anguish in her heart roared up her throat and exploded out of her in a scream.

The scream wrenched Noelle from that dark street and back onto a hard wood floor, her body twisted in blankets. She blinked at the blurry ceiling above her, an afterimage of that awful night burned into her vision.

Tears squeezed up her tightening throat, and she struggled to breathe beneath the crushing weight of grief on her chest.

Tay was gone, his precious life snuffed out by a screech of tires and a blaring horn. Noelle wrapped her arms around the stuffed spider, wishing it was her little boy, and tried to swallow the tears.

In the quiet, Tyrese's voice slithered into her thoughts, bringing guilt and searing pain with it. *Our son is dead because of you.*

She tried to push away the words her husband had spoken to her the day of the funeral—words designed to grind the broken pieces of her into dust.

Get up, she silently urged. If she lay here much longer, she would sink into the waiting depression and never find her way back to the surface. *Get up and do something before you can't do anything.*

———————

The storm receded before dawn, leaving broken limbs and a fresh smattering of wet leaves on the ground.

The morning air smelled crisp and damp as Noelle breathed it in, the chill invigorating even as it made her long for a warmer jacket. It wasn't cold enough to freeze her nose hairs together, but the mist numbed her cheeks.

She'd considered going for a run to work through her emotions, but since there was no madman chasing her down with a knife, she couldn't find the motivation to move beyond a leisurely stroll.

She waded through the knee-high grass of the yard, acres upon acres of weeds and trees, and noted the details in the hazy morning light. A shed, the artesian well pump, the tips of a wrought iron fence that enclosed a small square of land. Was that a cemetery?

Something in the woods caught her eye, and she maneuvered past the prickly bushes to get a closer look. It was a tree house nestled in one of the large oaks. It might have been beautiful once, but now it was patched together with scraps—wood, metal, cardboard. There were even strips of cereal boxes.

Ladder rungs made of ragged and splintered boards trailed up the tree to a latch fastened in place by a padlock.

Children didn't lock tree houses. To a child, passwords and secret phrases were security enough.

Noelle stepped back to consider the structure from a different angle. There was a small window facing the far woods, and another that provided a perfect view of the house. *Her* house.

Anxiety threaded through her.

Was this the source of the mysterious light she saw last night? Had someone been watching her from the tree house during the storm?

Fresh mud caked the ladder rungs, indicating someone had been up there recently, but the entry flap was padlocked from the outside.

Noelle wrapped her arms around herself and scanned her surroundings. Walt had made it clear that he wanted her gone, and it wouldn't surprise her if he huddled up there with a lantern last night, waiting to see if their confrontation would send her running.

Where was he now?

Twigs snapped and wet leaves scraped across the ground as she turned, visually searching her surroundings.

Don't let him scare you.

She forced her eyes to stop bouncing between the trees. If he wanted to spook her, the best thing she could do was deny him the satisfaction. She turned and headed back toward the house, keeping her retreat relaxed.

Something bright blue and half-buried in leaves drew her eye. Dismissing it as garbage, she continued walking, but she barely made it five steps before her imagination whispered, *It could be buried treasure.*

"Or a potato chip bag." Which was likely, considering the rest of the trash strewn around the area.

Or the fragments of an old hot air balloon with a fascinating history.

"Hot air balloon?" Where had her creative brain dreamed that up? Something about this place had awakened her dormant imagination, and odd ideas like ghosts and balloons were spilling out.

She gripped the pendant resting below the hollow of her throat, remembering the childlike delight of discovering something beautiful and interesting. It was a delight she hadn't felt in a long time, one that rough life experiences had sanded away.

But she had moved here for a fresh start, so why not reconnect with the wonder-filled child she used to be?

She released her pendant and marched back to the object, crouching. "If this is a potato chip bag or a cigarette package . . ."

Using a stick, she pushed aside the matted leaves. Surprise flooded her. The object wasn't garbage at all. It was a blue notebook with a faux leather cover.

She plucked it from its soggy grave and brushed it off. "What are you doing out here?"

It was in good condition despite the rain. Peeling open the cover, Noelle studied the inscription written in permanent marker.

"To my little Firefly, the light of my life."

Noelle smiled at the nickname. She'd never seen a firefly glow, but her grandmother, Grammy, had been born and raised in a part of the country where fireflies lit up the summer nights. She said it was like fields of glitter, a sure sign that even in the dark, God shines a light.

The message in this diary must've come from a parent or grandparent, but there was no name to tell her who the notebook belonged to.

There might be names hidden somewhere in the childlike script that filled each line. If so, she would find it and return the notebook to the young soul who had poured her thoughts across the pages.

CHAPTER
Fourteen

Derek tied up the bag of trash left over from last night at the diner and heaved it out of the can. What did they fill it with, bowling balls?

Trudy eyed him as she tied an apron around her waist. "I'm perfectly capable of taking out the garbage."

"As heavy as this bag is, you'd go into labor midlift."

She considered her stomach and then glanced at the trash bag nearly bursting at the seams. "Well, one of us is sure to pop this morning, and I'd rather it be me. Move over and let me at it."

Derek swiped away her reaching hand. "Nice try."

Her mouth thinned, and she stuffed her apron pockets with straws, her movements more frustrated than usual. There was something more going on than what they discussed last night.

"Why don't I stay and wait tables while Joanna's out sick?"

An odd look crossed Trudy's face before she averted her eyes. "You don't need to do that. Besides"— she flashed him a teasing smile—"I'm not sharing my tips with you."

"You're just afraid I'll make more than you."

"The only way you would ever make more tips than me is if Janet Robinson came in for lunch. That woman would throw anything at you to get your attention—her life savings, her car, herself."

Derek laughed. Unfortunately, Trudy wasn't exaggerating. The woman had more tentacles than a jellyfish, and she always managed to wrap them around him at church. He was lucky if he escaped the building without tangerine lipstick on his face.

"Maybe I should give Janet a chance. We might make a good couple."

Trudy's eyes widened in shock. "Please tell me that's a joke."

"You want me to get married again, she wants to marry me . . . it's like a match made in—"

"Absolutely not. I will not have that woman as my sister-in-law. Don't even joke about something so heinous."

"Heinous seems a tad extreme."

"When I first started showing, she accused me of having early-onset middle-aged spread and tried to sell me a drink that would melt away the 'layers of fat.' Layers, Derek. She didn't just call me fat. She called me fat with *layers*. Like I'm a big ole chunky cake."

Derek pressed his lips together to trap the laugh that wanted to escape.

Trudy's cheeks flamed with anger. "I can't even look at a cake without thinking about that woman." She grabbed a lighter from beneath the register. "I'm going to go light the candles . . . which make me think of cake, which makes me think of Janet. And now I feel fat."

Derek smiled and shook his head as she waddled into the dining room to light the mason jar candles at the tables where her breakfast regulars preferred to sit. Trudy always had a flare for the dramatic, but with her pregnancy hormones, she was an entire theatrical performance on her own.

He hefted the garbage bag and carried it toward the back door, pausing to pick up a piece of paper on the tile. He expected it to be trash, but it was a bill with "Past Due" highlighted in red.

Trudy must've forgotten to pay it.

Setting down the trash bag, he returned the bill to the desk in the office. Several more bills stared back at him with a "Past Due" or "Late" notice marked in red. Derek picked them up and flipped through them, worry tightening his chest—gas, electric, trash, produce. Everything.

Trudy's shoes squeaked on the tile as she appeared in the doorway, and she folded her arms above her rounded stomach.

"Why didn't you tell me you were struggling, Tru?"

Tears sparkled in her eyes. "Because you would've asked questions, and I don't have answers."

"What do you mean?"

"I don't know where the money's going. Brian's been squirreling it away for months. When I asked him about it, he said it's a surprise, but . . . I think he might be gambling again."

"And you were afraid to tell me because I'm his boss." There was a real chance Brian would lose his job if he relapsed. Derek dropped the bills back onto the desk. "Is Joanna actually out sick?"

Trudy rolled her lips between her teeth and shook her head. "I couldn't afford to pay her, and I won't ask her to work for free."

What was Brian doing? How could he put his wife in this situation?

Derek pulled his phone from his pocket. "I'm calling Noelle to let her know I can't come over today, and then I'm calling Brian."

"No, you are not. You agreed to help her, and the members of this family do not go back on their word." She pinned him with a look that reminded him of their mother. "And Brian is my husband. I'll talk to him."

"I can't leave you to handle this all on your own. You shouldn't be waiting tables."

"I'll manage for a few days or however long it takes. Tough times don't last forever. But if you want to help me clean up and close everything down tonight, I wouldn't complain."

"Of course I will."

"Now, you're going to help Noelle, and you're going to take her a pumpkin spice latte when you do."

His eyebrows lifted. "Oh really?"

"It's her favorite coffee. I did manage to get that much out of her during our chat. But before you go, you can take that trash out." She eyed the bag slowly slumping its way over on the floor. "It stinks."

With a smile, he kissed the top of her head. "We'll figure this out together."

"I know."

He scooped up the trash and shouldered open the metal door that led to the parking lot. His phone rang as he headed for the dumpster.

Rusty.

Derek tossed the bag into the metal bin before taking the call. "Hey, Rusty."

"Captain. I managed to get in touch with Ms. Eugenia Banks this morning. Good news—the ninety-seven-year-old woman was not driving the abandoned car."

"Small blessings."

A blue car turned into the parking lot of the law office across the street, and Perry Habrams climbed out. He grabbed a briefcase and then hurried toward the front entrance, his attention swiveling left and right.

Was he limping?

"Ms. Banks passed her car along to her granddaughter, Maddie Wingate," Rusty continued, drawing Derek's focus back to the conversation.

"What do we know about Maddie?"

"She's eighteen, a freshman at Akron University. Ms. Banks gave me her cell number, but every call goes straight to voice mail. I think the phone must be off."

That detail alone triggered alarm bells. "What teenage girl turns off her phone?"

"That's my question too. I can barely get my granddaughters to look away from their phones long enough to say hello and good-bye."

"What about the school?"

"Maddie's only been a student there since August, so they didn't have much to offer. They gave me the contact information for her roommate, but she's in class until this afternoon. The parents might know something. I'm expecting a call back."

It sounded like they were going to have to wait on other people's schedules to gather more information.

"Do we have a photo of her?"

"Yeah, give me a minute and I'll text it to you." Rusty muttered to himself before adding, "There we go. I think I sent it."

A photo loaded on Derek's screen, and he found himself staring at a pair of bright brown eyes, a shy smile, and a round face framed by silky blonde hair. Maddie Wingate had an innocent cuteness about her that reminded him more of a child than a woman.

Derek cautioned himself to wait for all the facts before leaping to the worst possible conclusion, but something dark and foreboding slithered through his stomach as he stared at her picture.

"I know that no one has officially reported her missing yet, but go through the car—gently. See if there's any indication of foul play," he instructed.

He didn't want the car dismembered or chunks cut out of the fabric for stain analysis if Maddie was going to pop back up on the radar after crashing at a friend's house for the weekend.

But if something had happened to her, and the sheriff's department dragged its feet . . . the consequences for Maddie could be life altering. Or life ending.

CHAPTER Fifteen

Noelle sat on the porch steps with a mug of hot green tea and stared at the gray sky.

She needed all the caffeine she could get if she was going to make it through the rest of the day without taping her eyelids open. Actually, as heavy as her eyelids felt, she might have to bypass the tape and go straight for superglue.

She'd been awake since six o'clock this morning, which wouldn't be a problem if she'd fallen asleep at a reasonable hour. Three a.m. was not a reasonable hour.

She'd called the electric company to let them know she needed the power turned on, but they said it would be a day or two before they could send someone out.

She was more concerned about the sewage and water pipes than the electricity, though. If new pipes needed to be laid, that was another pricey repair beyond her skill set. It might come down to a choice between the roof and the plumbing.

Worry only serves one purpose—to steal joy. Noelle's heart warmed at the memory of Grammy imparting those words with a shine of wisdom in her eyes.

Before the Alzheimer's stole Grammy's mind, she'd been a font of wisdom—a lifetime of experiences that became lessons for everyone she loved.

Joy. Noelle turned the mug restlessly in her hands as she pondered the word that had become a foreign concept in her life. Despite the fleeting hope inspired by the scripture last night, there had been nothing joyful about her morning.

"Joy isn't happiness, child. Happiness comes and goes with the breeze," Grammy used to say, when Noelle pouted that she was unhappy. "But joy is rooted so deeply in the Rock that it can't be uprooted even when a storm tears through your life."

"Well, the storm came, Grammy, and here I am standing alone, my joy swept out to sea."

Her thumb grazed her bare ring finger, a habit she was trying to break, and she curled her fingers into a fist.

How many times had she twisted those gold bands around her finger as she waited for her husband to come home? Sometimes Tyrese hadn't come home at all, and sometimes, when he did eventually walk through the door, she wished he hadn't.

He wasn't the man she married. He wasn't the man who promised to build a beautiful life together around the baby growing inside her. He changed. Or maybe he'd been that way all along, and she'd been too smitten to see the signs.

Mom warned her that Tyrese was a poor choice, that he didn't hold the same values as their family, but Noelle ignored her.

Naïve and foolish.

And she'd lost the only good thing to come out of that miserable, broken marriage.

She took another sip of her tea and tried to ignore the shadow of depression that plunked down beside her on the steps. If she didn't find something positive to focus on, he would slide closer.

"Positive, positive, positive," she muttered, searching for something—anything.

A thin ray of sunshine punched through the blanket of clouds, landing on the spiderweb above her and making the intricately woven strands glitter.

"Morning, Charlie." She raised her mug of tea to the little spider. "Nice threads."

Spiderwebs might be disgusting to run into, but they truly were beautiful works of art. They weren't as unique as snowflakes, but they were unique to the breed of spider.

She knew more about spiders than she ever wanted to because Tay had been obsessed with them, and he devoured and shared every detail he could find about them. Somehow, his passion became a part of her.

She'd given him the stuffed spider for his seventh birthday, and unsurprisingly, he named it Peter Parker.

Noelle's gaze trailed to the mysterious journal beside her, which, based on the feminine style of the inscription, was a special gift from another mother to her child.

The notebook lay open and drying, the pages flapping like boat sails in the wind.

She slid the journal closer, noticing ridges where half a dozen sheets of paper had been torn out. Her notebooks growing up had been similar. She couldn't simply scratch out a few lines she didn't like. She ripped out the entire page and started fresh. Her eyes slid from the torn pages to the first entry.

This is my secret diary.
If you're reading it, it's probably cause I tied it to the leg of a giant bird and he flew away and dropped it somewhere in the world. You can be my secret friend. If you want.

The mental image of a little girl trying to snatch a pigeon from her window so she could tie the diary to his leg coaxed a smile from Noelle's tightly pressed lips. The girl must have seen a movie or read a book that involved carrier pigeons, but with this anchor tied to his leg, that poor bird would sink like a boulder from the sky.

That did spark an interesting question, though—carrier pigeons aside, how had this diary ended up in the woods behind her house?

She took another sip of tea and continued reading, hoping the answers would appear somewhere in the text.

I think reading is one of my favorit things in the whole world cause I can go lots of places in my head even when I'm stuck in one place. Mom puts me in quiet time alot so I sit by the window and read on her kindle.

I learned somthing cool about elephants when I was reading today. They have long memries like people. But not all people. Mom forgets where she puts her lighter and her gum and sometimes her socks.

That was a woman Noelle could relate to. This morning, she couldn't find the vanilla lip balm she kept in her jacket pocket. It was still missing and presumed lost for all eternity.

At least she still had the lip balm in her purse, the one in her glove compartment, and a spare in the emergency kit in the trunk. She needed to buy a new one for her jacket before things exploded into chaos.

Mom accused her of having a "Chapstick obsession." One in every flavor and in every necessary location was hardly an obsession.

She wiggled the sphere of mint lip balm from the pocket of her jeans and applied a layer. Lips thoroughly moisturized, she turned her attention to the last paragraph of the entry.

I told Mom what I read about elephants cause I think it's pretty cool. But she says remembring things isn't always that graet and sometimes its better to forget. Sometimes she tells me to forget things and pretend I didn't hear something or see something bad but I'm not good at forgeting. I think I'm kind of like an elephant.

Noelle couldn't imagine telling a child to forget something bad that happened. Even bad experiences could lead to growth and understanding if handled correctly.

What was this girl being exposed to that she was supposed to forget and pretend didn't happen?

She started to turn the page, concern driving her to dig deeper, when an unfamiliar gray truck turned into the driveway.

The driver door opened, and Captain Dempsey climbed out. He'd traded in his sheriff's department uniform for jeans, an unbuttoned red flannel, and a gray T-shirt.

Axe-toting murderer or Hallmark movie love interest, Noelle mused. *Both seem to favor flannel.* She closed the journal and rose to greet him.

Even with his flannel, he was dressed better than she was. She'd picked ratty jeans with unflattering holes around the knees and an old, stained sweatshirt. In truth, she didn't have many nice clothes. There was never a need. Tyrese didn't invite her to his fancy work dinners, and her friends were imaginary. They didn't care what she wore while typing them into existence.

Her wardrobe was perfect for working on this house—painting, dusting, crawling through filth and spiderwebs.

She flicked an apologetic glance toward Charlie the spider. "Sorry if I kill any of your cousins today."

Captain Dempsey grabbed some things from his truck and then crunched up the driveway in well-worn work boots. The man wasn't gorgeous by any stretch of the imagination—and Noelle's imagination was pretty flexible—but he wasn't *unattractive* either. He was broad shouldered, and his blond beard, trimmed and neatly rounded, softened what might have been an angular face.

His hazel eyes sparkled with chipper energy as he climbed the steps onto the porch. "Good morning."

Oh, he's one of those people, she groaned inwardly. "Morning? Isn't it still yesterday?"

"I take it you didn't get much sleep."

She grunted. The bags under her eyes were so big that the airport would charge her extra to bring them on board the plane.

"Old houses make a lot more noise than I expected," she said, unwilling to share the real reason for her lack of sleep. The nightmares were more disturbing than the creaks, groans, and cracks of the house, and they were too private to share with a man she barely knew.

"Yes, they do."

"How about you, Captain?"

"This is my second time at your house in twenty-four hours. You're welcome to call me Derek, and the rest of my night was relatively peaceful."

He offered her one of the three cups from the tray he carried. Surely he hadn't invited a third person to this cleaning party.

She accepted the cup. "Thanks."

He held out a plastic bag. "I brought a little something I hope you'll like."

97

Setting the journal on the railing, Noelle took the bag and peered inside to find a bottle of pumpkin spice creamer. Her favorite. But how . . .

"Before you start wondering if I'm a creep, Trudy told me you asked about pumpkin spice lattes last night when you stopped at the diner for dinner."

"Trudy." She blanked on the name, but then a short pregnant woman with a messy bun of blonde hair materialized in her mind. "The pregnant waitress?"

"That's the one."

"So, you two are . . ."

"Brother and sister."

Oh. That wasn't what she expected, but with that clarification, she could see the similarity in their eye and hair color, as well as the kind disposition.

"I'm sorry it's not a latte, but hopefully it's the next best thing," he said.

He could've bought her a pet rock and it would've flooded her chest with the same warmth. She'd gotten so used to Tyrese's cold indifference that she'd forgotten how wonderful it was for someone to simply think of her.

"It's my favorite creamer actually, so thank you." She popped the lid off the coffee cup to find it half empty, and slid him a questioning glance. "Get thirsty on the way over?"

He set the tray with the two remaining cups on a chair. "Blame Trudy. I asked for two coffees, she gave me one full cup and two cups half filled. I have no idea why."

A half-empty cup left plenty of room for creamer, something she and Trudy had discussed last night.

Noelle preferred her coffee about 70 percent flavored creamer. If she were being honest with herself, though, she could drink this spicy cream straight from the bottle.

She twisted off the cap and filled the empty space in her cup, the dark liquid swirling into a creamy beige that made her mouth water.

Derek let out a low whistle. "I can look away if you want to chug that straight from the jug."

She screwed the cap back on and narrowed her eyes at him. "Don't judge. Or read my mind."

"Even if I had that superpower, I think I would avoid the confusing corridors of a woman's thoughts. I would never find my way back out."

"True. You would probably get lost in a memory of some awkward thing I said seven years ago that still plagues me today."

She had quite a few of those moments stored away.

Derek laughed, and it was a warm and inviting sound that somehow made him more attractive. Not that she was in the market for a relationship, or that he would even be interested.

She'd met this man twice—once while wearing pajamas, and now with a wasp's nest of untamed hair, holey jeans, and a sleep-deprived glaze over her eyes.

She was man repellant.

"You mind if I check out this door before we get started cleaning?" Derek fixed his sights on the front door. "I noticed it was unlevel last night."

Noelle couldn't disagree, but she wasn't sure the door could be fixed with the screwdriver he drew from the tool belt around his waist. "Knock yourself out. Not literally, though. My first aid skills are lacking."

Derek opened the door to inspect it and made a thoughtful noise. "The frame is rotted, and the wood isn't gripping the screws for the hinges. There's a lumber yard about twenty minutes away where we can get supplies to build a new frame. Or you might be able to find a prehung door that we could install."

That *we* could install. How much time and energy was this man willing to sacrifice for a complete stranger?

"So you work full-time for the sheriff's department *and* you're a handyman?"

He shrugged. "I inherited the handyman position when I was eight. My dad passed away, which left me as man of the house. I taught myself a few things so I could help out my mom."

He spoke as though losing his father were merely a fact rather than a traumatic, life-altering event. "That must've been hard."

He exchanged the screwdriver for a measuring tape. "I blackened a few thumbnails before I learned how to aim a hammer, and I nearly electrocuted myself once. But I eventually got the hang of things."

That wasn't what she'd meant, and she suspected he knew that. "That was a lot of responsibility thrust onto your small shoulders."

"As you can see, my shoulders grew to accommodate that responsibility."

She *could* see. As he bent to measure the frame, the flannel pulled tight across his back and shoulders, emphasizing thick muscle. If he ever had to make an arrest, criminals would probably offer to handcuff themselves to avoid tangling with him.

"What about you?" he asked.

"Sorry, what?"

"Your family."

"Oh, um, I have my parents and some aunts, uncles, cousins. I have an older half sister from Dad's relationship before he met my mom, but we never really connected."

"That's too bad."

She'd tried to have a relationship with her sister, only to be met with bitterness because their father chose to build a life with Noelle's mother rather than hers. If the situation had been reversed, Noelle might have felt the same.

She leaned against the railing and cleared her throat, trying to redirect her thoughts. "Do you happen to know if there are any children in the village who go by the nickname Firefly?"

"No, sorry, I don't. Why do you ask?"

"I found a diary, and I wanted to get it back to—" Something snapped and popped, and before she could do anything more than gasp, the railing behind her was gone, and she was falling.

Derek's hand shot out and wrapped around her wrist, but it was too late. She plunged over the edge of the porch and dragged him down with her.

101

The logical part of Noelle's brain knew it was only a four-foot drop, but her body panicked, as if she'd been thrown out of an airplane and was hurtling toward her death. Her heart launched into her throat, smothering a scream, and then she smacked the ground hard enough to rattle her teeth.

Ow.

A groan came from her right, and she turned her head to see Derek lying beside her, half in the overgrown yard and half in what remained of the flowerbed.

Noelle lifted her head and examined him with concern. "Are you okay?" she choked out, still trying to recapture her breath.

He rolled onto his side in slow motion. "Never better. The surprisingly hard ground broke my fall."

She winced sympathetically. "Sorry to take you down with me."

Amusement danced in his eyes. "You should be sorry. It's completely your fault that I grabbed your arm."

Noelle dropped her head back into the grass. "I guess I need a new railing."

"I have crime scene tape in the back of my truck. No one will notice the difference."

A rusty sound escaped her throat, creaking into a wheezing laugh. She couldn't remember the last time she'd laughed, but there was no ignoring the absurdity of this situation. This poor, kind man had offered to help clean her house, and she'd repaid that thoughtfulness by pulling him off the porch into the mud.

And to think, a few minutes ago she'd been worried about looking a wreck because of her hair and holey jeans. Now she was going to have a mud-streaked backside.

She pressed a hand to her stomach as the fading laughter left a delightfully familiar ache in her sides. "I can't remember the last time I laughed like that."

He smiled. "Been a while, huh?"

"Nearly a year."

Concern dimmed his smile, and questions swirled in his eyes, but Noelle spoke before he could voice any of them.

"Where'd my coffee go?"

"To find that, you're going to need a machete and a jungle tour guide."

Meaning it was lost in the knee-high grass. Wonderful. "Good thing I have a spare."

Derek propped himself on an elbow. "What am I lying on?" He reached beneath him and pulled out the blue journal, now covered in mud. "Yours?"

She took it from him and sat up. "Sort of. It's the diary I found in the woods this morning." She swiped a hand across the top of the notebook, flinging aside the mud and leaves.

Derek grunted and looked down at his beard, where a glob of muddy leaf had landed.

Heat rushed to Noelle's face. "I'm so sorry."

He picked it from his beard and flicked it away. "It's not bad enough that you threw me off a house? Now you're slinging mud at me?"

She narrowed her eyes. "It was a porch, and I didn't throw you."

His mouth curved into another easy smile. "I think that's a matter of perspective." He got to his feet and offered a hand. "Let's try this again, without the falling."

She took the hand that was as dirty as hers and let him pull her to her feet. She started to brush the leaves and dirt from her clothes when something moved at the edge of her vision.

A skeletal figure stood beneath the shade of a large tree. The morning light stripped Walt of the ghostly quality that clung to him last night, but there was still something about him that made Noelle's nerves flutter.

A muscle writhed in the hollows of his cheeks as he stared at the two of them, until his attention snagged on the journal in Noelle's hand.

He stepped forward, shifting his grip on the rifle that rested on his shoulder.

"Derek." Noelle touched his arm to get his attention, but when she looked back toward the tree, there was nothing but reeds of grass swaying in the chilly morning breeze.

CHAPTER Sixteen

Derek approached the maple tree flanked by two ancient pines, searching for any sign of the old man. Noelle was certain she'd seen Walt, but he disappeared in an instant.

Derek parted the sagging branches of the pines and peered inside, frowning when he found a man-made cavity. Interior limbs had been trimmed to create a comfortable space, and a log sat in the center, a ring of cigarette butts around it. One of those cigarettes still smoldered where it had been pressed into the damp bed of needles.

Derek's eyes drifted upward to where a worn tarp had been tied to notches in the branches to create a canopy above the clearing.

Walt was nowhere in sight. He must have walked out the other side, unseen from their position by the porch.

Derek released the branches, and they closed like curtains over the hiding spot. He needed to have a conversation with Walt about criminal trespass and invasion of privacy.

How was he going to explain this to Noelle without scaring her?

He glanced over his shoulder to see her on the porch, fixing her second cup of coffee. A smile tugged at his tight lips when he noticed a brightly colored leaf bobbing in her hair—a leftover from their fall.

That experience certainly gave new meaning to the expression "falling for a woman."

He thought for sure he could catch her, but gravity had the upper hand. His back still ached from the landing, reminding him that he was months away from turning forty.

Flinging a wet leaf off the tip of his boot, he walked back to the porch.

Noelle swirled the cup in her hand, mixing the contents. "Anything?"

"No Walt. But there's a man-made clearing inside the two pines and a smoldering cigarette. He was definitely there, and recently."

The cup stilled in her hand. "I'm sorry, what?"

Smooth, Derek. Ease right into the fact that an old man has been creeping on her from the trees in her front yard. Sometimes he could kick himself for not being more tactful.

"Walt has always been abnormally protective of his family's home, and he has watching posts hidden throughout the property. No one knows where all of them are, but it looks like he turned the space between the trees into one of them."

Her gaze slid past his shoulder to the old pines.

He waited for the instant recoil he'd been concerned about, for her to retreat inside behind the safety of a locked door, but it was outrage rather than fear that colored her next words. "What is wrong with him?"

Derek scratched at his beard. "My guess is a lot. If we could get him to speak to a psychiatrist, I suspect she would discover, at the very least, a paranoid personality disorder."

"Yeah, well he's going to make other people paranoid, namely me. Hiding in my trees." Her hand moved to the necklace she wore, the pendant slipping between her fingers. "Do you think he's dangerous?"

How to answer that . . .

Walt was an outcast by choice, and he operated based on his own sense of right and wrong. He wasn't above physical and psychological intimidation to get his way.

Almost everyone in the department knew Walt was a loose cannon, and they were waiting for him to cross a line so they could force him to get the help he needed.

"I would like to think he wouldn't cause any harm, but you're the first person to live here since his family. Unfortunately, that makes it impossible to know how he'll behave."

"Great." She sighed. "Just what I need in my life right now."

"I'll talk to him as soon as I can, make sure he understands the consequences for trespassing and harassment."

"Thanks."

She lifted her eyes to his, and the sunlight highlighted flecks of amber and root beer brown in her irises, creating a mesmerizing depth. Trudy described Noelle as cute, but that word didn't quite fit her.

Noelle shifted against the door frame, her hand moving to touch the knot of hair on top of her head. "Do

I have another cobweb in my hair?" She probed self-consciously with her fingertips. "I've been dodging them all morning."

He realized he was staring and smiled. "No, but you do have a leaf. May I?"

She moved her hand, giving him permission, and he plucked the bright yellow leaf from her hair, letting it flutter away in the breeze.

"Ready to get started?"

"Sure." She pushed away from the door frame and retreated inside, with him only a few steps behind.

———

Derek was as hardworking as Noelle expected. He scrubbed the floors in square patches, as though he were performing a grid search rather than cleaning away dust and dirt.

The unusual clean streak on the floor vanished beneath his fast-moving brush, but it remained in Noelle's mental vault of mysteries to be solved.

With a pair of rubber gloves she found in a cabinet, she scooped dishes from the sink into a trash bag. If only the makeshift mask over her face could block the odor as well as the mold particles.

Derek sat back on his legs and swiped an arm across his forehead. "If you don't mind my asking, what brings you all the way from Washington to Ohio?"

Noelle paused with a plate in her hand, giving herself time to think, then set the dish in the bag. "I needed a fresh start."

She should've taken an extra second to consider her words, because somehow those ones made her sound like an ex-con trying to escape a bad reputation.

"I don't mean that I *had* to leave. I didn't do anything illegal that sent me on the run. I'm not a criminal or an ex-con or anything."

Derek dried his hands off on the towel draped over his knee, a smile playing at his lips. "If you have a problem with criminals, you're not going to like me much."

"*You* have a criminal history?"

"Unofficially. No charges were ever filed."

Intrigued, she leaned against the counter. "What did you *unofficially* do?"

"Stole a car when I was fifteen. Turned out the car belonged to the wife of the local sheriff."

"You don't aim small when you commit a crime, do you?"

He grinned. "It was a nice car. The sheriff's deputies tracked me down and hauled me into his office. Sheriff Duncan was a big man, and I wasn't exactly small at fifteen."

"So you were quaking in your little boy boots?"

"Tennis shoes, but yeah, definitely. I thought he would lock me up with all the murderers right then. I gave him a sob story about how my family needed money, and I was trying to help my mom."

"Was any of it true?"

"All of it, actually. Dad had been gone for years, and I was struggling with his death and absence. Mom worked three part-time jobs to keep the heat on and put food on the table. A lot of nights we went to bed hungry and cold anyway. I was too young to get a job and help out financially, so I stole a car that I thought I could sell to help pay the electric bill and buy groceries."

"You didn't consider the consequences?"

"I thought I was smarter than I was." He grinned, and she could imagine that mischievous expression on a teenage boy's face. "That illusion came crashing down pretty quick. Sheriff Duncan gave me two options: prison time or mentorship. If I went to prison, there would've been no one around to protect my mom and three sisters."

"*Three* sisters?"

"Yep. My older sisters moved out of state, though, so now it's just me and Trudy."

The poor boy had grown up surrounded by nothing but estrogen. "What was the mentorship with Sheriff Duncan like?"

"He took an interest in my life. Helped fill a pair of shoes that had been empty for seven years. He taught me to drive, came to my football games, encouraged me to get involved in church. He could've had me thrown in prison, which would've sent my life into a downward spiral, but he chose to invest his time and energy in me instead."

"He sounds like a great man."

"Yeah, he was." Sadness tinged his voice. "He died shortly after I joined the sheriff's department."

"That must have felt like losing another father."

"Very much like it, but I'm grateful for the years I had with him, for the difference he made in my life."

Noelle's heart ached at his admission, bringing her own grief to the forefront of her mind. "I can't seem to get there, to be grateful for the time I had and not be angry about the time I'm missing out on."

She tried to appreciate those seven precious years, but her thoughts always circled back to the fact that her little boy could've lived ninety or a hundred years. He could've experienced the world, fallen in love, become a father.

Derek's voice was gentle when he asked, "Who did you lose?"

Noelle pulled the corner of her lips between her teeth, biting down in an effort to control her emotions. "My son, Tay. Eight months ago."

Sometimes she could still hear his little feet running down the hall, like an echo from the past. Other times she could almost feel him, like he was playing in the other room.

"I'm sorry." Derek's eyes shone with compassion. "I can only imagine how hard it is to lose a child."

She drew in an unsteady breath and blew it out in an effort to calm her raging emotions. If she didn't get them under control, Derek would be cleaning *her* up off the floor.

"When I lost my wife five years ago to cancer, I was exactly where you are—hurt, angry, frustrated. First my dad, then my mentor, then the woman I loved more than anything in this world."

He'd lost his wife too? How was this man still standing after so much loss?

"What did you do with all that emotion?"

He grunted, half-amused, half-embarrassed. "Yelled at God. He knows everything we're thinking and

111

feeling, so He wasn't exactly blindsided by my outburst. During that one-sided argument, I invited Him to walk through the grief with me. More a challenge than an invitation, to be honest, but when He was walking through it with me, He taught me to see things differently. It took me about a year to reach a point where I could look back at that time with Lacey and be grateful that God gave me a chance to know her and love her before she was gone."

"A year?" Did that mean she had four more months of pain and anger before her world made sense again?

"It's different for everyone. Give yourself some grace. And even though it might be hard right now, trust that God will use your grief and tears as fertilizer to grow something new and beautiful. It's what He does."

"That's the first time anyone's ever referenced fertilizer while offering me advice."

An unabashed smile curled his lips. "Welcome to the country."

She nudged up her glasses with a wrist and dabbed at her eyes with her sleeve. "So you joined the sheriff's department because your mentor inspired you to, and then worked your way up to captain?"

"Pretty much sums it up."

"Any interest in becoming sheriff?"

"Sheriff is an elected position, which means I would have to convince people to like me. That's too much work." Derek dunked the scrub brush into the bucket of water beside him and started in on the floor again. "What about you? When did you become a writer?"

"About . . . thirteen years ago."

112

"Who inspired you?"

"No one I ever got to meet." Noelle readjusted the rubber gloves on her hands and resumed clearing out the sink. "But it started with my parents' career. They flipped houses when I was a kid, and I spent most days at work with them."

"No school?"

"Homeschool, which amounted to a lot of reading and trips to the library. I researched the history of every house, going back to the year it was built."

"How many houses?"

"Nineteen. Some of them blur together now. But I enjoyed getting to know the people who'd lived there over the years, their personal stories. Some of them were fascinating and heartwarming, and others were tragic. My imagination filled in the gaps between facts, and I decided I wanted to try to write a fictional novel based loosely on some of their lives. After that, I found other interesting real-life experiences and built fictional stories around those. Eventually, that turned into ten novels."

"Ten novels." He let out a low whistle. "So what you're telling me is, I'm cleaning the floor of a famous person, and I could sell this scrub brush on eBay for thousands of dollars."

Noelle snorted back a laugh. "Good luck with that. I'm hardly famous, and that"—she waved at the layers of gunk on the floor—"isn't even my dirt."

"I hate to be the bearer of bad news, but you paid for this dirt. Every speck of it."

She shook her head with a smile. "Well, if you sell that scrub brush for thousands of dollars, I expect at least half."

"Deal."

She appreciated Derek's sense of humor. He was easy to joke with, and the lighthearted banter and personal stories kept the hours of cleaning from dissolving into tedious misery.

He was sweeping the cobwebs from the ceiling when his phone rang. He grabbed it from his belt, glanced at the screen, and then leaned the broom in the corner.

"Excuse me a minute." He took his call out onto the back porch.

Noelle melted into one of the dining room chairs and tossed aside the rag she'd been using to clean the cupboards. It was as good a time as any to take a break. Her body ached in more places than she knew she had.

She took a sip of water as she watched Derek through the window. He wrapped a hand around the porch post and stared out at the backyard, the baritone of his voice a soothing hum in the air. There was something about his presence that was comforting.

And that was dangerous. For her slowly mending heart.

She tuned out his voice and the feelings that left her conflicted, and pulled the little girl's diary toward her for a distraction.

She opened it to the second entry and smiled at the way the girl started this one with a question, as if she hoped her secret friend would write back.

Do you know who god is?

That was the kind of simple yet complicated question children had a tendency to ask. Tay once asked why no one got dizzy from the earth spinning. She tried to explain that they were moving *with* the earth, as if they were moving with a running car, but Tay insisted he was sitting perfectly still. As if that boy *ever* sat perfectly still.

Noelle smoothed a hand over the crinkled page and continued reading.

There's lots of books about god but their to hard to read. I asked mom about him. She says he's a fairytail. If he was real she wouldn't be trapped doing something she hates.

She says God's not real but she was talking to her friend about him. I'm not spose to read her chats but sometimes I do when she goes pee. She's got lots of online friends. I wish I could have friends but mom says I'm not spose to talk to anyone but her, not even the other girls in the house cause they're sick. Mom says quiet will help them get better but they never get better even when I'm extra extra quiet.

Firefly's words painted a dismal picture—a bitter and controlling mother, a lonely child with no one to speak

115

to or play with, and rooms filled with sick people. It was no wonder Firefly enjoyed books. They were windows out of that house, where she could meet new people.

Noelle turned the page and began reading the next entry, hoping for more insight.

The man with the gray hat is here again. He comes to our house alot. mom says he's a doctor and he's here to check on the sick girls. I don't know his name so I call him dr. Gray. Do you think he gives them shots? I don't think I like shots.

When he comes to visit mom says to stay in the bedroom and not make any noise. She says to be as quiet as a mouse with a cat in the house so he can ~~consen concern~~ so he can focus. Sometimes his boy nurses come to check on the girls instead but I still have to be a mouse in the bedroom and listen to headphone music. It's hard to be quiet all day but I get to read books so that helps.

I asked mom today if I can go outside and play with the little girl across the street while the doctor and nurses work but she said no. It's not fair. She's always outside jumping rope in her blue coat. I wish I could have a blue coat.

A sheet of paper was folded into the crease, and Noelle opened it to find a colored pencil drawing of a man in a gray hat. Doctor Gray's face had two dark dots for eyes and a grimacing slit for a mouth. Nothing about his depiction exuded the warm compassion of a doctor, but a lot of children were frightened of the people who gave them shots and ran tests.

It was unusual that he was making house calls, though. Were the sick residents unable or unwilling to go to a hospital? Were they illegal immigrants, afraid they might be reported and deported? And why did Firefly need to stay in her room when the doctor or his staff came to tend to the sick? Was she being sent to her room to keep her from getting underfoot, or was there something else going on?

Quiet as a mouse with a cat in the house.

It could be nothing more than a silly rhyme, but Noelle couldn't help but wonder if it held a deeper meaning. Cats were born predators, and they preyed on anything smaller than them. A mouse's best defense was to stay out of sight.

Noelle tugged at her bottom lip with her teeth. Maybe she was reading too much into it, but a niggling doubt in the back of her mind told her something wasn't right about this little girl's living situation.

CHAPTER
Seventeen

Derek picked at the chipped white paint of the railing with his thumbnail as Rusty updated him on Maddie Wingate.

"I got a hold of the college roommate, Chandra. She said Maddie left Friday evening around eight to meet up with a boy."

"Another college student?"

"No, some guy she's been corresponding with online."

Derek closed his eyes, a sinking feeling in his gut. No matter how many school seminars and videos law enforcement did to raise awareness of online predators, kids never fully grasped the danger.

"Did the roommate tell you where Maddie and this boy were meeting?"

"She didn't know," Rusty said. "The two girls were roommates but not friends, and according to Chandra, Maddie was shy and didn't socialize well."

"Which is why she gravitated toward someone she met online." Derek peeled off another chip of paint. "Do we know what program or app they were using to correspond? Dissecting their conversation might give us a lead."

"No idea, but it must've been something she could access on her phone, because she doesn't have a personal computer. She checks out a campus laptop or goes to the computer lab whenever she needs to write a report."

Unfortunately, they didn't have her phone, so they couldn't check to see what app she was using. "Did she pack anything?"

"According to her roommate, all she took with her was her purse. Too small for much more than a wallet and phone."

Maddie was eighteen, which gave her the right to disappear if she wanted to, but the details were leaning toward a suspicious disappearance. A girl didn't take off for the weekend without packing for the trip, and she certainly didn't leave her car and her keys on a secluded trail.

"Anything from the parents?" Derek asked.

"Her mom called me back. She and her husband haven't heard from Maddie. As far as they were aware, she was still on campus. The last communication was Friday morning. She sent her mom a cheesecake recipe over the Facebook messenger and requested it for Thanksgiving."

That didn't sound like a girl who planned to disappear. "Do we have anything from the car yet?"

"The rain washed away any usable prints on the outside, but hair and prints are at the lab. When I mentioned that we found the car, Mr. and Mrs. Wingate were surprised. Apparently, they asked Maddie not to drive it because it's got some problems, one of which is a tendency to stall. They were worried it would do that in the middle of a busy intersection."

"But she was driving it anyway."

"I guess so. They did officially report her missing, and they're driving over to meet with me as soon as possible. They live in Cleveland, so they should be here around three. You want to be there?"

This was the kind of case that could blow up in the media and paint his hometown in a dark light. Derek *needed* to be there.

"Yeah, I'll join you. Tell forensics they can dig into the car without reservation now. We need anything and everything as quickly as possible."

"All right. I'll let you know what they find." Rusty disconnected.

Derek rested his forehead against the vertical beam of the porch as the slithering feeling in his stomach returned. As much as he was enjoying getting to know Noelle, he was going to have to cut this day short.

He found her at the dining room table, her brow creased as she read the notebook she'd placed on the railing earlier.

She looked up when he entered and closed the diary, marking her spot with her hand still between the pages. "Is something wrong?"

"I'm afraid I have to cut our cleaning day short. We have a missing teenage girl, and until we figure out where she is and if she's all right, it's going to be all hands on deck."

Noelle straightened in her chair. "Is there anything I can do to help?"

"Her car was found abandoned about two miles from here, near the cemetery. She could be anywhere in town. I know you haven't been here long, but you might've seen her."

He showed her the picture on his phone, and she studied it, disappointment crossing her features. "I honestly don't know. With so many new faces around me, everyone kind of blurs together."

"If you don't mind giving me your number, I can send you the picture. That way you can keep an eye out for her."

"Of course."

He handed over his phone, and she added her name and number to the contacts before passing it back. "I'm sorry to leave after promising to stay and help, but . . ."

"No, you should definitely go. Finding her is more important. Besides, the dust and dirt will still be here a week from now."

He appreciated her understanding and offered to come back and help on his next day off.

———

Derek hated missing person's cases, especially when they involved young women or children. The possibilities turned his stomach inside out, giving him heartburn.

He popped an antacid into his mouth and squatted beside the damp tire tracks on the trail where Maddie's car had been found.

Without slowing, she'd driven through the thick chain that cordoned off the trail. The snap of it against the grill of her car should've shocked her into hitting the brake, and yet she drove another two hundred yards.

That didn't make sense to him. The idea that she might have driven to this unlit, secluded path to meet a boy made even less sense. It was naïve and reckless. But then, after months of talking with him online, it would be easy to convince herself he was trustworthy.

Derek rose to his full height, twisting a few blades of grass between his thumb and middle finger.

Unless this wasn't the intended meeting place, but a desperate detour to escape a boy who turned out to be a threat. That would explain why she didn't stop when she hit the chain. She drove until the car stalled and then fled on foot, not wasting a second to pull the keys from the ignition.

The storm had washed away most of the tracks and impressions, erasing any evidence of a pursuing vehicle or physical struggle.

Derek climbed to the top of one of the dirt hills nearby so he could see the nearest paved road. If a pursuer forced her to flee north, she would've found fields and trees straddling a dark road.

Even if she wasn't being followed, and she was out trying to find someone to help with her car, anyone could've come around the bend and spotted her wandering alone. Maybe someone from the Copper Penny Bar who'd had enough to drink that he wasn't thinking about consequences.

He knew of one man who lived in the trailers outside town whose preference for young blondes had landed him on the registry. Paying Nick Nelson a visit was on his list of things to do today.

Derek shredded the pieces of grass and tossed them into the breeze, his focus on the surrounding trees. They would need to search every inch of them for evidence.

CHAPTER
Eighteen

Noelle tore off a strip of duct tape and smoothed it over the crack in the dining room window to stop the hiss of cold air.

There were six rolls of duct tape beneath the kitchen sink, which the previous residents had used to "fix" everything. There were strips of it all throughout the house, holding things together like silver triage bandages. If she started peeling it off the walls, tiles, and fixtures, the house might fall apart.

But until she could afford to replace things, she would have to do some patchwork. She touched up the kitchen window as well, trying to quiet the pane that rattled with every gust of wind.

Her gaze trailed to the woods that wrapped around the back of the property, and she spotted a half dozen blackbirds circling above the treetops. Were they enjoying an air current, or were they homing in on something?

A sharp thump from the front of the house made her jump, and she dropped the roll of tape. It wobble-rolled across the floor into the wall and fell over.

Noelle picked it up and placed it on the counter before going to check on the strange noise. She lifted the curtain over the foyer window, checking for unwelcome visitors, then opened the front door. Her feet froze on the threshold as she took in the scene.

Someone had smeared mud across the porch to shape a single word—LEAVE—with a round rock placed as a period.

They must have slammed the rock down when they were finished scrawling their message. Did the rock come with its own meaning, a threat that things would become violent if she didn't heed the warning, or had its sole purpose been to draw her attention?

She folded her arms against a chill. This had to be Walt's doing. The kitchen door flying open last night might've been his doing too. Scare tactics from someone who liked to hide and spy on people.

Anger burned away some of her fear, and she stepped out onto the porch to smear her shoe through the message. "I'm not leaving!"

Birds lifted from the surrounding trees, startled by the echo of her voice, and their departure sent fresh leaves raining to the ground.

"If you have a problem with me, then come out so we can talk about it."

No one answered, and the silence only fueled Noelle's anger. She picked up the rock and hurled it at the tall pines. A squirrel scampered from the massive branches into the maple, but if Walt was in there, he didn't startle easily.

A quiet swishing sound came from somewhere inside the house, one of the many mysterious sounds Noelle heard in the middle of the night, and she turned back to the foyer.

It was probably mice chasing each other through the walls or some other critter making himself at home. But with her luck, Walt had pushed his way through her flimsy barricade in front of the back door, and she would find him sitting at the dining room table, prepared for another confrontation.

She closed the door and leaned against it as she considered how to approach the old man if he'd let himself into the house.

Maybe I should've kept the rock.

Her gun was in her purse in the kitchen, so she walked back down the hall armed with nothing but her phone.

The faint scent of cinnamon and sugar tickled her nose, but the aroma evaporated as spontaneously as it had appeared. Noelle's stomach rumbled with hunger, reminding her that all she'd eaten today was a protein bar.

She checked the time on her fitness band—one in the afternoon, well past time for the frosted cinnamon rolls her imagination was teasing her with. She'd always had a fondness for breakfast foods, but she would have to settle for a peanut butter and banana sandwich.

She stopped at the edge of the dining room when she found the window open again, jammed in the same position as last night.

Her eyes flicked left, taking in the hallway, and then right, visually clearing the kitchen.

That explained why the rock didn't startle Walt from his hiding place. He was busy sneaking around back so he could pry open a window.

"This doesn't scare me either," she muttered. But in truth, the uncertainty of how far the old man would take things to drive her out left a quiver at the base of her spine.

He might be nothing more than a nuisance she had to shoo away each day, but there was also the possibility he might be unhinged and violent.

She muscled the window shut and locked it, for all the good that would do. The locks in this place were so old they were useless. A little jiggling or a hard shove and the windows and doors popped right open.

Her phone dinged with an incoming message, and she checked it to see a text from Amy.

Hey girl, haven't heard from you and I'm starting to worry. Also, the publisher needs your new address so they can ship author copies and bookmarks to you.

Noelle sat on the edge of the table, sadness cutting through her chest like a dull scalpel.

Her latest book was due to hit the shelves any day now, and she dreaded the snapshots Amy would email to her—reviews, photos of the novel on bookstore shelves, social media posts by readers.

Ordinarily, she loved the feedback, but this book was different. Not because of the storyline or the amount of research it required, but because it memorialized the worst night of her life.

She'd sent in the final draft for publication minutes before her life imploded with screeching tires and screams. She never wanted to see that book again. Her publishing house could keep all the author copies as far as she was concerned.

Noelle shoved the phone back into the pouch of her hoodie and released a breath that shivered under the weight of the tears.

It was as good a time as any to make a supply run, and listening to music in the car always calmed her frazzled nerves.

CHAPTER Nineteen

Derek pounded the side of his fist against the metal door of the trailer. "Sheriff's department!"

He hated coming down to this trailer park anymore. It used to be filled with families, but now it was full of ex-cons and drug addicts. They destroyed the communal playset and left trash everywhere.

Swearing and stumbling came from inside the trailer, and Derek backstepped to avoid the door that swung open.

Nick Nelson stood in the opening in boxer shorts, a tank top, and saggy socks, the tip of a cigarette glowing between two fingers. Recognizing Derek, he threw up both hands. "I haven't gone anywhere near the diner again. I swear."

Shortly after his release from prison, Nick wandered into the diner for lunch and made the mistake of leering at the little blonde behind the counter.

Derek hauled him behind the building and laid out some ground rules—stay away from Trudy and stay away from the diner.

"Glad to hear it."

Nick lifted a socked foot and scratched at his shin. "I haven't done nothing wrong."

Derek lifted his eyebrows.

"I mean recently. I take full responsibility for the wrongs I did before, but I did my time, I'm sticking to my parole, and I'm in therapy now."

Nick should still be behind bars, in Derek's opinion, but he was paroled a year ago due to overcrowding at the prison. Now this threat to society was the sheriff's department's problem.

"If I remember correctly, both of your victims were pretty teenage girls, and both were blonde."

"One was more ash brown, really, with blonde highlights and . . ."

Derek cut him a warning glare, and Nick closed his mouth. Derek brought up the picture of Maddie. "Recognize her?"

The man's face turned as gray as the ash curling from the end of his cigarette. "No, never seen her before."

"Convince me."

Nick swallowed like there was a grapefruit stuck in his throat. "I've never seen that girl. I never even went near her. You ask her."

"There's a problem with your suggestion, Nick. We found her car abandoned, but she appears to be missing."

"M-missing?" He shook his head, greasy strands of black hair sliding back and forth across his forehead. "N-no, that's . . . I've never . . . you can't really think I would snatch someone."

Kidnapping wasn't in Nick's history, at least not his known history. The crimes he did time for were acts of impulse rather than premeditation, but that didn't mean those were his only crimes.

"Maybe you noticed her walking down the road after her car broke down and saw an opportunity."

Nick shook his head. "I haven't seen any girls on the road."

"Where were you Friday night? And don't tell me you were home. It'll take me thirty minutes to find out where you really were."

The sheriff's department was always receiving calls from concerned parents who kept a close watch on the registered offenders who lived near their children.

Nick's mouth fell open. "I . . . I went . . . to get a late dinner."

"A liquid dinner?" When Nick started to sputter an objection, Derek held up a hand. "All I have to do is ask the bartender if you were at the Copper Penny Friday night, Nick, so do you really want to lie to my face? We both know you like to drink."

Nick scratched at his bare leg again, nearly toppling over. "Don't jam me up for this. Please."

"I don't care if you had a couple of beers. I do care that you drove home afterward. Even more than that, I care about this missing girl." He showed him the picture again. "Did you offer her a ride?"

"No, man. No. I didn't even see her. Check my trailer. Ch-check my car. You won't find nothing. I didn't take that girl."

Derek pushed past him into the trailer. The claustrophobic space was a disaster of dirty clothes and garbage, and Derek kicked through the mess. "Where you working these days, Nick?"

"The local factory. Part-time."

Derek checked the bathroom, drawing back the shower curtain. He grimaced at the mold and soap scum coating the walls and floor. "Ever heard of a scrub brush?"

"I'm not much for cleaning," Nick called back.

"Clearly." Derek glanced at the man in the kitchen before checking the bedroom. Nothing but clutter. There was nowhere to hide a person in this place.

"See?" Nick puffed on his cigarette, leg bouncing with nerves. "No chick." When Derek shot him another hard look, he stammered, "Eh . . . girl . . . lady. There's no ladies here."

"Show me the car."

Derek followed him outside to the off-white car, stitched together like Frankenstein's monster with different colored parts. He searched the interior and the trunk, finding nothing obvious that could connect Nick with his missing teenager.

Derek slammed the lid and leaned against the trunk, folding his arms. "Tell me what you know, Nick."

"W-what do you mean?"

"Even if you didn't hurt her, you know someone who knows something."

Nick scoffed. "It's not like we have a weekly perv meeting. Unless group therapy counts, and I don't think I'm supposed to talk about that."

"Nick," Derek said with impatience.

"Honest, I know nothing about a girl. The last thing I want is to end up back in prison, so I'm going to do right by you. If I learn anything, I'll tell you first thing."

"I'll hold you to that." Derek pushed away from the car and left the trailer park. Hopefully, the townsfolk would have more information to offer.

———

Noelle swung into a parking space in front of the Cherry Creek Market, the only grocery and supply store in town.

It was quaint, with a cowboy mural on the side of the building and a fall display along the front window. Though, after meeting Walt last night, she doubted she would look at a scarecrow the same way again.

She dug the chai lip balm from her purse and added a little shine to her lips. The scent reminded her of crackling fires, a warm blanket, and spicy hot tea with a hint of cream.

Dropping it back into the zippered pocket, she clutched her purse and climbed out, hiking the strap up onto her shoulder. She reached for the glass door plastered with handwritten signs about bargains, one in particular standing out: "Fresh worms with any six pack of beer."

Was that supposed to be a bargain or a warning?

She pulled open the door and walked inside, grateful for the warmth of the heater vent overhead.

The store was divided, one half hardware and household, and the other half grocery. To fix the house, she'd probably have to buy out the hardware section.

She reached into her purse and groped for the list of supplies and groceries she'd finished pulling together this morning, but she didn't feel it. She pried open her purse with both hands and peered inside, only to find she had everything *except* the notepad with her list on it.

"I could've sworn . . ."

She remembered picking up the notepad to put it in her purse, but couldn't actually remember following through.

She had a bad habit of that—thinking about doing but not actually doing, all the while believing she did. It led to a lot of dishes stuffed into a dishwasher that was never turned on and frozen dinners slowly thawing in a cold oven she was certain she preheated.

She sighed and looked around the store, trying to remember what she needed, but it was like a vacuum had sucked the mental list right out of her head. She stood beside the row of carts, staring vacantly at the shelves of food and hoping the mental list might spontaneously reappear in her brain.

Nope, nothing.

She would have to wander the store until she saw items that triggered her memory.

———

Somehow, Noelle always picked the shopping cart with a bum wheel. This one kept veering to the left like a NASCAR driver, and she'd nearly taken out a corner shelf of taco shells.

She wrestled the dysfunctional cart full of groceries and supplies through the glass doors and out into the parking lot. As she scrounged for her car keys in her purse, her fingers brushed along the diary.

She'd asked the cashier as well as the woman in line ahead of her, who worked as a substitute teacher, if they recognized the diary or knew of a child in town with the nickname Firefly. Neither of them knew anything.

In a village with less than twelve hundred people, there must be someone who could identify the girl.

Noelle frowned when she spotted a piece of paper tucked beneath her windshield wiper. Great. Even small towns had solicitors who shoved ads beneath people's car wipers.

She yanked the sheet of paper loose, prepared to crumple it and toss it in the trash, when she realized it wasn't an ad. It was a folded piece of notebook paper.
She unfolded it and read the note that someone had written in black marker, a chill curling around her spine like a snake: "You're not alone in that house."

She searched the parking lot for the person who left it. Her gaze swept over a horse and carriage tied to a post, an old woman sweeping leaves from the sidewalk, a man sitting in his truck cab.

Did one of them leave the note? What did they mean she wasn't alone in the house?

She had checked every room last night, and so had Derek. Unless there was a hidden entrance Walt was using to slip in and out.

The possibility sent her anxiety spiking. *One thing I can control in this moment*, she reminded herself.

She could put the groceries in the trunk.

She forced herself to push the cart toward the back of the car, popped the trunk, and placed the groceries inside. The next thing she could do was pay the lawyer a visit.

If anyone ought to know whether or not there was a hidden way in and out of the house, it was the lawyer who handled the auction. And if this note was nothing more than someone's way of trying to scare her into selling, then it was left by someone with an interest in the house.

She wasn't sure how many bidders there had been during the auction, or even who they were, but she'd swooped in at the last minute and outbid all of them, which was tantamount to cutting someone off in traffic. If any of those people were resentful about her winning the auction, she needed to know who they were and if they were dangerous.

CHAPTER
Twenty

The stand-alone building had been many things before Trudy moved in—a small church, a video store, a thrift shop. Trudy had transformed it into a local gathering place with homecooked meals and small-town pride. There were always local sports updates and team pictures on the bulletin board just inside the door, and on Christmas Eve, one of the local church choirs sang Christmas carols in the corner while Trudy passed around homemade eggnog and hot chocolate.

Derek greeted a few of the patrons with a nod as he made his way to the front counter.

Trudy's attention was on her phone, her lips silently shaping the words she thumbed into a text: "Brian, please come by the diner when you're back in town. We need to—"

Derek's shadow stretched across the countertop, and she looked up from the unfinished message.

Her eyes narrowed. "There is no way you're done tidying up that house already. Did you man-clean, or did you say something wrong and get yourself kicked out?"

"No, I didn't get kicked out, and what in the world is man-clean?"

"Shuffle things from one place to the next and call it done. It's Brian's favorite way to *clean*. Also known as the clutter shuffle."

"No, believe it or not, I didn't do that either."

Trudy finished her text and set down her phone. "How'd it go then?"

"Fine."

"That's it? That's all I get? You were there for three hours. There has to be more to the story than *fine*."

He leaned on the counter, shrinking to her height. "I'm not here to talk about Noelle."

She mounted her hands on her hips, popping her pregnant stomach out even further. "Well, you should be. I've been waiting all morning for details. What did you learn?"

He pressed his lips together. "Your hunch was right about her being sad. She's grieving."

The excitement on her face dimmed. "That explains what I found on her social media. I was sort of stalking her author profiles today and—"

"Trudy."

"What? Not in a creepy way. It's not like I went through and hearted all her Facebook photos for the past thirteen years or tried to find her address . . . not like that's a mystery now. But I noticed she was super active and engaging, and then eight months ago, crickets. Not even an 'I'm going to be gone for a while' post. She just dropped off the face of social media. That's when she lost someone, isn't it?"

"If you're that interested to know, why don't you talk to her yourself?"

"Or, since people find my personality a smidge overwhelming at first . . ."—she interlaced her fingers on the counter—"you could have dinner with her tonight and then tell me all about it."

"I have work to do, which is why I'm here."

She sighed theatrically. "And here I thought you came by to see your favorite sister."

"Is Tina in town?"

"Ha-ha."

Trudy had always been his favorite sister, and she knew it. He adored her sweet and caring nature, even if she occasionally stressed him out.

"Wait a minute—what do you mean you have work to do?" she demanded. "This is your day off."

He lowered his voice so the customers wouldn't overhear. "We have a missing girl."

"A miss—" Trudy bit off the word and swept her eyes over the patrons before whispering, "A missing girl? Like a child? From the village?"

"No, she's an eighteen-year-old college student, but we found her car, and the last anyone saw or spoke with her was Friday."

"Friday?" she gasped. "It's Monday."

"I know, and it looks like her car has been parked back behind the cemetery since before the rain started Friday night." He showed her the picture of Maddie on his phone.

Trudy's hand flew to her mouth. "Oh my word, she's so young."

"She could be in town willingly. We don't know that anything bad happened to her. Her car could've stalled, she could've gotten a ride from a friend and decided to unplug from technology for a few days."

His explanation didn't soften the creases of worry around her eyes. "She hasn't been in here. With that blonde hair and those big brown eyes, I would remember her."

"I figured you would. I need to meet with Rusty and her parents, but before I do, I'm going to see if any of your regulars have seen her. Would you mind whipping me up one of your nutritious protein smoothies for the road?"

"Sure."

He pulled some cash from his wallet to pay for the smoothie. Trudy frowned at the five-dollar bill, then took it. She hated charging family for food, but she needed the money more than he did. Her frown morphed into a scowl when he added a twenty to the tip jar.

"Any word from Brian?"

She tapped her phone screen, but there were no notifications. "Nothing since this morning. He sent me a message to let me know his mom is feeling a little better and he would be heading back sometime today."

Good. Derek wanted to talk to him about his reckless and irresponsible behavior when he had a baby due in three weeks.

"I'll be right back with your smoothie." Trudy turned toward the kitchen, then paused to shoot him a stern look over her shoulder. "And don't put any more money in that jar."

He waited until she retreated into the kitchen, then stuck a handful of ones and fives into the jar with a smile.

He turned toward the patrons in the diner and cleared his throat. "Ladies and gentlemen, I'm sorry to interrupt your meals, but I need to show you a picture." He approached each of the tables, letting the patrons see Maddie. "If you crossed paths with this young lady or think you might have seen her, please let me know."

One of the older women drew in a worried breath. "Did something bad happen to her? Our granddaughter is supposed to come stay with us this weekend, but if there's a chance she might not be safe—"

"Was she kidnapped?" One of the men broke in, silverware clattering on his plate. "My little girl walks home by herself after school."

A flurry of questions erupted, and Derek held up his hands. "I don't think there's any reason to worry. At the moment, all we have is an abandoned car and a young lady not answering her phone. Our goal is to make sure the lack of communication is voluntary and that she's safe." He waited for the room to quiet. "Did any of you notice anything unusual or suspicious the past few days?"

Heads shook, and couples murmured to each other.

A man Derek didn't recognize shifted in his seat by the picture window and readjusted the beanie on his head.

Derek approached his table. "You're not from around here."

The guy looked up at him, onion ring in hand. "Is that a crime, Sheriff?"

Derek had changed into his uniform even though it was his day off. "It's Captain, actually. Mind if I sit?"

The man placed a foot on the chair opposite him and pushed it back from the table. "Make yourself at home, Cap."

Derek sat, hoping to keep this interaction cordial despite the undertone of tension coming from the stranger. "What's your name?"

The man hesitated a beat too long, and Derek knew the name that came out of his mouth would be a lie. "Cody."

Derek placed his hat on the table. "What brings you to our small town, *Cody*?"

The left side of the man's mouth quirked up at the emphasis on his fake name. "Passing through."

"How long you been passing through?"

Cody dusted the greasy crumbs from his hands and leaned back in his seat, blue eyes narrowed. "You ask every outsider these questions or only the people who look different than your small-towners?"

Derek glanced at the tattoos that covered both of the man's pale forearms and traveled up his neck. "Your appearance has nothing to do with my questions."

"Sure it doesn't. I've seen the looks some of the other customers in here are throwing my way. Half of them think I'm going to rob the place, the other half think I'm in a gang. The only one that hasn't given me the stare of judgment is prego Barbie." He indicated Trudy in the kitchen with a tip of his head. "So, what crime do *you* think I committed?"

"I'm just trying to get to know you a little."

"Right. Well, I hate grits, I think soccer is for pansies, and it's not a party without onion rings." He shoved one of the onion rings into his mouth and asked around a mouthful of batter, "Anything else you want to know, Cap?"

"I'd like to know what you saw."

"No idea what you're talking about."

"When I asked if anyone saw anything suspicious the past few days, you shifted in your seat. What do you know about this girl?" He showed him the picture again.

Cody glanced at Maddie's face and then away. "Never seen her."

"Are you sure? Because if you did see something, it could help us find her."

"You seem awfully worried for someone who told a roomful of people there's no reason to worry."

"I have no reason to suspect her disappearance is anything other than an isolated incident. But I am worried. For her. My gut tells me she's in trouble."

Cody pushed back his beanie and scratched at his head. The tattoos covered his scalp as well, filling in where there should've been hair. "I saw *a* blonde girl Friday night. From a distance. I don't know if it was her."

"Go on."

"I was driving around, hoping to find a place to park my truck for the night. That was around nine. And there she was, standing at the edge of the road when I came over

143

the hill. As soon as she saw my truck, she took off into the trees."

"You didn't think that was odd?"

"Yeah, but what was I supposed to do, chase her down so I could ask her if she was all right? You really think she wouldn't panic seeing a guy like me running after her?"

"Did it seem like anyone else was chasing her?"

He shrugged. "She was the only one I saw, but I'm not sure she was alone."

Derek leaned forward. "If you didn't see anyone else, what makes you think she wasn't alone?"

"You know those reflectors you find on bikes, buggies, shoes. My headlights caught something in the woods. There could've been someone else out there."

Could it have been Maddie's mystery boy, or had someone else been with her Friday night?

"Did you call the police?"

"I don't really get along with your kind."

Derek pressed his lips together. This guy assumed everyone in the world was judging him, and yet here he sat, judging everyone else in the world.

Derek brushed aside his annoyance and focused on the matter at hand. "Did you see where she went?"

"Well, there were trees, dirt, leaves . . . I'm thinking the woods."

Derek bit back a sigh. "What road was this on?"

"I don't know. All these country roads look the same to me. There was another car on the road that night, coming from the opposite direction. Blue. They slowed down, like they saw the girl too."

"Did you get a license plate?"

"I was busy being blinded by high beams, so . . ." He spread his hands wide. "Sorry, can't do that part of your job for you."

Derek struggled to hold on to his patience. "Dark blue or light blue?"

"Dark. Kind of like that one." Cody threw a thumb toward the car parked in front of the law office across the street. "But I'm not saying it was that particular car."

Derek checked his watch. He didn't have time for a lengthy chat with Perry Habrams before meeting with Maddie's parents, so that would have to wait.

"I need to know where you're staying and how to reach you in case I have more questions." Derek slid his notepad and pen across the table.

Cody scoffed. "You mean in case you decide to frame me as a suspect."

"Right now, I don't even know if a crime has been committed."

Cody shifted his jaw and grabbed the pen, scribbling down his information before slamming the pen on the notepad and sliding it back to Derek. "I live in my truck, the only thing I own, so no address."

Derek nodded. "Thank you for your help."

"I didn't do it for you."

Derek tucked away his pen and notepad and pushed back from the table. "You know, not all law enforcement is bad, Cody."

"Yeah, that's what you all say." He tossed a twenty on the table before rising and grabbing his coat. "Save the

145

party lines and social media dance videos and focus your energy on finding that girl before something bad happens to her. If it hasn't already."

Cody brushed past him and out the door. Derek watched him climb into an oversize truck, the license plate conveniently obscured with mud.

Was the mysterious man as innocent as he seemed or a really good actor? Had he given Derek a lead to follow, or was he sending him on a wild goose chase so he could slip out of town?

Uncertainty churned in Derek's gut as the truck peeled out of the parking lot and rumbled down the street.

CHAPTER
Twenty-one

The scent of pine air freshener hung in the air as Noelle opened the glass door to the law office, taking her back to the years before she bought her own car, when she had to take taxis to run errands.

The waiting area furniture looked cobbled together from yard sales and thrift shops, each piece different and worn, and the pictures on the walls were better suited to a doctor's office.

There was no receptionist, or even room for a receptionist, so she made her way back to the glowing office she'd visited last night.

Perry Habrams was in his mid to late fifties, but it was clear by his toned physique and dyed but thinning hair that he was fighting to forestall the effects of aging.

Noelle knocked on the door frame. "Mr. Habrams."

He turned from the filing cabinet he was sorting through, his expression darkening. "Ms. McKenzie. I don't have time to talk right now. Call and make an appointment."

Noelle dropped her purse into one of his guest chairs. "I just need a few minutes."

"I believe our business is concluded. The sale of the house was final, in as-is condition. If you're dissatisfied—"

147

"You did leave out a few details. Like the murders, the animal graveyard, Walt."

He closed the metal drawer with a screech, and she tried not to cringe. "I provided all the information I was legally required to provide."

"A heads-up about a surviving family member would've been nice."

"You didn't ask."

Annoyance flickered through her. "Any idea how to smooth things over with him?"

"I would recommend avoiding him altogether." He turned toward her. "Walter Bechtel isn't someone you want to mess around with. Even his sister kept her distance."

"Why didn't she will the house to him instead of auctioning it? He's her only surviving family, isn't he?"

"I imagine there are any number of reasons. She could've been trying to force him to move on with his life, or perhaps she didn't want anything to do with him. I didn't ask her reasons. Elizabeth Bechtel hired me to handle her affairs after she passed, and I did so according to her wishes."

"Why not tell me everything from the start? About the house's history, about Walt."

"As I said, I provided all the information I was legally required to provide."

She studied him. He wore a charcoal suit with a blood-red tie—a far cry from the sweat-stained white button-up and tweed jacket he wore last night. He'd splurged on an expensive suit, like a person who expected to come into a decent chunk of money.

"She arranged for you to receive a large percentage of the sale, didn't she? And you didn't want to scare away the highest bidder."

His lips thinned in a smile that was anything but kind. "I believe we're finished here. You know where the exit is."

Noelle didn't budge. "How many other bidders were there?"

"Several."

"I need to know their names."

"Unless there is a criminal act or a legitimate threat, that's private information."

She'd expected something like that. She grabbed the note from her pocket and placed it on his desk. "Someone left this on my car. Either the person who placed it under my wiper is trying to warn me, or it's one of the other bidders trying to frighten me."

He leaned forward to read the note, a necklace with a purple crystal slipping out around his tie. "'You're not alone in that house.'" He straightened. "And what, this single statement makes you think someone might be hiding in the house?"

"I don't know." Yesterday afternoon she would've thought the idea of hidden doors and concealed rooms was ridiculous, but then she moved into a house where three people had been murdered and the sole surviving family member haunted the grounds like a ghost. "I checked the house, so if someone is getting in and out or hiding inside, it would need to be a concealed space."

149

"Ms. McKenzie, it was thirty-four degrees last night and thirty-six the night before. Do you really think anyone could survive beneath the floorboards or in the walls of an unheated, damp house in these temperatures?"

She hadn't considered that. "Probably not, but I'd like a blueprint of the house so I can check for myself."

He sighed. "George Bechtel was a paranoid man. If there were blueprints, he hid them so that no one else would have access to the layout of his house. You could tear up every floorboard trying to find them, or you could pay to have new ones made."

"But that wouldn't include any concealed spaces or hidden doorways that might've been in the original plans."

"No, but if there's anyone in that house with you, it's not a living person. It's something much darker."

Noelle's fingers tightened on the back of the guest chair. "Meaning what?"

"Everyone knows that house is stained by the blood shed there." He tucked the crystal back beneath his tie. "If you're going to live there, you should consider some protection."

Derek told her that there were people in town who believed the house was cursed, but she didn't expect the lawyer to be one of them.

"You're not telling me you think the house is cursed, are you?"

"Evil is alive and thriving in this world, Ms. McKenzie, and it latches on to everything it can."

She couldn't disagree on that point, but it wasn't the kind of evil a colored stone on a chain could protect someone from.

"You think the house is somehow infested with evil, but you sold it to me anyway?" she asked.

"Don't make the mistake of thinking your uninformed decisions are anyone's responsibility but yours. Now, if there's nothing else, I have an appointment."

Irritated, Noelle snatched the note from the desk, grabbed her purse, and walked out.

————

Noelle thrust open the law office door and stormed out of the building and into the blustery fall day, the sprinkle of rain on her face cooling some of her ire.

Perry Habrams wasn't a lawyer. He was a self-serving shark.

A gust of wind snatched the note from her hand, and she grabbed for it, but it tumbled and skittered into the street, landing in a rain puddle.

She blew out a breath. She didn't need the cryptic note anyway. Pulling her keys from her purse, she unlocked her car and reached for the handle.

"Excuse me," a male voice said, and she turned to find an unfamiliar man a few feet behind her.

Wariness crept through her as she studied the thirty-something man with unusually thick eyebrows and a rough scar on his top lip that might've been a cleft when he was a child.

151

She shifted her keys in her grip. "Yes?"

"I saw this escape, and it looked like you were considering going after it before it landed in the road." He held out the limp slip of paper, the permanent marker as bold as ever despite floating in muddy water.

Noelle relaxed at the kind gesture, even though it had been unnecessary. The only thing she planned to do with that note was toss it in the trash. "Thank you," she said, taking it from him.

"Not to intrude into things that aren't my business, but that's kind of a creepy message."

"Yeah." She grimaced at the note. "Thanks for diving into a puddle to get it for me."

His lips curved into a crooked smile. "Not a problem. I hope everything works out."

Noelle frowned. "Everything?"

He gestured to the office. "Most people don't come here unless there's an issue that needs sorting out. I'm here because my girlfriend left me and took our daughter. I have no idea what to do."

Noelle couldn't imagine how awful that must feel. "I'm sorry."

He shrugged, but there was a glimmer of some deep emotion in his eyes. "I guess you never know what to expect from life. If the good lawyer here couldn't provide a solution to your problem, people around here offer a lot of good advice."

When he started past her for the law office door, she asked, "Do you know anything about the Bechtel house?"

He paused, fingers wrapped around the handle. "Only what I've heard. Some say it's haunted, some say it's cursed. Others say the man who built it added hidden rooms where he stored all his money."

"Do you believe there might be hidden rooms?"

He frowned. "I've never really given it much thought. I'm sure there's a blueprint somewhere with the answer to your question."

She sighed. "There isn't. I asked."

"You could always sneak into the place and take a look around, see what you find, but watch out for the old guy who creeps around the property. He doesn't like people over there."

"And if I were trying to find hidden rooms, what would I look for?"

He shrugged again. "I wish I knew. But if you look long enough and hard enough, I'm sure you'll find something." He tipped his head toward the glass door. "I need to get to my appointment, but it was nice chatting with you."

"You too." She smiled and turned her attention back to the mysterious note as he slipped inside.

————

Derek held the door for the elderly couple leaving the diner, his eyes fixed across the street. He'd seen Noelle burst out of the law office in frustration.

His plan was to cross the street and make sure everything was all right, but as soon as he stepped out, the

153

older couple decided to follow. As much as he wanted to keep going, he couldn't let the door slam on them.

He watched Noelle's interaction with the man who handed back something the wind had stolen from her grip, and waited for the old woman to maneuver her walker through the opening. Her wheel snagged on a stone, and Derek helped her get past it, trying not to be impatient even though he wanted to be somewhere else.

"You're such a gentleman," she said, offering him an appreciative smile. "Your mother raised you right."

"She did her best."

Once the elderly couple was clear of the doorway, Derek jogged across the busy main street. The man Noelle had been talking with retreated into the office building, leaving her alone in the parking lot.

Recognition and something that might've been interest sparkled in her eyes as he approached. "Hey."

"Hey."

She stuffed whatever was in her hand into her pocket and smiled. "Is this what life is like in a small town? Always bumping into the same people?"

"Pretty much. I was grabbing lunch from the diner before I head to the department, but I wanted to make sure you were okay. You looked upset."

"Oh, yeah, I'm fine. I was hoping Mr. Habrams might have a blueprint for the house, but . . ." She noticed the green smoothie in his left hand and her eyes narrowed. "Wait, you think my tea tastes like weeds, but you drink grass?"

He swished the liquid around, stirring up dark sediment on the bottom. "I don't actually know what Trudy puts in these things, but I doubt it's grass. It tastes more like mint, and it's great when you're short on time, which" —he glanced at his watch—"I unfortunately am. I wanted to make sure you were okay before I go, though."

She smiled. "I am. Thanks for checking."

"Anytime." He turned to leave, but some internal string jerked him back around. "How would you feel about having dinner tonight?"

She blinked, as surprised by his question as he was. But now that the words were out in the open, he was glad he'd broached the subject.

She looked down at her keys in her hands, scrutinizing each one. "Like . . . a date?"

He didn't miss the uncertainty in her tone, and his gaze trailed to the indentation on her ring finger, questions about her husband resurfacing. He'd assumed she was divorced, but what if she was separated but still married? There was the possibility that her husband died along with her son and that she was grieving them both.

"I'm sorry," he said. "Not for asking, because I would still love to share a pizza with you sometime, but I'm sorry for making you uncomfortable. I haven't dated anyone since Lacey passed away five years ago, so I understand not being ready."

Noelle studied him. "Five years is a long time."

"I have my dog, Elsa, to keep me company. She's great, except she snores, eats all the corn chips, and occasionally chews up my shoes."

Noelle let out a surprised laugh. "As far as relationship problems go, those aren't too bad."

"I can't complain."

"If I decide to warm up a can of vegetable soup with crackers and eat alone, what are *you* going to do for dinner?"

He couldn't ignore the trickle of disappointment as she laid the groundwork for a refusal, but he masked it. "Grab something from the vending machine and eat at my desk while working Maddie's case. It's probably what I should do anyway."

"No break? Won't that wear you out?"

"With cases like this, I'm not great at taking breaks." He was terrible at it actually. The most balanced he'd ever been was with Lacey. No matter what he was working on, if she dropped in, he would let her drag him away for dinner to help him retain his sanity.

Noelle fidgeted with her keys. "In that case, I don't like green peppers on my pizza. Or olives of any color."

She surprised him yet again by accepting his offer. "That's a yes for tonight?"

She smiled and shrugged. "I'm tired of soup, and you'll need a break, so . . . yes."

"I'll see you around six then?"

She pressed her lips together and nodded.

He wasn't sure whether or not sharing a pizza qualified as a date, but it was dinner with a beautiful woman who intrigued him, and Derek's nerves buzzed as he walked back to his cruiser.

CHAPTER
Twenty-two

Fat raindrops splattered across the windshield as Noelle drove home down the back road. Doubt nibbled at her decision to have dinner with Derek.

"It's a friendly meal. Not a lifetime commitment," she told herself, flexing her fingers on the leopard-print steering wheel cover.

Still, she glanced at her phone sitting in its holder on the dashboard and considered sending him a text to cancel. Something simple and vague like, "Change of plans," or "Something came up."

But the only thing that had come up was her anxiety level, bringing doubt and fear with it.

She needed time to rediscover who she was before adding anyone else into the mix. No longer a wife, no longer a mother, no longer an author. What did that leave?

"I don't know who I am anymore, God," she said into the quiet of the car. "I don't know what I'm supposed to do or who I'm supposed to be."

For months she'd searched for a new identity in the Scriptures, but they felt as flat as the instructions on a cereal box. She begged for answers, but her prayers bounced off the ceiling.

"Where are you?" she demanded, tears distorting her vision. "These past eight months, I have felt so alone and so lost."

Her life had been far from perfect before, but she had her son for company, she had writing projects to distract her from the fact that her husband was never home, she had God, whose words would wrap around her like a blanket.

Where was that God now? She longed for Him to reopen the communication between them, to offer even a drop of comfort and direction.

A blur of movement in the corner of her vision was her only warning before a deer dashed out of nowhere and across the road in front of the car.

She swerved to avoid the animal, and something popped, sending the car veering to the left. She slammed on the brakes, snapping forward against her seat belt as the car ground to a stop in the dirt.

The deer frolicked past her car into the field, white tail flashing, seemingly unaware of how close it had come to death.

Noelle released a trembling breath and rested her head on the steering wheel, heart pummeling her now-aching ribs.

She'd read about the perils of living in Ohio in the colder months, but she didn't think she would ever get used to wild animals leaping in front of her car.

At least she hadn't hit the deer. She wasn't sure her little Volkswagen would survive a head-on collision with an animal that size. The antlers alone would probably take out her windshield. And possibly her.

With a sigh, she flung open her door and climbed out, only to find that her left front tire had been flattened by a sharp piece of metal.

"Great."

She ran a hand over her hair and looked around. She was in the middle of nowhere. Did they have roadside service in the country? Would it arrive five hours later on horseback?

The visual of a man riding up with a tire strapped to the horse's rear end amused her, and despite the inconvenience and frustration of this situation—or maybe because of it—she laughed.

"Oh, I'm losing it," she said as the amusement dwindled.

She unclipped her cell from the holder in the car and called a local tow company. They could at least get her home. She could worry about finding a replacement tire tomorrow.

The receptionist told her someone would be out in about twenty minutes.

Noelle dropped back into the seat and stared at the stretch of nature ahead of her. Why couldn't this town have a Starbucks for people to break down next to?

She glanced at her purse in the passenger seat and then reached over, pulling the diary from inside. After Walt's peculiar behavior when he saw it in her hands this morning, she decided to keep it with her. She opened it to the spot where she'd left off, and shifted into a more comfortable reading position.

Do you ever have bad dreams?
I do sometimes but mom has them alot. Almost every night. Somtimes I wake up cause the blankets are all twisted up around her and I'm cold. And sometimes I hear her talking in her sleep like she's whispring to someone.

"I'm sorry, I'm so sorry." She says that alot and I wander what she did in her dream that she's sorry for and who she's talking to. But she never remembers in the morning. Or maybe she does and just doesn't want to tell cause it makes her sad.

On bad days I help her light her cigaret cause she's shaking so much she can't hold it. I tell her it'll be okay but I don't think she hears me cause it doesn't make her feel better. I try to make her smile but all she does is cry. Mostly I lay down beside her and cry too cause maybe then she won't feel so alone but it's like she doesn't even know I'm here.

The scene the little girl described sharpened in Noelle's mind—a despondent woman curled on her side in bed, a child huddled against her back, willing comfort into her mother through her own silent tears.

Noelle's heart broke for Firefly, and she wished she could pull her into her arms and smother her with love. No child should have to comfort a parent like that, to fight to make their world better so they can simply be noticed and loved.

Firefly's mom didn't seem *un*loving, but it did sound like she was consumed by post-traumatic stress or . . . grief.

The moment the thought struck Noelle, the scene in her mind changed, and she saw herself in the woman's place, weeping and resistant to the comfort being offered.

I tell her it'll be okay but I don't think she hears me. I try to make her smile, but all she does is cry. I lay down beside her and cry too cause maybe then she won't feel so alone but it's like she doesn't even know I'm here.

Firefly's words reached straight through her, twisting into her soul.

"Oh God." Tears burned her eyes, and she lifted her gaze heavenward. "Am I that woman so consumed by her own pain that she can't recognize and accept the comfort being offered?"

Was God *her* Firefly, trying to shed light into the darkness that had consumed her life? Was He whispering love and encouragement that she couldn't hear? When His words failed to reach her, did He curl up alongside her on those sorrowful nights and weep silent tears so she wouldn't be alone?

All these months, she thought her unanswered prayers meant God had abandoned her, when in truth she'd been so focused on all that was wrong and all that was missing that it was impossible to see how God was working in her life.

Maybe He was trying to comfort her even now by offering a friend to soothe the ache of loneliness, a man who understood the pain of loss because he'd experienced it. Was God still reaching out to her?

She squeezed her eyes shut, letting the tears fall. "Lord, I'm sorry."

She used to know God's character better than any character she'd ever written, but when tragedy turned her life upside down, she forgot who He is—a loving father who comforts and fights for His children. Not a worldly father who walks out when things get difficult.

She might not be able to hear Him right now, but He was here with her. That was His promise to His children.

A tap on the car window drew Noelle's head up, and she found a man standing outside her driver's door.

He was stocky, with a crooked jaw and a nose that must've been broken a time or two. He looked like someone prone to parking lot fights after too many drinks at a bar. Not that she was judging.

Was he the tow truck driver?

She wiped the tears from her face and glanced in the rearview mirror at the blue car twenty feet behind her. It wasn't a tow truck, and he wasn't wearing a company uniform.

"Can I help you?" she asked.

He motioned for her to roll down the window. He could be a concerned citizen, but he could also be a crazed serial killer.

"I'm fine, thank you."

He tapped the window again and swirled his finger through the air. Could he not hear her through the glass?

He could be deaf.

She pressed the button for the window, and the pane of glass whirred down a few inches, damp, chilly air swirling into the car and sending a shiver through her.

She made sure her lips were visible, in case he had a hearing deficit. "If you stopped to see if I need help, I appreciate it, but I'm fine. There's a tow truck on the way."

He leaned down to speak through the crack. "Could be a while. They have a bad habit of being late." Alcohol clung to the breath that steamed her window. "I can give you a lift home."

She wouldn't get into the car of a sweet and cuddly grandmother whose breath smelled like a bar. She certainly wasn't climbing into this man's vehicle.

"Thank you, but I wouldn't want to inconvenience you."

"No inconvenience. I go right by your place on the way home."

She started to decline again, when his words registered. He knew where she lived.

An urgency to end this conversation now and put some distance between them washed through her. "I think I'll wait with my car. I wouldn't want the tow truck to take it to the wrong address."

"It's hard to confuse the Bechtel house with any other house in this town. They'll find it easily enough. Come on, I'll drop you at home so you're not sitting out here until dark."

When he reached for the exterior door handle, Noelle's heart leaped into her throat, and she hit the lock button. All four locks snapped down simultaneously.

The man's features tightened, and he released the handle. "I'm trying to help you out."

"I'm not getting out. I said I'll wait for the tow." She unclipped her phone from the dashboard holder. "And I have some calls to make, so if you don't mind backing away from my car . . ."

He didn't back away. "I only want to talk to you."

"Please. Go." She rolled up the window. She wasn't sure how much more polite she could be.

"We need to talk!"

If she ignored him, would he leave peacefully or continue to escalate? Her imagination churned out terrifying scenes of him smashing her car windows and dragging her out. She could end up in one of those trash bags on the side of the road that inspired passing drivers to wonder, *Is that trash or is there a dead body in there?*

She decided ignoring him wasn't the best course of action. "I asked you to leave. If you don't, I'm calling the police."

"You're overreacting."

She dialed 9-1-1 and held up her phone for him to see, thumb poised over the send button.

He swore under his breath and backed away, running his hands through his unkempt hair. "I just need to . . ." He glanced at her thumb prepared to hit the send button and swore louder.

He stalked back to his car, climbed in, and slammed the door. Noelle's heart hammered against her sore ribs as she watched him in the side mirror. He pounded his hands on his steering wheel, convulsing with anger, and then turned over the engine.

He pulled out around her, and the glare he threw her way as he passed by made her want to shrink in her seat. She gripped her phone and her purse with her gun inside, unable to relax until the tow truck rolled to a stop beside her fifteen minutes later.

CHAPTER
Twenty-three

Derek wasn't surprised to discover that the cell number Cody gave him was out of service. Had he bothered to give him an address, it likely would've been as fake as his name.

The man's distrust of law enforcement could be warranted based on a bad experience, or he could be hiding something.

Derek input his approximate age and features in the criminal database, hoping something would kick back for the tattoos, which would've been noted if he was ever booked for a crime. He didn't hold out much hope for results with so few criteria.

Rusty appeared in his office doorway, gray hair damp as if he'd tried to smooth down the tousled mess in the bathroom. "Gary and Beverly Wingate are here."

Derek's gaze trailed past his deputy to the couple standing in the squad room. Grief and fear shrouded them, weighing down their shoulders and haunting their expressions.

He motioned Rusty in. "Shut the door." As the door snicked shut, he asked, "Are we sure they weren't involved in Maddie's disappearance?"

"I spoke with both of them, and I didn't get the sense that either is involved. They strike me as genuinely concerned for her well-being. Beverly Wingate is barely holding it together."

"How much did you tell them?"

"That we found their daughter's car abandoned. Any leads on your end?"

"Nick Nelson, one of our registered predators, is awfully nervous. I did a quick check of his trailer and vehicle, but nothing obvious stood out. A possible witness . . . or suspect . . . claims to have seen an unidentified blonde female crossing the road Friday night."

"What road?" Rusty asked.

"He didn't say."

"Who's the witness?"

"Fake name, fake phone number, obscured license plate. Supposedly passing through."

"You blink and pass through Cherry Creek. It doesn't take three days."

"My thoughts exactly. That and his reluctance to provide any accurate information makes me suspicious. I'm running his details now, but I'm not holding my breath. Here's the make and model of his truck as well as his description." He pushed his notes across the desk.

Rusty picked them up and reviewed them. "I'll let everyone know to keep an eye out for him."

"He also mentioned another car on the road that night. Dark blue, and he used Perry Habrams's car as an example."

"Meaning it might not have been that specific car."

"It was conveniently across the street from the diner, so it might've been an easy way to deflect attention from himself. But if Perry was on the road that night, I want to know what road he was on and every detail of what he saw."

"I'll talk to him, and I'll look into any other dark blue cars in the area." Rusty's head gradually tilted to the left, as though the thought forming in his brain tipped the scales. "Doesn't Brian drive a dark blue car?"

"He's in Cincinnati."

"Huh, I guess he needed to blow off some steam."

"Why would he need to blow off steam?"

"From what I overheard in the break room, he was planning to buy the Bechtel estate and transform it into some kind of haunted attraction. He was pretty excited about it, so I'm guessing losing that auction hit him hard."

Derek clenched his teeth. That was where all the money was going—toward some half-thought-out plan to buy and remodel that house into a business? And when Brian lost the auction, he suddenly needed to go to Cincinnati and visit his sick mother. If that money went into a casino, it was never coming out.

"Are you ready for the Wingates?"

Derek leaned back in his chair, twisting a pen between his hands, and tried to refocus. "Yeah."

Rusty ducked out and reappeared a moment later, pushing open the glass door and holding it for Mrs. Wingate, whose resemblance to her daughter was shocking. If Maddie walked into his office twenty years from now, she would be identical to her mother.

Derek tossed down his pen and rose to greet her. "Mrs. Wingate."

She took one of the guest chairs, her red-rimmed eyes glazed with shock. Not unusual for a parent who recently learned that one of their children has been missing for three days.

When Gary Wingate extended a hand, Derek shook it. "Thanks for coming in."

"We left our son, Robbie, with my sister. He thinks Maddie is still at college." Gary took the remaining guest chair and reached over to grip his wife's hand. "What can you tell us?"

Derek sat and nodded to Rusty, who stood by the glass wall. "Deputy Ramone is heading up the investigation into her disappearance."

"Something must've happened to her." Beverly pressed a wadded tissue to her left eye. "She worked hard to earn her scholarships, and she wouldn't throw them away by running off."

Derek interlaced his fingers on the desk. "At the present time, we're treating her disappearance like an abduction."

Rusty rested his hands on his belt. "I know you both want answers about what happened to your daughter. So do we. The more we know about Maddie, the better."

"What do you need to know?" Gary asked.

"Anything you can tell us."

Gary swiped a hand over his face. "Um, Maddie is . . . she's kind to everyone. She's not even competitive because she doesn't want anyone to lose. She's the type of person who would give away her shoes to someone in need."

"She filters everything through her lens of faith," Bev added. "She is very intentional about helping people."

"Is she trusting?" Derek asked, and they exchanged a look before silently nodding.

Trusting victims were easier to abduct, because they walked into situations that a cautious person might question or avoid—like driving to meet a boy they only knew online.

"If Maddie's car broke down, would she call for help?" Rusty asked.

"She would've called us to come pick her up," Gary said. "That was the deal when she got her license. No matter where she was, what happened, or what she'd done, she was to call one of us. She promised she would."

"Even if she was doing something you wouldn't approve of?" Derek asked.

"She's a good girl. She would never—"

Gary interrupted his wife. "Yes. I told her that even if she'd been drinking or partying, I would pick her up without consequences. I didn't want to give her any reason *not* to call if she needed help."

"You thought she might be drinking?" Beverly gasped. "And you didn't tell me?"

"She wasn't drinking, but there's a lot of pressure to try new things in college. I would rather pick her up at three a.m. because she experimented a little too much than get a call that she died in a drunk driving accident. Wouldn't you?"

Beverly wilted in her chair. "You're right."

"To be clear, she didn't call you Friday night after eight o'clock?" Derek asked.

Gary shook his head. "No, we checked. Please. Tell us what happened to our girl."

Rusty took the lead again. "From what we've gathered so far, Maddie left the dorm Friday evening to meet up with a boy she'd been chatting with online."

Beverly twisted in her chair to see him, a frown pulling at the corners of her mouth. "Maddie wouldn't do something like that, not without talking to us first."

All parents thought that about their children, but in Derek's experience, parents rarely knew their kids these days.

"According to her roommate, Maddie has been talking to this boy for months," Rusty explained.

"Months?" Beverly paled and glanced at her husband. "Did you know?"

His left hand fisted in his lap. "No."

"Well, who is he?"

"We don't know his name yet," Rusty said.

Beverly shook her head. "We raised her to be smart. I can't believe she would take off to meet a boy that no one knows anything about."

Her husband squeezed her hand. "She was lonely, Bev. Two months at that school and she hadn't made a single friend. We can't blame her for wanting one, and we can't blame her for . . . for whatever's happened."

"I'm not blaming her. I just don't understand how any of this could happen."

Before Derek or Rusty could respond, Gary's expression darkened, and he demanded, "Did this boy use

171

her trust and kindness against her? Did he lure our little girl somewhere and . . . do something to her?"

"Ohhh." His wife pressed a hand to her mouth to stifle the trembling exclamation.

Derek wished he had something to say that would offer them a reprieve from the dark possibilities haunting them, but the truth might be as dark as they feared.

"It's possible that her online friend is a genuine person, and that whatever happened to her happened before or after meeting him," Derek explained. "But the opposite is also possible. Until we can get a hold of the transcripts from their conversations and dig into his identity, it's hard to say for sure."

Gary shifted forward in his seat. "What do you need from us? What can we do?"

"Her phone wasn't in the car, and it appears to be turned off. But there may be some helpful information in her text messages or last GPS location. If you're willing to help us get that information from your service provider—"

"Absolutely. Anything you need."

Derek retrieved a picture of the car's interior from his case folder and passed it to them. "From what we can tell, there was no sign of a struggle in the car, but considering what you told us, Maddie may have gotten out of the car willingly to meet or help someone. Forensics is still going through it for evidence. Do you notice anything missing? Anything out of the ordinary?"

The couple leaned forward, heads bent together as they studied the picture.

Beverly pressed her fingertips to her lips. "There was a small unicorn dangling from the rearview mirror. It was a decoration on the outside of the gift we gave her on her sixteenth birthday, but Maddie actually liked it more than the present. She's always loved unicorns."

"That's good. Can you describe it?"

"White, with a rainbow mane and a yellow horn."

Derek made note of it.

"I'm going to reach out to the community to see if they know anything that can help us. If you could write down any information you can think of—names Maddie mentioned, concerns or feelings she's expressed recently, locations she might like to visit, any username and passwords of hers that you know. The smallest detail could be helpful."

He slid a notepad and pen across his desk. Beverly took both with trembling hands.

"Our baby disappeared on Friday. It's Monday. What are the chances—"

"Bev." Her husband placed a hand on her shoulder, but she ignored him.

"What are the chances she's still alive?"

Derek's insides twisted at the question. Statistically, they weren't going to find Maddie alive . . . if at all.

"We're going to do everything we can to find your daughter. I promise you that."

It wasn't the answer she wanted, but it was the only answer he could give that wouldn't destroy her.

CHAPTER
Twenty-four

Noelle waited on the porch as the tow truck driver unhooked her car in the driveway, her gaze slipping past him to the road.

She half expected the man with the crooked jaw to show up and demand to have his conversation. Now, safely removed from the uncomfortable situation, she wondered what it was he wanted to discuss. Or had "conversation" been a euphemism for something else?

She rubbed her arms at the frightening thought.

The driver scribbled on his notepad, tore off the top sheet, and handed her the bill. She couldn't bring herself to look at the total—more money down the drain when she had a house to repair.

Maybe she should call Amy back about the book. She was going to need the income from sales, which meant re-engaging with her readers and promoting it to anyone who enjoyed based-on-a-true-story fiction.

Either that, or she would have to go back to waiting tables, like she'd been doing before she published her first book. Surviving on tips and living in an apartment similar to the one she left behind in Seattle.

A small town job and a small town life might not be so bad, as long as she could chip away at the repairs and pay the bills. At least until another problem blindsided her.

The tow truck clunked and rumbled out of the driveway, and Noelle sighed, cramming the bill into her back pocket. She would deal with it tomorrow, along with the tire and thoughts about books.

She plodded down the steps to retrieve her groceries from the trunk, and scowled at the deflated flap of rubber around her front wheel. She managed to avoid hitting a deer the size of a moose, only to run over a jagged piece of metal the size of a thimble.

Ridiculous.

She popped the trunk and ducked her head beneath the edge of the lid to avoid the pinpricks of icy rain on her scalp. She could make several trips to the porch with her grocery bags, but there was some unwritten rule against that kind of common sense.

She grabbed the groceries and supplies, plastic bags swaying from her wrists and fingers like pendulums. Now the conundrum of closing the trunk lid when she couldn't raise either overloaded arm.

Hmm . . .

If only she were flexible, she could lift a leg and kick it shut. But if she tried that, she would sprain her entire body and fall backward into the mud.

Trying to shake some of the bags from her wrists only twisted them around one another. Before she could peel them off layer by layer, the trunk slammed.

She sucked in a sharp breath and turned to find a figure standing beside her car, one hand still resting on the pink lid.

"You should never have your hands so full you can't defend yourself," Walt said, his presence sending tension crackling all the way down to her toes.

She eyed the rifle dangling from his left hand and shifted her feet, the mud sucking at her shoes. "Is there some danger I need to defend myself against?"

Like you.

If he tried anything crazy, she could bludgeon him with the overstuffed bags still clinging to her wrists.

"I told you to leave. I won't warn you again." The growl in his voice sounded more like a threat than a warning.

When he turned to leave, she blurted the question that had been nagging at her since this morning. "Are you watching me from that tree house?"

Silence stretched before he answered, "Not you exclusively."

Her muscles tightened with fear. She hadn't known for certain it was his tree house, or that he was actually watching her. Until now.

Wait . . .

If not her exclusively, then who or what else was he watching?

Before she could ask, he said, "I suggest you stay out of the woods." And then he turned and walked away, disappearing around the house.

———

Derek leaned back in his desk chair and rubbed at his eyes, his vision blurred from scrolling through Maddie's social media profiles.

Unsurprisingly, her poor privacy settings left her entire life on display for the world—her thoughts, feelings, even dressing room photos with outfits she uploaded to share with "friends." She never modeled anything inappropriate, but she had received comments from people who weren't on her friends list.

If Derek ever had a daughter, he would monitor her social media accounts like a hawk. He knew far too well how many predators were out there.

He closed the Facebook tab and logged into the department's Instagram account, looking up Maddie's profile: Madz4unicorns.

She had uploaded a picture Friday night, fifteen minutes after leaving the dormitory. Derek sat up straight and read the text she'd included with the picture of her rainbow-painted fingernails.

> Today I get to meet someone who sees me and appreciates me, who loves to talk about God as much as I do. Here's hoping Nate still wants to be my friend after he meets me in person.
> #FellowChristiansUnite
> #RainbowsRock

Derek's eyes zeroed in on the name of the boy she was meeting: Nate. He jotted it down and then searched her followers for a match. Nothing. He checked her other social media accounts but came up empty on the name.

He sighed and tossed his pen on the desk, frustrated by the lack of answers.

Maybe the Wingates would have more information, but he doubted it. There was no Nate on the list of names they provided. He sent a text to Rusty anyway and asked him to check with them.

He radioed Linton, who was overseeing the search for Maddie in the area near where her car was found.

"Nothing yet," Linton reported back. "And with the weather, I'm not sure any trail or evidence would still be intact. But we'll keep looking."

Derek glanced at the clock. He had time to record and upload the social media update to the department's Facebook page before ordering dinner. Hopefully, it would generate some leads.

———

Eyes are watching me. And I think there are secret rooms in my house because someone left a vague but spooky note on my car.

If Noelle shared those thoughts with Dr. Mills during their weekly online counseling session, her laid-back therapist would probably suggest antipsychotics.

She rested a hip against the counter and stared through the kitchen window in the direction of the tree house. What had Walt meant when he said he wasn't watching her exclusively?

The buzzards circling above the trees drew her attention. He could be a bird watcher. An image of Walt with binoculars and a pocket-sized notebook, scribbling down the names of birds that landed near his tree house, formed in her mind.

"Yeah, not likely." She plucked an orange from the bag of fresh fruit and funneled her anxiety into tearing off the peel with her fingernails, scraping away the bitter white layer that clung to the fruit.

Most likely Walt meant that he was watching the house she happened to be in. That was comforting in a way, because it meant that his obsession wasn't with her. It was with an inanimate object, which . . . wasn't a testament to his state of mind.

She popped a sliver of orange into her mouth.

He could've attacked her in the driveway if he wanted to. She'd foolishly left herself vulnerable. But he "warned" her instead. What would happen when he grew tired of telling her to leave?

She popped another slice of fruit into her mouth, chewing mechanically.

One thing was for certain: that was the last time she would try to carry all the groceries in at once.

She set down the orange and licked her sticky fingers before picking up one of the live mouse traps she'd gotten from the store. Most people would think she was crazy for trying to catch the mice rather than kill them, and before Tay, she would've agreed.

179

She used a regular mouse trap once, only to discover that her son had befriended and named the mouse living in their garage. Tay was inconsolable for days after he found the body. They had a burial ceremony in the backyard for Mick the Mouse. The name made the mouse sound like a mobster, but Tay hadn't been satisfied with Mickey.

Stuffing some crackers and cheese into her sweatshirt for bait, Noelle grabbed the lantern she'd brought down from the bedroom. The one she'd intended to keep downstairs had vanished between last night and this afternoon. Like her Chapstick and her notepad. Next, the mates to her socks would start disappearing.

"I swear this house has a black hole in it," she muttered. Surprisingly, nothing important had been swallowed up.

As she made her way to the basement door, she caught herself visually searching for places where a hidden space might be—behind a bookshelf, beneath the living room area rug, inside a cabinet. She suppressed the itch to tear the house apart.

Well . . . more apart.

She headed down the staircase into the basement to place the trap. Dank and dark, with skittering creatures, the space reminded her of a windowless dungeon. Cold seeped from the stone walls and concrete floor, cutting through the thin fabric of her sweater.

Old furniture had been stored down here, and cardboard boxes lined one wall, mold crawling up the sides. Some people found basements creepy, but Noelle had always liked them. They captured the overflow of life.

Her family never stayed anywhere long enough to collect excess boxes of decorations, clothes, or toys, which made the contents of people's basements that much more fascinating to her.

She set the mouse catcher on the floor and turned her attention to the boxes, which had been labeled based on their contents. There was a stack marked "Walt's Toys" and another stack marked "Holiday."

Some of the boxes had been opened recently, probably by teenage scavengers digging for souvenirs. Peeling open the bent cardboard flaps, she peered into the first box. Metallic tree branches still wrapped in tinsel greeted her.

She smiled and rubbed the coarse needles between her fingers. A similar tree had stood in Grammy's living room every winter, adorned by ornaments she'd made or collected throughout the years.

It would be time for Christmas decorations soon, but Noelle wasn't sure she had the heart to put up a tree. What would be the point without gifts for a little one beneath it?

She closed the box back up, not ready to face Christmas, and started for the steps when she noticed one of the stones in the basement wall protruded farther into the room than the rest.

You're not alone in that house.

The words of the note echoed in her mind as she approached the wall. If she ever built a secret room, she would add it to the foundation—like a bomb shelter or hidden stock room for supplies during a war.

She pressed a hand to the stone, but nothing happened. It didn't move or open some secret passageway. Habrams was right about it being too cold for someone to hide in the house, but she felt along the wall for seams and latches anyway.

"This is insane. I'm going insane."

Next, she would be looking for a magical land in the upstairs wardrobe. That note had clearly been left by someone who wanted to make her nervous or paranoid. There was no one else in the house, and there weren't any hidden . . .

One of the stones behind the staircase shifted beneath her probing fingers, and she froze. "That . . . didn't just happen." Sleep deprivation paired with her imagination must be playing tricks on her.

She stared at the stone in question and then ran her fingers over its surface, grazing the barest sliver of something that didn't belong—leather. She pinched it between her fingertips and squinted at it. It was the same shade of gray as the stone it disappeared into, practically invisible to the eye.

"How did you get in there?"

The leather ribbon was frayed, as though it were the remnants of a longer piece that had snapped off. She tugged to see if it would come free from the stone, but the stone moved with it. Another gentle tug, and the stone slid further from its resting place in the wall, dropping without warning. Noelle barely managed to catch it before it could hit the floor and crack into a dozen pieces.

"Oh crud. Did I just break the wall?" She looked between the opening and the stone in her arms. The leather ribbon had been threaded through a small hole in the center and secured on the inside with an anchor to prevent it from slipping all the way through. "Clever."

Setting the piece of wall aside, she picked up the lantern, brightening the alcove under the stairs. There was an actual hidden space in the basement wall, concealed by a thin stone with a string.

"Right. That's . . . I mean, why not?"

Murder mattresses, pet cemeteries, hidden spaces. Next she would find a body in a cardboard box. Or maybe just a toe.

She bent down to examine the opening. The space was smaller than a toaster, but there was something inside. After a moment of girly hesitation, she stuck her hand in the hole to remove the object. It was wrapped in old, water-stained Christmas paper. Cautiously, she unwrapped the layers, blinking at the contents.

It was full of money.

She examined the chaotically arranged bills. Apparently George Bechtel *was* paranoid. Enough that he would rather hide his money in the walls of his house than in a bank.

Except . . . this style of currency didn't exist until the 1900s. George Bechtel died in the 1800s. And the dates on some of the bills . . .

This money had been placed here *after* Walt's family was murdered and the house abandoned.

CHAPTER
Twenty-five

Cleaning cobwebs and dirt off the old couch, Noelle stretched a blanket over the cushions and sat down. Mildew and dust assaulted her nose, but it was nice to sit on something soft. Her tailbone was still furious with her for sleeping on the floor last night.

She placed three half-burnt candles, which she'd scavenged from around the house, on the coffee table and lit them, glancing at the mysterious bundle of money she'd brought up from the basement. Hopefully, Derek would know what to make of her recently discovered buried treasure.

Rubbing her cold fingers together, she picked up the diary and tried to relax against the cushions. She still hadn't found anything to help her identify the little girl who wrote it, but after reading about how difficult her home life could be, she was even more determined to find answers.

A receipt marked her place. Firefly's personality shone bright in the next couple of entries as she shared her favorite color, animal, and superpower. She wanted to teleport around the world so she could make friends, play outside, try every ice cream flavor, and be home before anyone noticed she was gone.

Noelle didn't miss the undertone of loneliness. Why was she never allowed to go outside and play with other children in the neighborhood? What about school? She never mentioned anything about school.

Firefly's favorite memory was the night that no one came to check on the sick girls, because it meant she got to spend the evening in the kitchen making macaroni and cheese with her mom—a moment so rare that it was cherished.

As she read, her mind conjured an image of the child behind the heartfelt words and the flower doodles in the corner of each page.

A nine-year-old girl materialized on the living room floor a few feet away, her back to Noelle as she hunched over a notebook. Black box braids brushed the warm, dark skin of her cheek as she tilted her head back and forth as she wrote.

The doctor is back again. I saw his gray hat coming up the porch steps before mom made me get away from the window.

I'm tired of hiding in our room. I hate never seeing anything new. Always here in this house with the same houses and signs and cars and people outside the window.

Today I got bored and snuck to see what the doctor was doing. I was real quiet but he saw me through the crack in the door. I never saw him up close before. He has mean eyes and I don't like the way he looks at me. It makes my stomach feel like it's full of wiggly worms. He offered me a cherry sucker but Mom took it away.

"Not her. Anyone but her" she said and she was shaking all over when she pushed me back in our room. I know I was sneaking when I wasn't spose to, but why can anyone but me have a sucker? It's not fair.

Noelle reread the part about the mother's reaction to her daughter being handed a sucker.

Not her. Anyone but her.

Even if Firefly had disobeyed the rule to stay in the bedroom, even if she had health problems like juvenile diabetes, her mother's reaction seemed extreme. Granted, Noelle didn't know all the details, but her behavior didn't fit the situation.

Maybe the woman's emotional struggles led to irrational outbursts, or she didn't trust doctors any more than her daughter. Some people with psychiatric disorders believed there was poison in anything medical professionals tried to give them.

Or maybe it was simpler than that, and there was something off about the doctor.

Noelle readjusted the diary in her lap, and a second folded picture slipped out. It was a colored pencil drawing of a few houses and a distant sign with the word "Mart" on it. Scrawled across the top of the drawing in Firefly's handwriting was a single sentence: "I hate this place."

How many times had Noelle thought that about her various homes? While she had been locked in a cycle of moving and never being anywhere long enough to make friends, Firefly was locked in one place and not *allowed* to make friends.

Light dragged her attention to the foyer. It pierced through the curtain like a spotlight, announcing a vehicle in her driveway. Setting the diary on the coffee table, Noelle rose and walked to the window.

The headlights flicked off, and darkness rushed back in with blinding force. She couldn't see the person stalking toward the house, and fear that it might be the man from the road began to stir. But then he came near enough for her lantern to catch his features.

Derek.

Relaxing, she unlocked the door and opened it. If she'd had any remaining doubts about having dinner with him, they would've evaporated the moment she glimpsed the exhaustion and worry in his eyes. He needed this.

He lifted the pizza box in his hands. "It's a deluxe— a mixture of meats and vegetables. Unfortunately, I think they forgot to remove the olives."

They had. She could smell them through the cardboard, but she could pick them off.

"You can set the box on the coffee table. I'll be back with some paper plates and drinks."

She strode down the hall into the kitchen. It still surprised her that he wanted to spend the evening with her, especially after a difficult day at work. Apparently, neither of them was flush in the friend department.

Did the worry in his eyes mean he was no closer to finding Maddie? She couldn't imagine shouldering that responsibility.

She was pouring warm water into two mugs when a muffled thump nearly made her drop the hot kettle. A mental image of Derek passing out from exhaustion on the living room floor flashed through her mind.

"Derek, are you—"

"Everything all right?" Derek asked, his voice mingling with hers as he came down the hall. He appeared in the kitchen doorway.

"I'm fine. I thought I heard a thump and wanted to make sure you didn't pass out or something."

Amusement colored his voice. "Still on my feet, but it's interesting to know you worry about me fainting like a goat."

"I don't . . ." Her mind blanked as his words sank in. "I'm sorry, did you say fainting like a goat?"

"You've never seen a goat faint?"

"I've never even seen a goat in person."

He leaned against one side of the frame and folded his arms. "I have some videos to show you after dinner."

"Why *after* dinner?"

"Because I don't feel like giving you the Heimlich maneuver when you inevitably swallow and laugh at the same time."

Fainting goats. She tried to imagine it as she gathered the plates and two mugs of warm tea and followed him into the living room.

"Not that I'm worried you're a bank robber or anything, but why does it look like you robbed a bank?" He nodded to the stack of cash as he dropped onto one end of the couch.

"I . . . found that. Hidden in the wall of the basement."

"Likely story." He stared at her for a moment before his eyebrows lifted. "Oh, you're serious?"

"Believe it or not."

"That's . . . strange."

"Imagine *my* surprise." She sat down on the opposite end of the couch, praying the rotted frame wouldn't collapse beneath their combined weight, and set the mugs of tea on the coffee table. "I thought the money might belong to George Bechtel, but the style of the currency is recent, and one of the print dates on the bills is from 2017."

Derek picked up the stack of bills and sifted through it. "There's probably five thousand dollars here."

"More, actually." It was an absurd amount of cash to find anywhere, let alone stuffed in a wall. And she couldn't deny that she'd been briefly tempted to keep it and use it for repairs, but she wasn't the kind of person who took something that didn't belong to her. "My grandmother used to hide her money in books instead of using a bank. Do you think Walt might be doing something similar?"

189

Did he want her out of the house because he was afraid she would find where he stashed it?

"I don't know where Walt would get this kind of money."

"Then who does it belong to, and how did it get into the wall?"

"All good questions." He dropped the money back on the table. "If you want, I can take it back to the department and hold it until we figure out who it belongs to. Or, if we discover it has illegal ties, we'll admit it into evidence."

"Illegal ties?"

"Maybe someone did rob a bank," he teased.

"Well, either of those works for me." She didn't want the temptation lying around. She picked up one of the mugs and offered it to him. "Here, try this tea. I think you'll like it better than the dandelion root."

The expression on his face mirrored what she would expect if she were asking him to sip curdled milk, and she laughed.

"I promise it's good."

He took the mug, and his lips twitched as he read the script on the side. "'Tears of My Readers.' Well, that should taste interesting." He tried it and swallowed, pausing before giving a verdict. "Hmm. Not as salty as I expected. It tastes a little like cranberries."

"It's hibiscus." She tucked her feet beneath her on the couch and held her own mug of lightly sweetened hibiscus tea. "And the mug was another gift. From a reader. Apparently, she cried through the climax of my third book."

"She didn't provide a free sample of her tears along with the mug, did she?"

Noelle laughed. "Thankfully, no. She sent along a note and a box of tissues."

"Do you usually receive odd gifts from readers?"

"There's nothing odd about tissues. Unless they're used. That would be off-putting. But I have received a few questionable gifts and letters, from men and women, including some awkward declarations of love I never responded to."

"Your husband didn't mind people sending you love letters?"

"My husband . . ." Her thumb grazed her bare ring finger, and she corrected herself. "My *ex*-husband couldn't have cared less."

Derek placed pizza on two plates and handed her one. "If you don't mind me asking, how long have you been divorced?"

"Officially, seven months." And the viciousness of the divorce still scalded her insides every time she thought about it.

"I take it separating wasn't cordial."

"What makes you say that?"

She followed his attention to her lap, where she gripped the paper plate so tightly that it had begun to fold in on itself, her pizza one spasm of anger away from sliding to the floor.

"Oh." She loosened her fingers.

"I've never been divorced, but I've seen the devastation it can cause, so if you'd rather not talk about it, I understand."

And yet she sensed he was desperate for a conversation that would distract him from the worries swimming behind his eyes.

"Just a little light conversation over dinner?" she asked.

"Pizza makes everything better."

Except my waistline. She resisted the urge to excuse herself so she could slip into some stretchy leggings before chowing down.

She set her mug of tea on the table. "The divorce wasn't a surprise. Our relationship was a mess from the start. We were looking for two different things."

He relaxed back against the couch and propped an ankle across one knee, his willingness to listen to her personal story as endearing as it was unbalancing. He was such a contrast to her self-absorbed ex-husband.

"Mom saw Tyrese for what he was, but I couldn't see past his charm. He had a way with words, which is no doubt helpful in his career as a lawyer."

She couldn't keep the bite of bitterness from her tone. She'd helped him pay for school so he could become a lawyer, and he used it to stab her in the back.

"I fell for him, and before I knew it . . . I was pregnant. Tyrese adamantly pushed for an abortion." She'd been a Christian then, too, and the condemning stares and judgmental whispers from fellow church members almost

192

drove her to the abortion clinic. But they would've condemned her for that too.

"But you decided to keep your son."

"It was . . . a hard decision at the time. My church ostracized me until I couldn't take it anymore. I left. My mother looked at me with disappointment, and Tyrese was pressuring me. But I knew in my spirit that I couldn't end my unborn child's life to make mine easier."

"That was a courageous choice."

She lifted her gaze from the slice of pizza she was picking apart. "No one's ever phrased it that way before."

"You made the right decision in the face of what I imagine was uncertainty and fear. Courageous is the only way to describe it."

This man dumbfounded her. "I suppose. I thought Tyrese would leave me, but instead, he apologized for panicking and said we should move forward as a family. It wasn't exactly romantic, but we got married."

"Juggling motherhood and a new marriage at the same time must've been hard."

"It was, but Tay was worth it. I can't imagine those seven years without my little man being a part of them. Even when things felt impossible, he made everything better."

She paused, with a sliver of green olive between her fingers, noticing she didn't feel a rush of anger and loss at the memories. It was as though they were being reframed in her mind as beautiful gifts rather than tragic losses. Was that God answering another prayer?

She added the olive to the growing pile on the side of her plate and continued. "Tyrese graduated from law school and landed a job at a firm. He started spending less time with me and more time with other women. I don't know how many affairs he had, and truthfully, I don't want to know."

Realizing she wasn't enough for the man she loved had shredded her heart and self-esteem. So many nights, when he was at a "business meeting," she stood in front of the bedroom mirror and searched for the flaws that must have driven him into the arms of other women—stretchmarks from carrying a child, the weight that clung to her hips no matter how much she dieted, the dark freckles on her face.

"I tried to make it work for Tay, because I didn't want him to grow up with a broken family, but it was . . . miserable. *I* was miserable. The last year of our marriage, we ghosted around each other in silence."

"What made you eventually file for divorce?" Derek asked.

"I didn't. He did."

Most women probably would've left their husbands years before, but her only thought had been for Tay, who loved his dad with unrequited fierceness. Without those passing moments under the same roof, Tyrese would never have bothered to set aside time for his son.

"When Tay died . . . I think Tyrese saw that as an opportunity to be free. Our son was always an unexpected twist in his plan. With him gone, he could divorce me without any sense of guilt." *And he wouldn't have to pay child support.*

"I'm sorry he didn't treat you the way you deserve," Derek said, and the sincerity in his voice gripped her.

She rolled a green pepper between her thumb and forefinger. "Even though the timing was cruel, it was for the best."

"Where did you go?"

"I found a cheap apartment in a not-so-great neighborhood." Tyrese, with his connections, had taken everything in the divorce, unwilling to sacrifice a penny for her benefit. If not for her separate bank account with book royalties and her car, she would've been destitute. "And then one day, when I was searching for a new place, this property popped up. When I realized it was in Ohio, and that I'd forgotten to narrow the search parameters, I almost backed out of it. But there was something . . . I can't explain it."

"Well, whatever it was that drew you to this outstanding piece of architecture, I'm glad."

A reluctant smile touched her lips. "It really is one of a kind. And the company's not awful."

"Are you talking about me or the mice?"

She grinned and took a bite of pizza, giving herself an excuse not to clarify.

"Nice. I can't believe I'm going to ask this, but did you come up with names for them?"

"I still have to catch them, but I'm thinking Tom and Jerry."

"You do realize one of those was a cat. I guess we'll know which one is Tom when he eats the other one."

"What about Ben and Jerry?"

"John and Wayne."

She laughed and he joined in, some of the tension draining out of him. They tossed around a few more ridiculous names for the mice as they finished their pizza—Sonny and Cher, Bert and Ernie, Hansel and Gretel.

Derek's phone buzzed, and some of the tension returned to his features when he checked the notification.

"Is it about Maddie?" Noelle asked.

"Possibly. The search team found a woman's shoe." He pocketed his phone and pushed up from the couch. "I should get out there to help search."

Noelle set aside her plate and stood with him. "I could help."

He shrugged on his coat. "I appreciate the offer, but some of the terrain is hard to navigate at night, especially if you're not familiar with it."

"Do you have a specific search area?"

"Pretty much Cherry Creek."

Noelle crossed her arms. "I guess we'll save goat videos for another time."

"I look forward to it," he said, and judging by the smile that curled his lips, he meant it.

Warmth flooded her chest, and she walked with him to the foyer.

He turned his hat in his hands, absently tracing the brim as he lingered on the threshold. "Thank you for letting me join you for dinner. I've gotten used to having my meals alone the past five years, so it was a nice change of pace."

Her throat tightened with empathy, because she'd grown accustomed to eating alone these past months too. "I appreciated the company too. Maybe we can do it again sometime."

"I'd like that." He turned to leave, but paused to add, "Oh, and the tea . . . not bad this time."

She bolted the door behind him and leaned against it, a smile lingering on her lips.

CHAPTER
Twenty-six

Noelle settled in at the dining room table and looked up the sheriff's department website to see if there was any mention of how locals could aid in the search for Maddie.

A link directed her to a video, and she was pleasantly surprised to see Derek on the screen. He wore his uniform, name and rank clearly visible, and judging by the décor in the background, he'd filmed it in his office.

She clicked the play button.

His posture was stiff behind the camera. "Last night, an abandoned car was found on the dirt trail behind the Cherry Creek Cemetery. The young woman driving the vehicle, eighteen-year-old Maddie Wingate, is presumed missing since Friday night. Since her car was found inside village limits, it's possible she was or is somewhere in Cherry Creek." He held up a picture of Maddie. "Maddie is five foot six, approximately 115 pounds, with blonde hair and brown eyes. She was last seen wearing dark jeans and a pink-and-white striped sweater. If you have any information or believe you may have seen her, please call the Cherry Creek Sheriff's Department. You can find photos of Maddie and any additional information on our Facebook page. Thank you."

Noelle sat back in her chair with a sigh. He hadn't provided any information about how to actively help. Tapping her fingernails on the dining room table, she considered doing a little research into Maddie.

Something about this house, this diary, this missing girl—they rekindled her desire to dig deeper and string details together, to build the story around Maddie's disappearance until she could piece together the mystery.

You already have one mystery waiting to be solved, she reminded herself, glancing at the diary to her left.

But they could be connected, her imagination chimed in. *Maddie and Firefly could be the same person.*

No, that didn't make sense. Firefly was a child.

When Noelle visited elementary and junior high schools to talk to some of the classes about her life as an author, she had the students write a short story based on a prompt she provided. Firefly's entries reminded her of the nine-to-eleven age group. She could be older if she had a mental delay, but she certainly wasn't an eighteen-year-old college student.

It was unlikely that the diary and the missing teen were related, but something inside Noelle wanted to connect them.

"This isn't some complex book plot, you're not an author anymore, and you're not an investigator, so stay out of it."

She pushed the laptop screen halfway down before desire overrode her resolve. With a groan of surrender, she pushed it back up.

"Ten minutes of research, and then I'm working on the house. There's too much to do to sit around on my computer and make up stories."

She visited Maddie's Facebook page and browsed some of her photos. There were a lot of them—selfies, family group photos, an entire album dedicated to rainbows. Noelle clicked on the rainbow album and read the description:

When I see a rainbow, I don't just see beautiful colors. It reminds me that when God makes a promise, He keeps it. I know not everyone believes He talks to people, but sometimes I swear I hear Him in my head. Every night I pray that someday I'll have a chance to save lives and make a difference in this world, and God promised me I would.

And now this beautiful soul was missing. It left an ache in Noelle's chest. She backed out of the album and clicked through some of the family photos.

She sucked in a breath and clicked on an image of Maddie opening a birthday gift. She zoomed in, ignoring the faces and fixing her attention on the gift bag. A toy unicorn with rainbow-colored hair was tied to the ribbons.

She'd seen that unicorn before, minus the horn. She'd kicked it down the hallway last night.

But if the unicorn was here, then . . . Maddie had been here, in this house.

Pulse quickening, Noelle pushed back from the table and looked around. Where had she put the unicorn? She'd picked it up last night, but she couldn't recall where she'd set it down.

She tried to mentally retrace her steps from the night before. After closing the dining room window, she'd set out to make sure all the other windows were closed.

"Bedrooms."

She hurried down the hall and peered into the first room, which was bare but for the furniture and curtains. Last night, she'd assumed the lack of personalization meant it was a guest room, but after seeing Walt's toys boxed up in the basement, she realized it must be his room. At twelve years old, he'd probably outgrown most of the things he played with.

She moved to the last bedroom on this floor. Elizabeth's room was a dusty time capsule.

The bookshelf was still cluttered with things that represented young Elizabeth, from stuffed animals and flowery teacups to books that spanned the gap of childhood to adulthood.

Clean outlines on the shelves indicated missing items, things that had been moved after sitting in the same place for decades. Books, stuffed animals, obscure knickknacks.

She visually traced every object in the room, but there was no unicorn. She moved from one room to the next, searching, pushing and tossing things aside, but she couldn't find it.

Running her fingers over her hair, she dropped back against the kitchen counter. Should she call Derek and tell him about her discovery?

The discovery you don't have? her inner voice mocked.

Right. She had nothing to show him, and there was no guarantee the unicorn had been Maddie's. It didn't even have a horn, like the one in the picture. It could belong to any little girl who wandered through here. She couldn't pull Derek away from the search for that.

But she could look for Maddie herself by searching the land behind her house. If the teen had been in the house, then she might still be in the area.

If Noelle found nothing, it would be an hour or two of exercise, but if it were her child missing, she would want every available pair of eyes searching. She opened the shallow closet off the kitchen and grabbed her jacket. She pulled on the warm layers, tucked her gun into one of her pockets, and clicked on her flashlight.

The moon was full tonight, bathing the tree branches and tall grass in silver, and it spilled into the kitchen as she opened the back door.

If Maddie had been out there for three days, possibly injured, she would need water and food. Noelle stuffed a water bottle and two protein bars into her other coat pocket before trotting down the steps and through the grass.

She swung the flashlight, the beam landing on the warped, wooden shed no bigger than a porta potty. It reminded her of something from a horror film. If she opened the door, would she find chains and bloody knives

202

hanging from the ceiling or a body strung up like a marionette?

Or Walt sitting in a chair with his rifle, peepholes drilled into the side of the shed so he can watch the house.

Derek said the old man had turned the pine trees out front into *one* of his watching posts, which meant there were more scattered throughout the property.

As much as Noelle wanted to ignore the shed, she should check to make sure Maddie wasn't hiding inside. She wrapped her fingers around the rusted handle and, steeling herself for whatever she might see, whipped open the door.

She relaxed when nothing flew out of the shadows to attack her. The shed was filled with ordinary things—gardening tools and what looked like metal traps of some kind. Her gaze lingered on the muddy shovel for a beat and then moved to the overturned bucket in the center, surrounded by dry, dirty shoe prints. Someone was using it as a bench.

"Figures." She kicked the bucket onto its side with her shoe. She didn't check for a peephole in the wall facing the house because she honestly didn't want to know.

Slamming the door shut, she abandoned the shed and fixed her sights on the woods.

"Maddie?" she called out, her voice echoing. She'd walked part of the area this morning, so she branched out to cover new ground. "Maddie!"

The wind shifted, carrying an odor that made Noelle's breath hitch and brought to mind the buzzards she'd seen circling earlier in the afternoon.

An animal must have died out here.

203

She wove her way through the nearly naked trees, the stench growing stronger with every step. She pressed a hand to the back of her nose and cleared her throat, trying to dislodge the scent of decay, but another gust of wind whipped it into her face.

She swept the beam of her flashlight back and forth over the collage of fallen leaves, determined not to step on the poor creature.

Cracking twigs from somewhere nearby jerked her to a stop, and she turned, casting light all around her.

"Maddie?" Another snap brought her focus forward, and her throat tightened with fear. "Walt?"

The moon that had seemed so warm and bright when she first stepped outside now felt cold and dim as it filtered through the tree branches, leaving pockets of darkness that pressed in from every direction.

A whisper of warning slithered up Noelle's spine—the same one she felt while standing on the porch. Someone was watching her.

She fumbled the gun from her pocket, her panting breaths rising in clouds from her open mouth. "Walt, if that's—"

Another crunch, and she turned, searching for movement. Whoever was out here with her remained in the shadows beyond her sight.

She stepped back, stumbling over an unexpected mound of earth, and crashed to the ground, the landing jarring the gun and flashlight from her grip and knocking the glasses from her face.

Pain and blood flooded her mouth as her teeth sank into her tongue, and she sucked in the breath that whooshed from her lungs on impact.

Sweet oxygen, tainted by death, scraped along her gag reflex, and she dry-heaved as she groped frantically at the leaves for her gun, flashlight, glasses—anything.

Her right hand bumped cold metal and she grabbed her gun, whirling to aim it at the surrounding darkness.

She squinted at the shifting shadows. Without the flashlight or her glasses, the details around her blurred together.

Something rustled to her left, and she snapped the gun in that direction. "Who's there?"

What did they want? Were they toying with her? Did they intend to hurt her?

It could be another deer.

But the anxiety tap-dancing along her nerve endings and the passing whiff of alcohol told her it wasn't a harmless animal having an evening snack.

She lifted her left hand to support her grip on the gun, but her fingers were tangled in something—some kind of netting. The more she tried to pull free, the more the thin strands tightened around her fingers.

Giving up on her left hand, Noelle tried to steady the gun in one sweat-slicked hand. "Come any closer, and I'll shoot."

A chorus of snaps and crunches erupted as someone took off into the trees.

She didn't doubt for a second that whoever had been watching her would come back. Setting down her gun, she fumbled her phone from her pocket and switched on the flashlight feature so she could free herself from the netting.

The substance tangled around her fingers nearly made her heart stop in her chest. It was hair. Long, blonde human hair.

CHAPTER
Twenty-seven

Derek inspected the broken branches of a bush. Something or someone had collided with it at a quick pace.

Angling his flashlight, he leaned closer to make out a foreign object caught on one of the jagged pieces. It looked like woven material. From a sweater.

Maddie had been wearing a sweater Friday night. If she'd deviated this far left of where they found her shoe, she'd been headed out of the village.

"Got something!"

The beams of light crisscrossing through the woods swung in his direction. The search shouldn't be taking this long, but something was interfering with the canines' ability to track. Even with the T-shirt that had been collected from Maddie's laundry hamper at the college, they couldn't pick up her scent.

Derek indicated the bush and then backed away to let his deputies work. He spotted Rusty heading his way.

"I figured you would still be out here," Rusty said. "How's the search coming?"

"There's no blood, no crime scene. Just a shoe and a piece of fabric in a bush."

Rusty's mouth turned down at the corners. "I wish I had better news. Mr. and Mrs. Wingate don't recall Maddie knowing or ever mentioning a Nate."

"So the mystery man remains a mystery. What about Perry Habrams? Did you have a chance to speak with him yet?"

"He says if there was a blue car on the road after seven thirty Friday night, it wasn't his. He claims he was on his couch, browsing for new suits online. I'll compile a list of blue car owners to speak with tomorrow."

At the rate this search was going, Rusty would make it to the end of his list before they figured out where Maddie was headed.

"If she was running from someone, and she made it this far, why didn't she run to a house to ask for help? There are plenty along this next road she could've gone to."

Rusty rested his hands on his belt and squinted toward the road. "It's possible she did go to one of those houses for help, and she picked the wrong one."

"Someone chasing her *and* she happened to knock on the door of a psycho?" Derek shook his head. "I don't buy that."

"He could've herded her toward his place, like a twisted hunt."

Derek grimaced at the thought.

"Oh, I almost forgot." Rusty pulled a folded piece of paper from his jacket pocket and handed it to Derek. "The Wingates still aren't sure what the login information is for Maddie's Google Maps account, but these are the possibilities they've come up with. If one of these pans out, and we can see the last address Maddie typed in, it might tell us who our predator is."

Derek skimmed the list of email addresses and possible passwords. He supposed it was too much to hope that Maddie's parents would know all her logins. If none of these combinations worked, he would try resetting the password, even if he had to call the Wingates for answers to any security questions.

His jacket started ringing, and he juggled the paper and his flashlight as he reached for his cell phone, surprised to see Noelle's caller ID. She knew he was out searching for Maddie, so it was odd that she would call. Unless Walt was giving her problems.

He answered. "Hey, Noelle, is everything—"

She cut in, her words sending dread all the way to the soles of his feet. "There's a body . . . in the woods."

———

Noelle sat numbly on the steps in the foyer, rubbing at the dirt embedded in the creases of her palms.

Everything around her felt surreal, like the sounds were being filtered through a layer of water—the static rattle of windowpanes, the fuzzy tap of raindrops on the roof.

Shock, she realized. *I'm in shock.*

There was a human body beneath the mound of dirt and leaves she tripped over, buried in a shallow grave.

It wasn't just the tangled strands of blonde hair that betrayed the ground's contents, but the pale, feminine fingertips popping out of the dirt like flower buds in the spring, nails chewed to the quick.

The contents of Noelle's stomach burbled, threatening to surge into her throat again, and she swallowed.

She'd thrown up beside the grave before groping at a tree to drag herself up onto wobbling legs, only to lose her stomach a second time.

She found her glasses and sprinted frantically toward the house, tripping over tree roots and colliding with tree branches she didn't duck in time to avoid.

If she hadn't been able to find her glasses, she might've wandered around in the woods for hours, unable to see where she was stumbling. A deep scratch bisected the left lens, but she didn't feel steady enough to put in her contacts.

Something slammed outside, followed by muffled pounding that reverberated through the floor beneath Noelle's muddy sneakers.

Her heart crawled into her throat, and her hand fell to the revolver on the step beside her.

Whoever had been in the woods with her must've known about the grave—it was impossible not to smell it from that distance—and they must know she discovered it. If they buried the girl there, would they try to silence Noelle before she could tell someone?

Too late for that.

She'd called Derek the moment she reached the yard, but she hadn't stopped running until she was barricaded inside the kitchen. It was a wonder he understood her words through her desperate gasps.

"Noelle?"

The voice carrying through the front door was distorted by the watery layer of shock drowning her brain.

"Noelle!" came again, accompanied by hammering fists.

The familiarity dragged her off the steps, and she limped across the foyer, her bruised knees and irritated ankles protesting every step.

She unlocked the door and swung it inward to find Derek on the porch, silhouetted by the blazing headlights of his cruiser in the driveway.

Simply seeing him brought her a sense of comfort and safety, as though some unseen force poured out of him and wrapped around her.

He looked her over. "Are you okay?"

She considered her jeans, one knee torn open and the other caked with mud, and then adjusted the scratched glasses on her nose. "I ran into a few tree branches."

Derek blinked at her matter-of-fact tone. "We need to get you to the hospital so a doctor can take a look at you."

She shook her head. Even if she could afford an ER visit with her dwindling income, the scents and sounds of hospitals reminded her of the worst night of her life.

"No." She sank back onto one of the steps. "I don't like hospitals."

Derek studied her. "Are you sure you're okay?"

How was she supposed to answer that? Aside from the acidic burn in the back of her throat and a few aches, she was physically fine, but emotionally . . .

"I don't know. How should I be doing after finding the dead body of another human being?"

He sat down beside her on the step. "It's normal to be scared, horrified, even nauseated. We all feel it the first time."

Horrified. That was the word slipping through her mental fingers. Finding human remains in the woods behind her house that might belong to a missing teenage girl was horrifying.

"I can't believe I didn't know she was out there." Her voice hitched under the pressure of tears, and Derek wrapped his fingers around hers, offering steadiness.

"There was no way *to* know until you stumbled across her."

Logically that made sense, but she'd gone for a walk in the woods this morning. She should've sensed . . . something. Shouldn't she?

"Do you want to tell me what happened?" Derek asked.

Noelle drew in a shuddering breath and released it. "I know you told me not to help with the search because it's dark, but I thought I could at least check the woods behind the house. I honestly didn't expect to find anything, but there was this . . . smell."

It was worse than anything she had ever smelled before, like some part of her mind recognized the scent and screamed at her body to flee even as she stepped closer.

"I thought it was a dead animal. As I got closer to the source, I heard a sound, like sticks crunching beneath feet. I called out several times, but no one answered. I was starting to get anxious, so I drew my gun. And then I tripped and fell over a mound of dirt. My left hand got . . . tangled . . . in her hair."

Her voice broke, and Derek squeezed her icy fingers.

She sniffled and drew herself up. "I should take you to the grave."

"We'll get to that. My people are on the way. Right now, what's important to me is making sure *you* are okay."

His face blurred behind a veil of tears. "I was so scared, Derek. I think . . . I think there was someone else out there."

Derek's brow furrowed with concern. "A second grave?"

"No, someone alive. Watching."

His shoulders stiffened. "Did you see this person? Did they say anything?"

"No, it was more of a feeling. Someone was moving nearby, or . . . maybe some*thing*." She sighed, her doubts spilling into her words. "It could've been a deer, I guess. I don't know. Maybe I'm losing my mind."

"You're not losing your mind. If someone was out there with you, I'm sure we'll find evidence of it."

She lifted the glasses from her nose and wiped at the moisture collecting on her lashes. "Her hair, Derek." Her throat tried to close against the words she was about to speak. "It was long and blonde. Like Maddie's."

213

His grim expression suggested that he'd already braced himself for the possibility.

"There was something I was going to tell you. I remember thinking you needed to know, but . . ." She rubbed at her forehead, trying to unscramble her thoughts. It was something important, but all she could think about were those awful moments in the woods.

"It'll come to you."

More sheriff's department vehicles arrived.

Noelle straightened her slumped shoulders and dried her face with the sleeve of her sweater before gripping the banister to pull herself up. "I should show you where the body is."

If she could remember the way back. Her path to the grave had been wandering, and her path away from it had been frantic chaos. There were too many leaves on the ground to leave tracks, which meant they couldn't use her foot or face-plant impressions in the mud to backtrack.

Derek stood with her. "The dogs should be able to pick up the scent. You don't need to go back there."

Her determination to help wavered. She wanted to be braver, but she wasn't made the way the rest of these people were. Death and crime were something they faced daily. She'd only ever written about it from the comfort and distance of her laptop.

"If the dogs can't find it, I'll come back and get you," Derek suggested, and when she relented with a nod, he motioned one of his people inside. "Stay with her."

"Derek."

He paused in the doorway and turned back to face her. "Yeah."

"I don't know if it's related, but I found an old shovel in the shed behind the house. Someone used it to dig recently." And she could only think of one person who used that shed.

She saw the same thought cross Derek's face— could Walt be responsible for what happened to this girl?

―――――――

The dogs sat down, alerting the team to what they already knew—they had reached the grave.

The odor of death rose from the ground and permeated the air, and Derek pressed the back of his hand against his nose as he swung his flashlight over the area. Overturned clumps of leaves indicated someone had dug and clawed at the ground, probably Noelle in her haste to escape.

"Tread carefully," Derek instructed. "I want everything preserved and photographed."

If Noelle was right, and someone else had been here, she might've stumbled into the killer's private revisiting of the grave. There might be something here to help them identify him.

Rusty knelt beside the mound of earth, a grim set to his mouth as he pulled out a camera. All of Derek's deputies were trained to collect evidence and preserve crime scenes. "I was really hoping to find this girl alive."

"Me too."

The grieving faces of Maddie's parents floated through Derek's mind. He didn't want to deliver this news any more than Rusty did.

"This is what, a little over a mile from where we found the shoe?" Rusty snapped a picture of the blonde hair tangled in the leaves. "Is it possible she ran all this way?"

"Or she was dumped."

"He didn't think out the spot too well. Tree roots make digging a grave hard, and between Walt and the neighborhood kids traipsing through on the way to the haunted house over there, it was only a matter of time before she was discovered."

Derek placed the end of his flashlight in his mouth as he snapped on gloves. He didn't think the killer gave much thought at all to the location of the grave. It was shallow and mounded, making it obvious that something was buried there. Kicking foliage over it didn't disguise it.

"I think this grave was dug by someone desperate and in a hurry," Derek said as he removed the flashlight from his mouth. "There's a footprint here." He pointed toward a partial impression in a patch of mud.

Rusty approached with an evidence marker and his camera. "Does it look like Ms. McKenzie's?"

"I don't know, Rusty, I didn't memorize her feet."

Rusty shrugged. "Some people are foot people. That widow who's always bringing baked goods to the department—Carol—she has cute pixie feet."

Derek blinked. "I'll take your word for it."

Rusty bent down to get a closer look. "Ms. McKenzie mentioned a shovel in the shed with dirt on it. You think it was used to bury this girl?"

"Given the proximity of the body to the shovel, chances are good. I sent someone to collect it. If it belonged to the Bechtels, I doubt the handle is in good enough condition to lift prints, but rough wood means possible skin cells, so long as the killer didn't wear gloves."

Rusty rose and searched for more evidence, taking pictures of a broken flashlight—likely Noelle's—a bottle of water, a flossing stick, and another shoe print, this one smaller than the first. "I'm thinking this was the work of an outsider. A local would know this area is frequently visited. But an outsider might see an abandoned-looking house from the road and nothing for another half mile and think it was a good place to stash a body."

"Or I was wrong about the killer not giving much thought to the location of the grave, and she was buried by someone who expected to win an auction and own the land by now. After that, he could enclose the property so no one could ever find her."

Rusty looked up from his camera. "This is part of the Bechtel property?"

"If we're where I think we are, right on the edge of it. Another couple hundred feet or so and they would've buried her on village land."

"That's a risky move, and not all that smart."

"We're talking about a guy who dug a grave that can't be deeper than two feet, in an area where kids snoop around, with a shovel that he probably got from the shed and then put back. I don't think smart is on his resume."

"We need to find out who was bidding on the house then." Rusty tapped a finger on his camera. "If Ms. McKenzie was a man, we would be looking at her as a suspect right now."

"She arrived from Seattle yesterday. Judging by the smell, this grave has been occupied for days."

Maddie had probably been dead before anyone realized she was missing. The thought squeezed Derek's heart, and he looked up at the dark clouds drifting overhead.

Lord, please don't let her have suffered.

"I'm sure you've considered this already," Rusty said, recapturing his attention. "But when I request that list of bidders from Habrams, Brian's name is going to be on it."

"Yeah, I know."

And if his brother-in-law had something to do with what happened to Maddie Wingate, his badge and his relationship to Derek wouldn't protect him from the consequences.

CHAPTER
Twenty-eight

Noelle folded her body into the corner of the couch and stared at the dust bunnies rolling across the floor in the draft, as the scene in the woods looped through her mind.

Despite the fact that she had no proof, she couldn't shake the feeling that someone else had been out there. Tyrese would tell her she imagined it, that she'd shaped monsters out of shadows, and maybe she had.

It was possible no one had been there at all, and she'd panicked over nothing.

Nothing? Her imagination punched her brain with the image of the girl's hair and fingers rising out of the earth.

Those details were going to haunt her dreams. But nighttime imaginings weren't a concern right now; the concern was that someone violent and twisted had been in those woods only days ago and might still be in the area.

And she'd gone out there alone. After dark. Without telling a soul.

Stupid, Noelle. Stupid.

Whoever murdered that girl could've killed her and buried her in the woods alongside the other unmarked grave. He could've knocked her out and dragged her away for some purpose better left unimagined.

219

She rubbed at her face and released a trembling breath, drawing the attention of the female deputy standing like a century in the foyer.

"Miss, you all right?"

Just having an emotional meltdown, Noelle thought, but she smoothed away the dampness beneath her eyes with her fingertips and nodded. "I'm fine."

But she wouldn't be if she continued to sit here with nothing but her thoughts for company. She could feel depression inching closer, waiting for an opportunity to wrap around her. She was too tired for an emotional battle, which meant she needed a distraction.

———

Derek knocked on the back door, pausing a beat before stepping into the empty kitchen.

Four mugs of tea steeped on the counter, the scent of peppermint and vanilla filling the room. Brewing tea must be one of Noelle's coping methods for stress. A handwritten note sat beside the mugs.

> In case you guys need something warm to drink that won't keep you up all night.

Derek smiled at her thoughtfulness, even though she clearly didn't realize that a badge came with a caffeine addiction. It would take a truckload of coffee to keep any of them up at night.

He added a few drops of honey to one of the mugs and picked it up, turning it to see if there was another comical saying. This one was blank.

Deputy Angel Jimenez strode into the kitchen, carrying the Reader's Tears mug he'd used earlier.

She was a small Hispanic woman with a disposition that unsettled some of the men in the department. She didn't let her size or her gender prevent her from taking down a suspect twice her size. She evened the playing field by going for the ankles first.

"How is she?" Derek asked, mixing the honey into his tea with a plastic spoon.

Her dark eyes drifted toward the ceiling. "She's currently upstairs, trying to scrub fifty-year-old stains from the wallpaper in the main bedroom, so . . . I'm going to guess she's not great."

After the events of this evening, anyone would be rattled. "I'll go talk to her." Derek slipped past Jimenez and headed for the stairs.

Noelle was so focused scrubbing a spot on the wall that she didn't notice his approach.

Derek tapped knuckles on the door frame to draw her attention. She'd exchanged her scratched glasses for contacts, though he thought the thick, red frames suited her better.

He nodded to the dusty streams of water running down the stained wallpaper. "I don't think that wall is going to come clean."

221

Noelle plucked two earbuds from her ears and draped the cord around the back of her neck. "You're probably right."

"What are you listening to?"

"Nineties' pop music." She tapped a button on her phone screen to pause the music. "I guess I'm aging myself with that admission."

"I'm a Johnny Cash fan, so if that's how aging works, I must be rolling up on seventy."

"That explains the graying hair," she teased.

"Gray hair comes with the job, but at least I still have my hair. Not everyone is so lucky."

She dropped the sponge into the bucket of water, drying her hands on her jeans. "Since you're here and not out there, I'm guessing you didn't find the grave."

"We found it."

Her shoulders relaxed, no doubt in relief that she wouldn't have to lead them to the grave after all. "And Maddie?"

"They're excavating now. It's a meticulous process, so it'll take some time. And then we should know for sure."

"Her poor family." She sank onto the old blanket chest at the foot of the bed. "There's no worse feeling than finding out your child is dead."

There was a rawness in her voice. Was she thinking about when she received the notification about her son?

He gestured to the wooden chest. "Is there room for two on there?"

She slid over, and he dropped down beside her, squeezed so close that their knees brushed. She still smelled like pine, dirt, and dead leaves from the woods.

She drew in a breath. "I just realized that you'll probably be the one who breaks the news to Maddie's family. I've never considered how hard that must be for the person delivering it."

"I've had to do it before, and it's . . . difficult isn't really a strong enough word for it." Anyone with a degree of empathy struggled with that part of the job.

"I'm sorry."

"How are *you* doing?"

She rubbed her left hand on her thigh, pausing to pick at a spot of dried mud. "Tylenol took care of the aches from running into so many trees, but the rest of it . . . it's going to be a while before I can get that out of my head." Silence stretched before she asked, "Do you have more questions about what happened out there?"

"A few, but mostly I was checking in to make sure you were doing okay."

She flicked a clump of dirt across the room. "You and my dad both. He calls every day, but I swear he has a sixth sense with his timing. He called shortly before you came upstairs."

"He worries about you?"

"It's become a chronic condition for him since I lost Tay."

"That strikes me as more of a mother thing."

"Those first months after the funeral, I blamed myself for what happened, and things got pretty dark. Dad's been there and . . ." Her brow crinkled and then smoothed, as though she'd brushed the troublesome memory away. "It's a long story."

He rested his mug of tea between his knees. "I've got forty minutes or so before I need to get back to the grave."

"You sure listening to this is how you want to spend your forty minutes?"

"I'm sure." The more time he spent with her, the more he wanted to know.

She tucked her hands between her thighs and rubbed them together, her eyes fixed on the wallpaper. "It started when Dad was a cop. He responded to an armed robbery at a corner store. The robber was out-of-his-mind high, and he started shooting. Dad fired back. Instead of staying down, the teenage cashier got scared and ran. One of my dad's bullets hit and killed him. It was ruled an accident, but it nearly destroyed him. He quit the force. I remember him being sad, but I was too young to realize how bad it was. He blamed himself, and he sank into such a deep depression that he started considering suicide."

"Oh man." Derek couldn't imagine the trauma of killing a human being, let alone an innocent one he was there to protect.

"Mom got him help, and he slowly worked through it all. He doesn't want me to end up in that same dark place, so he checks on me every day."

Worry expanded in Derek's chest. "Do you have those kinds of thoughts?"

"Not anymore. But I do still struggle with depression." She cast him a sidelong glance to gauge his reaction. Seeing no judgment, she continued. "Back then, losing everything and believing it was my fault . . . it was too much."

"Why would you think it was your fault?"

Lantern light glinted off the tears in her eyes, but she kept her gaze averted. "Tay was hit by a car while I was finishing up a manuscript. The what-ifs tormented me to the brink of madness. What if I had closed my laptop and gone outside with Tay when he asked? What if I hadn't told him to wait ten minutes while I finished the manuscript corrections? What if I'd listened more carefully for the sound of the front door opening when he snuck out?"

"What-ifs can be dangerous. They trick us into thinking we had more power and control over the situation than we really did. We can't change something we can't foresee or control every variable that leads to that outcome, and we can't know everything or be everywhere. We're not God. Hindsight is meant to help us understand and learn from the past, not punish ourselves with knowledge we have now that we didn't have then."

She dragged her eyes away from the wallpaper and looked at him. "Are you sure you weren't meant to be a counselor?"

"I'm partial to my gun and handcuffs, and something tells me not every client would appreciate me carrying those during sessions."

She huffed a laugh. "Probably not."

"In case you have any doubts, your son's death wasn't your fault. It didn't happen because you were finishing up a manuscript."

A tear slid down her cheek, and he resisted the urge to reach out and wipe it away.

"Some days it's harder to ignore those thoughts, and I can't figure out how to separate my writing from his death, which is probably why I don't have any ideas or any passion for writing anymore."

"Is that why you haven't interacted with any of your readers in the past eight months?" When her brows pinched curiously, he clarified, "Trudy told me."

"Your sister's Facebook-stalking me?"

"If you're going to have a stalker, you can't go wrong with one who offers free hugs and bakes you pies."

"Clearly you're not a suspense writer, because I can see a dozen different ways for that to end in disaster."

He smiled. "If not writing, what do you have a passion for right now?"

She gripped the edge of the blanket chest, thoughtful. "A little girl whose name I don't know."

"The diary?" He'd seen it on the coffee table with a bookmark in it. "Still no clues about her identity?"

"No, and I asked almost everyone I saw today. I want to piece together her story." She glanced over her shoulder at the window, and he followed her gaze to the floodlights blazing in the trees, where his people worked. "Speaking of piecing things together, you said you had more questions about what happened out there."

"A few, yeah." He drank the last of his tea and set the mug on the floor. "Do you happen to know how many bidders you were competing against for this house and what their names are?"

"No, I asked Habrams for the list, but he wouldn't give it to me."

"Why did you want the list?"

"I knew there were other bidders, and that I came in at the last minute and bought the house. I imagine the person who had the top bid before me was pretty upset. With the back door being kicked in, the strange noises, someone smearing the word *leave* in mud on the porch, and then—"

"Wait, when did that happen?"

"After you left around noon. I heard a thump from the front porch, and when I opened the door to check on the sound, the message was scrawled there. I assumed it was Walt trying to spook me. After that, I drove into town for supplies, and when I came out of the market"—she pushed up from the bench and walked to the dresser, returning with a crinkled piece of paper—"I found this under my windshield wiper."

He took the slip of paper and read the ominous message: "You're not alone in that house." He looked up at Noelle. "I checked the house thoroughly last night."

"So did I. I thought one of the other bidders might be trying to scare me, so I went to Habrams for names. On the way home, I swerved to miss a deer and flattened my tire. A man approached my car while I was waiting for the tow truck, and he smelled like he'd been drinking. He was .

227

. . insistent on giving me a ride home, and he knows where I live."

Concern rose in Derek, and he stood. "When you say insistent . . ."

"Nothing physical. I don't think he was trying to kidnap me or anything, though he did try to open my door. I locked it, rolled up the window, and told him to leave. He was irritated, but he left."

The tight muscles in Derek's shoulders softened. "Did you get his name or license plate?"

"No, but he drives a blue car, and he looks like he gets into a lot of fistfights. His nose has to have been broken several times, and his jaw is asymmetrical."

Derek's brother-in-law was supposed to be out of town, but between the description and the car, the man sounded an awful lot like Brian.

"I know you didn't see anyone else, but you sensed someone in the woods with you. Do you remember any specific sounds or smells?"

She toyed with one of the drawstrings on her sweatshirt and those adorable quotation marks appeared between her eyebrows again. "I remember the sound of running—something or someone taking off. And there was a passing scent. You know the kind that's so faint you question whether you actually smelled it?"

He nodded. "Did you recognize it?"

"Alcohol, but I've never been a drinker, so I can't narrow it down any further than that." She sighed and looked around the room. "I think I need to get out of here for a while. Is there anything interesting to do in this town?"

"Um, eat. The ice cream shop, the diner. I think there's a football game going on at the high school."

"Wow, I'm overwhelmed by the options."

He grinned. "I imagine it's not quite what you expected when you decided to move here."

"Truth be told, I was disappointed to learn that this village isn't made up of tiny cottages around a communal well, with horse-drawn carriages bumping along dirt roads. You do have horse-drawn carriages, though. I saw one."

He suppressed a laugh. "Those are called buggies, and they're owned by local Amish families."

"I know. I saw a TV show about the Amish community once."

Derek cringed inwardly. Those shows were far from accurate.

Noelle tilted her head in thought. "What are the chances I could get a ride in one of those buggies sometime?"

He'd never met anyone over the age of ten excited by the idea of riding in a buggy, and it was . . . cute. "I know a family who might be willing to arrange that."

She smiled. "You're very good at making people feel better."

"I do what I can, especially for people I like."

Bashfulness crept into her expression. "Is there anything else you need from me?"

"No, that was it for now. Do you want a ride to the diner or football game?"

"If you don't mind, the diner would be nice. I'll need to change first, though."

He considered her muddy, torn jeans. "I hear grunge is making a comeback."

"There's a difference between grunge and grun*gy*."

"True." When she stood there, waiting, he sucked in a breath of realization, heat crawling up his neck. "Right, I'm in your bedroom, and I should leave and let you change."

He stepped out and closed the door, stifling a groan at his own awkward behavior. He was nearly forty. It wasn't like he'd never been around an attractive woman before.

Refocusing on the matter at hand, he dialed Brian's number. He needed to find out where he was and what was going on with him. The call immediately went to voice mail. Another attempt had the same result.

Fine, if Brian wanted to ignore his calls, Derek would call his mother to find out if he really went to Cincinnati to see her. And if he lied and was still in the area, he would send deputies to track him down and bring him in for questioning.

CHAPTER
Twenty-nine

The diner had a cozy atmosphere—pictures of locals spanning one wall, old wooden booths and tables, and a candle at the center of each.

Noelle dropped her purse in a booth near the kitchen. The warm scent of honey wafted up from the mason jar candle, the heavenly aroma tempting her to draw in an even deeper breath.

She unwound the scarf from her neck and wandered over to investigate the artfully arranged pictures. Some were old and faded, while others were newer. Generations of families.

There had been too many customers in here last night for her to appreciate the photos without intruding on people's meals, but most of the tables were empty now.

The last of Noelle's anxiety drained away as she observed the pictures, the frightening ordeal from the woods fading to the back of her mind. Her eyes caught on a vaguely familiar face. A man surrounded by his wife and four children. Something about him tickled a memory—the sharp angles of his face, the softness of his eyes . . . his smile.

"I see you found my family."

Noelle jumped at the unexpected voice and whirled to see the pregnant waitress shuffling her way, both hands pressed to the small of her back. The poor woman was so far along that she was almost as round as she was tall.

Trudy's face scrunched in apology. "Sorry, I didn't mean to scare you."

Noelle's heartbeat slowed. "You're fine. I'm a little on edge today."

"Is everything all right?"

Noelle opened her mouth to answer, then reconsidered. If Derek hadn't filled his sister in on the dark turn his investigation had taken, there was a reason. "Um, moving here has come with a few surprises."

"I imagine that's true of any place you move. I moved to Tennessee for several years, and it was full of surprises."

"Tennessee, huh? That explains the accent."

"I have an aptitude for accents. I can't speak a lick of a foreign language, but accents slide on and off my tongue like an ice cube on a hot day. I became Tennessean real quick. It's a lot easier to pick up the twang than it is to lose it. Can't figure that one. I'd like to visit Ireland someday, but my tongue would start dancing an Irish jig two hours off the plane, and I'm sure they would think I was mocking them. I would never do such a thing." A slow grin spread across her face. "Well, okay, not *never*."

Noelle returned her attention to the photo that had captured her attention. "You said this is your family?"

"That was right before Daddy died. I was only a few months old." She pointed to the baby girl in the photo, who rested on her mother's hip. "That little chunker is me. Can you believe I weighed ten pounds, two ounces when I was born?"

With her petite build, Noelle couldn't imagine that at all. But there she was in the photo, cheeks so plump that her nose was little more than a button between them.

"The other two girls are Tammy and Tina. And then, of course, Derek."

"Trudy, Tammy, and Tina."

Trudy shrugged. "Mom had a thing for T names, but she could never keep them straight. I couldn't tell you how many times I got called Tam-tin-Trudy. Mom would get it right eventually, but unfortunately my nickname became Tamtin. Derek still calls me that sometimes."

"How did he escape a 'T name'?"

"Daddy. Nonconformist."

Noelle smiled. The name Derek suited him better than Tommy or Timmy or whatever other T name his mother might've had in mind.

"Derek looks a lot like Daddy. Except for . . ."

"The beard," they said at the same time. That was what made it difficult for Noelle to recognize the face.

Trudy puckered her lips in thought. "Personally, I think he should shave it, but some women really go for the beard and badge."

Studying the features that Derek shared with his father, Noelle had to admit that he looked better *with* the beard. It made him appear softer and more approachable.

"He's single, you know. Derek." Trudy tilted her head to see Noelle's face, a glint of mischief in her eyes.

"Uh . . ." What was she supposed to say to that? Thanks for letting me know? That's good to hear? She cleared her throat and defaulted to her usual I-have-no-clue-what-to-say phrase. "I see." Noelle's gaze caught on another picture, an old black-and-white family portrait wrapped in a simple wooden frame. "Is that . . ."

"The family who used to own the house you moved into, yeah. It took a while to track down that picture, but after what happened to the Bechtels, I thought they deserved a place on this wall."

Noelle inched closer, drawn to the faces of the people whose story lived on in her home.

The entire family exuded joy, except for the little boy, who looked like he would rather clean the bathroom toilet with a toothbrush than pose for the camera.

"What do you know about Walter Bechtel?" Noelle asked, studying the boy's grim expression.

"Not much more than anyone else, I guess. He usually keeps to himself, except for coming by to pick up his meals. He was agitated when he came by Friday night, though."

"He was agitated when he came to the church that night too." The plump woman hunched over her bowl of soup twisted in her seat to see them.

"Church?" Trudy asked, probably thinking the same thing as Noelle: *He doesn't seem like a churchgoer.*

"He was asking for extra blankets and nonperishable foods. We gave him what we could, but it's a food kitchen. We don't have many spare blankets lying around."

234

Frustration sharpened Trudy's voice. "I wish someone had said something. I have plenty of spare blankets at home. He must be freezing at night this time of year."

"His camper doesn't have heat to get him through the colder months?" Noelle asked, unexpected compassion threading through her. Could she be creeped out by someone and be concerned for them at the same time?

"I don't think his camper has anything," Trudy said.

The front door swung open, sucking the warmth from the room like a vacuum.

A woman shuffled inside, rubbing her hands together against the cold, and Noelle's breath caught in her lungs. If she hadn't just stumbled over the grave, she would think it was Maddie strolling into the diner.

But then she noticed the soft lines around the woman's eyes and the touch of gray in the blonde hair she tucked behind her ears.

She turned to her husband as he followed her inside. "I don't want to be here, Gary."

His face softened. "You need to eat, sweetheart. Your blood sugar's low."

"I don't need food. I need my daughter." Desperation laced her voice. "We should be out trying to find her. Knocking on doors or something."

"You know we can't do that."

The woman choked on a sob and pressed a hand to his chest, his fingers coming up to cover hers.

No one in the diner moved, not even the old woman with her spoon hovering soundlessly above her

235

bowl of soup. There seemed to be an unspoken agreement to afford these two parents a moment of silence to grieve.

Gary broke it with a whisper. "We need to let the sheriff's department do their job."

Maddie's mother wiped a tear from her cheek. "That's the problem. It's a job to them, another paycheck. If something happens to her, they'll still be able to sleep at night."

Noelle slid a glance toward Trudy. It was her brother they were talking about.

Trudy's soft mouth was compressed into a hard line, but it was compassion rather than anger that sparkled in her eyes. She straightened her shoulders and strode toward the couple. "Mr. and Mrs. Wingate."

Two faces turned her way, visibly surprised to be addressed by name.

"My name's Trudy, and my brother, Derek Dempsey, is one of the officers looking for your daughter."

Regret flashed across Mrs. Wingate's face. "I'm sorry for what I said, I only—"

Trudy touched her arm. "You don't need to apologize. But you do need to know that my brother cares about what happens to your little girl. The moment he realized she might be missing, he started investigating because he didn't want to waste a moment. And every second he's not able to bring her home to her family is agonizing for him, so trust me when I tell you, it's more than a job for him. He will go above and beyond to find your daughter."

Tears streamed down their faces, and it was Gary who choked out, "Thank you."

Trudy smiled and rubbed Mrs. Wingate's arm before donning her hostess persona. "Now, let's get you two something to eat. How do you feel about warm apple crisp with vanilla ice cream?"

"That sounds perfect," Gary said.

"Sit wherever you like. I'll be right back." Trudy bustled off to the kitchen.

The couple shed their jackets and sat down in the booth by the picture window.

Bev leaned into her husband for comfort, mascara tears streaking her face. "They're going to find her, aren't they, Gary?"

Noelle's thoughts turned back to the body in the grave, and her heart constricted in her chest. But it wasn't her place to tell them that their daughter had already been found.

———

There were things in the world that Derek wished he could unsee, and a girl in a shallow grave, wrapped in a tarp like a grisly gift, was one of them.

He studied the girl in the glow of the floodlights. Between the ravages of time and the fetal position of her body, all he could discern was that she was young and blonde with pale features.

"I can't tell if it's Maddie."

Rusty snapped a picture of the girl's profile. "Who else would it be?"

Derek tamped down the instinct to brush the strands of hair from the girl's face as Rusty repositioned for another picture. She was gone; the hair wouldn't bother her.

"She's the only blonde girl around this age who's been reported missing from the area," Rusty pointed out.

"True, but something doesn't fit."

"Yeah, her shoes."

Frowning, Derek aimed his flashlight at the sneakers on the girl's feet. The light blue material bulged, stretched too tight over her toes. "What size does Maddie wear?"

"According to her mother, between an eight and nine, depending on the cut of the shoe. The one we found in the woods is an eight-and-a-half."

Derek pressed down the mud-encrusted tarp so he could get a better view of the size marking on the bottom of the shoes—size 7. "There's no way these are hers. They're at least a size too small."

"I would ask why she's wearing someone else's shoes, but I think she's wearing someone else's clothes too. This isn't what the roommate said she was wearing when she left the dorm room Friday night."

She'd left in jeans and a pink-and-white striped sweater. Now she was dressed in loose black leggings and a tan threadbare sweater that engulfed her slim frame.

"She could've changed her clothes between leaving the dorm and meeting her killer, but considering the too-small shoes, I'm wondering if *he* changed her clothes,"

238

Rusty said. "Wouldn't be the first time a preferential predator adjusted his victim's appearance."

"No, it wouldn't."

"What should we tell the Wingates?"

"For the moment, nothing. I don't want them coming here, and it'll be an hour or so before we get her to the morgue. There's no sense in distressing them."

No parent should have to see this.

"Good evening." The voice preceded a gangly man, whose skin was as pallid as most of the corpses he examined. Karl Abbott, the county medical examiner, could blend in at a vampire convention—appropriate, since he interacted better with the dead than the living.

Derek greeted the man with a nod. "Abbott."

"Captain." Abbott set down his bag near the grave site. "I haven't seen you at a crime scene in quite some time. Must be something special to draw you out from behind your mountain of paperwork." He opened his case and pulled out rubber gloves, squatting beside the body. "Hello, pretty girl."

Rusty grimaced and stepped away. He, like many others, found Abbott's habit of speaking to the dead disturbing. Derek wouldn't deny that the man was odd, but he excelled at his profession.

Abbott's expression pinched with sadness. "You are a young one. Late teens to early twenties, by my estimation."

Derek wanted to ask how long she'd been in the ground, but Abbott would get to that detail in his own time.

The doctor lifted one of her hands, studying it. "There's been some animal activity."

"Her fingertips and hair were exposed when the witness stumbled across the grave. Probably coyotes," Rusty said.

Abbott didn't acknowledge his explanation, his focus on Maddie's remains. "Judging by the flexibility and the breakdown of the skin, you've been here about three or four days."

Abbott shifted to peel the hair from her face and neck, but Derek's attention lingered on the hand now resting in the dirt. There was something wrong with it, with the pale fingernails that had been chewed to nubs.

Abbott carefully repositioned Maddie's head, his expression turning thoughtful. "Well, that's unexpected."

"What in the . . ." Rusty bent down to get a closer look.

Derek was at the wrong angle to see what held their attention, so he stood and rounded the grave, sucking in a breath when he saw the right side of the girl's face. A scar traveled from her hairline all the way down to her mouth, narrowly missing her eye. And he knew, then, what bothered him about the fingernails—no rainbow nail polish.

This was not Maddie Wingate.

CHAPTER
Thirty

They found the grave.

 He rubbed his hands together as he paced, sweat pooling in the creases of his palms even as the temperature dipped toward freezing.

 No one was supposed to find her. He'd wrapped her in a tarp from the shed to mask the smell that would inevitably rise and disguised the grave by mounding leaves over it. It had blended into the forest floor seamlessly.

 "Obviously not," he muttered.

 This entire situation could've been avoided if she had listened to reason. But she resorted to screaming and struggling, and the rest wasn't his fault.

 He did his best to clean up the mess so no one would know, but he'd clearly missed something. No, he hadn't missed anything. It was that woman.

 Noelle McKenzie.

 His molars ground together. She had moved into the house and complicated everything. He needed to fix this. If he didn't fix it and soon, it was going to destroy his life.

CHAPTER
Thirty-one

Firefly's diary entry swept Noelle out of the diner booth and into a dark hallway that smelled of sickness, Noelle's imagination pulling together details to paint the scene:

Firefly stretched out on the hallway floor, cheek pressed to the cold wood as she strained to see beneath the door into one of the other rooms. She wasn't supposed to go near them because of the illness, but the cries of one of the girls drew her from her room.

Firefly whispered into the gap, "It's okay. You're going to get better. And then you can come out and we can be friends."

The other girl whimpered, "Please, help me."

"What's your name?"

"Emma. My name's Emma."

"And I'm Sarah," another girl said. "Please. We need help."

Firefly opened her mouth to share her name, but a man's hand wrapped around her arm and yanked her to her feet.

"What are you doing? You know you're not supposed to be near these rooms."

Firefly shrank in the man's painful grip. "But I heard crying. I only wanted to make her feel better."

A glass broke in the diner, shattering the imagined scene along with it, and Noelle found herself back in the booth, watching brown bubbly liquid stretch across the tile as a customer fretted over her clumsiness.

"Don't worry, it's all right," Trudy said, approaching with a broom and dustpan to sweep up the glass shards.

Before Noelle could slide out of the booth and offer to help, the burly cook appeared with a mop. They had the situation under control.

Noelle reviewed the diary entry she'd been reading, but she couldn't find her way back into the scene. The spell had been broken. She focused on the details instead.

This was the first time names had been mentioned—Sarah and Emma. If Firefly would've had the chance to share her name with her newfound friends, what would it have been? And who was "he," the man who grabbed her so roughly and wrenched her away?

Noelle took a sip of her lemon water and turned the page.

Moms in truble again. When I'm real quiet I can hear them arguing downstares. Maybe she's in truble cause I was peaking under the door across

243

the hall. Mister got real mad about that. Now he's yelling at mom and saying someone wants to see me. What if I'm sick now to cause I got too close to Emma and Sarah's room and Dr. Gray is going to come give me shots? I don't want shots or medicine.

Mom says she can find someone else, but Mister says no. Mom is crying now and asking him not to let this happen, but he says it was going to happen someday. I'm scared. I don't want the doctor to come see me.

Noelle's eyes drifted from the page to her water glass, trying to make sense of what she'd read. Firefly was frightened of someone coming to see her, but there wasn't enough detail to understand what that visit would mean. She turned to the next entry—the *last* entry.

Something's wrong with Mom. She put all my close in my backpack last night and took it away. And she made me put on all my socks. They make my feet sweaty but she says I have to wear them to protect my feet cause I don't have shoes.

Noelle frowned. What child in this country didn't have shoes?

She's making peanut butter sanwiches but she keeps looking at the window like someone is spose to be there. I'm scared she's waiting for the doctor. She said we have to go cause he wants to see me. Maybe I have to wear all my socks cause we're going outside but I don't want to go see the doctor. I don't think he's a nice man even if he has suckers.

Mom is shaking again like she does with her bad dreams. She says not to tell anyone we're going but that when she says so we have to go as fast as we can. And she says I should keep going even if they stop her. But I don't know where to go. What if I go the wrong way and I get in trub—

That was the last word in the diary, interrupted as the graphite from the pencil zigzagged from the letter "b" to the far edge of the page, like the little girl had been dragged away while writing.

Every fiber of Noelle's being told her something was wrong, that this little girl was in more danger than she realized.

The details clawed at her imagination, urging her to analyze and piece them together. She needed to understand this little girl's story so she could help her.

She doesn't need an author. She needs a social worker.

Except without a name or address, Children's Services wouldn't be able to find her. No one would be able to find her.

Before taking the diary and any theories to the authorities, she needed to have some idea what was happening in that house and where it was located.

The last time you got involved, you tripped over a grave, her inner voice reminded her, and for a moment she questioned her decision to dig deeper.

But if she did nothing, what would happen to Firefly? Unlike Maddie, no one was searching for this girl because no one knew her. This diary might be the only proof she existed.

No, even if pursuing this path led her to another grave, Noelle needed to find Firefly. And there was only one way she knew how to figure all of this out, the way she figured out every story—with an organized, colorful storyboard.

Except she didn't have any of her supplies, because she thought this part of her life was behind her. She never expected a child's diary to reawaken her desire for storyboarding.

She searched through her purse before remembering that her notepad was missing. She'd picked up a new one at the store, but it was back at the house.

She searched for Trudy, who was leaning on the checkout counter, frowning at her phone. Noelle slid out of the booth to join her. "Everything okay?"

Trudy darkened her screen and set her phone on the countertop. "Fine, I'm waiting on a call that feels like it might never come." She adjusted her wedding ring absently, telling Noelle without words who she was waiting to hear from. "Do you need a refill on your lemon water? Or I could get you something sweet."

"Actually, I was hoping you might have some plain paper and colored pens I could use."

"Let me check the office. You go relax."

Trudy disappeared into the kitchen, and Noelle returned to her table. She glanced at Maddie's parents, who had barely touched the food in front of them. Every minute without news must be torture.

Trudy returned to Noelle's booth and set down a box of crayons and a few paper menus that were white on one side. "I'm afraid this is the best I can do."

"It'll work, thanks."

Trudy sank down on the opposite side of the booth, pausing to catch her breath. "What are you going to draw?"

Noelle unboxed the crayons. "Actually, I'm going to make a storyboard."

Trudy's eyes brightened. "Like for a book? Because I know your fans are desperately waiting for one."

Noelle smiled, remembering what Derek had said about Trudy snooping around her author pages. "No, I'm not writing a book right now, but I'm trying to make sense of one."

Trudy touched the diary. "This one?"

"Yeah. It was written by a little girl, and I'm worried she might be in danger. There's nothing specific in there to tell me who or where she is, but I'm hoping I can figure that out. You'd be surprised how much information is in a few details."

Trudy studied the inscription on the inside cover. "It looks like there might've been a name written here. Someone tried really hard to erase it." She pointed to the top left-hand corner. "Right there. Does that look like the first two letters of a name? Big *E*, little *m*."

Noelle squinted. Sure enough, beneath the inscription written in permanent marker, there were faint impressions left behind from erased pencil. Em.

"It could stand for Emily, Emerson, Emilia . . ." Trudy listed off.

Or Emma. Noelle ran a finger down the ragged edges of torn-out pages. She had assumed Firefly ripped them out, but what if this notebook belonged to the sick Emma before it belonged to Firefly? What if her mom tore out the used pages, erased the name, and passed it off to Firefly as a gift?

But why would someone do that?

It could've been a thrift-store purchase, and Firefly's mom had tried to make it look newer. The Emma Firefly mentioned and the erased name could be unrelated.

"You don't know any children in town who go by the nickname Firefly, do you?" Noelle asked, though she already suspected the answer.

"Unfortunately, no. Most families do bring their kids with them for dinner, but I haven't heard that nickname, and I haven't seen any girls writing in a diary like this either. Most kids have phones nowadays." Trudy tilted her head to read the upside-down text. "She's got better spelling than most adults I know. How old do you think she is?"

"Between nine and eleven." Noelle wrote "Characters" in blue crayon and underlined it, then began listing the people in the diary:

> Mom
> Doctor
> Sick girls
> He/Mister
> Firefly

Beside the names, she listed the characteristics of each. Firefly's mom hated her job and her living situation, and she wanted to be anywhere else. She wrestled with nightmares, possibly PTSD, and she controlled everything her daughter said and did.

The doctor was a mysterious figure who came to tend to the sick girls in the other rooms of the house. But he didn't exude the warmth and compassion typical of a doctor.

Firefly didn't have much information about the sick girls, except that she wasn't supposed to disturb them, and one was named Emma and another Sarah.

He, Mister, seemed to be in charge of the facility or household, making the final decisions. Firefly viewed him as an authority over her mom—a boss, a husband, a boyfriend?

Firefly was a quiet and isolated child who lived her life in books and communicated through her diary. She longed to go outside and make friends, but she was forced to remain isolated.

Why? And how had her diary gotten here? Did she live in a house somewhere in town or outside town?

"What makes you think this little girl is in danger?" Trudy asked.

Noelle tapped the crayon on the paper. "I know it sounds weird, but from the moment I opened the diary and started reading, the feeling that she needs help started gnawing at me."

"Sounds like Godly intuition."

"I don't know about that. I haven't heard from God in a long time." She had no doubt He was present now, but she still couldn't hear His still, small voice the way she used to.

"You'd be surprised how often Christians say that, and I wonder . . . do they only communicate with their loved ones in one way?"

"What do you mean?"

"As a writer, I'm sure you know words are powerful, but they're not the only method of communication. We express ourselves without words all the time—with hugs, smiles, gestures, even simply being present. God uses different methods too. He reaches out through Scripture, dreams, thoughts, other people. And sometimes"—Trudy tapped the diary with a finger— "something as subtle as a gnawing feeling."

Trudy's words tumbled around in Noelle's head like clothes in a dryer, bumping into questions and getting tangled up with self-doubt. She couldn't even keep her own child alive. Surely, God wouldn't entrust the safety of someone else's child to her care.

The moment that thought formed, Tyrese's voice sliced through her mind: *Our son is dead because of you.* No, she couldn't let herself slip back into that destructive pattern of thinking. If Trudy was right, and God wanted her to help this child, she couldn't let those dark thoughts trap her in place.

"Well, I'll leave you to mull over all this in that writer-y way your brain works. I'm sure you'll figure it all out and find a way to help that little girl." Trudy started to push herself up from the table, when she let out a cry and grasped her stomach.

Noelle dropped the crayon. "Are you okay?"

Trudy released a slow, stuttering breath and sank back onto the cushion. "That one hurt."

Noelle slid out of the booth and rounded the table to her side. "Are you having contractions?"

"Just cramps, I think. I'm not due for another three weeks."

Noelle blinked down at the woman's enormous stomach. "Really?"

Trudy huffed. "Why does everybody say that with such surprise? I am no fatter than any other pregnant woman."

Noelle respectfully and *silently* disagreed. If Trudy was ten pounds when she was born, this baby was going to be eleven. "Are you having a C-section?"

The tension in Trudy's body started to ease. "Yeah. Apparently, even though my hips have widened like the

251

Grand Canyon, they're not wide enough to pass this baby." The bell above the door chimed as a customer left, and Trudy braced herself to stand.

"What are you doing?"

"I need to clean that table."

"You need to rest."

"If I don't do it now, I'll have to do it when I'm even more tired." She tried to push herself up, but Noelle placed a hand on her shoulder.

"I'll clean it up."

"Don't be ridiculous. I can . . ." She shifted and groaned. "If this spastic baby would quit kicking my internal organs around like soccer balls, I might be able to get up."

"Let me help. I used to waitress before I became an author, so I know my way around a restaurant."

"I thought you had a mystery to solve."

"Cleaning helps me think."

Trudy exhaled. "Okay." She untied her apron and handed it to her. "Have at it then."

Noelle tied it around her waist, feeling the straws and the order pad in the pockets. It took her back to her life before Tyrese, when she was waiting tables during the day and writing all evening, dreaming of one day becoming an author. She'd loved a lot of things as a child, but writing was one of only a few childhood loves she'd never outgrown. Maybe someday she would reconnect with it again.

She set to work cleaning and serving customers, sinking into an old, familiar rhythm.

CHAPTER
Thirty-two

Stretched out on a metal slab under the fluorescent lights of the lab, the girl was more gaunt than Derek had first realized.

Her cheekbones were cartoonishly sharp, emphasizing the sunken pits around her eyes, and her collarbone and ribs were visible even beneath her sweater.

It was clear that food was a rarity in her life. Whether that was self-inflicted or because she was being held against her will for a prolonged period of time, he didn't know.

"This scar . . ." Abbott studied the girl. "I've never seen a scar this vicious on a person's face. Whoever stitched you up didn't even try to minimize it, did they?"

Derek approached the autopsy table, feeling like he was intruding on the doctor's private, one-sided conversation with the dead. "How can you tell?"

Abbott looked up at him and blinked, his eyes owlish behind his glasses. "Sorry, I forgot you were here."

Derek had learned not to be offended. "It's fine. I was asking how you can tell proper care wasn't taken with the scar on her face."

Abbott pointed to the small bulges. "Puckering. And the scar thins and widens like a river as it travels down her face. I would guess they used fifteen stitches when they needed about eighty and left it at that. It's a wonder she didn't die of an infection. There's no way this girl was taken to a hospital or even a clinic."

"Back alley?"

"That would be my guess. The original wound looks like it was clean-cut, which means the scar could've been easily minimized."

"Do you think it could've been an accidental wound?"

"The length of this wound, the way it curves along with her face . . . it wasn't a glancing cut. I would guess someone dragged a knife or a piece of glass down the side of her face."

Derek grimaced as he imagined the gory scene. "Can you tell how old the scar is?"

"All I can tell you is that it's more than a few years old."

Derek smoothed a gloved hand over the girl's blonde hair, revealing an uneven, habitual part that would've left her blonde hair hanging like a curtain over the scarred portion of her face. She tried to conceal it.

"I don't understand why someone didn't take her to the hospital," Abbott said, a hint of outrage in his voice.

Derek could imagine numerous reasons—an abuse situation, an inability to pay hospital bills, an illegal lifestyle. Any of those reasons could deter someone from seeking proper medical treatment, but there was another possibility.

"Can you tell if she was held captive for a prolonged period of time?"

Abbott nudged his glasses up the bridge of his nose. "You're thinking she was abducted?"

Derek rubbed at the tense muscle in the side of his neck. "It's a possibility."

Maddie had been abducted—he was almost certain of that—and there were too many overlaps between her and this girl for them to be unrelated. Maddie disappeared three days ago, around the same time this girl was killed. Her car was found abandoned within two miles of this girl's buried body. They were both young, pretty blondes. One died, and another disappeared.

Lord, please don't let this be a serial killer scenario in the making.

Abbott considered the girl. "A blood test will tell me if she's vitamin D deficient, which would indicate limited exposure to the sun. I can also run tests on her hair and teeth and see what they tell me about her environment and nutrition. But none of that is definitive proof of captivity. It could be a result of self-inflicted deprivation. A disfiguring scar like this could lead to depression and self-isolation."

The doors to the morgue creaked open, and Rusty slipped inside. "I called Habrams and asked him to come by the department with that list of bidders. Also, it turns out you were right about Brian. He's not in Cincinnati."

Derek had gathered that much from the phone call with Brian's supposedly hospitalized mother. She was home and healthy, and she hadn't seen him in months. "Where is he?"

"Aaron found him drinking down by the creek behind the school, raving about a woman who wouldn't listen to him. Are he and Trudy having problems?"

They were having a lot of problems, but Derek doubted Brian's rant about a woman had anything to do with Trudy. She hadn't spoken with him since yesterday. So who was it that wasn't listening to him?

"Aaron's bringing him in for questioning," Rusty said when Derek didn't answer.

"Tell him to take a picture of Brian's shoe prints. Someone besides Noelle and our team was at that grave site tonight."

Rusty sent a quick text, then asked, "You don't really think he did this, do you? Gambling and drinking, sure, but murder?"

"I hope he had nothing to do with it." *For Trudy's sake.*

"What about Walt? Should I send someone over to his place to bring him in for questioning? He practically lives in those woods. Either he buried this girl, or he saw who did."

Walt would open fire on his deputies before he would allow them to put him in the back of a cruiser.

"No, I don't want anyone getting hurt if we can avoid it. I'll talk to him first thing in the morning." Hopefully Walt enjoyed Trudy's meatloaf enough that he wouldn't shoot him.

Rusty crossed his arms and studied the victim. "Anything more you can tell us about her, Doc?"

"She's a nail biter. There are scabs around the nail beds. Whoever this young lady is, she was no stranger to anxiety." Abbott tugged up her right sleeve and then her left. A dark bruise banded the creamy pale skin of her left wrist.

Derek leaned closer. "Is that from a restraint?"

Abbott bent over the girl's arm. "Of sorts." Abbott shifted to wrap his hand around the mark, his thumb coming to rest on his middle fingernail. "Someone with a large hand and a tight grip had a hold of her."

He lowered her arm and picked up a pair of scissors, splitting the sleeve all the way up to the collar. Three more bruises marred her skin, one oddly placed around her elbow.

"They were grappling," Derek realized, because it didn't make sense to pin someone by their elbow. "She was fighting to get away, and he was trying to keep a hold of her."

"That would be my guess. It would also explain why several hairs with root balls attached shook out when we moved her. They were probably ripped loose in the struggle. She might've lost in the end, but she put up a good fight. There's skin under some of her nails, likely from her attacker. I'll send the samples to the lab."

Hope sparked in Derek's chest. It could take a while to run the DNA, but if there was a match in the system, it might lead them to the killer, and if his hunch was right, to Maddie. It also meant that her killer would have physical marks on his body.

Abbott parted the girl's lips and peered into her mouth. "Teeth are intact. If she's had dental work done in the past, that should help us identify her."

Dental records, fingerprints, DNA—hopefully something would give them a name for this girl.

"Cause of death?" Rusty asked.

"Anything I tell you at this point would be a guess. I need to do a full examination to be sure."

Derek was desperate for answers, but all he could do right now was go have a chat with his brother-in-law.

CHAPTER
Thirty-three

Derek let the interrogation room door slam behind him, jarring the slumped figure at the table upright.

Brian blinked groggily at the lights and rubbed a hand over the cheek that had been pressed to the table a moment ago. "Derek?"

"Have a nice nap?" Derek set down a mug of coffee and a bottle of water for his brother-in-law, then dragged out a chair for himself.

Brian dug his thumb and forefinger into his eyes, trying to rub away the tiredness. "Why did Aaron bring me in?"

"Because I have a few questions."

Brian scrubbed both hands over his face and then let them drop onto the table. "If this is about me ignoring your call and not calling Trudy back—"

"We'll get to that." Derek removed a photo from the folder he'd brought in and slid it across the table. "This is a picture of the muddy boot print you left on the tile coming into the building."

Brian stared at the picture, bleary-eyed, then twisted to see the bottom of the boots he wore. "Guess I forgot to wipe my feet."

Derek slid a second picture across the table. "This is the shoe print we recovered from a crime scene. More accurately, a body dump site."

He waited for his words to sink through the layer of alcohol encasing his brother-in-law's brain and watched Brian swallow hard.

"Explain to me how your shoe print . . ."—he tapped a finger on the first picture—"ended up at my crime scene."

"I . . . went for a walk in the woods the other day."

"That would make sense except this print isn't from the other day. It's fresh. That means you were in the woods at the dump site before anyone from our department even knew about it."

"I'm not the only person who wears this type of boot."

"In a size twelve with the same wear patterns? You walk more on the outsides of your feet than on the pads and heel." Derek leaned back in his chair. "I know you were there, so why didn't you report the body?"

Brian grabbed the bottle of water and twisted the cap, his face downcast. "I didn't know she was there."

"I could smell that grave from a hundred yards away. You were standing ten feet from it. Try again."

Brian tossed the bottle cap on the table. "What do you want me to say, Derek?"

"The truth, if you can manage it."

Brian didn't object to the insinuation that lies came more easily to him than truth.

"I want you to explain to me why you discovered the remains of a human being and didn't think it was your duty as a deputy, *my* deputy, to call it in."

Brian shrugged. "I guess I'd had too much to drink, and I wasn't thinking straight."

"I don't buy that." He pulled out a picture of the dead girl and placed it on top of the shoe prints. "Know her?"

There was no disguising the fact that Jane Doe had been dead for days, and Brian swallowed, looking away from the photo. "No."

"You were standing right next to her." Derek dropped a third photo that highlighted how close the suspicious print was to the mound of earth. "How do you think she got there?"

Understanding sobered Brian faster than a slap to the face. "I had nothing to do with what happened to her. I'm not some sexual predator."

"I never said she was sexually assaulted." He didn't know whether or not she had been, and he wouldn't know until morning, after Abbott finished his examination.

"She's a young blonde. Talk to that pervert in the trailer complex, the one who used to eye Trudy before she got pregnant. Did you know he was still coming to the diner? He strolls right up to the back door for a free meal after closing. At least he did until three months ago, when I threatened to break his fingers if he touched my wife again."

Derek's pulse jumped. "He put his hands on Trudy?" Why hadn't she told him?

"Whenever he would take the food from her, he would make sure their fingers touched, like a creepy caress." He took a swig of water. "I don't care if he's in therapy. He's not better."

Derek tried to calm the anger pounding in his veins. It didn't surprise him that Nick lied to his face, but it did surprise him that he went back to the diner after Derek warned him away.

"Maybe he found someone else to creep on since Trudy's pregnant," Brian suggested.

"I'll send someone over to talk to Nelson again, but right now, let's you and me figure a few things out."

Brian scoffed. "Sounds like you've already convinced yourself I'm guilty."

"I'm not convinced of anything yet." He placed a picture of Maddie beside Jane Doe. "She look familiar?"

"From your social media post. I've never seen her in person."

"Where were you Friday night?"

"Work."

"Your shift ended at three p.m."

"I went home to relax."

"After you found out you lost the auction you'd been saving for, you went home to relax? I find that hard to believe."

Brian's brow wrinkled. "How do you . . ."

"Another deputy overheard you discussing your plans in the break room. You said you wanted to turn it into a haunted attraction."

"Do you know how many people visit that place to see if there are actually ghosts? Imagine if someone charged a five-dollar entrance fee. It could bring in a lot of extra money."

"Sounds like another gamble. One that, yet again, has done nothing but drain money and time from your marriage. And after all that, you didn't even win the auction. Noelle did."

At the mention of her name, Brian's fingers tightened around the water bottle, crunching the plastic. "She could've bought any place she wanted. Why that one?"

"Losing the auction made you angry."

Brian seared him with a glare. "Not angry enough to grab some random girl off the road and kill her."

Derek leaned forward. "Off the road. Interesting choice of words, considering a witness placed a blue car on the road at the same time a blonde girl was frantically running across it. I don't suppose you were driving around town Friday night."

Brian shifted in his chair, leaning against the backrest. "I told you I was at home."

"All evening?"

"If I'm not at work or the diner, I'm at home."

"Except tonight, when you were wandering around the woods behind someone else's house."

"I had good reason to be in the woods."

Derek motioned for him to continue. "I'm listening."

"I needed to talk to Noelle."

"How does pacing in the woods behind her house help you talk to her?"

"I'm sure she told you about the flat tire thing earlier today. I was trying to offer her a ride home. I thought we could talk about the house, maybe negotiate a price. But when I tried to open her door and help her out of the car, she freaked out and threatened to call the police."

"You tried to open her door *after* she declined your offer for help. What do you think goes through a woman's head when you do something like that?"

"I didn't mean to scare her. I thought if I could get her to listen, she might be willing to sell me the house, and maybe even let me pay for it in monthly increments. I needed time to work out what I was going to say."

"And you needed to do that in the woods behind her house?" Derek shook his head. "That doesn't make sense."

Brian slumped in his chair. "It did at the time."

"So you're telling me you happened across the grave because you were in the woods rehearsing your pending conversation with Noelle."

"Yeah, that's what I'm telling you."

Derek sighed. "The problem I'm running into, Brian, is that you lie. A lot. And your answers don't make sense."

"I'm not lying."

"You're not even supposed to be in town. You told Trudy you were going to Cincinnati to see your sick mother. And yet, here you are, in Cherry Creek, wandering around in the woods—even though you never leave the house unless you're working or at the diner—and happen across a murder victim but you don't tell anyone."

"I did go to Cincinnati."

"It wasn't to see your mother. I called her this evening, and she hasn't seen you in months. So what were you doing in Cincinnati?"

Brian set the empty water bottle on the table. "After losing the auction, I had all that money taunting me. I . . . I went to play a few games."

"You gambled." Derek kept his tone even, despite the anger building inside. Trudy was scraping together change to pay the bills, and Brian was tossing money down the drain of his addiction.

"Only a little, and then I started thinking. Maybe my plans weren't ruined. There was a chance I could convince whoever won the auction to sell the house to me. I drove back last night, but then I saw a deputy cruiser in the driveway."

Derek thought back to the kicked-in door and the prowler on Walt's property. Looking at his brother-in-law objectively, he was the right size and build for the man he'd seen disappearing into the trees. But he wasn't limping.

"You go for a walk in the woods last night too?"

Brian shook his head. "No."

"Why did you really want the Bechtel property so badly?"

"You already know."

"I know that someone buried a body there, and I think that person was expecting to win the auction and be able to keep the girl's remains hidden. But then they lost, so they started trying to scare away the woman who did win the property. Only it didn't work, and she found the grave."

Brian paled and pushed the pictures back across the table. "I didn't kill anyone."

"Where do you think Maddie is?"

"I don't know."

"Did you take her somewhere?"

Brian slammed his hands on the table. "No! I had nothing to do with either of those girls."

"Why didn't you go home last night?"

"Trudy thought I was going to be out of town, so I decided to stay at the Smithvail Inn and take advantage of the time to figure things out."

"Figure them out by drinking? Are you trying to fast-track your way to a second addiction?"

Brian's jaw clenched. "Noelle buying the house ruined my plans. I had—"

"I'm not interested in attending your pity party. You shouldn't have been buying a house without talking to your wife first. Do you have any idea the position you put her in?"

When Brian shifted in his chair, several shallow scratches peeked above the collar of his T-shirt.

Derek's breath hitched. "How'd you get those scratches?"

Brian lifted a hand to cover the marks. "I was running through the woods. I got sideswiped by a few sharp branches."

Or a few sharp fingernails.

266

Abbott said the victim had DNA under three of her fingernails and she would've left marks on her attacker.

"Look, I know you're mad because I could've handled things better with Trudy, but I didn't mean to hurt her."

"But you did." Derek slid the photos back into the folder. "I'll send someone in to take pictures of those scratches and your shoes. Then you can go."

Brian gritted his teeth. "You think I did it."

"I don't know what to think, Brian. I have a dead girl, a missing teen, and my strongest lead is one of my own deputies, my brother-in-law."

"What about Nelson?"

"I said I would send someone to talk to him."

"And Walt? He's an antisocial freak who's always in the woods where the body was found. You know we've all been waiting for him to snap. It's inevitable."

"Maybe Walt lashed out and killed her, or maybe he saw the person who did. I'll find out when I talk to him."

Brian paused, one shoe off and the other half untied. "You think he saw whoever buried her?"

Derek stood with his folder. "Time will tell." He left the interrogation room to find Rusty waiting on the other side of the one-way mirror.

"He's lying about something."

Derek looked through the mirror at Brian, who wiped sweat from his forehead and anxiously tapped his fingers on the table. "He's always lying about something."

Rusty frowned. "Habrams is waiting to speak with you in room three. Might just be me, but something's off about that guy too."

"You've never met a lawyer you trust."

"True, but he's dressed nicer than usual, like he recently came into some money. Makes me wonder what desperate soul he relieved of his life savings."

"If Elizabeth didn't will the money from the auction to her brother, maybe she divided it between charities and her lawyer."

"Doesn't seem right."

"Right or not, it isn't illegal. Finish up with Brian and then call it a night. It's going to be a long day tomorrow." He clapped Rusty on the shoulder and went to speak with Habrams.

———

Perry Habrams rose from the chair when Derek entered the room, displeasure stamped across his lined face.

"I've been waiting for fifteen minutes."

Derek took in the man's tailored suit and polished shoes. "Nice suit. Is that the one you were browsing for online Friday night?"

Habrams buttoned his jacket, a shine of pride in his eyes as he did so. "One of them, yes."

One of. That ensemble would eat up an entire month of Derek's salary. Maybe Habrams's take-home from the auction had been more than a small percentage. Aside from

Walt, Elizabeth didn't have anyone else to pass her worldly possessions along to.

"I'm sorry for the wait and inconvenience, Mr. Habrams. We're investigating a homicide, and it makes for a busy schedule."

"A homicide? I thought the teenage girl was only missing. You . . . found her body?"

"We found *a* body."

Habrams shook his head. "I tried to warn people that place was cursed."

Derek tucked his hands into the pockets of his slacks, interest curling through him. "What place would that be?"

"The Bechtel property, of course."

"What makes you think we found the body there?"

Habrams paused, then said, "Educated guess. There was a lot of activity on that road tonight."

The floodlights would be hard to miss if you lived in or commuted through the area, but Perry Habrams lived on the other side of town. Was he keeping tabs on the property or something else?

"As requested, the list of people who placed a bid during the auction, including Ms. McKenzie." Habrams passed him a document printed on professional letterhead, and Derek made a mental note of the man's wince and shifting weight.

"Thank you." Derek rested a hip on the edge of the interrogation room table. He had intended to retrieve the list and be on his way, but now his interest was piqued. "I couldn't help but notice you have a bit of a limp today."

"New exercise at the gym. Unfortunately, I got a little overzealous and irritated my knees."

Derek had his doubts about that, but he let it go for now. "When was the last time you were at the Bechtel house?"

"Yesterday afternoon. Elizabeth's will stipulated that her remaining relatives be informed about the sale and transition of the property. I would've called, but Walt doesn't have a phone. I parked in the driveway and waited for him to come to me."

"You didn't get out of the car?"

"Of course not. I had no interest in being shot for some perceived trespass."

But he had no problem letting Noelle walk blindly into that very situation? She said he hadn't told her anything.

"Why not meet Walt at his place?"

"Aside from the risk of being killed, his camper is inaccessible from the road. I would've had to hike through the woods. I'm a man of fitness, but I don't hike."

Was it possible his limp had nothing to do with the prowler who limped into the trees last night?

Derek studied the list of six names, including Brian's and Noelle's. He would need to look into the others. "Did any of these people strike you as desperate to win the auction?"

"Only Brian Mason. The others didn't put forth much effort. Except Ms. McKenzie, of course."

"Are there any names omitted from this list?"

Habrams narrowed his eyes. "If you're suggesting that I might've removed my name, it was never there to begin with."

Derek *hadn't* been suggesting that, but his quick leap to that assumption made him curious.

"I had no interest in the Bechtel property beyond selling it. I certainly didn't want to be saddled with it for the rest of my life."

"Because you believe it's cursed, and that Walt poses a serious threat."

"Yes."

Derek dropped the document back on the table. "If you truly believe that, why wouldn't you warn a woman who was about to leave your office and go there alone, after dark?"

Habrams heaved an annoyed sigh. "Of course that's what this is about. I should've known. Ms. McKenzie believes I wronged her, and you, having an . . . affinity for her, decided to take up the fight. But I did not endanger her life by withholding vital information. I provided everything I was legally required to provide. As I told her when she burst into my office this afternoon without an appointment."

Derek wasn't sure what interested him more—the man's bizarre conclusions or the distaste in his voice as he delivered them. He folded his arms. "An affinity?"

"Rumor has it you were with her this morning as well as last night, and I saw you with her outside my office."

Why was Habrams paying such close attention to who Derek spent time with? "If you're keeping an account of my activities, don't forget pizza this evening."

Habrams grimaced. "You may want to consider whether or not it's appropriate for the two of you to be spending so much time together."

"Why wouldn't it be appropriate?"

"I should think that would be obvious."

It took Derek a moment to catch his meaning, and he had to tamp down his rising anger. "Is it Noelle you have an issue with or the idea of her and me together?"

Habrams lifted his coat from the table and draped it over one arm, choosing silence.

"A word of advice, Mr. Habrams—if you feel the need to judge someone, judge them on the content of their character and not their appearance. That skin-deep eyesight of yours will deprive you of a lot of amazing interactions and relationships."

Habrams's mouth hardened. "If you have any other questions for me, you can make an appointment and come by my office."

"Thanks for coming in. And Mr. Habrams," Derek said, recapturing the man's attention before he could leave, "how I spend my time and who I spend it with is my business. Not yours. Try to remember that."

He watched the man limp from the room. Rusty was right—something was off about Perry Habrams, something more than his prejudices. It could be his disregard for Noelle's safety that rubbed Derek the wrong way. Or it could've been his smooth and practiced answers.

He was guilty of something. Maybe not the murder of a teenage girl, but Derek would bet he manipulated a frail and dying woman into willing him everything, even the money from the auction. A man with thrift-store furniture in his office building and no budget for a secretary couldn't afford suits with that price tag.

"Sir."

Derek looked toward the voice to see Deputy Kara Grisham approaching. Kara and Angel were the only female deputies in the department, and the two women couldn't be more different. Angel Jimenez was outspoken and self-assured, while Grisham was quiet and uncertain.

She had recently graduated with a degree in forensic art, and tonight she had the opportunity to lend her skills to the department.

"I think I'm finished." She handed him the folder, and he opened it to find a detailed sketch of their Jane Doe.

He needed to see if the Wingates recognized her, but he didn't want to further traumatize them by showing them a photo of her remains. No doubt their imaginations were already generating horrifying images. He wouldn't give them another one that they could overlay their daughter's face on.

"Dr. Abbott said you think this girl might've been abducted," Grisham said. "I can do a second sketch and age-regress her. If she disappeared when she was a child and there's an open case, it might help us identify her faster."

"You can do that?"

"I think so, sir."

273

He studied the near perfect likeness in his hands, then said, "Remove the scar in the regression. Judging by the lack of care taken with it, I doubt it happened while she was living at home with her family."

Grisham nodded and then left to get started on her second sketch. Derek closed the folder. He had a distraught family to talk to and a restaurant to clean.

CHAPTER
Thirty-four

Derek pulled into the diner parking lot, exhausted all the way to his bones. It had been a long day, and he had more questions than answers.

Hopefully, Abbott would have something for him in the morning.

He was certain the girl with the scarred face and Maddie were connected—if not to each other, then to the monster who intersected both of their lives. If Abbott could find something to help him narrow in on Jane Doe's killer, it might lead him to Maddie.

"God, please help me find this girl before . . ."

He couldn't bring himself to finish the sentence, even though the possibility had plagued his thoughts since they discovered the grave.

He spotted the Wingates sitting by the window, Gary holding his wife's hand as she stared vacantly at the mason jar candle in the center of the table.

Trudy had sent Derek a text three hours ago to let him know they had come in for dinner. When he reached out to Gary before leaving the department, he was surprised to learn they were still at the diner.

But where else would they go, when their daughter disappeared from this town? They were waiting for answers—answers he didn't have.

Unbuckling his seat belt, he grabbed the folder from the passenger seat and dragged his tired body out of the car.

Surprise washed over him when he stepped inside and found Noelle with an apron tied around her waist, clearing and wiping down tables. He searched for Trudy and spotted her slumped in a booth, snoring softly.

Noelle finished with a table and strolled over to greet him. "Hey."

"Hey. Is Trudy okay?"

"She was having some cramps, so I told her to rest."

Worry darted through him. "Cramps? Is it the baby?"

"I don't think so. She's just worn-out and needed a break."

So Noelle decided to take over cleaning and serving to give her one? He couldn't find the words to express his gratitude. "You didn't have to do this."

Noelle shrugged. "She needed a hand. I happen to have two. And after what I stumbled across this evening, I could use the distraction." She glanced at the Wingates and then back at him, a question in her eyes.

He shook his head and lowered his voice. "The body in the grave is a girl, but it's not Maddie."

Her brows drew together. "Then who?"

"I don't know. She's not local."

"How old is she?"

"Looks to be late teens."

Noelle's gaze drifted to the table where Trudy slept, handwritten notes and crayons scattered across the surface, and he could see her thinking.

"Do you know something?"

She wadded the damp rag in her hands and shook her head. "No, just trying to make sense of things."

"That makes two of us. We'll chat more after I talk to Maddie's parents, and then I'll help clean up and close everything down."

"Okay. Oh, um, the cook stacked containers of food on the warming rack before he left. Any idea what I'm supposed to do with those?"

"If you hear a knock on the back door, hand the person a container of food. Or four, if they're feeding a family."

"Do I collect any sort of payment?"

"No, it's Trudy's charity."

As if on cue, someone rapped on the metal door, the sound echoing through the nearly empty restaurant.

"Good thing I asked." Noelle turned on her heel to get the door.

Derek approached the window booth. "Mr. and Mrs. Wingate. May I join you?"

Gary waved him toward a seat. "Of course."

Derek snagged a chair and placed it at the end of the table so he could sit facing both of them.

"I know you said on the phone that you have more questions, but are you any closer to finding Maddie?" Beverly asked.

Derek gentled his voice. "No, not yet." Her face crumpled, piercing him with regret. "I wanted to touch base with you, since I'm sure you'll hear the news around town soon. We discovered the remains of a young woman this evening, but it isn't Maddie."

Beverly's hands flew to her mouth to stifle a cry, and Gary released a measured breath before asking, "Are you sure?"

"Without a doubt. The young woman shares some of Maddie's physical characteristics, but she has blue eyes and a prominent facial scar."

Beverly dragged her hands down her face to the table, clutching her napkin and balling it in her fist. "What happened to her?"

"We're still gathering details, but it would be helpful if you could tell me whether or not she has any connection to Maddie."

Derek placed the sketch on the table. It was a near perfect rendering, including a touch of color to the hair and irises. Derek could imagine the young woman with a sparkle of life in her eyes.

Gary studied the drawing, his throat working. "What happened to her face? Did someone do that to her?"

Derek heard the underlying question: *Does the monster who disfigured this girl have my daughter?* Gary met his eyes, searching for the truth.

"The scar appears to be old, possibly from early childhood," Derek explained, leaving out the probability that someone—possibly a captor—had intentionally inflicted it.

"Who is she?" he asked.

"We're still trying to identify her."

"We've never seen her, and Maddie never mentioned a girl with a scar like that." Beverly dabbed beneath her eyes with her napkin. "Look, I know you're doing your job trying to identify this girl, but . . . she's dead. Our Maddie is still out there somewhere. Shouldn't your resources be focused on finding her?"

"Bev," Gary chided. "She's someone's daughter too."

"I know. I know it sounds terrible and heartless, but . . . you can't help this girl anymore. She's gone. Maddie is out there waiting for someone to rescue her."

Gary's neck flushed with embarrassment, but Derek understood his wife's point of view. When your child was missing, bringing them home became the only thing that mattered.

And in truth, as much as he cared about finding this girl's killer, Maddie was his priority. She was missing, presumably in danger, and after combing through her life, she was no longer a stranger. He needed to find her alive.

"I promise you, Mrs. Wingate, we're doing everything we can to find Maddie."

"You're not doing enough."

"Bev—"

"Excuse me." She pushed back from the table and dashed toward the bathroom, brushing past Noelle, who followed her retreat with concerned eyes.

After only a second of indecision, Noelle slipped into the restroom after her, probably to comfort her mother to mother.

Gary plucked the baseball cap from his head and tossed it on the table, rubbing a hand over his thinning hair. "I'm sorry, she's not usually like this. This is . . . hard for both of us."

"Neither of you need to apologize."

Gary picked up the sketch. "It's crazy how much she looks like Maddie. Except Maddie's not a natural blonde."

"She's not?"

"She's got my brown hair, which she always says is ashy. She and Bev have a salon day every month to do a dye touch-up or something. I don't know what all they do there, but for what it costs, they should come home with gold-plated hair." Tears clung to his lashes. "I'll pay for her to dye her hair every week if I can have her back." He set the sketch back on the table between them. "You think whoever killed this girl took our Maddie, don't you? That's why you're trying to find connections."

"We're considering every possibility."

"What did he do to her? What's he doing to our daughter right now?"

"Mr. Wingate—"

"I need to know."

He *thought* he needed to know. But in truth, most parents didn't want to know the dark details.

"There's nothing I can tell you. I have to wait for the medical examiner to finish. I'm sorry."

He wished there was something he could say or do to offer comfort to Maddie's parents, but nothing short of wrapping their arms around their little girl would bring them peace.

———

Noelle locked the back door after handing out the last premade meal to an old man with a cane and a cast on his leg.

The old man regaled her with a story about how he broke his leg fighting off the trespasser in his cornfield with nothing but his cane and force of spirit. The trespasser squealed and scrambled into his truck, taking off.

She doubted much of the story was true, but she smiled and listened. When interest twinkled in the old man's eyes, and he started talking about how he would marry a girl like her if he were thirty years younger, she told him good night and shut the door.

Fingers still wrinkled from hot, soapy water, she untied the apron around her waist. She'd forgotten how tiring it was to wait tables. Of course, she was ten years older now, and her body was beginning to creak and groan as much as her new house.

"Last one?" Derek asked.

"Yeah, I placed the out-of-food sign on the outside of the door like you said. That last guy missed his calling as a storyteller. Apparently, even at eighty years old, he fought off a truck driver parking in his cornfield without permission."

Derek placed both hands on top of the broom he was sweeping the tile with. "Really. Did you catch his name?"

"Chester, I think. But as far as stories go, I can see a few plot holes."

Derek's mouth twitched into a half smile. "I suppose you would be good at spotting those." He shifted his grip on the handle. "I wanted to thank you for helping Mrs. Wingate."

She draped the apron over the counter. "All I did was listen while she vented." She hadn't known what to say, but she understood the fear and pain the woman was going through.

"Well, whatever you did, it helped. And thank you for what you did for Trudy."

Noelle looked past him at the woman who still slept, face buried in her arms, at one of the tables. Trudy's exhaustion had been palpable, and Noelle was more than happy to give her a few hours of rest.

"She kept trying to get a hold of her husband. I thought I might get to meet him tonight, but he never came by or called her back."

"You've already met him. Brian. He's the man who stopped when your car was on the side of the road."

Noelle blinked. "Your sweet, funny sister is married to that guy?"

"I tried to talk her out of it. I think he might also be the person who was in the woods with you when you found the grave."

Confusion flooded her. "Why would he have been in the woods? And why didn't he say anything?"

"I don't know why he didn't say anything, but he claims he was out there because he was working up the nerve to ask if you would sell him the house."

"Was he one of the other bidders?"

"Yeah."

Her fingers grasped the pendant at her chest, turning it over along with this new information.

"If he bothers you in any way, even if he seems perfectly polite and says he only wants to talk, call me," Derek said.

"Do you think he had something to do with that girl?"

Derek paused before answering. "I can't say anything for sure yet."

When he glanced at Trudy, Noelle's gaze followed. She hadn't even considered the danger Trudy might be in if her husband was a killer.

"We should finish cleaning so I can get Trudy home," Derek said.

Noelle released the pendant and followed him back into the dining room. The sound of bristles swished behind her as she wiped down the salt and pepper shakers at each table.

Music, soft and relaxing, broke into their quiet cleaning. Noelle glanced at Derek, who slid a perturbed look at Trudy when lyrics transformed the relaxing tune into a love song.

"Trudy."

Trudy lifted her head from her arms and smiled. "You know the rule in our family, Derek. When a slow song comes on, grab your partner and dance."

"Now isn't the time, Tru."

"I think it's the perfect time." Her smile widened into a mischievous grin. "Absolutely perfect."

Derek narrowed his eyes at her and then turned to Noelle, shrugging off his reservations. "Ms. McKenzie, may I have this dance?"

Noelle's lips moved soundlessly as she floundered for a response. "Um . . . right here in the middle of the diner?"

"My partner's either going to be a broom or a beautiful woman." His forehead creased with mock pain. "Please don't make me dance with the broom."

The image of him twirling around the room with the wooden broom was almost temptation enough to say no, but she cleared her throat and took pity on him. "Okay."

Derek set aside his cleaning tools and waited for her to wrap her hands around his neck. Butterflies fluttered through her at how close it brought them, her nose brushing his whiskers, her fingertips grazing the short hair at the nape of his neck. When he placed his hands on her waist, heat crawled from beneath his fingers all the way up into her face.

"So," she began, trying to redirect some of the blood in her face to the brain cells required for speech. "Tell me about this rule that forces you to dance with random people at random times."

Derek guided her into a gentle sway. "It's a family thing. It started with our grandmother. She taught dance, and she believed that it could unite any two people, even enemies."

She stepped on the toes of his left foot and winced. "Sorry."

"Feeling more united by the second," he teased, and she smiled as she moved back into her own space.

"Why did she think dance could unite people?"

"According to her, dance requires getting to know your partner, their strengths and weaknesses. It requires observation and teamwork. And when you stand nose to nose with someone, staring into their eyes, it's hard not to see them and connect with them." He studied her. "For example, I can tell that you're tense."

She tried to relax her muscles. "Sorry, it's been a long time since . . ." *A man has held me with such gentleness,* she thought. It felt foreign and comforting at the same time.

Physical affection between her and Tyrese faded away long before the divorce, and there were moments when she desperately craved his touch—something as small as a brush of hands or a passing kiss on the cheek. But he sated his need for physical affection elsewhere, leaving her to starve without this simple but vital connection.

"I get that," Derek said, as if he could see the internal struggle on her face. After their conversation about her marriage, maybe he did understand. "Anyway, Mom adopted Grandma's beliefs, only she used it as a form of punishment."

"That's a unique punishment."

"Derek danced *a lot*," Trudy chimed in. "I think he's good enough to teach lessons after all that practice."

"Thank you for your input," Derek threw over his shoulder. "What Trudy is alluding to is that if us kids were fighting or arguing, Mom would turn on a slow song and make us dance together until we stopped quarreling." He grinned. "Sometimes that took five songs."

"By that reasoning, this should be a punishment, and we should've quarreled about something. Should I insult you so we have something to work out?"

"You did stomp on my foot."

"Step. I *stepped* on your foot. Unintentionally."

"That's not how my toes remember it."

"Your toes remember wrong."

"Then I guess it's a good thing we're working through our difference in perspective."

Noelle laughed. This was not how she envisioned her evening playing out. She'd been prepared to classify the entire day as a disaster, but this made her reevaluate.

"As it turns out, Grandma and Mom were wrong, and dancing doesn't resolve every conflict." Derek swayed slower as the song drew to a close. "It did teach us kids to fight quietly so Mom would never find out, though. My middle sister and I were the worst. She would put salt in my Kool-Aid, and I would dunk her hairbrush in the toilet."

"Vengeful, aren't you?"

"Don't worry. I've outgrown my retaliatory tendencies, so I won't throw you off a porch into the mud when no one's looking."

Noelle rolled her eyes and smiled.

286

The song faded away, and Derek slid his hands from her waist as she unwrapped her arms from his neck.

"Thanks for the dance," he said, offering Noelle a smile that reignited the warmth in her cheeks.

She'd been as wooden in her movements as the broom, but she still felt unexpectedly disappointed that the song had come to an end.

"We should lock up so I can get you ladies home," Derek suggested, and Noelle agreed. They were all tired.

They finished tidying up the diner and rolling silverware in napkins for the breakfast crowd tomorrow morning. Derek dropped her home first, walking her up to the front door of her house like the kind of gentleman she'd only read about.

As certain as she was that she wasn't ready for dating, she was less certain than she'd been this afternoon. Something about Derek made her feel safe, comfortable, and relaxed enough to laugh. Eventually, she would have to figure out what to do about that.

CHAPTER
Thirty-five

Noelle locked the front door and switched on the lantern that sat on the side table to her left. Something felt different about the house, wrong somehow, but she couldn't put her finger on it.

It could have something to do with that murdered teenage girl you tripped over, her inner voice offered. *Or the fact that her killer might still be lurking in the area.*

One thing she knew for certain was that something strange was going on in this village, and it was beginning to feel like her house was at the center of it—one girl dead, another girl who vanished two miles away, Firefly's diary that dropped out of obscurity into the woods.

"How does it all connect, God?"

She waited for a whisper or a feeling to give her direction, but all she could feel was the nagging sense that something was wrong.

Grabbing the lantern, she walked through the house, looking for anything out of place.

Were the couch and half bookshelf sitting further from the wall or was she imagining things? The refrigerator might be sitting slightly crooked. And her barricade against the back door . . . it was too far to the left, wasn't it?

Someone had been in the house, and they were looking for something.

But if she called the police about a slightly off-kilter refrigerator and a trash can in the wrong spot, they would think she was insane.

Maybe you are.

She stared at the closet off the kitchen, the door resting a few inches from the frame. Did she forget to close it after fetching her coat this evening? Was it open when she stood here brewing tea for Derek's team?

She couldn't remember.

Creeping forward, she peered through the crack and then widened the door, finding the small space as empty as it was when she left—nothing but a coat hook on the back wall.

She was definitely going crazy.

With a sigh, she shrugged off her coat and hung it. Carrying her purse into the dining room, she stopped dead in her tracks, gaze fixed on the window.

A bloody handprint was splattered in the top left corner, and it streaked downward, like the person who placed it there had melted down the glass.

Heart thudding, she rushed forward and looked out. Moonlight, seeping through cracks in the clouds, highlighted a dark shape sprawled in front of the window. A person. There was a bleeding person lying on her back porch.

For a moment, she stood frozen; then she drew her gun and phone from her purse, shoving the weapon in her waistband, and darted for the back door. She dialed 9-1-1 with trembling fingers as she shoved aside the barricade with her legs.

"9-1-1, what is your—"

"There's someone incapacitated and bleeding on my porch."

"What's your address?"

Her mind blanked, and it took her a moment to find the information. She grabbed her lantern as she rattled off the address and stepped outside. Cool light bathed the porch, and she took in the scene.

A man lay crumpled beneath the dining room window, crimson expanding around his body. Blood was everywhere—on the porch, the railing, smeared down the siding.

"Ma'am," the calm voice said through the phone, and Noelle realized she'd missed whatever the woman had been saying. "Are you all right? Are you in any danger?"

The word *danger* was like a bucket of ice water over Noelle's head, and she looked around, every pocket of darkness a potential hiding place for threats.

"I . . . I don't know. I didn't see what happened."

"Do you know who the person is?"

She was about to say no, but as she inched closer, she recognized the too-thin fingers limply resting on the butt of a rifle.

"I think it's Walter Bechtel."

———

Noelle's house faded away in the rearview mirror, and Derek pulled his eyes from the road to frown at Trudy in the passenger seat. "I can't believe you did that."

Her lips twitched. "What ever do you mean?"

"You know what I mean."

She removed a large clip from her hair and rubbed at her scalp. "All I did was turn on a song. You didn't *have* to dance with her. It's not like Mom or Gran were watching."

Derek couldn't imagine having that spiked thing stabbing him in the head all day. No wonder women always had headaches. "You set me up. If I refused to dance with her, she might've taken it personally. She might've thought . . ."

"That you don't like her?" Trudy finished for him. "But you *do* like her."

"As a—"

"If you say 'friend,' I will smack you upside the head. She likes you and you like her, but I've never seen two people more hesitant to do something about it."

"We just met yesterday, Tru."

"I'm not saying put a ring on her finger after twenty-four hours, but there's nothing wrong with dinner and a dance. It's called a date, something normal people do."

"She's not ready for dating."

"She's not ready or *you're* not ready?"

Her question punched him in the chest. Noelle was a wonderful person, but he wasn't sure he was ready to let himself care for another woman. Loving Lacey had been a whirlwind that ripped his heart out in the end. After so

291

much loss in his life, a part of him was afraid to build more relationships he would only lose.

"When Lacey said she didn't want you to be alone for the rest of your life, she didn't mean get a dog," Trudy pointed out.

"Elsa is great company."

"Elsa probably peed on your floor."

After how long he'd been gone today, probably. She had a doggy door into the enclosed backyard, but when he was gone too long, she became anxious and left a puddle on the kitchen floor.

"I do like Noelle, but I need you not to push." He glanced at her. "She's got a lot of healing to do."

Trudy tugged at the seat-belt strap around her lower abdomen. "All right. But you two dancing together was still cute."

A reluctant smile curled his lips because he agreed. Having his arms around her had felt nice, and they had been close enough that he could smell the cinnamon and spice in the lip balm she wore.

Trudy shifted in her seat and watched the trees pass by. "I thought you were taking me home. You missed my turnoff."

"I was hoping you might spend the night at my place tonight."

"We're a bit old for sleepovers, don't you think?"

Derek knew she would resist coming home with him, but if he dropped her off at her trailer, where Brian might show up at any moment, he wouldn't be able to sleep.

"Brian call you yet?"

She checked her cell. "No, but he should be home by tonight. I'm going to try to talk to him about what he's doing with our money before any more of it disappears."

He flexed his fingers on the steering wheel, bracing himself for a difficult conversation. "He's been in Cherry Creek since last night."

Silence stretched. "No, he's in Cincinnati visiting his mother."

"I called his mother. She hasn't seen him in months. And he told me himself that he's been in the area since last night."

Breath left her in a whoosh, and she turned toward the window. "Do you think he's having an affair with someone in town?"

Derek hadn't expected her to leap to that conclusion. "I doubt it."

"Look at me, Derek. I'm as big as a freight train. I have been for months." Tears glistened on her cheeks when she turned toward him. "And we both know he's always looking for the next best thing. What if the next best thing is a pretty woman who's skinny enough that she can still see her toes?"

"I don't think he's having an affair."

She wiped at her tear-stained cheeks. "Wait, when did you talk to him? I haven't even talked to him since he le . . . since he said he was leaving."

"We had a chat this evening at the department. He's gotten himself into some trouble."

Wariness tinged her voice. "What kind of trouble? Like, spent all our money at the blackjack table trouble?"

Derek hadn't planned this far into the conversation, and he tried to rally his thoughts. "I can't tell you everything yet. I need you to believe me when I say that you staying with me is the best option right now."

"What did he do?"

"I can't tell you." He hated the way the lie tasted on his tongue, but telling her that her husband might have murdered a teenage girl and buried her body in the woods would only paint images in her head that she wouldn't be able to erase. He loved her too much for that.

Tears clogged her voice. "Whatever happened, it has to be a misunderstanding."

Derek held his tongue. He didn't want Brian to be guilty. Someone he knew, someone related to him couldn't be a monster. And yet the doubt was there.

"It could be a misunderstanding," he agreed. "But until we know for sure, I need you to trust me. I've earned that."

She swallowed and dried her face with her fingers. "You have. But if we're having a sleepover, I'm going to need some things."

"We'll get them first thing in the morning."

He turned into the driveway of his house and cut the engine. He was about to pull the key from the ignition when his radio crackled, dispatch issuing an alert for a break-in and assault.

Trudy sucked in a breath at the address. "Noelle's house?"

Derek's heart pounded against his ribs, and he grabbed his radio. "Dispatch, this is Dempsey. You're sure on that address?"

"Yes, sir."

He had dropped Noelle off and walked her to her door minutes ago. What could've happened in that short time? But he knew. Every officer knew how quickly a situation could change.

He looked at Trudy. "You still have my spare key?"

She fumbled her keyring from her purse. "I do."

"Go inside and lock the door. And if Brian comes by, don't open it."

"But he's my hus—"

"Trudy, please."

She swallowed and gripped the keys in her fist. "Okay."

He waited until she was safely inside, then reversed out of the driveway so quickly that it flung gravel in every direction.

———

Blood gushed from a wound on the side of Walt's head, but there was nothing on the porch that Noelle could use to staunch the flow.

She set down the phone and twisted out of her sweater, wadding it up and pressing it to his head, the pressure drawing a groan from him.

"Walt, can you hear me?"

Had he been attacked, or had he fallen and then made his way here, hoping she would help him?

His eyes fluttered, and a garbled word escaped his lips. Noelle leaned down, pressing her ear close to his mouth. "What did you say?"

"Didn't mean . . . for it to happen. I'm . . . sorry. So . . . sorry . . . Skyler."

Didn't mean for what to happen, and who was Skyler? Noelle's thoughts immediately turned to the girl in the grave. No one knew her name or how she'd gotten there, except the man who put her there and possibly the man who watched everything.

Movement snapped her attention to the dining room window. The lantern light reflected off the glass, but something, or someone, stirred behind it. Her heart thudded in her chest, and she snatched the gun from her waistband.

"Who's there?" she demanded, but the only sound in the quiet night was her heavy breathing. "I'm armed," she announced, a tremble in her voice.

Something rustled and thumped in the kitchen.

Noelle wanted to pick up the phone and scream to the dispatcher that someone was in her house, that she was in danger and they needed to hurry, but she would have to release pressure on Walt's wound or lower her gun, neither of which she was willing to do.

You don't owe this creepy old man anything. Run, hide, a part of her mind demanded, dredging up their disconcerting interactions.

But she couldn't. She wouldn't abandon him when he was unable to protect himself, and she prayed that if she were ever in a similar situation, someone would do the same for her. She kept her gun trained on the door and waited for the threat to come for them.

CHAPTER
Thirty-six

Derek arrived before the ambulance and responding units, and his cruiser skidded through the mud as he slammed on the brakes in Noelle's driveway.

The front door of the house stood wide open, but he'd seen her close it before he left.

Fear darted through him, and he drew his sidearm as he sprang from the car. He pounded up the steps, pausing only to grab his flashlight before gliding into the pitch-black house.

"Noelle!"

"Derek!" Her shrill voice carried from around back.

He bypassed the staircase and side hallway, checking around every corner as he cut through to the kitchen. Noelle's purse lay on the floor, the contents scattered across the linoleum. He stepped over them and out onto the porch, unprepared for the scene.

Walt lay facedown, blood soaking the sweater Noelle pressed to the side of his head.

Derek scanned the area for threats, then holstered his sidearm and knelt beside her. "Are you okay? What happened?"

"I don't know. I found him like this. I can't stop the bleeding."

"Head wounds bleed a lot, but that doesn't mean the wound is fatal." He placed two fingers to Walt's neck, measuring his pulse. Weak, but present.

Noelle shifted on her knees, wincing. She was already in pain from falling in the woods, and kneeling on this hard porch was only making it worse.

"Why don't you let me take over?"

She was shaking her head before he even finished offering. "No, if whoever did this is still here, I would rather you be able to use your gun if they come after us."

"You think he was attacked?" He shrugged off his coat and draped it over her shoulders.

Uncertainty clouded her face. "I don't know. He could've fallen and hit his head somewhere. But why stumble all the way here instead of calling an ambulance?"

"He doesn't have a phone."

She exhaled a slow breath and looked back at Walt, pity in her expression. "I don't think this was an accident. Someone was in the house. I'm sure of it. Maybe Walt tried to scare them off, and they came up behind him."

"Did you see anyone?"

"No. But someone moved past the dining room window, and I heard a thump in the kitchen. And things were . . . moved."

Approaching sirens cut off, and flashing lights reflected off the trees. Doors slammed and voices echoed.

Derek walked to the corner of the porch and called out, "Back here!"

299

Two paramedics stomped up the steps and came their way, carrying a gurney. The female paramedic demanded, "Give us some room to work."

Noelle stared at the woman with shocked horror, and for a moment Derek didn't think she was going to give them the room they needed. Then she uncurled her fingers from the sweater and scooted away.

Derek helped her to her feet, and she stumbled into him, pressing her hands to his chest to steady herself.

Tears streamed down her face, and she struggled to catch her breath as she watched the paramedics work.

Realization struck Derek. Her son had been hit by a car. Had she been beside him when the paramedics rushed in and dragged her away so they could administer first aid? Was she back on that street rather than this porch?

Father in Heaven, she needs your comfort, he pleaded silently, and the thought that whispered through his mind in response caught him off guard. *I sent you.*

Derek reached up and touched the side of Noelle's face. "Hey, look at me."

"He's not going to make it."

Derek turned her face away from the scene. "Whatever happens, it's going to be okay."

"It's not okay," she choked out, looking at her bloodstained hands. "None of this is okay."

Derek wrapped his arms around her and pulled her into a hug, holding on even when she fought not to touch him with her bloody hands and forearms. When he didn't let her push away, she melted against his chest and buried her face in his shoulder, sobbing. He held her and wished he could rewind this day to pizza and hot tea on a musty couch.

The paramedics transferred Walt's limp frame to the gurney.

"Where are you taking him?" he asked.

The female paramedic didn't look away from her patient as she answered. "Weston Community."

Derek rested his head against Noelle's as he stared at the dark liquid glistening on the porch. Hopefully, Walt was as stubborn about staying alive as he was about everything else.

———

By the time Noelle finished scrubbing off all the blood, the bucket of water was pink. She dumped it down the toilet and then studied her reflection in the broken mirror above the bathroom sink.

She was exhausted, and with the way the past twenty-four hours had played out, she didn't foresee the future being any less exhausting. She should've stayed in Seattle.

This abandoned house had more action than her city apartment, which was quite a feat considering her neighbor across the hall sold narcotics at all hours, usually concealed in toothpick boxes. The guy probably had enough toothpicks in his apartment to build a bonfire. Either that or he had really clean teeth.

A quiet tap of knuckles on the door drew her from her dismal thoughts. "You okay in there?"

Derek. The one unexpected bright spot in this entire disaster. For reasons she couldn't fathom, he went out of his way to make her feel welcome and safe. Even if that meant holding her when reality collided with her memories and reduced her to a sobbing, shivering mess.

Embarrassment flooded her as she remembered the way she collapsed into him, burying her face in his shoulder.

"Noelle," he said when she didn't answer.

"Yeah, I'm all right."

"We did a thorough search of the house. If anyone was here, they're gone."

If. First the sense that someone was watching her, then the back door flying open, and now nothing to prove that someone was in the house even when she saw . . . something.

What if the movement she thought she saw had been a trick of the light? What if the thump in the kitchen was her purse falling off the counter onto the floor? She'd shrugged it off without a care for how close it was to the edge.

Or maybe someone was intentionally messing with her mind. Walt wanted her gone, Trudy's husband wanted the house, something about the lawyer bothered her, and then there was the mysterious person who left the note on her car.

The more she thought about that note, the more it felt like a scare tactic. If the person who left it knew she wasn't alone in this house, why not elaborate? There had been plenty of room on the paper for useful information, but they opted for one cryptic line.

Murmuring came from outside the door. Derek must've been talking to someone else. "Thanks," he said, ending the conversation. His voice grew louder as he returned to the door. "I thought you might want to know Walt made it to the hospital. Deputy Grisham is there, and she said he's conscious and requesting to speak with you."

Noelle pushed away from the grimy, chipped sink and opened the bathroom door. "Me? Why would he want to talk to me?"

"You did save his life."

"That's a bit of an exaggeration."

"Regardless, he's refusing to speak to anyone but you."

"You're kidding." But nothing in his expression indicated humor.

"We found blood on the ladder rungs of the tree house. We don't know if someone hit him or if he fell."

She'd seen those ladder rungs. They would be dangerous dry, let alone while slicked with rain. "You think he wants to tell me what happened?"

"He says he has something important to discuss with you, and that's all he would say."

Could it have something to do with the words he murmured tonight? She hadn't told anyone about that yet, but she should. Disoriented or not, Walt's apology sounded dangerously close to an admission of guilt.

"On the porch tonight, Walt was apologizing to someone named Skyler. He said, 'I didn't mean for it to happen. I'm sorry, so sorry.'"

303

Derek straightened from his relaxed position against the wall. "Skyler?"

"I think it might be the girl in the grave. Earlier today, he told me to stay out of the woods, that they're dangerous, but now I wonder if he was worried I would find her."

"Walt doesn't strike me as a murderer."

"It's possible he didn't mean to hurt her. You know how possessive he is of the house. What if she was inside, exploring, and he wanted her to leave? They could've argued and things went badly."

Had that girl died here in this house, her limp body dragged out the kitchen door, leaving the mysterious clean streak on the floor? Did Walt bury her with the family shovel?

"He might want to confess."

"If he killed her . . ."

"What does that mean for Maddie?" she asked, finishing the thought she assumed was responsible for the worry etching grooves into his forehead.

"Yeah."

Noelle retreated back into the bathroom, trying to fix her hair because she didn't know what else to do. The idea of setting foot in a hospital again turned her insides to jelly. The smell of antiseptic, the beeping of machines, the doctor coming toward her to tell her that her world just died.

"I know you don't like hospitals." Derek leaned in the doorway. "You don't have to go, no matter what demands he makes."

"Don't I?" She turned to face him, resting a hip against the sink. "If he knows something about either of those girls . . . I saw how devastated Maddie's parents are. If there's the smallest chance I can help reunite that family, I need to do it."

He regarded her with something that might've been admiration. "You're a kind and caring person, Noelle McKenzie."

Heat flooded her face. "Um, I should probably change into something else." She offered his coat back.

He took it and stepped aside so she could slip by. "I'll be downstairs when you're ready."

She went into the bedroom to strip out of her bloodstained layers. Between graves, blood, and spills off the porch, she was running out of clothes. Tomorrow she would need to find a laundromat.

Dressed and as composed as she could make herself, she glanced at the knot in the ceiling. "Don't let me fall apart in the hospital. Please."

Two embarrassing emotional collapses was all she could handle for the day. Her sneaker laces needed bleaching, so she pulled on her calf-high boots and joined Derek in the kitchen.

He held out her purse. "Since we didn't find any indication of an intruder, this isn't evidence. Unless you notice something missing."

She took it from him. "Thanks for picking it all up." She opened it and scanned the contents, but everything appeared to be accounted for.

"Ready?"

"I guess so." She was about to face one of her fears, and she prayed it wouldn't all be for nothing.

CHAPTER
Thirty-seven

The automatic doors sucked the air from Noelle's lungs as they whooshed open, and she stood frozen outside the hospital emergency entrance.

This is where the living come to die, she thought, that awful day pushing its way to the front of her mind.

She should flee back to the car and refuse to see the old man. Derek would figure out how to get answers out of him.

A gentle hand touched her elbow, startling her, and she looked over at Derek whose brow furrowed with concern.

"Are you having second thoughts?"

And third, fourth, and fifth thoughts. She'd been arguing with herself the entire ride here, but she always found herself back at the beginning of her reasoning—this was about helping Maddie and the mysterious Skyler.

"We're wasting time," she said, with a bravado she didn't feel, and passed through the doors into the emergency room.

Sounds rushed in around her—coughing, crying, machines beeping, phones ringing—and anxiety throbbed in her veins.

Derek's reassuring hand between her shoulder blades propelled her toward the reception desk. "Excuse me, we're here to see a patient. Walter Bechtel."

The nurse grunted and slid the sign-in clipboard toward them. "Good luck with that one."

They signed in, and she directed them through the doors to a room. Noelle's heart pounded in her ears as she walked alongside Derek, the curtains and room numbers blurring together. Her mind flashed back to another hospital, where a nurse led her down a hallway to a room much like these to see her son's body.

God, I can't do this.

Nausea churned in the pit of her stomach as they approached the striped curtain that had been tugged almost closed.

Eight months and four days ago, a nurse had drawn back a similar curtain, her gentle assurance that Noelle could stay as long as she needed doing nothing to calm her full-body trembling. Noelle had barely made it to her son's bedside before her legs gave out.

Derek lifted a hand to open the curtain, and Noelle gripped his wrist on reflex. "Derek . . ."

Compassion shone in his eyes, but before he could say anything, a woman's voice came from inside the room.

"Mr. Bechtel, you need to lie down."

The curtain hissed along the metal track as Derek opened it wide enough to see Walt climbing out of bed in his hospital gown.

"I have to go."

A petite older woman in green scrubs pressed him back into the pillows. "No, you need a CT scan."

He swatted at her hands, his reflexes as slow as someone fighting under water. "Get your hands off me. I have to go home. I shouldn't even be here."

"You suffered a serious head trauma. This is exactly where you should be."

"You can't keep me against my will."

The nurse reared back, her wrinkled lips pressed into an unforgiving line. "Now you listen to me—"

"Are we interrupting?" Derek asked, attracting the attention of anyone within earshot.

Walt squinted, the same way Noelle did when she was looking at something without her glasses. "Well, color me surprised."

The nurse excused herself, announcing that she would be back in ten minutes to take him for his CT scan.

Noelle folded her arms against the chilly memories seeping from the hospital walls. "Why am I here, Walt?"

His eyes flicked left, focusing on Derek. "You and your minion aren't welcome for this conversation."

Minion? Noelle noticed Deputy Grisham for the first time, sitting in a chair in the hallway. The woman was quiet and willowy with dark freckles, as if a painter coated his brush in shades of brown and flicked it, spraying dark specks across every pale surface. She was uniquely beautiful.

She had a sketch pad open in her lap, using the photo on her phone as a reference point to sketch a child's face.

Noelle stole a longer look at the picture on the phone, and her stomach rolled sideways. The pallor of the girl's face, the lifeless glaze over her eyes . . .

Grisham darkened her phone screen and offered Noelle an apologetic grimace before turning her attention to Derek. "I asked if what happened tonight was an accident or an attack, but Mr. Bechtel won't tell me. He says people with badges can't be trusted."

"Did you show him the pictures of Habrams, Brian, and Nelson?" Derek asked.

"I did, but he wouldn't confirm whether or not one of them attacked him. He wouldn't even acknowledge knowing them."

They thought the lawyer or Derek's brother-in-law might be behind this attack?

Derek turned back to Walt. "Noelle agreed to listen, so say what you have to say."

"I'm not talking in front of you or that woman out there. Neither of you can be trusted."

Walt sank back against the pillows and sealed his lips.

Noelle dipped her head toward Derek and whispered, "If he'll give me information about the girls that he won't give you, it might be better for you to wait in the hall." When he drew in a breath to speak, she preempted his argument. "He couldn't even fight off a nurse the size of a seventh grader. I don't think he's dangerous."

Reluctantly, Derek left them to speak alone. Grisham gathered up her drawing materials and chair and followed him out into the hall.

Walt licked dry lips. "The curtain."

"Stays open." She would give the man an inch, but she wasn't giving him the mile. "Why do you trust me all of a sudden?"

"The way I hear it, you went out of your way to help me. Bad people don't do that."

If he assumed everyone was bad and untrustworthy until they proved otherwise, he was going to lead a lonely life.

"Do you want to tell me why I came home to a horror movie on my back porch?"

His nostrils flared when she said "my back porch," but he didn't argue. "Someone hit me."

"One of the men the deputy showed you?"

Considering his enraged pounding of his steering wheel after she refused to speak with him, Noelle could imagine Brian lashing out. The lawyer was more difficult to imagine, and she didn't recognize the third name—Nelson.

When Walt remained silent, she asked, "Was it the same person who was in the house tonight? The one who moved things?"

"What sort of things?"

"Furniture."

He propped himself up against the pillows, a glimmer of fear in his eyes. "He was looking for something."

"For what?"

"Something I hope he didn't find." He stared at the blankets, visibly wrestling with a decision, then asked, "Was the closet near the kitchen open?"

311

"Yeah, how did you know?"

"Did he take anything?"

"There hasn't been anything in that closet since I moved in. It's just an empty space."

As if that were the answer he hoped for, he relaxed back against the pillows, all traces of fear gone. "Why did you help me tonight?"

Noelle wanted to probe more about the closet, but she doubted it would do any good. "Because it was the right thing to do."

He chewed on that. "Is that how you live your life—based on what's right?"

"Most people do."

"No they don't," he spat. "They live life based on what's right *for them*, no matter who else gets hurt."

Noelle sat on the edge of the visitor chair against the wall. "That's a dismal way to look at things."

"Would you do the right thing even if it was dangerous?"

"I'd like to think I would. Now, would you tell me what happened tonight?"

"I already told you. I was coming out of my tree house, and someone clubbed me over the head."

"Someone."

"Some sissy-armed punk. If he didn't hit like a preschool girl, I'd be dead. Instead, I woke up with a face full of dirt. Made my way to the house. Last thing I remember is stumbling up the steps onto the porch."

Noelle leaned forward, resting her elbows on her thighs. "When you were lying on the porch, and I was trying to stop the bleeding, you mentioned a name. Skyler."

His throat bobbed as he swallowed, and he averted his eyes. "I don't know any Skyler."

Noelle wasn't an expert on human behavior, but she knew from experience that secrets, emotional pain, and guilt made eye contact difficult. She had a hard time meeting her therapist's eyes when they touched on painful subjects, and after coming home from a night out with one of his lovers, Tyrese avoided her gaze like it would turn him to stone.

"You do know a Skyler. Is she the girl buried in the woods?"

Silence.

"Did you see what happened to her?"

Walt tapped his fingers on the blanket draped across his waist. "What does it matter? She's dead."

So cold and detached—and yet, when he was disoriented, he apologized to Skyler for something he didn't mean to happen.

"Did you kill her accidentally and then bury her?"

"You really think I'm foolish enough to confess to murder with Deedee and his minion outside in the hallway?"

"If I'm not here so you can tell someone what happened, then why am I here?"

He licked dry lips again. "You're not here to help them frame me for murder. They tried to do that before, and they'll try it again."

Exasperated, she said, "All I want is the truth."

"Answer the rest of my questions, and I might answer yours."

She could leave now and be done with this maddening conversation, but then it would all have been for nothing. "Fine."

"Why did you move into my family's house?"

"Because it was for sale."

Walt's eyes narrowed. "You say you live your life based on what's right, but then you lie when I ask you a simple question. What's the real reason you moved in?"

She stared at the white tile beneath her feet, and her throat tightened painfully against rising tears. "I lost my son and my marriage, and no place felt like home anymore. When I saw the photos of the house on the auction website, I felt drawn to it, like I was meant to be here."

Walt paused. "You lost your child?"

"He died. Eight months ago in a hospital." She shot him a look that conveyed how angry she was with him for putting her in this situation. "So, being here is really hard, and I would like to leave. If we could speed things along, that would be great."

"I don't want you here either, but I needed to look you in the eyes when you answered my questions." He pushed himself up against the pillows with a pained groan. "You have a gun."

She blinked at the abrupt change of subject. "What does that have to do with anything?"

"You know how to use it?"

"Of course."

"Good, 'cause you might need it."

314

She opened her mouth to demand an explanation, when the petite nurse appeared with an empty wheelchair.

"Time for your scan, Mr. Bechtel." The nurse pushed past Noelle with the wheelchair. "I'm sorry, Miss, but you'll need to leave."

Noelle had come all the way here, to a place that made her insides quiver, and it couldn't be for nothing. "I need answers, Walt. Give me something."

The nurse's mouth pinched into an impatient line as she helped the rail-thin man up and into the wheelchair. "Miss."

Noelle clenched her teeth and pushed up from the chair. As the nurse wheeled Walt past her, he reached out and caught her wrist, his grip unexpectedly strong.

"Go back to the house and stay there," he whispered.

"This afternoon you wanted me gone. Now you want me to go back? Why the sudden change of heart?"

"Because I'm not there." He released her wrist, and the nurse started to wheel him from the room.

"Wait." Noelle pulled the diary from her purse and held it up in front of Walt. "No one in this town that I've spoken with recognizes this diary, but you do. I saw the way you reacted to it this morning. Who is Firefly?"

Walt's dark eyes shifted to the nurse and then past her to the hallway, where Derek and his deputy waited.

Leaning closer to Noelle, he said, "Be careful who you trust with that." Then he straightened. "Let's make this quick, nurse lady. I need to get out of here as soon as I can."

Noelle followed them out of the room and watched them stroll away. Walt's words carried back down the hall to her ears, and she wondered if they were meant for her rather than the nurse. "My family's house can't be left alone."

———

Derek met Noelle outside the hospital room. She slid her necklace pendant between her fingers, an anxious habit he was learning to recognize.

"Nothing he said makes sense," burst from her, frustration lacing each word. "All he did was ask me a bunch of random questions and then tell me to go back to the house and stay there."

"Going home to rest might not be a bad idea. It's been a long day." And the circles of exhaustion beneath her eyes were darkening to bruises.

"But he didn't tell me anything about Maddie or the girl in the grave." Quotation marks formed between her eyebrows. "He did say that someone hit him when he was coming down from the tree house, and I think that *someone* was in my house."

Derek doubted anyone had been in the house tonight. His people had searched for intruders when they arrived, and there was no indication anyone else had been there. "What makes you so certain someone was inside?"

"They moved things—the couch, the bookshelf, the refrigerator."

"What would someone be looking for by moving those things?"

She paused to think and then released an exasperated breath. "I don't know."

"It's been a chaotic day, and you barely slept last night. Why don't you go home and get some rest."

She dropped her hand from her necklace and conceded with a nod.

"I'll drive you."

"No, Walt knows more than he's saying. Even if he didn't kill that girl, he knows something about what happened to her. I saw it in his face. You need to make him trust you enough that he'll tell you."

"That's easier said than done."

"You have to try."

He knew she was right, and as frustrating as it would be, he *would* try because a girl's life might depend on the information the old man was withholding.

Noelle readjusted the purse strap on her shoulder. "I'll take a taxi, assuming you have those around here."

"You know this is the country, not the wilderness."

"Sometimes I wonder." She flashed him a tired smile. "Good night. Again."

CHAPTER
Thirty-eight

Noelle missed Seattle and the hazy glow of lamplight on every street. She used to think *that* was darkness, but as the taxi's headlights faded, pitch blackness closed in from every direction, engulfing her driveway.

Lighting the way with her phone, she started toward the porch, her steps brisk. She raced up the staircase so no one could reach out and hook her ankles. It was an irrational fear—the steps were solid, not backless—but after this crazy day, there was no room for rationality.

She ducked inside the house, feeling as jittery as she had last night after meeting the Scarecrow, and turned on the lantern on the side table.

"Relax, Noelle. Everything is fine."

The false positivity tickled the back of her throat, and before she knew it, she was doubled over with exhausted and slightly unhinged laughter.

A missing girl, a dead girl, a diary written by a child no one seemed to know, an old man who might be a killer, a phantom who broke into her house . . .

All fine. Perfectly fine, normal problems. Nothing to worry about.

She wheezed as the giggle fit faded, leaving her drained and weary. She sighed, then thumped her head back against the door. Derek was right—she needed sleep.

Except with sleep came vivid dreams, and after her visit to the hospital, she had no doubt she would find herself back in that curtained room, clinging to her son's limp fingers.

She stared up at the second story, wrestling with the physical need for rest and the emotional need to avoid the nightmares that would overwhelm her dreams.

Firefly. If she was going to dwell on a child, then she would rather it be one she could help. If she funneled her attention into connecting the dots, she should be able to make sense of the girl's story.

Putting thoughts of the hospital from her mind, she walked into the dining room, the best place for her storyboard.

Shrugging off her coat and draping it over the back of a chair, she fixed the characters and their descriptions to the wall with duct tape, then pulled the box of crayons from her purse.

Characters were blue, descriptions were green, so plots would be . . .

"Eeny meeny miney mo." She plucked the pink crayon from the box. Fitting, considering pink was the perfect color, and all good ideas should be written in pink.

She stepped back to survey her notes.

Her mind kept circling back to the same question: how did Firefly's diary end up in the woods behind the house?

319

Her drawing of what she saw every day from her window depicted a residential city street rather than the country, which meant the diary was a long way from home. It didn't simply slip out of Firefly's backpack when she was walking home from school.

If the girl even went to school. She must've had some kind of education because she knew how to read and write. Noelle added the question to her notes on Firefly: *Homeschooled?*

Noelle pressed the crayon to her lips, barely catching herself before biting down on it like she did her pen caps. A mouthful of wax would be the icing on the moldy cupcake that was her day.

Did the unknown teenage girl in the woods have something to do with the diary being so far from home? Did she steal it, or . . .

Noelle tapped the crayon against her lips in thought. If she tried too hard to connect the teenager with the diary, she would end up tangled in a web of unanswerable questions. She needed to focus on the content first.

The doctor was a regular character in the diary, and Noelle was certain that if she could figure him out, the rest of the story would fall into place.

"Who are you, Dr. Gray?"

She sank into her chair and grabbed the chai lip balm from her purse, applying a spicy layer of comfort as she considered the little she knew about the man.

It was rare for a doctor to make house calls, and yet he popped by the house regularly. It could be a halfway house, a shelter, a home with hospice care patients. All of

320

those situations might involve people who needed on-site medical treatment or consults.

The girls never getting better, as Firefly had noticed, could mean that their illnesses were terminal. Dr. Gray could be doing biweekly checkups to document their conditions.

But the doctor scared Firefly. There was something more to that than a child frightened of needles and exams. She could feel it.

Rubbing at her tired eyes, Noelle mulled over the possibilities.

If he was a doctor without scruples, Gray could earn a lot of money using his skills outside the law. The criminal underworld provided plenty of work—illegal medical procedures, experiments, consults, medical care for criminals.

"He could be a doctor who's also a serial killer, and he has a house full of victims," she muttered, overlapping her arms on the table and resting her chin on them.

She stared at her notes, one unlikely possibility after another whirling through her mind until sleep dragged her under.

————

Derek had never met anyone more stubborn than Walter Bechtel. He could understand the old man refusing to speak about the dead body for fear of incriminating himself, but he wouldn't even describe or identify his own attacker.

Derek finally called it a night, and since they had no evidence that Walt was guilty of murder, he sent Grisham home as well. She seemed distracted, almost dazed, as she stared at her half-finished sketch. When he asked her if everything was all right, she muttered something about déjà vu, packed up her art supplies, and left. Hopefully she would have the sketch finished by tomorrow.

Derek walked into the living room to find Trudy asleep on the couch with a book in her lap. He moved the book so he could drape a blanket over her and was surprised to recognize the author photo on the back cover. It was one of Noelle's books, published under her maiden name.

"It's a really good book," Trudy said, her eyelids cracking open.

"I'm sure it is." He set the book on the side table.

"She puts so much heart into her writing that you can feel it. It's incred—"

Violent pounding erupted at the front of the house, and a bellow pierced the thick wooden door, carrying to the living room. "Derek!"

Trudy straightened at her husband's voice, the blanket slipping down to pool on her stomach. "Why does he sound so angry?"

"Did you tell him you were staying with me for the night?"

"I sent him a text, but he never responded."

He was responding now, pounding on the door and shouting for Derek to come outside.

"Stay here. I'm going to talk to him."

She caught his wrist. "If he's drunk, leave it alone. Let him sober up. He makes really bad decisions when he's been drinking."

"He makes really bad decisions when he's sober. Don't blame it on the alcohol."

Anxiety flashed through her eyes. "If you go out there, he might pick a fight with you."

"Don't worry. I'll try not to hurt him."

She huffed and released his wrist, wrapping her arms around herself. Derek whistled for Elsa, and she trotted out of his bedroom and over to the couch.

"Stay."

Elsa sat down beside Trudy, ready to protect if the threat made it into the house. Derek left the girls in the living room and padded down the hall in his socks. He glanced at his gun, debating whether or not to arm himself for this confrontation.

Lord, please don't let this escalate to violence.

He unlocked the front door and swung it open to find Brian steaming in the rain, the neck of a beer bottle clutched in one hand. There went any hope of rational conversation.

"Where's Trudy?"

Derek stepped out into the sprinkle and closed the door behind him. "Why don't you go home and come back when you're sober."

Brian's left hand curled into a fist. "I have a right to see my wife."

"You're a suspect in the murder of a teenage girl, and now you're drunk and pounding on my front door like

323

a Neanderthal. What makes you think you have the right to see her?"

Brian stepped forward. "I didn't kill that girl."

"I'm sure you also didn't try to bludgeon Walt to death shortly after I told you he might've seen who killed and buried that girl. It's purely coincidence."

Brian blinked a few times before Derek's accusation processed. "I didn't do that either. And you have no business interfering in our marriage. I—"

"If you were being the husband you're supposed to be, I would agree with you. But you're not."

"You think you're so high-and-mighty with your religion, but at least I still have a wife. One who isn't dead."

Rage scorched through Derek's veins, and his fingers curled so tightly that the bones ached. "Do you even know what a husband is supposed to be?" he gritted out, fighting to contain the urge to pound his brother-in-law into the sidewalk.

Brian spread his arms wide. "I think I'm doing all right."

"Then you're not paying attention. When your wife worries that you might be having an affair, you're doing something wrong."

"I'm not cheating on her."

"What about honoring, supporting, and protecting her? You're not honoring her when you lie about where you are and what you're doing. You're not supporting her when you run off to do what you want and leave her to do life alone. You're not protecting her when you funnel your household income into some addiction or secret scheme

324

she never agreed to, causing her stress because she can't pay the bills." Derek stepped forward, the rain like ice on his feet. "A boy puts his own wants and dreams first. A man, a husband, puts his wife's needs before his own desires. You need to reevaluate what's important in your life, because this person standing in front of me doesn't deserve Trudy."

Brian swallowed. "I love her."

"I'm sure you do. But it's not what you're showing her."

Anger twisted Brian's face again. "You never liked me. You tried to convince Trudy not to marry me. I know that."

Derek sighed, unclenching his fingers. "She made her choices, and you've made yours. With your addictions, you're a sinking ship tied to my sister, and I won't let you pull her down with you."

"You . . ." He shoved a finger in Derek's face, and Derek slapped it away.

"Get off my porch, Brian."

"We're not done."

"We are for tonight." He snatched the keys from his brother-in-law's hand. "Now walk home and sober up. Think about what we discussed. And if you come back here drunk and raging, I'll arrest you for trespassing."

"Give me my keys."

"Tomorrow." Derek closed his fingers over the ring of keys. "Try not to pass out in a ditch."

Brian shook with anger, but he turned and left, staggering down the road in the direction of his and Trudy's trailer.

325

CHAPTER
Thirty-nine

Tay's little feet ran straight out of Noelle's dreams and into the waking world, pattering away down the hall on the other side of the bedroom door.

Except, as she peeled open her eyes, she realized she wasn't in the bedroom. She was in the dining room, where she'd dozed off at the table. With a groan, she lifted her head, a sheet of paper from the diary clinging to her cheek.

She blinked blearily at the collage of notes on the dining room wall, and the night before came trickling back. She'd been trying to piece together the story behind the diary, but she hadn't gotten far.

Pushing to her feet, she tried to stretch the kinks from her body. The one in her neck might require some Vicodin and a massage. She rubbed at it as she shuffled into the kitchen to make some thinking brew. Most people dove straight for the coffee, but she favored green or peppermint tea.

As she waited for the water to warm, she checked her phone. There was a missed text message from Derek at seven this morning:

I wanted to make sure you could use your car if you needed to, so I replaced your tire with a spare.

You'll need a new tire eventually, but this one should get you wherever you want to go today.

His thoughtfulness sent a warm tingle all the way to her toes. She'd never met anyone quite like him. She sent a text back, thanking him, and after a moment of silently arguing with herself, she added,

And thanks for the dance last night. It was unexpected and nice.

She pulled at her bottom lip with her teeth as she waited for his response. Was it awkward for her to send that? His response came a moment later, bringing a smile to her lips.

I had a nice time too, even though you stomped on my foot.

He punctuated the message with a winking smiley face so she would know he was teasing.

Noelle smiled and shot back,

Stepped, not stomped. I think we're having another one of those differing perspect—

She sent the message, not paying attention to whether or not the last word was complete, because her mind was already somewhere else. *Perspective.*

She walked back into the dining room, attention fixed on her notes. She was treating the diary entries like facts, when they were anything but.

Firefly was an unreliable narrator—a child with an isolated and limited understanding of the world, trying to describe the events going on around her. Her perceptions were shaped by the single adult influence in her life: her mother.

The man in the gray hat was a doctor because her mother said he was. The girls were sick because her mother said they were. She couldn't talk to or see the girls because her mother said they needed quiet to get better.

"Her mother said," Noelle muttered.

But despite her mother telling her he was a doctor, Firefly never documented anything about him that supported that. She never mentioned him carrying a medical bag when she watched him coming up the steps, an essential item for house calls. She never saw him perform any kind of exam or procedure. There was nothing in the picture she drew of him that suggested he was an actual doctor.

He was just a man in a gray hat, which begged the question, What if "doctor" was a title fabricated by her mother to keep a curious child from realizing the truth?

How many times had Noelle lied to Tay to keep him from realizing that his father missed dinners and birthdays because he was out with another woman?

Too many times.

It was easy to sate a child's curiosity and soothe their fears with a lie. They didn't know any better.

Noelle's phone slid from her hand onto the table as she studied the storyboard. If Firefly's mother lied, and the doctor wasn't a doctor, then maybe the sick girls weren't sick.

Firefly mentioned one of the girls crying out, but she never mentioned any other sounds from their rooms— no coughing, sneezing, or retching. Sick people weren't silent . . . unless they were sedated.

It was possible Firefly heard other noises and chose not to note them, but given how she reacted to that single cry, sounds coming from those rooms were important to her. Those girls were her potential friends, and she cared about them enough to break her mother's rules when one of them cried out.

Noelle dragged the diary closer and flipped back through the entries, searching for that particular encounter. Emma had said, "Help me," and Sarah had echoed her plea with, "We need help."

Neither of them asked for a doctor or a nurse, for medicine or pain killers. They asked for help. Firefly's mother said the girls were ill and needed quiet to heal, and yet none of them ever got better, a curious fact that Firefly noticed even if she didn't question it.

Was the illness a ruse to prevent Firefly from talking to them and finding out something her mother didn't want her to know?

The teapot whistled, drawing Noelle's attention to the kitchen. She set down the crayon and went to fix her thinking brew. She breathed in the minty aroma as she returned to her storyboard.

Setting her tea on the table to steep, she picked up the pink crayon and focused on Firefly's mother. "What's going on in that house? What are you doing?"

If the entry about the argument was accurate, Firefly's mother wasn't in control of whatever was happening in the house. But she *was* complicit.

Are you sure? Noelle's inner voice whispered, challenging her to reevaluate what she thought she knew once again.

Firefly's mother hated her job, and she was plagued by nightmares, during which she desperately apologized to someone. To whom—the girls?

"If she hated what was happening in that house, why not take her daughter and leave?"

Maybe she couldn't.

"She was chatting with people online. If she was in a dangerous situation, she could've asked for help."

Sometimes victims don't know how to ask for help.

"Victim?" That was a ridiculous thought. "How is this woman a victim? She was obviously involved in something awful. She was probably lying to her own daughter about everything." She picked up the diary and turned back through each entry. "Lying to her, controlling her relationships, never letting her outside, confining her to their room . . ."

To protect her.

The thought struck her as she reached the inscription on the inside cover: "light of my life." This woman's daughter was precious to her, a bright spot in what she must've felt was a dark and miserable existence. What if everything she did was to protect and preserve that innocent light.

She told Firefly to forget the bad things she saw or heard, to listen to music whenever "the nurses" came to check on the girls, to stay quiet and out of sight when the doctor or his nurses—always men—were in the house.

Not her. Anyone but her, Firefly's mom had pleaded, stepping between Dr. Gray and her daughter. It was something Noelle might say if she were stepping between her child and a threat. Not him, not my child.

It was after that incident that someone told Mister they wanted to see Firefly. Her mother pleaded for a chance to find someone else—someone other than her daughter.

She was doing everything she could to protect her child from their dark world, even if that meant essentially imprisoning her in their room to separate her from people she perceived as dangerous, and lying to shield her from the truth. A truth that gave her nightmares and left her riddled with regret.

Nausea crawled the walls of Noelle's stomach as the pieces began clicking together, and she thought she might vomit.

Lord, let me be wrong. Maybe I'm interpreting the details incorrectly. Maybe this isn't what I think it is.

But something told her she wasn't mistaken.

The man in the gray hat caught a glimpse of Firefly, and then he approached Mister to make arrangements to *see* her.

"It was going to happen someday," Mister had said, a pronouncement that reduced Firefly's mother to tears.

She was so terrified of what that man was going to do to her daughter that she offered to find a replacement. And when that didn't work, she planned to send her little girl out into the world, a place she'd apparently never been, because she thought it would be safer than the doctor's company.

Noelle's stomach lurched again as she visualized the eerie way Dr. Gray must've looked at Firefly when he handed her the sucker, a predatory gleam that made Firefly nervous.

Those "sick girls" in the other rooms weren't ill, and they didn't have round-the-clock care from a doctor and his nurses. They were kept in those rooms so that men like the so-called doctor could come *see* them—men Firefly's mother tried to hide her from.

Noelle picked up the crayon, blinking as the phrase she added to the storyboard flooded her eyes with tears: sex trafficking.

If she was right, then Firefly was living in a house of horrors, and her mother could no longer protect her.

————

Derek scrubbed his hands over his face and leaned back in his desk chair. He had no new leads on Maddie Wingate. No remains or evidence had been found in the search, and none of the "tips" he'd received after his social media video led anywhere.

He hadn't gained much ground on Jane Doe either.

He flipped open the medical examiner's report and studied the details again, his eyeballs aching from too little sleep. Abbott narrowed the young woman's age to early twenties.

Aside from the DNA beneath her fingernails, there was no foreign DNA on her body and no sign of sexual assault.

Derek read the handwritten note slipped into the folder.

Captain, I know how much you hate medical jargon, so here is a layman's summary. An X-ray of Jane Doe revealed a skull fracture and broken neck, which likely would've resulted in paralysis. Impact bruising on the body suggests the skull fracture and broken neck were caused by a fall during which the body repeatedly struck a hard surface. However, cause of death was asphyxiation. I recovered soil and leaf particulates from her mouth and airway.

Jane Doe had been buried alive. Either her killer was cruel enough to bury her while she was still breathing, or, confusing her paralysis for death, he panicked and tried to hide the body.

Brian's shoe print was at the grave site, but there was only one person Derek could think of with motive to hurt the girl.

If Jane Doe broke into the Bechtel house to explore and refused to leave when Walt confronted her, there could've been a struggle.

Derek could envision the two grappling, Jane slipping and falling down the staircase—each strike against the steps leaving an impact bruise on her body—Walt panicking and dragging her body out to the woods.

He needed to pay Walt another visit at the hospital, but he doubted the man would be any more forthcoming than he had been last night.

If he was right about Jane's death, though, then Noelle's house was a crime scene. A crime scene that he unknowingly helped clean yesterday morning.

But then there were details that didn't line up with his theory—like Jane herself.

She wasn't a local. She was wearing shoes that were so small for her feet that they had to be painful. Hardly something she would wear to break in and explore an abandoned house.

Her left foot was covered in lacerations and dirt, like she'd been running barefoot through nature, but her right foot was unmarked.

"Because she lost a shoe."

Derek opened Maddie's file to find the photo they had taken of the left shoe in the woods. They assumed it belonged to Maddie, along with the sweater fibers recovered from the bush. They'd been searching for Maddie's trail and stumbled across Jane Doe's.

What could've terrified her so much that she could run over a mile, debris slicing into the bottom of one of her feet? She had to be running for her life, but from whom?

Jane was likely the girl the witness saw on the road Friday night. He said he didn't think she was alone. Someone was with her or following her.

"Who were you running from?"

He doubted it was Walt. Her pursuer was most likely young and fit—like Brian or the mysterious Cody. Derek's search for the man's identity using his physical description kicked out dozens of local results, but none of the photos matched. And no one had seen him. He must've decided to finish passing through town after the conversation at the diner.

God, none of this makes any sense. Please help me see what I'm missing.

A knock on the door pulled him from his frustration, and he looked up to see Rusty. He waved him in.

"I thought you might want to know the cell company sent over the information from Maddie's phone."

"Anything useful?"

Rusty pulled a chair around the desk to sit beside him so they could view the information together. "The only text messages she sent were to family and high school friends, none of whom were named Nate, and she didn't place or receive any calls the day she disappeared. She must've communicated with him through a phone app."

Which complicated matters. If they could figure out which app, and *if* the company stored communications between users, they could get a warrant for those records. But that would take a lot of time.

Even then, Derek doubted Nate was the man's real name. Online predators usually lied when creating their profiles—names, pictures, histories, everything. Sometimes they even went as far as to pretend they were women to put potential victims at ease.

"From what the cell company can tell, Maddie didn't have any of those fancy tracking apps downloaded on her phone," Rusty said.

"And none of her social media photos are geotagged." Derek had checked. Her profiles were open for public viewing, but she was smart enough not to broadcast her location with her uploads.

"Right, but the phone company was able to provide a last-known approximate location. Summit Lake in Akron."

A lake, where it was easy to dump a body after dark.

Rusty's grim expression indicated he was thinking along the same lines. "You think she actually went to a lake when it was forty degrees and dark?"

"No, I don't. But maybe her phone went to the lake."

"You think someone dumped it there so that when we pinged her last known location, it wouldn't lead us to them?"

"It's a safe bet. I think whoever she was meeting was between the university and the lake."

Rusty frowned. "There's something that doesn't make sense."

"Just one thing?"

Rusty conceded that point with a sideways tilt of his head. "If she was meeting someone in Akron, and her last known phone location was Summit Lake, how did her car end up here in Cherry Creek?"

Yet another puzzle piece that didn't fit. The dogs hadn't been able to pick up Maddie's scent, and aside from her car, there was no indication she had ever set foot in the village.

"I'm not sure Maddie was ever in Cherry Creek," Derek said. "I'm starting to think that whoever took her dumped her car where they hoped it wouldn't be found."

"And what, walked forty miles back to Akron?"

"They could've asked an accomplice or friend to give them a ride. Or they could've called a cab. Check with the cab companies in Weston, and find out if any of them had pickups in or around Cherry Creek Friday night."

Rusty made a note in his phone. "If our abduction area is between the university and the lake, that's what . . . a three-mile stretch?"

Derek opened a digital map of Akron, Ohio, studying the possible routes from the university to Summit Lake. "Depends on which route she took."

"The search radius for that distance is huge. We can't narrow it down any further than that? What about that Maps app for smartphones? If she'd never met him before, she probably put in an address where she was supposed to meet him."

"I finally managed to log into her Google Maps with her email and password this morning. Someone deleted the history. It's completely wiped."

If Maddie's phone fell into the hands of her abductor, he had quick access to the app, no email or password required. He could simply wipe it and toss it, erasing all traces of himself.

Rusty's phone rang, and he turned away to answer it. "Deputy Ramone." He paused, and then excitement

337

lifted his voice. "You're sure?" Rusty covered the mouthpiece of his phone. "Maddie used her debit card for gas at a BP station in Akron on Friday. Her parents called to get more information on the charge. The gas station was on Grant Street, and the charge was at 8:20 in the evening."

"After she left the dorm room. That gives us her route and brings us down to . . ."—he typed the gas station into the digital map—"2.6 miles from Summit Lake."

Whatever happened to Maddie Wingate likely happened between those two points. It was a lot of area to search, and there was no guarantee she was still in it, but at least they had a starting point.

A text message from Noelle lit up Derek's phone screen:

> I know you're busy, but when you're free, I'd like to talk to you about the diary. It's important.

He texted back that he would call her when he could, then silenced his phone so he could focus on the case.

"I'll contact the Summit County Sheriff's Department and fill them in. We have Maddie's car, but Maddie might still be in their jurisdiction."

Noelle paced the dining room, popping Chex Mix into her mouth and waiting for Derek's call, her anxiety growing.

She could call *him*, but he had a murder and a missing person's case demanding his attention. She had a hunch based on a diary written by a child.

She rubbed her hands together as she reached one wall, spun on her heel, and marched back the other direction, her gaze attached to the storyboard.

Am I really going to dump all this on Derek and try to convince him there's a third person he needs to worry about—a child? All based on my interpretation of that child's diary.

She couldn't prove anything, even with the diary, because it was her interpretation of what was written that led her to her conclusion. Derek might not see the same thing when he read it. He might think she was reaching with her imagination.

But she was certain, all the way down to the ball of nausea rolling around in her stomach, that her conclusion wasn't a result of her creative brain.

Still, indecision warred within her. She needed to focus on something else while she waited, or she would end up pacing herself into an anxiety attack.

"One thing, one thing . . ."

Ben and Jerry. She needed to see if her furry roommates had found their way into the live mousetraps.

She started to leave the dining room, then closed the diary and stuffed it into her back pocket. This house ate things, and with her luck, she would return to the dining room to find it gone, taking all of her nonevidence with it.

Grabbing her lantern, she descended the steps into the basement. She bent down and peered into the live trap to see a brown mouse with oversize ears roaming the inside edges.

"Well, hello there." She tapped a fingernail on the container. "Are you Ben or Jerry?"

Should she take him to a field and let him loose or buy an aquarium so he could enjoy cheese and toys for the rest of his life? What did mice even play with?

Tay would've begged her to keep him, but locking him in a plastic cage didn't seem fair. Of course, neither did releasing him into a field where he might get picked off by predators he didn't have to worry about here.

"What's your preference, Jerry?"

Something thumped above her, and her heart fluttered as she eyed the unfinished ceiling.

It's only the house settling, she reminded herself.

Except, in her experience, houses didn't make the noise she'd just heard. They groaned, creaked, and even whistled, but they didn't thump.

A series of creaks traveled through the floorboards, the rhythm reminiscent of someone walking. Only . . . there were no footfalls.

Fear kicked Noelle's heart into her throat, and she held her breath, listening to the ghostly footsteps.

Someone else was in the house, sliding their feet across the floor like Noelle used to do when she would sneak around at night to explore the off-limits rooms of the houses her parents were renovating.

The only reason to walk like that was to avoid drawing attention to yourself. The intruder knew Noelle was here and was trying to be quiet.

How did they get in? The back door was barricaded, the front door was locked. Did they climb in through a window again? Maybe that was the thump she'd heard.

Noelle reached for her phone or gun, patting herself down, only to realize she had neither. Her gun was in her purse on the dining room table, next to her phone. The only thing she had on her was the diary.

Great. She could give the intruder a paper cut.

She had no way to defend herself down here. She needed to get out of this basement and to her gun.

CHAPTER Forty

Despite the chill hanging in the air, sweat slicked Noelle's palms as she gripped the metal tree rod like a spear and crept up the steps.

She stared at the cracked door, afraid of what she might find on the other side.

With a trembling hand, she pushed the door. It yawned open, and a breath quivered from her lungs as she slipped out of the basement.

She lingered with her back to the wall, trying to gather her nerve. She'd made it up a handful of steps, but it would be a long dash to reach the dining room—to reach her gun.

I can do this.

One step sent a spiderweb of crackles through the floorboards, and she froze, heart fluttering around in her chest like a crazed bird.

If whoever broke in was still inside, there was no way they didn't hear that. She listened for the thunder of approaching footsteps, but the house was silent.

Releasing a tense breath, she tiptoed toward the dining room. She set down the Christmas tree rod and snatched up her phone and gun.

She raced to the back door, pushing everything aside and flinging it open, but then the closet off the kitchen caught her attention. It was open. Again.

Walt had mentioned the closet at the hospital, worried that something had been taken. This was the second time she found it unlatched when it should be closed. What was so important about that space?

It was empty, without so much as a shelf to make it useful as a pantry. A lone hook on the wall for a coat, and nothing more. Unless there was another hidden space stuffed with money, like the one in the basement.

Call the police and run, her inner voice screamed. *Let the police figure it all out.*

But someone from the sheriff's department had searched this house twice and found nothing. If she called them now, they would search and then leave, whispering to each other about the crazy woman who moved into the haunted house.

Heart thudding, Noelle inched forward, wincing with every groan of the floorboards. She shifted the gun in her grip as she reached the closet door. Nudging it the rest of the way open, she peered inside.

A sliver of light seeped between two of the vertical boards of the rear wall, so dim it could've been the glow of a dying candle.

Why would light be coming from a wall?

Noelle ran a hand over the vertical panels, and the rough wood shifted. Her mind lurched. That . . . didn't make sense.

343

She pushed on the wall and the boards realigned, snuffing out the light. When she lifted her fingers, the wall drifted back open—like a door.

Gripping the hook on the rear panel, she pulled, and to her horror, the wall opened with the eerie swishing sound she heard every night, light from behind it flooding the closet.

There was a hidden room behind the false wall, the closet-sized space outfitted with layers of blankets and mounds of pillows.

Memories connected in her mind—the note on her car warning her that she wasn't alone in the house, the rumor about hidden rooms, the unexplainable noises in the middle of the night.

Someone was living inside her walls.

Panic pulsed in her chest where her heart should be, and she fumbled the phone from her pocket and dialed Derek's number. The call went to voice mail. Noelle blew out a slow breath to steady her voice before leaving a message.

Hopefully he would listen to it and get back to her soon. If he didn't, she would call the department and request whoever was available to come check it out.

She disconnected the call and crouched to study the contents of the space more closely.

Her missing battery-operated lantern lit the room, reflecting off protein bar wrappers, empty food cans, and drained water bottles. Crumpled balls of yellow paper sat in one corner, and she scooted forward to reach one, unfolding it to find her grocery and supply list for the store, the one she thought she'd put in her purse.

She *had* put it in her purse on the kitchen counter, and someone had taken it out when she went upstairs to change.

But why?

Lifting the edges of the blankets, she found the vanilla lip balm that disappeared from her coat pocket, a book, and a woman's shoe.

A backpack was stuffed into one corner, and she pulled it closer to examine it. There were reflective strips on the back, probably to catch headlights if the person was walking or riding a bike down a dark street. She rummaged through the contents. Clothes, a dead phone, and the plastic horse she'd kicked down the hall the first night she was here. There was a hole between the ears where a horn used to be.

Maddie's unicorn.

Then she noticed the faded name written on the inside of the backpack: Sarah.

A diary that might've belonged to Emma and Firefly found its way into the woods, a backpack that belonged to a girl named Sarah was stuffed into the wall, Maddie's unicorn was in the house, and an unknown girl was dead.

What did it all mean?

The edge of Noelle's yellow notepad peeked out from beneath the blankets, and she dragged it out, when something behind her creaked and slid.

A band of fear tightened around her chest. Someone was in the kitchen. Releasing the notepad, she squeezed her gun and backed out of the closet, fear seizing her body when she found the tip of a knife pointed at her face.

CHAPTER
forty-one

Noelle's gaze traveled up the length of the long serrated knife to the small girl, whose hands trembled around the grip.

She was barely more than a wisp, maybe nine or ten, with skin as pale as peaches, and white blonde hair tangled in knots.

Could this be Sarah or Emma, or was this . . .

She stole a quick glance at the yellow notepad, recognizing the neat, round handwriting even though she didn't have time to read the words that stretched down the page.

"Firefly?"

The girl's shoulders stiffened, and she slid one foot back, prepared to spin and run.

Noelle tucked her gun into her waistband. "I'm not going to hurt you."

The girl threw her a suspicious look that didn't belong on a child's face.

"My name's Noelle." She retrieved the diary from the back pocket of her jeans and showed it to her. "Do you recognize this?" She opened the cover and pointed to the word *Firefly* inscribed on the inside cover. "Is this you?"

Tears gathered in the girl's blue eyes, but her lips remained pressed together.

Her reaction was confirmation enough, but why wouldn't she answer? Was she unable to speak, or . . .

Quiet as a mouse with a cat in the house, whispered through Noelle's mind, bringing understanding with it. Firefly's mother had instilled a habit of silence for her own protection. Anyone she didn't know and trust was a potential cat—a danger.

Noelle set the diary on the floor. "I don't know what you've been through, or even how long you've been here, but you don't have to be a quiet mouse around me. I'm not dangerous."

The girl's attention bounced from the diary to Noelle in question.

"Yes, I read it. I hoped I could give it back to the little girl who wrote it."

Firefly regarded the blue notebook with longing. It was a gift from her mother, filled with her thoughts and memories.

Noelle slid it across the floor, and it skidded to a stop beside feet covered in multiple layers of socks. "Did you drop it in the woods when you were running?"

Firefly dropped the book she must've taken from Elizabeth's room, along with an orange and a bottle of tea, and clumsily scooped up the diary without lowering the knife, hugging it to her chest.

Noelle considered her knotted hair and filthy clothes. Where was her mother? Why was she alone in this hidden space in a stranger's house?

If the last diary entry was moments before she and her mother planned to flee, then her mother should be here with her. Unless something went wrong.

"Where's your mom?"

Firefly's chin quivered, and she glanced at the open doorway, tears drawing clean streaks down her dirty cheeks.

Noelle followed her gaze to the trees, and confusion twisted through her. The girl in the grave couldn't be Firefly's mother. She was too young—late teens to early twenties. She would've had to give birth when she was twelve or thirteen.

Was it possible a child had given birth to a child, only to die trying to protect her from the same vicious existence that controlled her life?

Lord, why is this world so cruel?

She let her eyes drift heavenward before returning her attention to the wispy girl in front of her. "I'm going to call someone who can help us, okay?"

Firefly shook her head, her tiny face pinched in a fierce frown.

"It's someone from the sheriff's department. They're the good guys."

Before she could dial the number, Firefly surged forward and slapped the phone out of her hand, sending it skidding across the kitchen floor.

"Hey," Noelle protested, but her move to retrieve her phone was cut short when Firefly jumped between them, the knife trembling in her hand.

"Don't," burst from the girl's lips, a small voice laced with desperation. "You can't call anyone."

Noelle remained in a crouch, afraid that even the smallest movement would scare the girl silent again. "Why not?"

"'Cause you'll tell him where I am and he'll hurt me too."

Noelle frowned in confusion. "Why would you think that?"

"He . . . he was here. Before," she said, struggling to pronounce her Rs. "I heard him."

"You mean before I moved in?"

Firefly jabbed the knife at the air accusingly. "After."

The news caught her off guard, and she tried to compile a mental list of who had been to her house, but there were too many people—deputies, Derek, Walt. And that didn't account for anyone who slipped in uninvited.

"You said he'll hurt you too. Is that because he hurt your mom?"

"She told me to hide until she came back, but she never came back. I heard her fall down the steps, and then he dragged her away. I tried to be quiet so he wouldn't find me too." Tears dripped from her chin, and she wiped her nose on her shoulder.

Noelle's heart broke for her. It was bad enough that she lived as a shadow in the walls and behind locked doors, afraid to make a sound, but to hear her own mother be murdered?

"Now he's going to find me and kill me," she cried, her voice a squeak of terror. "I don't want to die."

"I'm not going to let anyone hurt you. Why don't you give me the knife, and we'll sit down at the table and talk. We'll have a snack."

Firefly's eyes trailed to the bag of oranges on the counter, hunger flickering in their depths. She was too thin. She had to be starving.

"I . . . I can't. Mom said not to trust anyone else, and I don't trust you. If I give you the knife, you'll call him."

"I promise you, I w—"

Footsteps thumped up the back porch steps, slow and dragging, and Noelle's heart flung itself against her ribs.

Was it him, the killer?

Firefly must've wondered the same, because panic crossed her face, and she looked around for a place to hide. "No, no, no, he can't find me!"

Noelle drew her gun and shot to her feet, sweat breaking out on her palms at the mere thought of pulling the trigger. But she could do it to protect a child.

The footsteps lumbered closer, one of the porch chairs scraping sideways as someone bumped it, and then a shadow stretched across the kitchen floor as a figure appeared in the doorway.

351

———

Derek filled his mug with coffee in the break room, sprinkling in some sugar for added energy. As he stepped into the squad room, he spotted Deputy Kara Grisham lingering by his office.

She saw him and headed his way, two folders clutched in her hand. "Sir."

"Grisham." He noticed her bloodshot eyes. "Did you sleep last night?"

"No, sir. I had too much on my mind." She pulled a sheet of paper from the top folder and handed it to him. "I finished the regression sketch."

A little girl with blonde hair and blue eyes stared back at him.

"As I was filling in the details, she started to look familiar. I thought I might be unintentionally pulling details from another face I'd seen somewhere, influencing the result. And when I was sketching Jane Doe last night, I kept thinking there was something familiar about her. Then it hit me. I've seen her before."

He gaze lifted to her in surprise. "You know her?"

"No, but I've sketched her."

"I'm not sure I'm following."

"When I was taking my Forensic Art class, the professor had us sketch real missing people, aging them forward and backward. I think we did twenty or so, all different ages, ethnicities, genders. One was a little girl with these physical characteristics, and we age-progressed her based on the last photo taken of her when she was twelve." She pulled out a second sketch and handed it to him. "This is the sketch I did two years ago, aging the girl from twelve to twenty-one."

Derek studied the image. The face was fuller, the hair styled differently, and there was no scar, but this two-year-old sketch was almost identical to his victim in the morgue.

"It wasn't until I started working her age backward that it clicked." She slid a printed photo from the second folder and held it up next to the sketch she'd finished last night. It was the same child, maybe two years apart. "This was the photo we worked from in class."

"I'm hoping you remember her name."

She handed him the second folder. "Natalie Jones. She's been missing for eleven years."

Derek set aside his coffee so he could review the file.

"She disappeared from her foster home in Columbus, Ohio, when she was twelve, which makes her twenty-three years old now," Grisham explained. "Natalie's foster family suspected she was pregnant at the time of her disappearance."

"At twelve years old?" he asked, unable to keep the horror from his voice.

Grisham nodded grimly. "The investigation notes are in there, but no one knows who the father is. When the foster parents confronted her about her pregnancy, she took off. Suspected runaway. I took the liberty of calling the medical examiner to ask if Jane Doe had ever given birth."

"And?"

"There was a bunch of unintelligible medical . . . stuff, but basically he said that Jane Doe's body did go through the birthing process. He couldn't say when exactly or whether or not the baby survived. If the baby did survive, it's possible she gave him or her away at birth. But since she was still considered missing, that adoption . . ."

"Would've been illegal." Meaning the child could be with anyone.

"And if she decided to keep the baby, there could be a ten-year-old child out there whose mother was just murdered."

And that child could be in the hands of a killer. Or worse, already buried in a grave they hadn't found yet.

Derek considered his exhausted deputy. "You stayed up all night to finish that sketch and put this together?"

"Dog with a bone, sir." She smoothed the edge of the empty folder still in her hand. "I know my sketch isn't hard proof like dental or DNA, but I'm certain Natalie Jones is your Jane Doe."

"Abbott will make the final determination, but I agree. Impressive work, Grisham. Now go home and get some rest."

"Thank you, sir." She smiled bashfully at the praise, then turned on her heel and left.

Derek grabbed his coffee and wandered back to his office, devouring the information in the file as he walked. According to her teachers, Natalie had been above average intelligence, compassionate, and timid, but was easily manipulated and pressured by outside influences.

The school counselor reported concerns that Natalie wasn't receiving enough attention in her overcrowded foster home, and that she would often seek attention and affirmation elsewhere, usually with older male students and faculty.

Derek looked at the school picture of twelve-year-old Natalie. Intelligent blue eyes, round cheeks, and no visible scars.

What happened to you, Natalie? And where's your child?

CHAPTER
Forty-two

He stood in the kitchen doorway, one hand against the frame, and the other wrapped around a gnarled walking stick he must've plucked from the yard. The hospital gown hung crooked on his frame, one side drooping down to meet the top of his muddy boot.

The gun shifted in Noelle's sweaty grip as she kept it aimed at Walt's chest. "How did you get here?"

"Hitched a ride." He shifted his weight entirely to the walking stick, planting it between his feet, a hairsbreadth from the threshold. "You can put your gun down. I'm not armed."

For all she knew, his rifle could be resting against the outside of the house like it had been the first night they met. "If you're here to hurt her—"

"I would never hurt Skyler."

Noelle blinked at the name. "I thought Skyler was . . ."

He followed her gaze to the woods. "That was Natalie, Skyler's mother."

Color flooded back into Firefly's panic-bleached cheeks. "What happened, Mr. Walt? Are you sick?" When she saw the white bandage peeking out from behind one ear, her voice pitched higher with fear. "Is the doctor coming?"

"No, no doctor, and no one's sick. It's only a headache." He fixed her with a stern look. "You want to tell me why you're pointing a knife at Noelle?"

"She found our hiding place."

Our *hiding place?*

Noelle looked between them as she lowered her gun. The hidden space was small, but two people could fit if they didn't mind tight quarters. Had Walt been sneaking in and hiding in the wall too?

"Put down the knife, Sky."

The knife dipped but didn't drop. "Mom said not to trust anyone, and she let him in."

"She didn't let him in. He let himself in."

Noelle itched to ask who *he* was, but she waited, watching the interaction between them. There was a warmth in Walt's eyes that she had never seen before. He was being truthful when he said he would never hurt her; he cared about this girl.

"Your mom said you can trust me, and I'm telling you Noelle can be trusted."

"But—"

"She's a good person."

What was happening right now? Walt had tried to frighten her into leaving, and now he was defending her character?

Firefly—or rather, Skyler—hesitated another moment before lowering the knife.

"Okay." She shuffled forward and held out the serrated weapon, her wide blue eyes shining with apology. "I'm sorry I thought you were a bad person, and that I pointed a knife at you."

Noelle floundered for words as she took the knife, but nothing came to mind. This entire situation was surreal.

Skyler rubbed her dirty nose and eyed the bag of fruit on the counter. "Can I have an orange now?"

Noelle waved a hand at the bag of fruit and returned her gun to the waistband of her jeans. She wasn't going to shoot a child, and Walt clearly intended her no harm. "Help yourself."

Skyler dashed to the counter, like she was afraid Noelle might change her mind if she didn't move quickly enough, and stuck a grimy hand into the bag of fruit, snagging an orange.

"Thanks for sharing," she said, and then she snagged a second orange before scampering into the dining room.

She plopped down at the table, her eyes darting to assess every creak and shifting shadow as she tore into her fruit. She was a child too aware of her surroundings, an awareness no doubt borne from the horror of overhearing her mother's death.

Sunlight filtered through the dining room window, highlighting the small bones that were too prominent beneath her pale skin, and Noelle's heart pinched.

"How long has it been since she's eaten?"

Regret deepened the lines of Walt's weathered face. "Too long."

He leaned on the walking stick so heavily that a breeze might blow him over. The weakness and pale complexion were likely from blood loss, but Walt was thinner than he had been two days ago.

"How long has it been since *you've* eaten?" She grabbed the chair she usually kept in front of the door and scooted it closer to him.

He made no move to accept it. "I can't come inside."

"Why not?"

His eyes roamed the walls of the kitchen, familiarity and longing sparking to life before grief and guilt chased them away. "I haven't been inside since my family . . ."

Empathy washed over her. After Tay was killed, she went out of her way to avoid hospitals, so she couldn't blame Walt for not wanting to enter the house where his family was brutally murdered.

"I understand that, but if there's a man out there waiting for an opportunity to kidnap or hurt Skyler, I need to secure this door. If you would rather stay outside, that's fine, but I think she would feel safer if you came in. She trusts you more than me."

The internal struggle played across his face, and then he slid a foot across the threshold.

When Noelle tried to help him to the chair, he swatted away her hand. "I don't need your help."

She gritted her teeth. He made it painfully difficult to like him. He gripped the back of the chair and melted bonelessly onto the seat, looking frailer than he had when she thought he was dead.

"You didn't answer my question." She closed the door, wishing she had taken the time and money already to replace it with something sturdier, and grabbed another chair from the dining room to wedge beneath the knob. "How long has it been since you've eaten?"

He dropped the walking stick to the floor beside him. "I ate last night at the hospital."

"And before that?"

"A few days."

"A few days?"

He was too thin to be missing meals. Then she remembered what the nosy woman at the diner had said about him asking for nonperishable foods at the church Friday night. If he hadn't eaten them himself, then . . .

She looked toward the hidden room, where empty cans were piled in one corner, and then at Skyler. "You gave her all your food, didn't you?"

"Children shouldn't go hungry."

All the times he dropped by, she assumed his sole purpose was to intimidate her, when in reality, he was bringing over whatever food he could scrape together for Skyler.

Noelle grabbed an orange and a bottle of sweet tea and handed them to him. "You could've asked me for help."

"I didn't know you from Eve. I wasn't going to tell you a secret that could get a child killed." He cracked open the tea and gulped down a third of the bottle.

"So all those questions at the hospital . . ."

"I needed to make sure I could trust you."

Presumably, she'd passed his test. "How did she even get here? And how long have you known she was hiding in the wall?"

"I knew she was in the wall because I told her where to hide. My great grandfather's father included that panic room in his building plans, and it's been a family secret for generations."

Understanding dawned. "It's where you hid when the man broke in and murdered your family, wasn't it? That's why no one could find you."

"Yes."

"All these years, people have wondered what happened to you that night, and why you were missing for two days. Why not tell them?"

He placed the cap back on his tea bottle, waiting to speak until it was screwed into place. "Because I was a coward. Lizzy tried to get in, but I was afraid to unlock the door. I hid in there for two days, with nothing but my fear and shame for company."

And he hadn't wanted anyone to know. Noelle reached out to place a comforting hand on his shoulder, but he shifted away.

"Keep your hands to yourself. I don't need your pity pats and sympathy hugs."

Noelle withdrew her hand and folded her arms, trying to squash her innate desire to comfort the hurting. "How did Skyler end up here?"

Walt tore a chunk from the orange peel with his teeth and spat it into his lap. "Sky and her mother showed up Friday night. I was in the pine trees out front when I saw movement around the house. I figured it was kids trying to break in, so I came to tell them off. Instead, I found two scared girls. Skyler's only ten, and Natalie looked like she was barely more than a child herself. She was in rough shape from running through the woods, clothes torn, missing a shoe. And she was terrified. When she saw me, she pushed Skyler behind her and begged me not to hurt her little girl."

They both looked at Skyler, who had discovered the bag of Chex Mix on the table and was shoveling the cheesy pieces into her mouth with hands that hadn't seen soap in days.

"I asked them what they were doing on my family's property, and Natalie told me they needed a place to hide because a man was after them. She said that man wants to sell her daughter, and she had no choice but to run."

Noelle's stomach cramped at the idea of human beings, let alone children, being sold.

"She offered me money, money she stole from them, to help her and Skyler survive. I told her to hide it."

"In the basement wall?"

"You found it then."

"Yesterday."

He grunted. "That was my favorite place to hide things when I was a boy, but you'd be surprised how many other places there are to hide things in this house."

Was there ever a point in his life when he didn't hide things or people?

"I told them they could stay here, and I told Skyler where to hide in case that man showed up while I was gone. I thought I could protect them, that helping them would somehow make up for not protecting my sister."

The admission floored her. "You were a twelve-year-old child, Walt. What were you supposed to do?"

"For starters, I could've opened the door and let her in. But I chose to do what was best for me."

His accusation in the hospital, that people tended to do what was right for them—he'd been talking about himself as much as everyone else.

"Lizzy never forgave me. She survived that night, but I lost her." He worked at the peel on the orange. "I wanted to do what I could for these girls. I walked into town to the white church to see if I could get some canned foods and blankets, and then I stopped by the diner to see about a few free dinners. Trudy's always nice. She fixed up three containers for me, even though it wasn't closing time. But when I got back, I knew something was wrong. I called out, but no one answered. The back door had been kicked open and the grass had been smashed down from the bottom of the porch steps all the way to the woods."

Noelle glanced at the area on the floor where the clean streak had been. "He'd already dragged her out to bury her."

He nodded. "It's a long hike on foot, but I was only gone a few hours. I don't know how he found them so fast. And he keeps coming back for Sky. He wants her and the money they took when they escaped. I try to balance keeping him out of the house and going to town to find food for her. I decided to make the trip to the diner Sunday night. Sky hadn't eaten a meal since Friday, and I knew the few cans of vegetables and beans I got from the church wouldn't be enough."

"Sunday, before or after we met?"

"After." He tore off a slice of orange. "I warned her to be extra careful until I knew whether or not you were working with *him*."

"When did you realize I wasn't?"

"I suspected you were who you said you were after we spoke Sunday night, but I needed to be absolutely sure. Skyler's life was on the line."

Noelle frowned. "If you were pretty sure I wasn't a threat Sunday night, why were you still trying to scare me off the property yesterday?"

Walt lowered his voice to barely above a whisper. "That man murdered Natalie. If you weren't working with him, he would kill you too."

Noelle swallowed her rising fear.

"I thought I scared him off when I shot at him, that it might be safe to leave for a few hours, but it turns out he's hard to scare."

"You shot at him?"

"After he kicked in this door." He tipped his head toward the back door.

Noelle thought she heard a gunshot that night, but the rolling thunder made her question it.

"I don't know if he intended to scare you or kill you that night," he said, "but I couldn't take the chance of him getting inside. Sky's good at being quiet, but she can't help but make some noise."

All the unexplained sounds Noelle couldn't pinpoint—the thumps, creaks, and cries she dismissed as old boards. The footsteps that came and went.

"He's tried more than once to get rid of me. I expect that's why he was sneaking around my property Sunday night." He touched the white bandage on the back of his head with a wince. "I'm always careful, but he got lucky last night."

"Why didn't you go to the police? They could arrest him and protect her."

He gave a derisive snort.

"I know you don't trust law enforcement because they treated you like a suspect before, but Derek didn't have anything to do with that. He's trustworthy."

"I don't trust anyone with a badge. Not even Deedee."

Deedee? She supposed the nickname was accurate, given Derek's initials, but Deedee brought to mind an old woman snapping beans in a back porch rocker while tapping her foot to gospel music, not a burly member of law enforcement.

"Besides," Walt continued, "Natalie begged me not to involve law enforcement."

"Why?"

"She didn't tell me much. Only that she was forced to work for some bad people, and one of the men who helps run the organization is a cop. She had no one to turn to, so she did whatever they told her to do as long as it kept her daughter safe."

Safe because she was locked away in a room with no life outside of her books.

"But then some man saw Skyler and decided he wanted her," Walt said with a growl of disgust. "Natalie tried to negotiate to protect her, but there was nothing she could do. So she packed Skyler up and ran."

Noelle looked at the little girl, who was now making patterns on the table with the remaining Chex Mix. "But how did they get here?"

"She didn't tell me that. I don't know where they came from, what his name is, where he is right now, or who else is involved. You know as much as I know now."

"If you were so worried about Skyler's safety, why not take her to your place?"

"My twelve-foot camper with no lock on the door?" he asked. "She was safer here where he couldn't find her."

She released a long breath as she worked through all the information he'd dumped on her. "If you had managed to scare me away, then what? What was your plan?"

"Protect Sky."

"How?"

"The same way I have been."

"By starving yourself to feed her while she spends weeks, if not months, in that hidden closet with no sunlight or fresh air? That was the best plan you could come up with?"

Walt clenched his jaw.

Of course it was the best he could come up with. For a man suspicious of everyone, and a child who trusted no one, what other plan was there except to hide?

———

Derek reviewed Maddie's and Natalie's cases side by side on his desk. Where was the connection? He was certain there was one, and yet, aside from their physical similarities, nothing stood out.

His office door opened without a knock, and a head popped in. "Sir."

With a sigh, he tore his attention from his work. "Jimenez."

She glanced at the blinking red light on his desk phone, which he'd set to "Do Not Disturb," and then blurted, "Your sister's having a baby."

367

"I'm aware of that. Anyone who's seen her is aware of that."

"No, I mean she's having a baby right now."

He turned his attention back to the case files. "She's not due until November."

"That doesn't negate the fact that a patron from the Cherry Creek Diner just called to tell us she's in labor."

Stunned, his gaze shot back to her. "Labor?"

"The painful process that happens before the baby pops out," she explained, simulating a popping motion with her hands and hips.

"I know what labor is, Jimenez."

"Okay." She shrugged. "You seemed confused, so I thought I would explain. There's an ambulance on the way. They're going to transport her to Weston Community Hospital."

"Okay."

He tried to think through what he needed to do. Call their mother. It wouldn't take her long to get to the hospital, but their sisters lived across the country. They were planning to be here next month, when the procedure was scheduled. And Brian was . . . well, who knew where he was and what he was doing?

He pulled his key ring from his pocket and twisted off the key to the diner. "Do me a favor and go to the diner. Tell Jared, the cook, to shut everything down and kick everyone out. And then lock up."

"I can do that." She drew in a breath to add, "If your sister tells you that she hates you and tries to break your fingers while in labor, don't take it personally."

"It's a C-section, but thank you."

"Oh, good, your fingers will still work for you to approve my time off next week."

"Go, Jimenez."

She grinned and hurried off.

Derek snagged Rusty's attention as he was walking through the squad room. "There's a file on my desk about our Jane Doe. We have her identity. Review it. I need to get to the hospital."

"Everything okay?"

"Trudy's in labor."

Derek grabbed his things and ran out of the building, unsure whether to be worried or excited that he was going to be an uncle sooner than expected.

CHAPTER
forty-three

Noelle pocketed her phone after leaving a message at the department for Derek. They said he was out of the office, but he would get the message when he returned. Along with her multiple voice mails. They asked if she wanted to speak to a deputy, but she didn't know any of them personally, and after hearing that law enforcement was involved in the human trafficking ring that held Skyler and her mother captive for years, she needed to be careful whom she trusted. Any one of them could be *him*.

Walt hadn't even wanted her to call Derek, but she had to call someone, and her father was out of state. She couldn't deal with this alone.

Walt had moved into the dining room, and he and Skyler were playing tic-tac-toe with Chex Mix crackers and pretzels.

Noelle pulled out a chair and sat down across from Skyler. "Who's winning?"

"Every time I almost win, she eats my pieces," Walt said, but there was no bite to his words. He didn't care whether he won or lost.

"It's a dog-eat-dog world," Skyler said with a grin. "I read that in a book." She popped one of his pieces into her mouth and crunched down.

Noelle smiled. "I noticed from your diary that you like to read. Did your mom teach you to read and write?"

"Yeah, and when I'm reading on her Kindle and I find words I don't know, it lets me look them up. I learn new words all the time."

"A Kindle. That's pretty cool."

"Yeah, it's better than paper books. Those don't let me look up words, so I have to skip them. Mom asked and asked and asked if she could have a Kindle, and they finally said yes. And if she does her job really good, they let us buy a book."

"What's your mom's job?"

Skyler shrugged. "She chats with people online."

"What kinds of people?"

"Other girls."

The unease in Noelle's stomach grew. If Natalie's job for the traffickers was chatting with other girls online, did that mean she was luring new victims? That would explain why she hated her job. Being forced to lure girls into a life of slavery would give anyone with a conscience nightmares.

"I bought *James and the Giant Peach* 'cause it's my favorite," Skyler said, placing a pretzel on the imaginary game board. "James lived in a bad house with mean people, too, but he makes friends and rolls away in a giant peach."

Noelle could see why she loved the book so much. It was similar to her own life, only James was able to escape.

"Can you tell me about your bad house?"

371

Skyler's shoulders scrunched inward, as though the memory of that place made her want to be smaller—invisible. "I don't know."

"Was there anything you liked about it?"

"Mmm, Mom and me had blue curtains in our room. They were see-through, but they were still blue, and we had our own bathroom. And sometimes I got presents. Like my diary and my backpack, and my drawing pad with colored pencils. It already had pretty pictures in it, and I hung them on the bedroom wall. It was like two presents at the same time."

It probably had drawings in it because it belonged to another girl. Noelle would guess her mother took whatever the victims were brought in with and recycled them so her daughter could have the experience of receiving gifts. The thought was heartbreaking on so many levels.

"What *didn't* you like about that house?"

Skyler slid a pretzel around on the table, stalling. "Always being stuck in the room and not being allowed to go outside. I wasn't allowed to talk to the other girls or see them. And I didn't like the doctor or the boy nurses who came over all the time."

Noelle glanced at Walt, whose expression mirrored the disgust she felt for those people. "Do you remember what the house looks like?"

"Boring white with ugly dead plants on the porch. And it has bars on the windows."

"Did any of the other houses you could see have barred windows?"

"No. When I asked Mom why we had bars on the windows, she said it was so bad people couldn't get in." She flicked the pretzel across the table. "But I don't think that was true, 'cause if it was, we wouldn't have had to run away."

They had finally reached the issue that concerned Noelle most: the looming threat. She needed to know who was hunting Skyler. But she would have to probe gently.

"Earlier, when you said they let you buy a book, who did you mean? Can you tell me who *they* are?"

Skyler lowered her head and shook it, unable or unwilling to talk about the people who made the decisions in the house.

"Bad people can be scary, but sometimes all it takes is a brave person to stand up and tell on them. I think you're pretty brave."

Skyler's eyes rounded. "You do?"

"I do."

"So do I," Walt agreed.

Silence lengthened as Skyler seemed to struggle with whether or not to talk about *them*. "There's a lot of bad people," she finally said.

"What about the man who yelled at your mom sometimes?"

Skyler rubbed her upper arm. "He gets real mad sometimes. He hurt my arm when I was talking to Emma, and . . . he yelled at Mom here too. And then . . . he pushed her down the steps."

Mister, the mystery man from the diary, was searching for Skyler himself rather than sending someone else. This must be personal for him.

"He wants to take me back so the doctor can hurt me. Mom said that's why we had to leave." Skyler looked between her and Walt with tear-filled eyes. "Why do they want to hurt me? I didn't do anything wrong."

Noelle's chest tightened with emotions she tried to hold back. "No, honey, you didn't. And we're not going to let anyone hurt you."

Skyler sniffled and smeared tears across her cheeks with her sleeve.

"Can you tell me anything more about the bad man? His name or what he looks like?"

"Mom calls him names I'm not s'pose to say. Bad word names. Sometimes she calls him Mister. And he's old. More older than you but not as old as Mr. Walt. And he has a weird mouth."

"What do you mean by weird?"

She shrugged again. "Funny looking."

No name, and nothing more to the description than old with a weird mouth. The man could walk right up to the house, and she wouldn't know he was a threat. But Skyler would recognize him.

"He was real mad the night we ran away."

Noelle rested her arms on the table. "What happened that night?"

Skyler shrank down in her chair. "We left Mom's friend."

"Your mom had a friend living there?"

Skyler shook her head. "They chatted online for a long time, talking about God, and Mom invited her over."

In the diary, Skyler mentioned her mother chatting with a friend about God. Could the girl she invited over to the house be that same friend? "Does your mom invite a lot of girls to the house?"

"No. She usually says she'll meet them somewhere else, but she never goes. This was the first time she invited someone to the house. But then she told the guys that Madz was going to meet them at a park. I was sad 'cause I wanted to meet her, but later, after two of the guys went to pick up Madz, she showed up at the house by herself. And it was just me and Mom and Mister and the other man."

If Natalie was planning an escape that night, she would've wanted to reduce the amount of resistance she would face. Her deception about "Madz" cut the resistance in half.

"This friend that came to visit that night, her name is Madz?"

Skyler nodded. "Madz4unicorns. That's her chat name."

Madz was a common nickname for Maddie, wasn't it? Noelle opened the picture of Maddie on her phone and showed it to Skyler. "Is this her?"

"Yeah. We were in the kitchen when she knocked on the door. Mister and his friend grabbed her when she came inside. They yelled at my mom for being stupid. But she wasn't stupid. She's really smart. She taught me to read

375

and write, and she even taught me to count, but I'm not very good with numbers."

Hope fluttered in Noelle's chest. Maddie's disappearance and the diary *were* connected, which meant Derek might be able to find her.

"Is Madz still at the bad house?"

"I didn't want to leave her," Skyler said, her voice cracking with tears. "She was scared and crying for help like Emma and Sarah. I wanted to help her, but Mom said we couldn't."

"It's okay, honey."

Walt dipped his head to meet her eyes. "That's not your fault. You were supposed to listen to your mom, and you did right."

"What happened next?"

Skyler wiped her nose on her sleeve. "Mister and the man with the badge took Madz upstairs."

Noelle's stomach cramped. *The man with the badge.* Was he the reason Natalie didn't trust law enforcement? Was he a cop, a deputy, some sort of security officer?

"Mom got the keys Madz dropped by the door and our stuff and dragged me out to the car with the unicorn in the window. We drove until the car stopped working."

"And then you ran here."

"Yeah. My backpack got stuck on a branch, and all my stuff fell out. I tried to pick it all up, but Mom said we had to hurry." She slid out of the chair and scampered back to the hidden room, returning with the plastic unicorn. "But I saved Madz's unicorn from the car, even though I accidentally broke the horn." She set the toy on the table between Noelle and Walt. "Do you think if I give it back to her, she'll forgive me for leaving her?"

Noelle wrapped an arm around her tiny shoulders and hugged her. "There's nothing to forgive, sweetheart."

Walt leaned toward Noelle and whispered, "She can't stay here while you wait for Deedee to call you back. *He* knows she's here, and as soon as he realizes she's no longer hiding, he'll come for her."

His words made her pulse quicken. She couldn't put Skyler back in that closet-sized space, and she couldn't sit here waiting for Derek. She needed to get Skyler somewhere safe. But where was safe, when she had no idea who was and wasn't involved?

CHAPTER
Forty-four

He sat on a chunk of wood in the cornfield, binoculars trained on the window that allowed him a glimpse into the house.

He'd opened the curtains when he was inside last night, and she hadn't noticed yet.

What he wouldn't give to be inside right now rather than hunkered in the field across the street, peering through windows like some hormonal teenager hoping to catch a girl getting ready for bed. He was tired of this. He had better things to do.

He'd considered arranging a fatal accident for Noelle, but then he remembered that everyone could be useful under the right circumstances.

The look on her face when she found his note under her windshield wiper still amused him. When he let her know she wasn't alone in the house, he expected her to try a little harder to find the places where someone could hide.

What woman wouldn't be paranoid that a pervert might be hiding in her walls?

He'd only been able to search the house twice, once the night he tracked the girls there with the spyware tracker he'd placed on Natalie's phone—should she ever grow a spine and try to escape—and last night.

He'd gone to all that work, watching the old man so he could bash him over the head and get him out of the way in order to get inside the house, and still he found nothing. The kid was in there somewhere, hiding in the walls like a rat, and now that Natalie was dead, she was the only one who knew where the money was.

He was running out of time. If he didn't bring the kid and the money back, someone would find his body . . . in a dumpster. Sophia didn't take kindly to her houses being in a state of disorder, and she would have him shot.

He squinted through the binoculars at the window when he caught movement. Was that . . . the kid? It was too small to be Noelle.

Excitement shot through him, and he shifted closer to the road. There was a chance he could fix this mess after all.

The door opened and Noelle stepped out, visually scanning the property. She was nervous, adjusting the strap of her purse on one shoulder and her fingers twitching around the gun in her other hand.

He let out a growl of frustration. That gun again.

When a blonde head poked into view behind Noelle's hip, his fingers tightened around the binoculars.

"Hello, Skyler."

Noelle turned out to be useful after all. It was too bad she wasn't younger, or he would find other uses for her. They did have one open room. Without Natalie, he was going to have to find other means to acquire new girls, but Noelle was too old to be worth the effort.

He leaned forward, eager to grab the kid and the money, but if he moved too soon, Skyler would disappear back

379

into her hiding place, and then he would have to torture its location out of Noelle.

Patience, he told himself. Once they were out of the house, there was nowhere to hide.

Noelle wrapped an arm around Skyler and ushered her down the steps to the car, helping her into the backseat.

A car trip. Perfect. Things were finally working out in his favor.

CHAPTER
Forty-Five

Noelle backed out onto the road, scanning every inch of their surroundings for *him*. Skyler described him as older with a funny mouth, but that could be anyone. Someone with bad teeth, a crooked jaw . . .

"Where are we going?" Skyler asked from the backseat, straining against her seat belt to see out every window.

The safest place Noelle could think of was the diner—full of people, with a windowless office in the back that locked. They could wait for Derek there. He could protect Skyler, and hopefully she could tell him something more that would lead them to Maddie.

She glanced in her rearview mirror, expecting to find the stretch of country road behind them empty, but there was a blue car closing the distance between them.

Fresh fear gripped her. She recognized that car. She looked for another road, but with trees on one side and a cornfield on the other, there was nowhere to turn off.

"Noelle," Skyler said, voice rising with anxiety as she twisted in her seat to see behind them. "There's a car."

"I know, honey." She pressed harder on the gas pedal, but there was no chance she could outrun the vehicle behind her.

Was he going to force them off the road so he could take Skyler? Would he kill Noelle to eliminate witnesses? Why was he doing this? Why get involved with such evil people when he had everything to lose? Peeling her tight fingers from the wheel, she dialed Derek's number again.

Please, please, please.

Voice mail.

She disconnected and tried speech-to-text, hoping he would take time to glance at his phone and see the urgency of her text. "Derek, I think Brian's following me."

A rumbling engine and a flash of movement was her only warning before a truck launched out of the cornfield to their left and smashed into the side of the car.

Noelle's head bounced off the driver's window, and the world blurred as the car skidded off the road and over the ditch, the front end folding around a tree.

Ears buzzing, Noelle groaned and tried to lift her head from the airbag. Her neck ached, and her forehead burned. Blood trickled down into her eyes, distorting her vision.

"Noelle." A small hand shook her shoulder. "Noelle, he's coming."

Noelle turned her head with a muffled cry of pain and blinked at the figure striding toward the car. She patted the passenger seat for her purse and gun, but the impact had sent them sliding into the floorboard.

No, she couldn't let this happen. She couldn't let him take her.

Get up. Get up, she cried silently, but her body refused to obey her commands.

The back door swung open, and Skyler screamed. A man's voice shouted, "What are you doing?"

Gunshots erupted, the booming exchange triggering an explosion of pain in Noelle's head. The shouts, gunshots, and screams melded into deafening white noise, and she thought her skull might crack apart.

The world blinked in and out—a ragged voice speaking, the wail of sirens, a whisper, "I tried. I'm sorry, I tried." And then everything faded into blackness.

———

Derek opened the door to Trudy's hospital room. He expected to find her distressed about her premature labor, but she had the air of a woman at the beach—reclined back, flipping through a magazine, and fanning herself with one of the magazine inserts.

"Tru, are you okay?"

She draped the magazine over her stomach. "They gave me something to stop the contractions, but they recommend delivering him sooner rather than later. He's developed enough that he'll be all right."

"He?" Visions of tossing a ball around and going fishing with his nephew played through his mind. "The baby's a boy?"

"I told them I wanted to be surprised, so don't go getting your hopes up. You could be playing hopscotch and attending ballet recitals."

"I'll be happy with either. As long as he or she is healthy." He took her hand. "Is there anything I can do to help make you more comfortable while you wait for surgery?"

She wiggled her toes beneath the blanket. "You can rub my feet."

"I'm not going near your feet."

"Why not?"

"Because I didn't bring a gas mask."

"Ha-ha. They don't smell *that* bad."

"Agree to disagree."

She smiled, but it quickly dimmed. "I know Brian's been . . . difficult lately, but I need him to be here. I need my husband here when I come out of surgery with our baby." Regret flashed across her face. "I don't want you to think you're not enough, but it's—"

He squeezed her hand. "I understand."

Her shoulders relaxed and the smile returned. "You really are my favorite brother."

"Even though I won't rub your feet?"

"Even though." She lifted her phone from the tray beside her bed and dialed, her lighthearted mood fading when Brian didn't answer. She didn't leave a message. "Maybe he's mad at me for not coming home last night. Can I try from your phone?"

"If he sees the call is coming from my phone, he might ignore it, but you can try." He passed his cell to her.

She unlocked the screen with the code only he was supposed to know and checked the notifications at the top. "Good grief, do you ever check your messages?"

"I've been a little busy investigating a homicide and kidnapping."

"Worst excuses I've ever . . ." Her eyebrows pinched as she stared at his screen.

"Are you reading my messages?"

A note of concern touched her voice as she scrolled. "You need to call Noelle."

"Why?"

"Something's wrong. One of her texts says she found a little girl in her closet, and the most recent one says, 'Derek, I think Ryan is following me.' Who's Ryan?"

Not Ryan. *Brian.* Derek snatched his phone and dialed Noelle's number, pacing to the doorway as it rang. It clicked over to voice mail.

"You've reached Noelle's voice mail. I can't—" He disconnected and redialed, only to receive the same message.

Why was Brian following her? And what did she mean she found a little girl in her closet? He listened to her voice mails, his sense of dread growing with the urgency of her voice.

He called Rusty, who picked up almost immediately. "Rusty, where are you?"

"I'm heading over to the Bechtel house. The more I think about it, the more I think that might be where Jane Doe, or . . . Natalie, was killed. The shoes she was wearing are a '60s design. There's a good chance they belonged to Elizabeth Bechtel and that she got them from the house. The impact bruises on her body could be from falling down a flight of stairs. There's only one flight of stairs within a half mile of where she was bur—"

"Rusty, listen to me." He stepped out into the hall and closed the hospital room door. "I got a bunch of voice mails and text messages from Noelle. She's not picking up when I call her back. I need you to find her and make sure she's okay."

Silence stretched, and Derek was about to repeat himself when Rusty let out a curse. A door slammed, and heavy breathing filled the line. Was he running or having a heart attack?

"Russ, what's going on?"

Urgency flooded the older man's voice as he spoke into his radio. "Dispatch, I need an ambulance on Benton Road near the Bechtel house." A gasping pause. "Make that two."

Rustling and muffled voices filled the background, and Derek's blood chilled as Rusty relayed the code every law enforcement officer dreaded—*officer down.*

———

A fist of fear squeezed Derek's chest as doctors and nurses swarmed the gurney that the paramedics wheeled into the emergency room. Blood and bandages were all Derek could see before they whisked the patient away through a set of doors.

This was the first time any of his officers had been shot. It was a fear that lingered in the back of his mind every time one of his people left on an emergency call.

And it was Brian.

His baby sister's husband.

Jesus, was the only thing that penetrated the chaos of his thoughts. No scripture, no prayer, just the name that represented everything he needed right now.

The emergency room doors hissed open, and Rusty walked in, blood smeared across his hands and one side of his face.

Derek crossed the room to meet him. "Are you all right?"

Rusty's expression was grim. "Better than everyone else."

"What happened?"

"I don't know all the details yet. Brian was shot twice, once in the abdomen, once in the shoulder. He was in and out of consciousness when I rolled up on the scene."

"Describe the scene to me."

"Ms. McKenzie's Volkswagen collided with a tree. She was unconscious at the wheel, but she's going to be fine, according to the paramedics."

Derek released a breath of relief.

387

"Brian's car was a few feet behind hers, but he was slumped against the outside of her driver's door."

"Did she wreck or did Brian force her off the road?" Derek asked, trying to stitch these pieces together with Noelle's last text message. Had she shot Brian to protect herself?

"Neither. She was hit from the side. The offending vehicle left black paint on the side of her Volkswagen, and judging by the height of the contact, it was a truck."

"Was she at an intersection?"

"No, it came out of the cornfield and right for her. The terrain kept him from picking up too much speed, or the outcome could've been worse."

"How did Brian get shot?"

Rusty tilted his head. "He wasn't making a whole lot of sense when he was trying to tell me what happened. Something about the truck driver taking a little girl. He tried to stop it, the guy shot him. There's no sign a child was ever in the car, and as far as I know, Ms. McKenzie doesn't have a daughter. I think he was delirious."

Derek shook his head as he tried to process everything. "Ten years ago, Natalie Jones gave birth to a child."

"And you're thinking if she was here, her child probably was too."

"According to one of the voice mails Noelle left me, she found a ten-year-old girl in a hidden room of the house."

"And someone ran Ms. McKenzie off the road so they could take her?"

"I'm guessing the same person who killed Natalie." Derek ran his hands over his hair and gripped the back of his neck. "Did Brian say anything else helpful?"

"It was a bit scrambled, but he said something about seeing *her* on the road, and when he found out she was dead, he was afraid how it would make him look."

That was what Brian had lied about during the interrogation. It was his blue car on the road Friday night. He saw Natalie when she was still alive. No wonder he drank himself into a stupor after the interrogation.

"And he was mumbling something about trying to be a husband who deserves his wife, making amends. He wanted Trudy to know that he loves her," Rusty recounted.

Derek squeezed his eyes shut. Had Brian been following Noelle because he was planning to apologize to her, to make amends for the easiest offense and work his way up to Trudy? Was he on that road, in the line of fire, because of what Derek said to him last night?

But if he hadn't been on that road, would the truck driver have killed Noelle like he murdered Natalie? Did Brian's presence force him to change his plans?

As if his thoughts had summoned her, Noelle limped through the emergency room doors. Derek's heart constricted at the sight of her, blood on her forehead, tears streaking her face.

Deputy Jimenez brushed past her and up to Derek, returning his keys to the diner. "She wouldn't come in the

389

ambulance, but that head needs looked at, so I insisted on giving her a ride."

Noelle limped toward him, and Derek covered the remaining distance, wrapping her in his arms. She cried into his shoulder. "He took her, Derek. He took Skyler."

"I know." He gave her a moment to cry before asking, "Did you see the driver or what he was driving?"

She drew back, wiping at her cheeks. "I didn't see him, but it was a black truck. We have to find her, Derek."

A black truck wasn't much to go on, but he couldn't tell her that right now. "We will, but first let's get you checked out by a doctor."

"No, there's no time."

"Noelle—"

"You don't understand what that place is, who those people are. They're holding girls in that house, Derek, forcing prostitution. Natalie and Skyler escaped, and that man who took her is a human trafficker. We need to find her now."

Derek's stomach bottomed out. "We don't know where to look."

Noelle ran shaking hands over her hair, thinking, and then something clicked in her expression. "The traffickers forced Natalie to lure girls. I'm not sure where, but the last girl she lured, she gave her the address to the house so she could use her car and the distraction to escape. That girl was Maddie. Wherever Maddie is, that's where he's taking Skyler." She searched both of their faces. "Please tell me you have some idea where Maddie is. If not a neighborhood, at least a city."

"We have a search area," Rusty said. "But we don't know what to look for *in* that search area."

Noelle sucked in a breath. "I do. I know what to look for."

CHAPTER
Forty-six

Noelle stared at the drawing in her lap, willing answers to spring from the page. But there was only so much detail in a ten-year-old's artwork.

The buildings were crooked scribbles of color with dark squares for windows, and an angled sign rose above them with what looked like the word "Mart" on it. It was hard to be sure with the letters smooshed together at an angle.

There were dozens of businesses in Akron with those letters in the name, but most smaller businesses couldn't afford that kind of raised sign.

Wal-Mart, a closed K-Mart, Drug Mart.

Noelle let her eyes wander over the streets and buildings as Derek drove, searching for anything to point them in the right direction.

"Come on, Skyler. Where are you?"

This city was too large, and their map wasn't as helpful as she'd hoped. What if they were too late to help Skyler and Maddie? What if the girls had already been moved somewhere else?

Skyler's abductor had a head start, further lengthened by the time it took Derek to fill Trudy in on her husband and then find an unmarked car that wouldn't stand out in this part of Akron.

"Noelle."

Derek lifted a finger from the steering wheel to indicate a distant sign. It was bright yellow with white letters that read "Mature Mart."

Noelle compared it to the drawing. "I think that's it, the sign she sees from her window every day."

"But she only sees the last part of the sign, which puts her somewhere east of it, outside of our original search radius." He turned onto an intersecting street.

Noelle closed her eyes, a prayer rising up from deep inside. *God, please help us. Please help us find Skyler.*

"What did she tell you about the house when you spoke with her?" Derek asked.

"That it's white with dead plants on the porch, barred windows, and sheer blue curtains."

"Barred windows aren't uncommon in high-crime areas, unfortunately."

Neither are white houses, she realized.

They crawled down one street after another, slowing in front of every white house, but the surroundings looked nothing like the drawing.

"What about that one?" Derek asked, lifting a finger from the steering wheel.

Noelle considered the house and then the brick duplex across the street. "Maybe, but . . . there's a balcony on the duplex that isn't in the picture. And the house to the right is pink, not yellow."

393

Derek offered her a sympathetic glance. "We need to consider that she might have used whatever colors she had, and maybe she doesn't know how to draw a balcony."

Noelle pulled the corner of her lips into her mouth, chewing so hard it was going to leave sores. He was right. Skyler was only ten. They couldn't treat this drawing like a map, because it wasn't one.

She studied the white Victorian with potted plants on the steps—live potted plants. "I don't know."

She rubbed at her aching head and tried to avoid the butterfly bandages the paramedics had applied. She needed stitches, but she could get those after Skyler was safe.

A flash of blue caught her eye as a little girl disappeared around the house at the end of the block. Something about her tickled a memory.

"Go around to the next street. I think I saw something."

Derek did as she requested, and they both studied the hopscotch squares drawn on the sidewalk in various colors of chalk. The children's game wrapped around to the next street, where the little girl with a blue coat hopped from one square to the next.

The sight of her brought the slippery memory into full focus. Skyler mentioned in one of her journal entries that she wanted to play with the little girl in the blue coat across the street.

Noelle took in the brick duplex and yellow house, hope pumping through her veins. Across the street was a white house with dried-up plants and metal bars over the upstairs windows.

"Stop. This is it. This has to be it."

She reached for the door handle, eager to rescue Skyler from these monsters, but Derek placed a hand on her shoulder.

"We can't barge in there, Noelle. We have no idea what we could be up against."

"Skyler only mentioned four guys in the house."

"That she saw that one night. That could change at any time. And not only that, this isn't my jurisdiction."

Outrage rolled through her, and her grip tightened on the door handle. "I don't care about jurisdiction. I care about saving that little girl before they destroy her. I care about finding Maddie before she's lost in that nightmarish world of human trafficking where the life expectancy is seven years." Tears burned her eyes. "We can't just sit here."

"I know you want to save them. So do I. But if we bust in there and something happens to either of us, these guys will disappear with those girls in a heartbeat, and we will never find them. We need enough people to cover every exit, so let me call for backup before you do anything."

She hated his logical, sensible approach to the situation, because it meant she had to wait, no matter what was happening inside that house.

She released the door handle, her fingers stiff from gripping so tightly. "Fine."

While he called in the local authorities, Noelle's gaze bounced between the upstairs windows. Where were the blue curtains? Had someone ripped them down after Sky and her mom ran away? Was this the wrong house? She desperately wanted to see Skyler's pale face and blonde hair appear in one of the windows. Was she okay? Had she already been hurt?

Hinges squeaked and a door slammed, yanking Noelle's attention down to the front porch. She froze in her seat when she recognized the man who slipped outside for a smoke. The friendly man with the cleft scar on his top lip who picked up the note the wind snatched from her fingers outside the lawyer's office. He was the one who mentioned hidden rooms in the house. She thought he was being helpful when in reality he was planting the idea because he needed her to find Skyler's hiding place for him.

He pressed a cigarette between his lips and lit it, his gaze tracking the hopscotch girl as she skipped down the sidewalk.

His attention drifted past the beat-up car Derek had borrowed for this trip, and then snapped back, recognition crossing his face. The cigarette tumbled from his lips, and he reached behind him.

Noelle sucked in a breath when he drew a gun from his waistband. "Derek."

"Down!"

Panic flooded her as her mind flashed to the hopscotch girl. "Where's the—"

Derek threw an arm over her and dragged her down in the seat an instant before gunfire erupted.

––––––––

The first shot shattered the driver's side window, sending a shower of glass into the car.

Derek kept a hand pressed between Noelle's shoulder blades, her body trembling beneath his palm, as bullets pinged against the car and ricocheted off the sidewalk.

Derek fumbled his gun from his holster with his left hand, his thoughts as rapid as the spray of bullets. *Assess the shooter's position and try to put him down with one shot, protect Noelle, check on the child playing on the sidewalk. Don't get shot in the head.*

A final bullet shattered the rear window and punched into the leather upholstery of the backseat.

A static hum filled Derek's ears, and then the sounds of the world rushed back in—a car alarm blaring, heavy breathing beside him, someone screaming in the distance.

Derek lifted his head toward the porch in time to see the shooter retreat through the screen door into the house.

With Walt and Brian removed as suspects, he expected to find Cody or Nelson, but the shooter was someone he hadn't given a second thought to—the man who spoke with Noelle outside the lawyer's office.

Noelle straightened, glass falling from her hair like glitter. She stared at him with wide eyes, a breath away from hyperventilating, but then her breathing slowed, and she choked out, "The girls."

Now that the house's location was exposed, any girls being held inside were a liability. It would be easier to kill them than take them, and it only took a split second to end a life with a bullet.

"We can't wait for backup," Derek said. They wouldn't arrive in time. If there were four assailants in that house, there wasn't much hope he could protect the girls until backup arrived, but he was going to try.

He wiped the back of his hand against the warm wetness of his temple, where a piece of exploding glass sliced him, and then flung open his door and climbed out.

Out of the corner of his eye, he saw the child in the blue jacket disappear into the duplex with a woman. Good, that was one girl safe.

Noelle rounded the car. "I'm coming with you."

He glanced at the revolver trembling in her right hand. She had no business being in a potential firefight, but he didn't have time to argue with her. "These guys won't hesitate to kill you."

"I know."

"Stay close." He sprinted across the street and up the steps onto the porch.

Heavenly Father, be our shield, he sent upward, because they were walking into a battle with no body armor and limited ammunition.

He opened the door and glided soundlessly into the house. Noelle followed, catching the screen door a second before the spring could slam it shut.

The inside of the house was as worn down as the outside—yellow wallpaper torn away in jagged strips, ash burns on the walls from snubbed cigarettes, stained carpet, and a lingering smell of smoke and liquor in the air.

Noelle gasped and picked up something from the floor, stuffing it into her sweatshirt pocket. Derek caught a glimpse of rainbow-colored hair before hushed voices drew his attention toward the ceiling.

"You let yourself get followed by a cop?"

"I wasn't followed. I don't know how he found us. But it doesn't matter anyway, because he's dead. I unloaded my clip into his car. There's no way he survived that."

"It doesn't matter? It doesn't matter?!" A grunt preceded the sound of stumbling feet. "You shot up the street. Even if you did manage to hit him, it's only a matter of time before more cops show up. We can't stay here."

"Don't push me."

"Really? You're worried about a little push? Sophia's going to kill you when she finds out about this mess. You cost her six good pieces of merchandise *and* lost her money."

"What do you mean six good pieces of merchandise? Natalie's the only one dead, and nobody wanted her ugly face anyway."

"These girls can identify us, and dragging them along is going to make it too hard to disappear."

Noelle sucked in a breath. They had confirmation that the girls were here—six of them—and for the moment, they were alive.

"Do you have any idea how hard I worked to get that little brat back? I'm lucky I don't have pneumonia, and my foot is still throbbing from that walking corpse's animal trap. And now you want to get rid of her?"

"It's not my fault you screwed everything up as usual. Now go take care of the girls. I'll get the money. We need to . . ."

The floor in front of the kitchen entrance creaked beneath Derek's foot, and he stilled.

"Did you hear that?" Silence stretched as the men listened, and then footsteps pounded down the stairs.

Derek nudged Noelle into the kitchen and backed in after her, ducking behind the edge of the wall with his gun at the ready. The bigger of the two men, the shooter, reached the bottom of the steps first.

The smaller man, whose cold eyes and hard posture exuded authority, fell in line beside him and squinted toward the front of the house. "Go make sure that sheriff's as dead as you think he is."

"Not dead, but solid effort," Derek called out. "Reinforcements are on the way. Put your guns on the floor so we can end this without bloodshed."

The smaller man spat in the direction of his partner, "No way he survived, huh? You can't do anything right." He raised his gun, but before he could aim, Derek squeezed off two shots. The first one hit the man in the shoulder, and the second one dropped him to the floor.

A bullet sizzled past Derek's head into the wall, dumping another shot of adrenaline into his veins. That was too close.

The big man scrambled through the living room archway and took cover behind the wall. "We can make a deal, Sheriff."

"The only deal I'm interested in involves you handcuffed in the back of a cruiser."

"That's not a deal, it's a life sentence."

"It's better than the life you planned to sentence these girls to."

Noelle tried to slip past him, her eyes on the staircase, but he held her back. This guy would shoot her before she made it to the third step.

"I give you the names of my superiors, and you get me a good deal. Like probation," the man negotiated.

Probation for murdering Natalie Jones and trafficking human beings? This guy was delusional.

"Put the gun on the floor, kick it away, and then step out with your hands up," Derek demanded.

"I want your word that I get a good deal."

"You can take your chances with me, or you can wait for the officers who are going to kick down your door any minute, angry and looking for a man who sells children. I don't think you'll have to worry about a life sentence at that point."

The distant wail of sirens promised reinforcements. With a curse, the gun came skidding across the floor, and the man stepped out with his hands raised.

Derek crossed the hall, weapon still poised to fire. "Any more of your people in the house?"

"No."

"The girls?"

"Upstairs."

Noelle took off up the steps at a run before Derek could warn her to be careful. The guy could be lying about there being no other assailants on the premises, but Noelle was smart—she would know to be careful.

Derek holstered his weapon and twisted the man's wrists behind his back, grabbing a zip tie from his side pocket. He was about to wrap it around the man's thick wrists, but someone hit him from behind.

———

Noelle reached the top of the steps, panting, and found herself in a hallway with closed doors stretching all the way to the window at the end.

She approached the first one, taking in the series of locks installed from top to bottom. Clearly the men feared a single lock might not be strong enough to imprison a desperate woman fighting for her life. Blessedly, they were too lazy to use locks that required them to carry keys—the slide and snap bolts were all facing the hallway.

She undid the locks on the first door and threw it open. With barred windows and bare mattresses on the floor, the room resembled a prison cell more than a bedroom.

The two mattresses had been pushed together, and two girls huddled together beneath blankets. One of the girls lifted her head and looked at Noelle with drug-glazed eyes, pushing hair back from her face and blinking. As if she sensed that their circumstances were about to change, she placed a hand on the other girl's shoulder.

"Emma, wake up." She shook her. "Emma."

Emma's lids fluttered open, then widened at the sight of Noelle in the doorway. She propped herself up on an elbow, cautious hope growing in her eyes. "Are you here to help us?"

Noelle could barely speak through the lump in her throat. "I am. You're going to be okay now, but I need you to wait here. Help is coming."

She backed into the hall, disoriented by the evil that hung over this place like an oppressive cloud. The next room was a bathroom. The one after that imprisoned two more girls.

By the time Noelle reached the room she was certain must be Skyler's, she could barely see through her tears. "Skyler?"

A small voice came from the other side of the wooden door. "Noelle?"

"Yeah, it's me, honey."

"They locked me in, and I can't get out."

"I'm going to get you out."

She opened the slide bolts at the top and bottom, twisted the lock on the knob, and then snapped open the dead bolt in the middle.

The door was barely open before a flash of blonde hair flew at her. Skyler flung herself into Noelle's arms with a desperate sob, and Noelle choked back one of her own.

She was safe.

Noelle dropped to her knees, cupping the little girl's face. "Are you okay? Did they hurt you?"

Skyler's bottom chin dimpled and quivered. "They hurt Maddie." She pointed to the remaining locked room. "They put us together, and then the doctor came. He wanted to see me, but Maddie started hitting him and kicking him. His face was bleeding when he left. And then . . ." Fat tears rolled down her cheeks. "And then they hurt Maddie and put me in here by myself."

Noelle pressed her forehead to Skyler's, relief making her want to smother her with hugs. "Okay. We're going to help her." She pulled the unicorn from her sweatshirt and handed it to her. "Look what I found."

Skyler hugged the toy to her chest.

Two more gunshots resounded downstairs, and Noelle's heart skipped. Derek. Did he fire the shots or was there was someone else in the house?

She stood and took Skyler's hand, pulling her to the last room. They needed to get Maddie and find a way out before whoever else was in the house made their way upstairs.

She unlocked and opened the final door. A petite young woman lay curled on one of the two mattresses, strands of oily hair hanging over her face.

"Maddie?"

The girl didn't respond.

Noelle bent beside her and brushed back the curtain of blonde hair, the knot in her throat expanding. The men *had* punished her for protecting Skyler, and judging by the unfocused gleam in her eyes, they had drugged her to the brink of unconsciousness as well.

Skyler shuffled forward. "I have your unicorn." She placed the toy on the mattress in front of Maddie. "You can have it back. I named her Lucy, but you can change it."

Maddie's finger stretched out and touched the rainbow mane, tears gathering in the corners of her eyes.

Noelle scanned the room for another way out. The window wasn't an option, which meant their only exit was back down through the house.

Rhythmic pounding erupted from the far end of the hall—feet running up the steps. Noelle hurried to the open doorway, seeing the other girls skittishly hovering on the thresholds of their rooms. She motioned them back inside, and after a moment of hesitation, they retreated.

Noelle closed the bedroom door and nudged Skyler behind her, dropping to a protective crouch in front of both girls.

Where were the police? Shouldn't they have arrived by now?

Her heart buzzed in her ears and sweat slicked her palms as she aimed her revolver at the door. She prayed she would have the strength to pull the trigger if one of the traffickers burst into the room.

Grunts and thumps, interspersed with a few curses, filled the hallway. The walls shook with the force of bodies slamming against them. After one last vibrating impact that Noelle felt beneath her feet, the hallway dropped into silence.

She waited, listening for sounds of a threat over quiet whimpers and the growing wail of sirens. Stumbling footsteps approached the room, and the gun began to shake in her grip. The knob turned and the door unlatched.

"Stay away from us!" Noelle shouted, her finger flexing on the trigger.

"Noelle, it's me."

Derek. She nearly dropped the gun in relief.

The door swung inward, and Derek sagged against the door frame, the skin under one eye swelling and blood trickling down the side of his neck.

Noelle sprang to her feet and rushed toward him. "Are you okay?"

He touched the back of his head, wincing. "Yeah, when he said there was no one else in the house, he lied. There was a third guy."

The sirens cut off and car doors slammed. Skyler peered out the window and gasped. "Badges." But it wasn't comfort in her voice, it was fear.

"Natalie told Walt they couldn't trust the cops, because there are cops involved in this," Noelle recalled, her own fear rising.

Derek motioned toward the man lying facedown on the hallway floor. "That piece of garbage still had his badge in his back pocket. Looks like he's a detective from another precinct. If any other members of law enforcement are involved, it won't be long before they're found out. Good officers have no tolerance for officers like him."

Noelle was too worn out to be disgusted with the man who betrayed his oath to protect and serve. "Is he . . ."

"I don't know."

Derek's eyes held a grief she remembered seeing in her father's eyes as a girl, and she felt the same ache of helplessness now as she had then. "I'm sorry for what you had to do today."

Derek's lips tightened, and she folded him in a hug, resting her head on his shoulder. They would leave this place alive, but none of them would leave unscarred.

EPILOGUE

(Four Months Later)

Noelle set the tray of muffins on the stove top and closed the oven, the smell of apple cinnamon warming the house. She leaned against the counter and gazed out the kitchen window, watching Skyler and Derek toss a football in the snowy backyard.

Those two were thick as thieves. Skyler loved it when he came to visit, and she bloomed under his attention and guidance.

She didn't have any other family, which meant she had no home to go to after they rescued her. She would've gone into foster care, and given her age, she probably would've stayed there until she was eighteen.

Noelle couldn't stomach that thought.

After losing Tay, she didn't think she would ever be ready for another child, but from the moment she read Skyler's diary, she adored her. Raising a child who had only ever known captivity, fear, and lies wouldn't be easy, but Noelle was taking the steps to adopt her, and Derek was keeping her safe while law enforcement agencies worked to dismantle what remained of the trafficking ring.

Derek's phone rang, distracting him, and Skyler's return throw of the football smacked him in the side of the head. She doubled over with laughter, and Noelle snorted in amusement.

A floorboard creaked, dragging her attention from the window to the old man who stood at the edge of the kitchen, arms folded over his thin frame.

Walt had become a regular guest, joining them for dinner and holidays. Skyler had grown to love him like family—a crazy, paranoid uncle if not a grandfather—and she brought a sparkle of light into his shadowed eyes. She had that effect on most people. Natalie's nickname for her daughter was perfect. Despite everything she'd been through, Skyler was a little firefly, splashing light into the darkness around her.

"I was thinking we should build her a tree house next to mine," Walt said.

Noelle tilted her head. "Mmm, don't love that idea."

"I won't teach her to spy on people."

"You already do. She nearly gave me a heart attack jumping out of the pine trees yesterday."

He stared at her, unrepentant. "Every child needs a tree house."

"I'll think about it." And she did, for about half a second.

Walt ran a hand over the kitchen doorway, his eyes shining as he traced the growth markers that his family had notched into the wall. They were a part of his history that Noelle couldn't bring herself to erase. She'd done repairs and upgrades, but much of the house remained the same.

She'd picked up a mattress and some bedroom furniture from a thrift store in Weston, transforming Walt's childhood bedroom into a guestroom. When the temperature dipped too low for him to sleep safely in his camper, he spent the night.

"I can still feel my family here," he said, and he swallowed hard as he added, "Thank you for that."

This man had spent so much of his life alone. She couldn't imagine how hard it must be to accept that he wasn't alone anymore. None of them were.

God was filling the empty halls of her life with the voices of friends and the patter of a child's feet. He was stitching her broken pieces together in ways she could never have foreseen. She was living in the country with a foster child soon to be her daughter, befriending an old man who once terrified her, and flirting with the idea of dating again.

The back door flew open, and a blonde-haired snow angel bounced in, cheeks flushed pink and eyes watering from the cold. Skyler stomped the snow from her boots. "I love the snow. And football."

Noelle smiled. Day by day, Skyler was learning what she loved and what she didn't. Shoes were on the "didn't" list. She'd never worn shoes until Noelle bought her a pair, and she hated the way they "squished" her toes.

"I'm glad you had fun. Go put on dry clothes."

Skyler struggled out of her blue coat. "Then can I have a muffin?"

"The muffins are for church tomorrow."

"Oh, okay."

Skyler kicked off her snow boots without regard for where they landed, hugged Walt, and then dashed past him down the hall to Elizabeth's old room, which had become hers.

Derek tapped the white powder from his shoes before joining them in the kitchen. Noelle was gathering up Skyler's boots when she noticed the unreadable expression on his face.

"What's wrong?"

He checked to make sure Skyler was out of earshot, then said in low tones, "They didn't get Sophia."

Fear fluttered in Noelle's chest. "They've managed to catch everyone else responsible for that trafficking ring, but they can't catch the leader?"

"Someone must've tipped her off. She was gone by the time the raid went down."

Noelle released a disgusted breath and set Skyler's dripping boots outside on the porch. "So she's still out there destroying lives."

Walt grimaced. "If she's coming for Sky, I can sleep in my tree house with my rifle. I don't care if it's freezing. I'm not letting anyone get near this house."

"I don't think she's a threat to Skyler. From what the other members of the ring have said, she never came to the house . . . any of the houses she runs. There's no way Sky could identify her. I suspect she's a lot more concerned about her people in custody who are cutting deals for information." Derek checked the hallway again, but Skyler was still in her room. "One positive. They managed to

411

identify and round up more of the clients. One of them is an old pediatrician who favors a gray hat."

Noelle sucked in a breath. "Dr. Gray? He's actually a children's doctor?"

"Had his own clinic and everything."

Noelle wrapped her arms around her queasy stomach. "I have no words for how much that disgusts me."

Skyler's bedroom door opened, bringing an end to their conversation, and she slid out in her socks, nearly colliding with the wall. "I heard a car. I think Trudy's here. I get to hold the baby!" And then she was off.

Noelle stared after her, bemused at how much energy she had after playing in the snow for an hour. Then suspicion threaded through her. "Who gave her sugar and how much?"

Guilt flashed across Derek's face, and he took a step toward the hall. "I'm going to go help Trudy with my nephew."

"Derek."

"Excuse me." He fled from her reprimanding tone.

Noelle shook her head and scooped the muffins out of the hot pan and onto a cooling rack. Skyler was going to crash in an hour, and Derek could be the one who carried her to bed.

The moment the front door opened, Trudy's voice floated in like Tennessee bubbles, drawing a smile on Noelle's lips. Trudy had become the friend she needed— someone to laugh with, bake with, and even cry with. Noelle cried a lot less these days, but there were still days when depression invited himself in like an unwanted relative and set up camp on the couch, and moments when Tay's absence hit her like a freight train. During those times, Trudy was quick to listen and offer a hug.

Her husband, Brian, still had a lot of room for personality improvement, but he was a work in progress. "I do miss working at the department," he said, his voice preceding him into the kitchen.

Brian had been forcefully retired from the department for conduct unbecoming a deputy. Because he was shot trying to save a child from being kidnapped, they didn't outright fire him. But they wouldn't let him stay either.

"I know you miss it." Derek cradled an armful of chubby baby as he spoke. "But sometimes you have to lose everything you think is important to you in order to see the blessings in your life." He looked at Brian. "Maybe working at the diner with Trudy is where you need to be right now."

Skyler appeared in the kitchen entrance behind Noelle and held up a letter she must've gotten from the mailbox, her eyes alight with joy. "Maddie sent me a letter! Can I go read it now, or do I have to talk to grown-ups?"

Noelle smiled. "You can go read it."

Skyler's face split into a grin, and she took off back toward the living room. When she wrote her diary, she wrote it like she hoped a secret friend would respond. No one ever did. Now she had a friend, and while they didn't share a secret, they shared an experience that changed both

413

of their lives, and they bonded by writing letters to each other.

Noelle loved Maddie for reaching out to Skyler and for mailing back the unicorn as a gift—not something taken from someone else, but a thoughtful gift just for her.

Trudy slipped between the men next, hugging Noelle. "Guess who came into the diner today?" She snatched her baby from Derek's arms. "Janet Robinson, your future wife."

"Future wife?" Noelle asked, as Derek rolled his eyes.

"I am never marrying that woman."

Trudy bounced the baby. "I think you're the only person she doesn't insult. You think if I grow a beard and build some muscle, she'll start showering me with compliments? Today she told me she has a cream that will erase the stretch marks on my postpregnancy stomach so it doesn't have ridges like a Goodyear tire. Who says things like that? She's got some sort of tongue dysfunction, I swear."

Trudy ranted about the woman's other creative insults, including something she said to another customer about the skin under his eyes drooping like stretched-out gym socks.

Derek sidled over to Noelle and leaned close. "When can I take you on a date that doesn't involve other people and muffins?"

Warmth spread through Noelle at his flirtatious whisper. "If we can find someone to watch Sky, Sunday night?"

She'd started writing again, working on a novel to shed light on the dark world of human trafficking, but Sundays were a day of creative rest.

"I think Trudy would love to watch her." He glanced over her shoulder at the muffins, and a thoughtful line creased his forehead. "Weren't there twelve muffins?"

She twisted to see the cooling rack and counted the pastries. There had been twelve, but now there were ten. Someone must've snuck back into the kitchen from the entrance behind them, snagged two muffins, and flitted away to share them with an old man who was also mysteriously absent. She shook her head and sighed with a smile.

Firefly.

DEAR READER

I want to express my thanks to all of you who took precious time out of your days to read this novel. If this is the first book you've read by me, I hope you'll check out my other books, starting with *Criss Cross*.

If you think you would enjoy excerpts from future books (as well as publication dates and the occasional short story about my life), I would love for you to sign up for my newsletter, which can be found at the top of my author website: **www.ccwarrensbooks.com**.

If you're not an email kind of soul, then you can find updates on book progress and interactive questions on my Facebook (**facebook.com/ccwarrens**), Instagram (**Instagram.com/c.c._warrens**), or on my website. If you want to chat with other readers about my books, check out the Facebook group "C.C. Warrens' Readers: Mysteries, Mischief, and Marshmallows."

If you love these stories, I hope you'll take a moment to share your thoughts and feelings on Amazon, Goodreads, and BookBub. I know everyone asks you to write reviews, and if you're an avid reader like I am, that's a lot of reviews. But trust me when I say, as an author who has poured out her heart into every book she's ever written, your reviews are cherished.

I would love to hear from you, so feel free to reach out through any of my social media sites, my website, or through email. Have a beautiful day!

ABOUT THE AUTHOR

C.C. Warrens lives in a small town in Ohio. Never a social butterfly, she enjoyed painting, sketching, and writing, with the occasional foray into theater acting. Writing has always been a heartfelt passion, and she has learned that the best way to write a book is to go for a walk with her husband. That is where the characters—from their odd personalities to the things that make them bubble over with anger—come to life.

HOW TO CONNECT

Facebook: facebook.com/ccwarrens/
Instragram: @c.c._warrens
Website: ccwarrensbooks.com/
Email: cc@ccwarrensbooks.com

Made in United States
Troutdale, OR
04/25/2024